CW01081355

Peacocks, Pedestals, and Prayers

By Dina Rae

ALL RIGHTS RESERVED

No part of this book may be reproduced or transmitted in any form or by any means, electronic or mechanical, including photocopying, recording, or by any information storage and retrieval system, without permission in writing from the author, except in the case of brief quotations embodied in reviews.

Publisher's Note:

This is a work of fiction. All names, characters, places, and events are the work of the author's imagination.

Any resemblance to real persons, places, or events is coincidental.

Solstice Publishing - http://www.solsticeempire.com/

Copyright 2021 – Dina Rae

Watchers: The term originated in the Book of Enoch. They were fallen angels who fornicated with human women.

Nephilim: Offspring of female humans and fallen angels.

And there was a war in heaven. Michael and his angels fought against the dragon, and the dragon and his angels fought back. But he was not strong enough. And they lost their place in heaven.
Revelation 12:7-8

The Bible and other sacred writings of Jubilees and Enoch reference a great war in Heaven waged by Satan. After his defeat, Satan was ousted from Heaven, but he was not alone in his betrayal. One third of all angels took his side in a feeble attempt to overthrow God. When these traitors were cast down to their new kingdom commonly known as Hell, Sheol, Hades, and Gehenna, Satan became their king. Determined to battle God on every front, he assigned his most talented warriors an earthly mission of collecting souls for his expanding army.

This is a story about Armaros, one of Satan's Fallen. He once deceived God, and now that he lives on earth with a plan on deceiving Satan.

Chapter One
January 2022

The only light in his enormous office was cast from a computer, making his face appear an eerie blue. Andel's intense brown eyes stared at the geometric bouncing shapes of the screensaver while contemplating his next move. His current problem was slumped on his office floor.

Andel's oval-shaped office had no windows. Custom curved bookshelves displayed an eclectic reading collection that ranged from fiction, religion, How-to, biography, and bits of everything in between. He deliberately stocked the shelves with such variety so that any client, visitor, or employee could relate to his reading, while simultaneously hiding his true preferences.

A hint of Andel's personality lay within his clock collection. Time was his biggest fascination. Clocks of all sizes, eras, and styles were showcased throughout the room displaying different time zones in every part of the world. Andel's time, 1:10a.m., took place in the quiet, wealthy, and religious Chicago suburb of Wheaton, Illinois during a sub-zero weekday in January.

The rest of Andel's office furnishings consisted of contemporary black leather and industrial accented with wood, giving off an austere and mysterious feel. To add a dash of intimidation to the room, a glass buffet table with a display light that encased several ancient knives and daggers sat next to one side of the double door entrance. Tonight, one of the knives was not inside of the table. He licked it clean and continued staring at his computer screensaver.

In the middle of the room was a fresh corpse of a beautiful twenty-six-year-old Spanish woman sprawled out on her back in her own pool of blood. In her limp left hand was a Glock she had pointed at him twenty minutes earlier.

Andel snapped out of his hypnosis and crawled over to the dead woman's body. A few moments passed, and then he lapped up her blood like a dog presented with a bowl of water on a hot summer's day. Once every drop surrounding her body and inside her veins was gone, he ate through her chest cavity until her heart tissue was exposed. He feasted on the organ, savoring every morsel. Still ravenous, he severed her left leg with his knife and digested her flesh. He had not eaten flesh in years, but tonight he was insatiable.

An hour later, her bones, some organs, and half of her mangled body were the only remains strewn in bits and pieces over the stained rug. Andel did not touch her face; it was too beautiful to eat. *You resembled your mother*, he thought, as he severed her head and placed it upon his lap. He stroked her black, long hair while fondly remembering the first time he met Lourdes, her mother. Her head would be preserved in the basement refrigerator, and then used as an example for anyone else thinking of betrayal.

He picked up his phone and rang his assistant, Marcus Reinsing. "Marcus, are you still awake?"

"Yes, Andel. What do you need?" Marcus asked.

"I need you to come and clean my office. Bring the usual cleaning supplies." Andel hung up and waited. Marcus never failed to let him down.

Chapter Two

At six o'clock in the morning, on a frigid Friday in January, Eve Easterhouse breathed in her first whiff of freedom after two and a half years of incarceration. She quietly faced the service road of Dwight Penitentiary, awaiting her sister to pick her up. Eve shivered outside of the entrance, wearing only a sweatshirt and jeans. She would have rather died of frostbite than spend one more minute in the clink. Her lungs felt like frozen metal pipes as she nervously chain smoked her last cigarette. At thirty-two years old, she questioned if she had the strength to start over.

As Eve reflected upon her mistakes, she spotted her sister, Julia, approaching the main gate of the prison in her black Lincoln Navigator. Julia slammed the accelerator and sped up to the entrance. She got out of the car as Eve threw herself into her arms and cried.

"Get in the car! It's freezing out here, you ex-con," Julia yelled as Eve wiped away her tears.

They both slid into the Lincoln and sped away. Five minutes of silence elapsed as they emotionally collected themselves. They racked their brains for something to say.

"So....leave any bitches behind? Ever have to bend over for the soap?" Julia quipped, as she flipped her long, platinum blonde hair.

Typical Julia, thought Eve. She always knew how to break the ice with a joke. She never had appreciated Julia more than this moment.

"Oh, you know me. This morning the tears were flowing for the ladies in cell blocks G and H. Them bitches couldn't get enough of me. Not bragging, but I am known as the best beaver eater in all of Dwight Pen," Eve joked.

Both women burst out laughing. "It's good to be out of that hell hole."

"I hope you'll stay with me and Bell at mom's house. It's now half yours, as you already know. We could try living together or, before we kill each other, we could sell it and split the cash. You know, I get 90% and you get 10%, right?" Julia asked with a smile. "Whatever you want to do. Now that you are out of jail, we have to make an appointment with Mom's lawyer and have the will read."

"That would be great. I would love to try living together. It's not like I have any other options. I can't wait to see Bell. I can't believe she's already six years old," Eve said. "She probably doesn't even remember me. Maybe that's a good thing."

Julia weaved in and out of traffic as if she was an ambulance driver. Her hands clenched around the steering wheel as she paused, and then said, "Bell is spending the night with friends. I thought we could.... catch up. I took the liberty of contacting your parole officer, or P.O.? that's what you cons call them? Anyway, I told him you would be staying with me. Eve, I missed you, but I've got to get this off my chest." Julia sped up the SUV to at least ninety miles per hour. "I am not putting up with your lying, whoring, thieving, and drugging. Your low-life crowd is not allowed in our home or around my daughter. If you refuse to respect me, I will rat you out to your P.O. in a heartbeat. Understood?"

Eve looked at her sister's cornflower blue eyes and sensed a profound fear and anger that she had never seen before. She was the source of that fear and anger. Bowing her head down in shame, Eve mumbled, "Understood. For what it's worth, I've been sober throughout my whole sentence. I know that doesn't sound like much, but I could have gotten high everyday if I wanted to. I'm trying."

"How was it?"

"Not too bad. The food sucked and it was really fucking boring. I met a lot of flawed individuals much like myself. Went to an AA or NA meeting every day. Watched TV during certain times and mostly worked out."

"You plan on continuing with your program, 'one day at a time', right?" Julia asked.

"Of course. I have to. It's a condition of my parole."

"You miss getting high?"

"I missed my freedom more."

Chapter Three

As Andel waited for his servant and slave, Marcus, to come and clean up his sinister mess, he noticed blood all over his Armani suit. He licked the sides of his face, still savoring the taste. The Turkish rug that lay under his daughter's corpse was also ruined. Unlike the suit, the rug was irreplaceable. He remembered the Imam who had gifted it to him hundreds of years ago. It was priceless, and now he had to part with it.

He looked at the decapitated, beautiful head one last time and remembered what a true bitch she turned out to be.

His intercom buzzed. "Come into my office," he hissed, as he remotely let Marcus inside.

"You called, Master?" he obediently asked, as he stepped into his office and gazed at the floor. He zeroed in on the remnants of the cadaver. Pieces of flesh, bone, and organs were chewed up and stringy. This was not the first time he had cleaned up Andel's mess.

"May I ask what she did that brought your wrath upon her?"

"I'm downsizing," Andel said with a smirk. "Did you know anything about her personal life?"

"No husband, roommate, or friends from around here. Parents were divorced. The mother lived in Atlanta, and the dad in New York. Not sure why she decided to settle in this area," Marcus answered as he rolled up the sleeves of his buffalo plaid flannel shirt.

"As of today, she quit the agency and no one ever saw her again, understood?" Marcus nodded. "She's been plotting on destroying my empire. That's why she was here. Please get rid of her car as well. It's the light blue Lexus.

Here are the keys. Oh, and Marcus, run an ad for a new exec."

Although feeble, Marcus used what little strength he had in his toothpick arms and rolled up the remains of the woman's body with Andel's priceless rug, and then dragged it to her car. He almost fainted from the exertion after lifting a rolled-up rug and jamming it inside of the trunk. Marcus sat down on the icy cold concrete of the parking lot with his back against the tire of the dead woman's car and waited to catch his breath.

As his heavy panting slowed down, he began to formulate a plan. The rug rolled with the dead woman's body parts would be weighted down to the bottom of the Chicago River. The car would be parked by the El station on Chicago's west side with the door open and key fob left on the driver's seat. Like a mosquito to perfume, a thief would come along and do the rest of Marcus' work for him. Before he headed off to the city, he went back inside to deep clean Andel's office. Andel was gone. As he bleached and Lysol-ed and Pine-sol-ed every square inch of the room, he manically giggled with glee. *One day he will change me from a weakling to a god.*

Marcus' eccentricities began early in childhood. Always a target for school bullies and cruel girls, his hatred for the living compounded with each passing year. Once he finished school, rejection continued in other forms. He resigned himself to isolation.

By the time Marcus was ten years old, he would trap squirrels, mice, chipmunks, and birds then dissect them in various ways, practicing for bigger things. As a teenager, he had animal mutilation perfected into a swift ritual. He moved up the evolutionary ladder and began trying new techniques on the neighbors' roaming cats and dogs. When the animals squealed in pain, he became sexually stimulated.

Strays became monotonous. To recapture the excitement of animal torture, Marcus abducted Maggie, the neighborhood Old English sheepdog that roamed around without a leash. He easily lured her into his garage, and then tied her onto the woodshop table. He began his dissection by cutting into her fluffy tail. Before he could completely sever it, Maggie ate through the tether and mangled his face, leaving permanent scars along his jawline. The dog made such a ruckus that a neighbor broke into the house and found the dog and Marcus who was profusely bleeding from dog bites.

The ambulance and police arrived with plenty of questions concerning his scalpel set and the dog's chopped tail. With an extensive look around the property, the police found more hacked up animals buried throughout his mother's flowerbeds. His parents were wealthy doctors who covered for him by claiming the scalpel kit was theirs. After they threw money at the neighbors for vet bills and other incidentals, Marcus ended up with a slap on the wrist with four psychiatric sessions to undergo. He knew how to play this game, telling his doctor exactly what she needed to hear. No one could have predicted the future monstrosities he would commit.

Chapter Four

Hours after their reunion, Julia and Eve pulled into the circular driveway of their elegant Cape Cod in Wheaton, Illinois. Grief hit Eve like a derailed train. *She's not coming out to see me. She died thinking of me as a criminal rotting away in jail.* Though prison time was the most heart-breaking news she ever gave her mother, she had been living the life of an addict for several years. Family, relationships, career, and possible romance were squandered away on good times that weren't all that good.

Eve's sentence was reduced because of her exemplary behavior, otherwise known as 'good time.' Despite her requests, the prison would not allow her to attend her mother's funeral.

As Eve stepped out of the car, she motioned to Julia that she needed a quick walk around the estate. The familiar pavers, landscaping, and other childhood landmarks of the backyard calmed her down and brought back warm memories. The walkways and patio were meticulously shoveled without showing age or need of repair. Not only had Julia maintained the large old house, but she also made expensive improvements that enhanced the charm of the exterior. On the northside of the house was a 'Welcome Home' banner that hung inside a crisp new white gazebo.

Most of Eve's life was spent envious of her sister. Even though Eve was a beautiful woman, she always felt secondary to Julia. Like their mother, Julia was a natural platinum blonde with vibrant, cornflower blue eyes and a body meant for modeling swimsuits. She was also smart, artistic, and kind. The only mistake Julia ever made was marrying the wrong guy. He left her and their six-year-old daughter for another woman.

How foolish I've been, Eve thought. *She's got problems just like everyone else. And she's the only one in my life who loves me.* Once her composure was regained, Eve went back to the front porch. Julia sat there shivering and smoking. "Didn't know you smoked?"

"Just around white trash ex-cons. No one else knows. I've got appearances to keep up," Julia teased.

"Can I have one?" Eve asked.

"At $11.00 a pack? You must be high," Julia said, as she passed her a Marlboro and lighter.

"Hey, thanks for everything. The ride, banner, taking such great care of this gigantic house. I love the gazebo," Eve said.

"I've made a lot of changes that I think you'll like. Much of the work I did myself. My D.I.Y. projects have kept me busy since the divorce."

"This place has got to be pretty expensive to keep up. I really need a job, huh? Does Bell like living here?" Eve asked.

Julia's face softened. "She loves it. There is something magical about the house, the yard, and of course, Mom. I hope we never sell this place. Mom left us with a few accounts, but I think we'll both need to work. Such a dirty four-letter word, w.o.r.k., isn't it? So far, I've been getting some support and maintenance. I also sold our old house and made a few bucks."

Although Eve's felony record would be posing problems in the job market, she was highly skilled. Innately gifted, she breezed through high school and college without ever opening a book. Her Notre Dame degree in computer science and marketing gave her more bragging points to put down on a resume. Besides a topnotch education, she also had great experience. However, issues such as not showing up, coming in late, or not completing her job duties plagued her work record. She wasn't sure if she was better off being honest in an interview or making something up in hopes of landing a job. The bad economy was unkind towards upstanding citizens, let alone felons.

Julia showed Eve some of the remodeling projects she tackled over the last few months with one being Eve's bedroom.

"Wow!" Eve exclaimed. The bedroom looked entirely different from what she remembered. Gone were the teen hunk posters, stuffed toys, trophies, and pink girly wallpaper. The walls were now a sophisticated sage green. The bed was now king-sized with a white comforter and colorful throws. The room was magazine worthy. Eve's large, deep brown eyes welled up with tears. "This is a little different from what I'm used to. My last room had a thin, lumpy mattress on the top metal frame of a bunk. My only blanket was basically a dishrag. I don't know…"

"Stop blubbering! This bedroom is my gift to you. Kind of risky.... What if you just wanted to sell the house? There's more. Let me show you this." Julia led her into an enormous walk-in closet. She took all of Eve's clothes from her tiny old apartment and hung them up. Next, she escorted Eve into the connected master bath.

"It's too much; I feel like a princess. You must have torn up the walls from the other two bedrooms next to mine." Julia nodded. "Thank you so much. You have no idea what this means…" Eve said as her voice broke off.

"Again, Eve, stop crying! I did most of it, but I hired some help for the more complicated steps, especially the plumbing. I also remodeled mom's room and took it for myself if that's okay. I'm willing to switch if you'd rather have the original master," Julia offered.

"Are you kidding? I love this! Show me all of the blood, sweat, and tears that you put into Mom's room."

Julia proudly displayed her own bedroom and then exclaimed, "Let me show you Bell's room, it's so cute!"

The two sisters slowly strolled throughout the second floor. Julia proudly showed off her renovations while Eve admired each detail. Eve asked, "Did you find anything interesting while you ripped apart the walls? These old houses usually have secrets."

Surprised Eve would ask such a random question, Julia shook her head. She wasn't ready to share her discoveries.

Chapter Five

While Marcus scrubbed Andel's office cleaner than an ICU room, Andel Talistokov carried Catalina's fresh head into the custom-made panic room he had built before occupying the building.

The room was twenty feet below the basement, and he and Marcus were the only ones who knew about it. Inside the room were a toilet, table, and kitchenette equipped with basic appliances. The freezer acted as a personal trophy case, displaying an array of severed heads from previous victims. He enjoyed looking at them. There were currently three other heads in the freezer. Andel bagged up the heads and put them inside of a tote. He only wanted Catalina's head to be inside, set in the middle of the top shelf. He didn't want her face to compete with his other victims. She was special. She was his daughter.

***

Throughout the centuries, Andel always worked alone. Marcus was the first human to pray to Armaros, Andel's angelic name, instead of Satan. Hearing his own praises and cries for help stoked his ego. He answered Marcus' prayer in person.

Twenty years ago, Marcus was committed to the Utica Psychiatric Center in upstate New York for murdering his parents. Andel appeared inside of his padded cell and introduced himself as Armaros. He saw a scrawny, pasty boy, barely a man, with a scarred face rolling on the floor. His hazy blue eyes still burned with fire despite large doses of Thorazine.

"You prayed for freedom. I'm here to grant it, but you must fight with me. Use this," Armaros instructed as he handed Marcus a machete.

The two men killed their way out of the hospital. Armaros attacked the guards with his razor-like teeth, while Marcus hacked up their torsos.

"Oh Master, you are so beautiful!" Marcus exclaimed. He witnessed Armaros transform from a tall, black-haired, handsome man into a monster covered in boils and cysts. His black, charred wings burst out of his back and flapped in splendor. Blood was splattered everywhere, almost glowing against the stark white walls and floor.

Once there were no more guards blocking their escape, Marcus opened the padded cells and let the other patients out of their cages. "This is the great Armaros! Bow down to him; he is your true master!" Marcus shrieked.

"Armaros, Armaros, Armaros," they cheered as they saw their oppressors mangled and bludgeoned to death in the corridor.

"Attention, new friends! You are free! I am one of Satan's Fallen! Remember me in your prayers! Someday I will need you. Will you be there for me?" He solicited his own personal worship, which was forbidden. However, he felt entitled to it.

Many patients bowed before him and showered thanks. Others cackled and screamed like wild hyenas. To add to the madness, all the alarms in the building rang.

"You are my savior. I vow to forever follow and serve you." Marcus knelt before him.

At that moment, Andel appreciated his offering. He gave Marcus a place to live and work. And in return, Marcus faithfully followed Armaros to five states and seven countries over the course of their twenty-year relationship. His service was impeccable. Promises of everlasting life and strength were frequently made. The time had come for him to deliver on his promise.

Andel returned to his office while Marcus was cleaning. He handed Marcus the tote bag of frozen heads. "Get rid of these, would you? Had to make room in the fridge." And Marcus understood.

Only temporary. I have big plans for you, my son, he thought with pride.

***

Since the invention of television, advertising's profound psychological impact changed the world. From the beginning Andel saw its potential. He convinced his master it could be exploited and manipulated for his own means. His sales pitch impressed Satan, which in turn extended his time on earth indefinitely. As Andel predicted, the advertising industry effortlessly drafted millions to their side of the battlefield.

Andel's first agency debuted in France, and quickly expanded across Europe and North America. Each agency he owned was more successful than the last. Advertising's influence on mind control worked at rapid speed. He was in great favor of his master.

Andel's newest creation, *The Evil Empire*, was part of his Midwestern chain. It opened three years ago and already was overflowing with clients. With the recent loss of Catalina, several important accounts were left unattained. He jotted down requirements needed to fill the newly open position for an advertising executive.

Chapter Six

Claire Jacobsen slept past 10:00 a.m. on a Saturday. Normally up before sunrise, after putting in a seventy-hour work week, she was exhausted. Her campaign partner left the company without notice and now she was stuck picking up the slack.

Beast, Claire's Anatolian Shepherd, jumped on the bed, begging for attention.

Now I've really got to get up, Claire sadly thought. She slipped on a track suit and a lightweight jacket, and then leashed up Beast for a long walk. For late January, the day's temperature was remarkably mild for northern Illinois. As she strolled down the bike path with her well-trained purebred, she admired and appreciated the upscale neighborhood she currently lived in. The path was busy, filled with other residents who also took advantage of the fluke weather.

Once back at the house, Claire showered and ate. Housework and laundry mounted to an unprecedented level. Looking around, not even sure where to begin, anxiety set in. She needed an AA meeting to clear her foggy head. As she brushed her caramel hair and weaved it into a French braid, she stared at her reflection in the mirror and saw a haggard woman. Her bright blue eyes had dulled with puffy bags underneath them, and her hollowed cheekbones from too much weight loss caused her to look several years older than her thirty-one years. Make-up concealed some of this new look, but it could not replace the benefits of sleep.

Claire arrived at her regular club a few minutes early. While making small talk with other attenders, a couple of new faces timidly entered the large meeting room, scanning for an open seat. They decided to sit at the open table next to hers. Both women did not want to attract any attention. Out of the corner of her eye, Claire noticed their body language. She was close enough to hear what they were saying, so she decided to eavesdrop. She could tell they didn't know each other, but both tried to fill the silence before the meeting by feeble attempts at conversation. *I know exactly how they feel.*

The younger woman of the two newcomers was stunning. Her long, silky, almost black hair matched her almost black eyes. She didn't look like the typical drunk that first walks into an AA meeting.

The club's readings soon ended with the final questions, "Is anyone here for the first time? Is this anyone's first meeting?"

"I'm Francine, and I'm an alcoholic," said the older newcomer. She had a washed-out look, bloated face, and a drinker's nose. Claire guessed her to be around fifty and completely hungover.

"I'm Eve, and I'm an addict and alcoholic." Eve did not exactly fit the stereotype of the group, but then neither did Claire. Claire was especially intrigued.

Groups were counted off, and then divided into assigned seating. Eve ended up in Claire's group.

Although the AA chairman brought up the topic of acceptance for the group's discussion, Claire's group preferred to talk about the first step, 'powerless over alcohol', in honor of the new face.

When it was Claire's turn to speak, she shared some of the loathsome details about her bottom. "Hi, my name is Claire and I'm an alcoholic. Thanks for being here. You bring me back to my first-time walking through those doors." Claire looked over to the entrance with tatty, black double-doors and frosted glass windows. "I can't imagine what I looked like, or what others thought, but I knew I was in the right place. At the time, I was on the verge of losing everything: house, car, job, and even my freedom, and ultimately my life. My drinking and drugging made me a liability for all who knew me. I was burning out and taking down everyone standing in the way. This program began as an obligation. Now, two years and one month later, I look forward to coming here. It gives me a grounded sense of peace that the rest of the world can't provide."

It was finally the new girl's turn. *Would she talk? Or would she pass? Newcomers usually passed,* thought Claire.

"Hi, my name is Eve and I'm an addict," she said with a peculiar air of confidence as she scanned the round table, looking everyone in the eye. "Alcoholic, too, but really screwed up my life with cocaine. I'm really nervous. Although I've been sober for two and half years, this is my first real meeting. I was released from prison a week ago for a cocaine charge. I'm so embarrassed, nice first impression. Anyway, I need my P.O. to see that I attend. If anyone could stamp my sheet, I'd really appreciate it. I also need to get a sponsor, so if you know of anyone who is willing, please send them my way."

The group closed with the Lord's Prayer and then zeroed in on Claire. It was her turn to help a new member, and it was also part of her recovery. She knew what was expected, but her work schedule demanded most of her time. The others' eyes bored into her soul. Peer pressure prevailed.

"Eve, what's your number? I could temporarily sponsor you."

Chapter Seven
Six months before Catalina Rojas' demise

Catalina Rojas was an attractive, bright, educated young woman who daily pounded the proverbial pavement of the Internet's superhighway looking for a job. Hustling drinks in a skimpy uniform was not the exciting career she had dreamed of.

On paper, Catalina had everything to offer the business world: a Tulane degree with honors, volunteer service, and glowing references from her prestigious internship. In person, she would have had a chance at a lucrative modeling contract had she not been so petite. What she lacked most was the insider connections needed for landing a decent job. With the economy in dire straits, jobs once considered secure were now eliminated. Her sports bar colleagues facetiously reminded her how lucky she was to have her high-paying waitress position. Although she was making more money short of taking off her clothes, she longed for a better life without men looking down her bra top and up her micro-mini. Advertising was her passion, but marketing or anything in business would be an answered prayer. Her mother, Lourdes, could no longer stand to see her daughter so unhappy. She hesitantly stepped in and made a phone call to Andel's newest agency in Wheaton, Illinois.

"Evil Empire Agency," the receptionist answered.

"Hello. Does Andel Talistokov own this agency?" Lourdes asked, already knowing the answer. She had been keeping tabs on him for decades. It had been twenty-six years since she last saw him. Miraculously, his website photo divulged no signs of aging. She assumed he had the picture air-brushed or even had cosmetic work done.

"Yes, Andel owns this agency. Can I take a message?"

Lourdes gave the receptionist her information and prayed she didn't make an irreversible mistake. Minutes later he called. Electric waves pulsated through her body. She would have recognized his deep, sexy voice anywhere.

"Hi Andel. It's Lourdes Rojas. Do you remember me?" she nervously asked.

"Of course I do. I called you back, didn't I?"

"Oh....this is awkward. It's so good to hear your voice. I'll skip the small talk since you're such an important and busy man. My daughter, Catalina, can't find a real job, or at least a position in the advertising world. Creating ads and commercials was all she ever wanted to do. I'm ashamed to admit this, but I've been keeping tabs on your fabulous career," Lourdes explained. She continued to boast about all of Catalina's accomplishments with motherly pride.

"So, she needs to get her foot in the door. Advertising is one of the most cut-throat rackets out there. Besides talent, you need an "in." Catalina is welcome to work for me. Based on what you say, she'd fit in perfectly. Lourdes, are you still married?" Andel inquired.

"No," she paused, very uncomfortable. "Andel, thank you. I'll put her on a plane tomorrow. You'll be able to meet her by tomorrow afternoon."

"Is she mine?" Andel asked, smooth as velvet.

Startled, Lourdes' first reaction was to lie. "No. She's Hector's."

Andel smiled. Lourdes couldn't be more unconvincing. Throughout the centuries, he fathered several children, but had relationships with few.

***

Catalina sashayed into Andel's agency the next afternoon as promised. Heads turned as she walked past the open cubicles towards his office. Polished from head to toe, she was prepared and determined to ace the interview. Once Andel saw her, he was captivated with her beauty. He would have hired her had she shown up with facial hair and a stained white shirt. She didn't know it, but she was family.

Andel offered Catalina an opportunity most people would kill for. After giving her a generous relocation allowance and enormous starting salary, he had his real estate agent find her a place to live.

Catalina began a week later. Andel immediately gave her the highly coveted PowderSlim account and paired her with Claire Jacobsen, one of his most talented agents. Catalina had all the right tools to succeed. Both women worked remarkably well together. The client was very impressed and hired the pair of women for a social media blitz and infomercial.

Office rumors quickly circulated over Andel's obvious favoritism towards his newest employee. Eventually, the other executives overcame their jealousy and began the slow process of respecting Catalina.

As the months rolled by, Catalina experienced a gradual, but physical change from inside. Sleep and food lost their appeal. Her sight and hearing improved at an impossible rate. Smells were detected at incredible distances. Her patience evaporated. Temper tantrums were expressed when frustrated, and full-blown rage took over her personality when others objected to her ideas.

Catalina's emotions got the best of her one night while working late at the agency. A woman from the cleaning crew came into her office and accidentally broke one of her sentimental knickknacks while dusting. Furious, she pinned the tiny, horrified cleaning lady against the wall, screaming obscenities. Andel burst into the office and protected the woman from further abuse. He apologized with words and hundred-dollar bills. Once she left, Andel said, "Quite a temper you have."

Shaking, Catalina tried to regain her composure, but cried, "I'm so sorry. I don't know what got into me. I can't eat, can't sleep. Everything and everyone agitate me. Something is terribly wrong."

Andel nodded. *Was it possible, the Adonite gene was recessive, but could it have mutated over time? If Lourdes was a carrier...? Transformation occurred in adolescence, but could have environmental factors prolonged it? There could be no other explanation.*

"Catalina, what cologne was I wearing yesterday?" Andel quizzed.

"*Obsession For Men*," she suspiciously answered.

"What did Ned have for lunch today?" Andel asked, as he walked over to Ned's cubicle.

With only a few steps out of her office, she could smell the residue of his Lean Cuisine pizza and answered.

"See that pick-up in the overflow parking lot? What's its license plate read?" Andel continued questioning.

"SJX67F," Catalina correctly responded.

Andel would remember this moment forever, but he'd have to wait before revealing his pride.

"You're going to need a few days off. Take tomorrow and Friday to get...well. We'll talk Monday. I've been working you too hard. Really, I'm not mad. Now go home," Andel said with a smile.

"I will. And thanks for not firing me, right?" Catalina confirmed.

"You're welcome."

Catalina again found herself too restless to sleep. After staring at the ceiling fan for several hours, she decided to go running. With speed exceeding an Olympic gold medalist, her feet took her to the Illinois prairie path. Knowing the dubious types that hung out at night on wilderness trails, she felt no fear. In fact, she never felt more invincible. She cleared ten miles in less than an hour and was just getting started. The chilly night air refreshed and relaxed her with every stride. A homeless man heard her approaching and hid. She smelled his body odor, bloody Band-Aid, metallic breath, grape juice shirt stain, urine-soaked pants-she smelled all of him, yet kept running in his direction. He lunged at her as she ran and knocked her down, as she knew he would. He intended to rape her.

Pinned underneath the large man, Catalina easily lifted his 250lb frame and slammed his head on a tree stump. While he shrieked in pain, she zeroed in on his neck. She had to chew through several layers of flesh to get at his carotid artery, but once found, she clamped down with her new knife-like canines and sucked.

Several hours later, Catalina awoke in her own bed partly recalling her nightmare. Thankful to be home, she got up to urinate. On the floor next to her bed were a sweatshirt and leggings soaked with blood. At first, she panicked thinking that she was bleeding to death. Seconds later, after examining her body, she concluded the blood had to be someone else's. Still disorientated, she stumbled to her bathroom mirror. To her horror, blood coated her mouth and cheeks. Her eyes darkened from medium brown to black. *What is happening to me?*

Chapter Eight

Eve was doing everything and more expected from her parole officer. In addition to attending three AA or NA meetings per week, she sent out over eighty resumes in hopes of finding employment. She bought a stylish black suit and black pumps to wear for an interview. With all her efforts, she had yet to receive any responses. Meanwhile, Julia closed one of their mother's accounts and slowly doled out Eve's share of the money. Drug addicts and cash were a dangerous combination. Eve was still earning back her sister's trust.

Most of Eve's days were filled with cleaning, cooking, minor home repair, and errands. Her favorite errand was walking Beast, Claire's dog. She loved every minute of the low-stress bubble she currently lived in but knew her situation was only temporary.

Eve was making acquaintances through her AA meetings. She and Claire, her new sponsor, especially connected. Besides their addiction, they were close in age, single, educated, and without kids. When Claire explained some of the computer problems she had been having on her personal laptop, Eve easily purged it of all the viruses.

"Eve, you're a genius. You just saved me $200, probably more. I was going to get it fixed at a repair shop. I just had an idea. Can I have your resume to give to my boss? We could use your expertise."

"Your advertising agency? I don't know. I'm an ex-con. I don't think your boss would be interested. Plus, I don't want to get you in trouble for referring someone like me," Eve said.

"Listen, we still don't have an I.T. person at the office. If there's a problem, we call someone from a different branch and wait. Time is wasted. Time none of us can afford to lose. I used to put in fifty or sixty hours a week, but since Catalina, my ad partner, left, I practically live there. She was almost as computer savvy as you are. Hey, are you good with graphic art design? Web design?"

Eve nodded.

"I really could use your help. You could work as my assistant, and be our I.T. Don't worry about your police record. Andel is very open-minded. I could have easily been thrown in prison, too, with all the fast ones I pulled. It's not like you are a serial killer or rapist, although Andel probably wouldn't care. He's cool as hell! We all worship him-a true genius. I'll fill him in about your past so that you won't have to lie. If he's not interested, then you're no worse off than you are right now. You need a job, right? It's worth a shot," Claire suggested.

Eve gave Claire her resume without any expectations. A week later Andel's secretary called to set up an interview.

"Julia, my first interview in years! Claire gave her boss my resume. She told him all about my sordid past, and his secretary still called. Just think, me....in the glamorous world of advertising," Eve announced.

"Congratulations on getting an interview. This sounds very promising. You always were the brilliant one of the family. Walk into that place and work it. Make them realize what an asset you would be. I'm very proud of you," Julia said.

"I will wear my new suit. But I don't want to get my hopes up. An interview hardly equals a job," Eve countered.

"Good luck. Not to change the subject, but I need a favor. Can you watch Bell tonight?" Julia asked.

"Sure, what's up?"

"I've got a date. I've got a date. I've got a date," Julia sang as she swirled around in the living room.

"Well, well. He must be pretty cute. You're acting like a teenager right now. Will I be watching Bell all night?" Eve inquired.

"No, no. It's the first one. After my divorce, I'm taking things slow. I'm embarrassed to tell you that it's our lawyer," Julia shared.

"Your divorce lawyer?" Eve asked, confused. Julia's divorce lawyer was a woman.

"OUR lawyer. Not my lawyer or your jailbird lawyer. He handled mom's estate. You need to meet him. Paperwork still needs to be addressed. Anyway, he called me to see how I was doing and then asked me to dinner and a movie. Typical first date stuff, but don't wait up."

"Thanks," Eve muttered.

"I should be the one thanking you, not the other way around," Julia said.

"I mean thanks for trusting me enough to watch Bell," Eve said. "It means a lot."

Eve and Bell peeked out the window to steal a glimpse of Julia's date. He was the epitome of tall, dark, and handsome. Besides his movie star looks, he drove a new Mercedes. *Julia always could snag 'um*, Eve thought. *She won't stay single for long. S*he was envious of her sister. It had been almost three years since she had sex.

Once Julia left, Bell and Eve played *Candyland*, puzzles, and *Uno*. They settled on watching *Toy Story IV* before turning in for the night. By the middle of the movie, Bell began to fidget.

"My toys kind of act like that. They're not as funny," Bell said.

"What's your favorite toy?" Eve asked.

"Auntie Eve, hold on. Let me go get him. His name is Lonnie. I'm mad at him right now, but I want you to meet him," Bell rambled and then scampered up the stairs. She came back carrying a Charlie McCarthy ventriloquist doll.

"Hi, my name is Lonnie. What's yours?" Bell asked in her best impersonation of a boy. She held the doll's hand out for Eve to shake.

"Hi Lonnie. I'm Bell's aunt. You can call me Eve. Glad to meet you."

Bell continued to do a comedic routine with a series of chicken-road jokes with the doll reciting the punchlines.

"Bell, you are quite the performer. I love it!"

"Lonnie was a bad boy. I locked him in my toy chest. He's being nice right now. Wait a minute." Bell put the doll's face by her ear. "What? Lonnie, why are you saying that? I'm not going to tell her that. Alright, alright. Auntie Eve, Lonnie says you're going to get that job at the Evil Empire."

Had Bell overheard me tell Julia about my interview? Even so, I don't recall mentioning the name of the agency. Bell's act was beginning to raise the hair on her arms.

"Lonnie, shut up! It's not true! Stop it! Do you want to go back in the box? You're being bad again! I love her!" Bell screamed directly at the doll. The little girl was on the verge of hysteria.

"Honey, calm down. Let's forget about Lonnie and go raid the fridge. How about some ice cream sundaes?" Eve placated, desperate to switch gears.

Bell dropped the doll, threw her arms around Eve, and hugged her with all her might. "Auntie Eve, don't take that job. Something bad is going to happen."

Chapter Nine

Andel contemplated the repercussions he might suffer after Catalina was announced missing. Her mother, Lourdes, would never believe she walked off the job. He felt a twinge of remorse for what could have been.

Andel pulled into the four-car garage of his vast estate that he purchased after the *Evil Empire's* doors opened for business. He had several homes throughout the U.S. and Europe, but this one fit his needs best.

Winfield, Illinois, the tiny neighboring town of Andel's business, had tracts of enormous custom homes set on acres of land. The town gave its residents a country feel with suburban amenities. The exclusive neighborhood was his favorite part of the home, but he also enjoyed other indulgences such as a wine cellar and indoor pool. He primarily lived in the immense, unfinished, cave-like basement that sprawled and winded beyond the house's foundation. He sparsely decorated it with European antique furniture. The lack of windows and concrete walls gave him a sense of security. He gave Marcus the rest of the brick mansion to live in and maintain. No one, including Marcus, was allowed in the basement.

Marcus preferred the coziness of the apartment over the garage, but occasionally enjoyed the home's gourmet kitchen, media room, and pool. The rest of the house was used for the occasional party Andel threw for clients and staff.

In Andel's basement, a twenty-foot long, granite altar took up the center of the largest room. Its purpose was to provide a respectful place to worship his master. Over the last couple months, he had neglected to utilize it. Once home, he relaxed by turning on the evening news.

Several flies hovered around Andel's ears. Their buzzing sound amplified as hundreds more swarmed into the room. His eyes teared with the smell of sulfur. A sudden heat wave filled the room. A voice inside his head called him by name, preventing him from hearing the television's broadcast. He recognized the ethereal sound of angelic language. Although he couldn't see anyone in the room, he knew he was not alone. Beelzebub, Satan's First Lieutenant, materialized in his basement. Andel shut the television off and knelt before the altar in complete submission.

"Armaros, he has sent me as his messenger. We seem to have a problem," Beelzebub thundered in both of their native angelic tongue. He only referred to Andel as Armaros, his celestial name.

Andel stayed on his knees to show the darkest angel reverence, unsure of where this was all going.

"Who are you serving on this earth? Our Lord? Or yourself?" Beelzebub roared. The house reverberated.

"I know I've neglected prayer, worship, and communication, but my allegiance remains faithful. Please forgive me..." mumbled Andel.

"Silence!" Beelzebub interrupted. "Armaros, you are a fool. Do you think he sent me all this way from the depths of Hell because you haven't been keeping up with your worship? There are so few rules for you to follow. Satan tattooed them onto our skulls after we fell. Part your black hair and read them! Your disrespect has grown into contempt!"

"Enlighten me, great Beelzebub. What have I done to cause such wrath," asked Armaros.

"Fornicating with women! To add to your rebelliousness, you have fathered your own children! But that's not the worst of it. You then kill them! Where do you think they end up? Nirvana?" Beelzebub, dripping with condescension, screamed.

Andel held his tongue. He slowly stood up and defensively explained, "She was going to destroy me. I killed her in self-defense. It was either her or me."

"Armaros, don't insult our lord. She was going to shoot you - hah! We're all immune to bullets. Your own daughter is with us in the pit. She told us everything. And we can see you up here, remember? If that were your only mistake, I wouldn't be here, but your horrendous behavior just continues to build. You have been drawing too much attention to yourself...to all of us for years. Besides the children, all your magazine interviews, flashy homes, such as this..., and then all the publicity you attract for yourself and your agency. Your picture is on the agency's website. Too many people know you. What are you thinking? You don't age! Someone is going to figure you out. In response to this, our master is ending your assignment here on earth. Your borrowed time is up. If it were up to me, you'd be back home today. But because your business has been such a catalyst for our cause, our lord has generously given you six months to get your affairs in order. He commands you to find a replacement, human of course, to continue with your work," Beelzebub announced.

"But..."

"I am just the messenger. Questions go directly to him. Good evening, Armaros," Beelzebub said with finality. He and his colony of flies vanished, leaving the smell of brimstone in the air.

Andel went up to the main floor to vent out some of his rage. He broke every fragile item within reach while screaming for Marcus.

In less than a minute, Marcus appeared. "Yes, Master?"

"Get me someone to eat!" Andel screeched.

Chapter Ten

Marcus had never seen his master this angry. Andel's brown eyes yellowed and his hands were scaled with claws.

"Yes, Master. I will be back shortly," Marcus said. Andel had occasionally let him watch as he drank. Marcus ran out of the house in such excitement that he forgot to dress for the February weather. He was eager to bring back food for his ravenous master.

Several blocks away, before he had turned onto a main road, Marcus saw a man walking his Golden Retriever. It was only 8:00p.m., but the cold and snowy night kept people inside.

Marcus paused. The dog walker would make his errand quick. Because of the proximity to his home, he feared the man might be one of Andel's neighbors. *Don't shit where you eat*, he thought. The icy wind and blustery snow prompted him to forget about the consequences. A night like this wouldn't produce any other opportunities.

The street was empty. Marcus pointed his tranquilizer gun at the man and accelerated his car. As he crept behind the unsuspecting man, Marcus lowered the passenger window and fired. He almost missed, but the dart dug deep into the victim's leg. Seconds later, the man became groggy and let go of the dog, falling to the ground. Marcus got out of the car and dragged the man into his passenger seat. Although his victim was short and thin, Marcus still struggled. He put the victim's arm around his shoulder for extra leverage. As he was positioning his victim to sit upright in his car, a mini-van drove by and saw Marcus without a coat belting his victim into the seat. His head was lopped to one side and he did not appear to be breathing.

The minivan pulled up. "Are you alright? Your friend? It's an awfully cold night. Do you need a ride? Car problems?" asked the woman driver through her partly rolled down van window.

"My brother had too much to drink, that's all. I pulled over because I thought he was going to vomit. He needs to go home and sleep it off. Thanks for your concern, but we are fine now," Marcus lied.

"Okay, then. Good night," the lady nervously said. Marcus wasn't sure if she believed him, but she drove away. High with anticipation, he hurried home.

Andel was still ranting. He had stopped breaking things and began punching holes into the walls. Frothing at the mouth, he looked maniacal. An under layer of avocado green peaked out from his skin. His hair parted on each side of his head, showing two small protruding humps.

"Master, I have your food. He's in the car," Marcus declared.

"I'll go get him. Would you like to watch?" Andel asked. His voice had changed into a gravelly sound akin to a heavy smoker dying of lung cancer.

Marcus enthusiastically nodded. "Where would you like to dine?"

"I've never eaten in my dining room. How about there? Prepare it for me and I will bring in your catch," Andel said. As he calmed his temper, his demonic features began to fade.

Marcus retrieved several sheets of plastic and lined the table and the floor below it for an easy clean-up. Andel set the unconscious man on the table as if he were weightless.

"Marcus, are you hungry?" Andel sinisterly said with a smirk.

"Yes, oh yes," Marcus answered.

"From hence forth, you will be introduced to bits and pieces of my world, and then, if you wish, I will change you," Andel stated, as he stroked Marcus' face. "I usually drink my meals, but lately I need something more substantial. You seem to know your way around the kitchen. Tonight, you will prepare our dinner. First, I will have myself a before-dinner cocktail." Andel leaned over the sleeping man's neck and bit in, quickly puncturing the jugular vein. Andel guzzled up his blood in record time. The victim was almost dry. Still, too many fluids leaked all over the table and floor. Marcus eagerly mopped up the mess his master was making. As Andel hacked up the flesh with his teeth, he handed Marcus small, but manageable pieces to prepare. Andel worked his way through the man's torso and fished out the tastier organs, such as the heart, liver, and kidneys. Once Andel was finished butchering their main course, Marcus began his culinary opus.

Marcus prepared the fresh meat in a variety of ways. He fried the flesh in batter and sautéed the organs in butter and shallots. Other hunks of meat were broiled with wine and olive oil. The kitchen smelled like a five-star restaurant. His mouth-watering feast was fit for a king... his king!

While Marcus cooked, Andel rolled up what was left of the body in the plastic then placed it in Marcus' car for him to dispose of the following day. Andel set the table with dishes that weren't broken, and then lit the candles; Marcus entered the formal dining room with two silver platters of meat. He and his master gorged in wicked silence.

Chapter Eleven

"She talks to Lonnie as if he's real. Is that how she normally acts with her doll? I know I don't know much about kids, but I found it kind of bizarre for a child, hell, for anyone. And then she became so emotional about my interview. After her reaction, I'm not sure if I even want to go," Eve reported as she summarized the previous night's strange happenings.

"As the only child, Bell gets lonely. Lonnie is like her imaginary friend. I thought she would forget about Lonnie since she had you all to herself. Guess not. Her father gave her the doll several months ago, after our divorce was finalized. The same day he introduced her to his girlfriend. I'm hoping this doll obsession will soon pass. I think she uses the doll as a means of communicate her feelings. It's not as scary when Lonnie speaks for her. She wants to be closer to you. The possibility of you gone, working all the time, upsets her. Don't worry. She's resilient. Go on that interview and as many interviews as it takes to score a job. Your parole officer insists that you be gainfully employed, and Claire went through all kinds of trouble to set this up. Don't let a six-year-old run your life," Julia said.

"I never considered the impact that your divorce and mom's death must have on her. That poor kid. I'll be more sensitive to her feelings. Maybe I'm making a big deal over nothing, but she did shake me up," Eve said. "So, tell me about your date? Was he a good kisser? A good feel-upper? Good fingerer?"

"Enough! A kiss goodnight, that's all! Potential sparks, maybe. Nothing serious. He wants us both to come in next week and settle mom's estate. Monday work for you?" Julia asked.

"Yeah, sure. I've got my interview today. I'm going to slowly start getting ready."

An hour later, Eve descended the grand, spiral staircase in her black suit and heels. Her dark hair was perfectly coiffed in a classy French twist. Her makeup and nails were perfect. She looked like an executive.

"Well, well, well. Talk about turning a 180! From an orange suit to a black one. You clean up nicely, like a million bucks worth," Julia said. Bell looked depressed and stood in the foyer. Julia turned to her daughter. "She will be fine. Don't worry. Aunt Eve needs a job. She's going to knock them dead."

***

The advertising agency was only minutes away on the other side of town. Eve's head began to pound. Several minutes early, she nervously waited in the reception area. Claire popped in to pump up her confidence. Andel Talistokov soon entered and introduced himself. The youthful, good-looking man was not what she expected.

"So, you're the famous Ms. Easterhouse who Claire can't stop talking about," Andel grinned as he extended his hand.

"Please call me Eve. It's so nice to meet you," she stuttered, unable to let go of the handshake. Andel was enjoying her quirky enthusiasm and insecurity.

"Please call me Andel. Let's go into my office," he gestured. Eve could hear a trace of an Eastern European accent. He led her through a maze of cubicles and then down a long hallway into his ultra-modern office. She could not help but be impressed.

"Sit down, make yourself comfortable. Tell me why you want to work in advertising," Andel inquired.

"There are so many reasons. First, it's all so glamorous and creative. Your accounts are amazing: perfume, cosmetics, cars, champagne, food stuffs.... I would love to be part of putting together those slick beautiful ads that you are known for," Eve gushed.

"Ah, yes. It is a very sexy business. Did Claire tell you about the parties and free products? That's another lure that we all enjoy. Your resume looks great. Claire speaks very highly of you. She tells me you are quite a technology genius. To be honest, I tend to hire people with strong business and marketing backgrounds. However, my advertising business has exploded on the Internet, especially social media. I could use someone with your expertise. Let me tell you about the job. It's really two jobs. First, you would be the tech expert of the building. Anyone with a computer problem would go to you. Of course, my problems are the most important, but then my executives' needs would follow. Everyone else would need to get in line for your help. You would also be Claire's assistant. Many of her clients are requesting customized ads for many social media platforms. She isn't as proficient in graphic design as you are. The two of you would make a great team. One of the drawbacks to the job is the hours. I expect nothing short of moving into the building when we are up against a deadline. Are you up for it?" Andel asked as she wildly shook her head.

"This sounds like an opportunity of a lifetime. I do come with baggage. Did Claire tell you that I am on parole?" Eve meekly asked.

"She told me you were incarcerated for a couple of years. Cocaine, right? Is there more to it?"

"No, but isn't that enough? I'm a felon and I understand if...."

"Relax. In my wild youth I was known to partake from time to time. It's not a big deal," Andel confessed. His eyes were a beautiful, bright reddish-brown and seemed to dance when he spoke.

In his wild youth, thought Eve. *How old is he? 30? 35?*

"I have no problem talking to your parole officer. With exception of Claire, no one else knows about your past. It's your choice to share it, not mine. Now, before I hire you, we need to discuss salary. This position starts at 125K plus bonuses or commissions. We've got all kinds of benefits: insurance, 401K, credit union, and even a company softball team. I'm hoping to start one this spring. Do you play?" Andel asked.

"For 125K I could learn. Just direct me to the nearest batting cage," Eve joked.

"So welcome aboard then. Let me show you around," Andel said.

"Thank you so much! You won't regret it!" Eve exclaimed.

Andel gave her a tour of the immense office while introducing her to his employees. He pointed out some of the many advertisements that framed the walls of the building. Eve recognized them. As he opened his trophy case and showed her his Clio award, her headache came back. She heard his voice, but it didn't match his facial movements. *Am I listening to his thoughts?* she wondered.

Marcus needs to go hunting with me this weekend. Maybe Wisconsin or Michigan. Somewhere far away....

Eve's head throbbed. The two distinct conversations from Andel that she was hearing were giving her a migraine. Confusion began to cloud her thinking. *I'm going crazy,* she thought.

"Eve, this is my assistant, Marcus," Andel said. *I'll let Marcus choose the location.*

Eve heard Andel's voice, but he hadn't spoken a word. She felt ill. "Nice to meet you, Marcus." She managed to extend her hand and shake Marcus' hand. He had dirty fingernails, ill-fitting khaki pants, and greasy hair- a foil to the extremely polished Andel. Eve forced herself to smile despite wanting to collapse. She continued to main floor with Andel. He led her into an immense office with a blazing fireplace.

"And this is Tony. He's one of my best ad execs," Andel said.

"Hi. Your head has got to be ready to burst. Information overload. Welcome to *The Evil Empire*," he grinned and then shook Eve's hand.

"Hi Tony. And yes, my head is really going to burst," Eve said. She still couldn't shake off nausea, but still noticed Tony's warm brown eyes and pearly white smile. His name would not be forgotten.

"So, how about starting this Monday?" asked Andel.

"Perfect, I mean...wait. I have an appointment to see my family's lawyer on Monday. Would Tuesday be alright? My mother died. We need to go over her estate," Eve explained, worried he already regretted hiring her.

"Not a problem. Sorry about your mother. Was she from around here?" Eve nodded. "Well then, I'll see you Tuesday. 8 a.m.," Andel said dismissively.

"Thank you, Andel. Thanks for giving me a chance. Any tech problems, please call me over the weekend," Eve offered.

On the short ride home, Eve's headache had escalated to an unbearable level. In addition to the pounding, she could hear Bell's tiny voice warning her. *Don't take that job, Auntie Eve.*

Eve rushed into the bathroom and quickly swallowed some Tylenol from inside of the medicine cabinet. The headache immediately stopped.

Am I losing my mind? How did I get this job? 125K to start? No big deal I'm a felon? The interview went too well. Eve feared this was all too good to be true. Deep in thought, the bathroom door burst open. She screamed.

"Oh, Bell, you scared me. You're crying. What's wrong?"

"Why did you take it? I love you Auntie Eve. Don't leave me," Bell cried, clutching onto her leg.

Julia hurried into the bathroom and scooped Bell in her arms. "Honey, it's okay. Auntie Eve loves you very much. She's not moving out. You'll still see her all the time. Most grown-ups have to work."

"Auntie Eve, this was Grandma's. Take this with you at all times. Put in in your purse, your desk. It will keep you safe. Promise me!" Bell instructed with maturity beyond her years.

Eve took the large flat rock from Bell and instantly recognized it. Her mother displayed it on her garden hutch. It had unique markings etched all over it.

"I'll take it, but there is one condition. You must quit worrying about me. Pinky swear?" Eve asked.

"Pinky swear." Bell locked fingers with her aunt and then hugged.

Chapter Twelve

The Chicago newscaster reported:

Phillip Krakowski, 39, of Winfield, was reported missing last Wednesday evening. His wife, Sara, turned to the police hours after Phillip left the house to walk their Golden Retriever. The dog was found the next day, but no leads have come up for Phillip's whereabouts. Although details are sketchy, a neighbor sited a dark blue Mercury sedan in the general path where Phillip frequently walked his dog. Police are hoping the man will come forward with helpful information. Phillip's neighbors and church members have formed a search party in addition to the efforts made by the police. John King, his next door neighbor, states, "Phil would have never left his wife, kids, and dog. Someone out there knows what happened and where he is. He's a good man and we're going to find him."

Phillip Krakowski was last seen wearing jeans, a blue down jacket, and Chicago Bears hat and scarf.

***

Holy shit, thought Marcus, as he overheard the news while cleaning. *I knew that woman didn't believe me. Master will be very angry.* Marcus remembered he gave the good Samaritan a bogus story about his brother being passed-out drunk.

This time Marcus was not dumping his car in Chicago, but an entirely different state without police and search parties looking for it. Thankfully, the car was registered under the agency as a company car. He hoped his car's plates were not reported.

Andel heard the news about his missing neighbor and shuttered with disappointment. Marcus should have known better. An act this careless would usually prompt him to terminate their relationship, but in light of the dismal news he just received from Hell, he decided to forgive his servant – a gesture he and the rest of the Fallen knew nothing about.

As Andel pulled into his garage, there sat the car everyone in town was looking for. His anger bubbled. *Forgive him, he's all you got,* said Andel's inner voice.

"Master, Master, I need to...run an errand. I will be home late. Is there anything you request before I go?" Marcus asked.

"Yes, there is. I need you to destroy your car. It seems our entire neighborhood is looking for the same make and model. Apparently, it was seen during the same time my neighbor on the NEXT BLOCK DISAPPEARED!" Andel screamed.

"I'm so sorry. You always told me that neighbors were off limits. Now I see why. In fact, I should have learned my lesson before you appeared to me. I ruined my own life over neighbors. And now, history repeats itself. Again, I'm in trouble but now you're involved," Marcus cried.

"You stupid, stupid man. But it's going to be alright. I take some of the responsibility. The sense of urgency I put upon your shoulders in finding me food caused you to act without thinking. I'm trying to forgive you. After twenty years of loyalty, you get one free pass for your incompetence. We'll get rid of the car tonight, and then you will scrub down the house again. I still want to follow through with our plans. Because you've always wanted to be like me, I will begin to reveal my ways. In time, once you are fully aware of what I am, you will be given a choice. Freewill is what the other side calls it. So tonight, I will hunt, and you will learn. You pick the city. We'll drive separately and then you can leave your car for thieves to take and drive back with me," Andel said.

Marcus, surprised to still be alive, questioned Andel. "Master, it would be my greatest honor to watch and learn your ways. After my recent failure, why do you allow me this opportunity?"

"Age has softened me. Actually, you're all I have. Soon I will have to go back and be with my master. In the past, I've told you very little about myself. You already know I am Armaros. What you do not know is that I was never supposed to be here for this long. My master's messenger came to me the night you took my neighbor. That's why I raged. He magnified my mistakes and belittled my success. My time is almost up."

Marcus dropped to the floor and bowed before Andel. He repetitively chanted, "My master, my savior, my life. To thee I give you all I have."

"That's enough. You still haven't picked your city," Andel reminded.

"Oh Master, I've never been to Philadelphia."

Chapter Thirteen

Eve was in a celebratory mood after snagging an exciting and highly paid position at the *Evil Empire Agency*. Her first day was put on hold due to a Monday appointment with her late mother's lawyer, Sean Slattery. Per Lydia Easterhouse's wishes, both her daughters' and granddaughter's presences were requested for the reading of her will. The three of them drove over to Sean's nearby law office to discuss their inheritance.

Sean and his two other partners converted an old Victorian into their office which sat across the street from the courthouse. The renovations preserved the original quaint ambiance of a charming old home, putting both employees and clients at ease.

Both Julia and Eve appreciated casual, cozy rooms and hardwood floors. It reminded them of a bed and breakfast with desks and file cabinets scattered throughout.

Sean greeted them in the foyer-reception area and escorted them into his second story office. His tall, lithe physique and vivid blue eyes were distracting. He handed Bell a coloring book and crayons to occupy her while reading the dry legalese of their mother's will. After he finished reading the document, he listed Lydia's assets.

"I don't want to keep you here the whole day, but you need to be clear about your mother's estate. Lydia came to me a little over a year ago to have her will drafted. She seemed...." Sean paused, searching for the right words.

"She seemed what? Did she know she was going to die?" Julia asked.

"Lydia never mentioned that, but she wanted the paperwork done immediately. When I told her, I'd put a rush on it and get it done within a week, she lost her temper. She offered me triple my fee if I could finish it before the end of the day. I agreed. She was adamant about you three getting her assets without any complications. Your mother was somewhat wealthy in real estate but didn't have much in liquid assets. There are three separate checking accounts totaling $9200, 2 bank CDs worth $20,000, and a savings account with $1600 in it. Her vehicle can be used by either of you or sold with the proceeds equally split. Her home in Lake Geneva...." Sean listed.

"Wait, Lake Geneva? What are you talking about?" Eve interrupted, then looked at Julia who was equally as confused.

"It's listed on page three. The property was purchased in 1999, cash. I have the deed and an extra set of keys for both of you. Your other house, the one here in town, is also owned outright. Here is the deed to it. Besides the two homes and all their contents, your mother had a painting that is now worth a great deal of money. The artist, Carlos Bacciani, died five years ago and the value has skyrocketed. Lydia wanted Bell to have it. She hoped it would remain in the family for generations to come. The only tricky part of the will involves this painting. Proof of financial problems is needed as a condition for its sale," Sean reiterated after reading it in the will.

"Where is this painting? And the summer house we never knew about it?" Eve asked.

"Maybe the painting is in the summer house. I don't know. The artist was known for his depictions of celestial images. It might be in your Wheaton house. Your Lake Geneva home's address is on the deed. It was last appraised at $1,400,000, but it's probably worth much more. Your mother wished that you both hold on to these properties until they become financially unfeasible. On another note, Bell, your grandmother left you her rock collection. She told me how you always admired them," said Sean.

"I miss Grandma. She loved her rock garden. I'll take real good care of them," Bell promised.

Sean had everyone sign the paperwork and then offered to treat for lunch. They took separate cars and pulled into Augustino's, a 1950's themed deli only a couple miles away. While they pigged out on Italian subs and fries, Sean became much more social.

"Lydia was such a beautiful woman. She would have easily passed for your sister. How old was she before the accident?" Sean questioned.

"She was very young when she had us, fifty-two when she died. We also had a brother. He was a year younger than me and one year older than Eve. He died years ago," Julia answered.

"Amazing. I'm so sorry about your mother, and also your brother," Sean said.

"Our mother was very lucky in the looks department. She never had any 'help' in keeping her young, just great genes. Hope we take after her," Julia said.

"I'm sure you lovely ladies will. I know this is none of my business and hate to pry, but my curiosity is taking over my manners. What did your mother do for a living? I know she didn't have a regular job. But the upkeep of her homes, especially the taxes, how did a single and seemingly unemployed mom manage? You have my confidence," Sean asked.

Eve became defensive and angry. "She was a hooker. You know, one of those $1000 an hour types. You even noticed how beautiful she was. Is that what you are implying?" Sean was getting much too personal, but she had often wondered the same thing.

"Forgive my sister's sarcasm. She's very private, like my mother was. We don't know how she made ends meet. There was our father, but we don't remember him. She might have had some boyfriends, but she kept all of that away from us. As for income, she was a very resourceful woman," Julia replied.

"Julia, can I take you and Bell downtown this weekend? A museum, perhaps?" Sean asked.

"That would be great," Julia accepted.

All three of them rode back home in silence. Eve was suspicious of her sister and their lawyer. Both were hiding something.

Chapter 14

During the middle of the night, Andel and Marcus headed towards Philadelphia in separate vehicles. Marcus could not afford to be spotted. Their neighborhood search party linked his make and model to the disappearance of their last victim. February's weather spiraled downward to Arctic levels. Andel, immune to all climates, wore his usual hunting attire: dark non-descriptive clothes and a hat. Marcus was dressed for the Tundra and still shivered in the sub-zero wind chill. They both reached Philadelphia's outer city limits by the middle of the following afternoon.

Their first task was ditching Marcus' car. After driving around for an hour, they found the perfect neighborhood for making it disappear. With keys in the ignition and both doors open, the car was left on a busy street next to a run-down park tagged with graffiti. Two blocks away, Marcus and Andel watched and waited. Twenty minutes later their car was gone.

"Marcus, we have a couple of hours before dark. How about a tour of this great city? I've always been fond of Philadelphia. I was here when it was the nation's capital," Andel said with pride.

"Master, exactly how old are you?" Marcus asked.

"I was made at the very beginning, with all of God's angels, but as a human, let me think. Oh, I've been back and forth for centuries, but my most recent visit to here, on Earth, started in 1769 and I have not been back home since." Andel's large, dark eyes saddened. "And I don't want to go back home."

Andel slowed the car and pointed to Marcus's passenger side. "On this street, there are many of the buildings still intact. Right at that corner is where I drank a beer with Ben Franklin. Years later, I dined with some other Patriots, General Washington for one. I have many American memories that all start here. Thank you, Marcus. This was a wise choice for our hunt."

Andel parallel parked and motioned for Marcus to get out of the car. He briskly walked towards an open table outside of a cafe, and Marcus followed.

"Please sit. I'm going to show you how I hunt. It's really an art form that requires patience and knowledge."

Marcus' teeth were chattering. Philadelphia was just as cold as Chicago. He wore a ripped up, stained, quilted down jacket, hat, and thick, heavy ski gloves. They barely made a difference in protecting him from the icy wind. "Master, I'm so anxious to learn, but I'm afraid the weather is unbearable. Can we begin our lesson inside? With something warm to drink, perhaps?"

"Yes, yes, of course. You and everyone are bundled from head to toe and here I am attracting attention outside in my sweater."

They went inside the coffee shop, bought coffee, and took a seat next to the window.

"There is much thought that goes into a hunt. The key aspect is picking the right prey," Andel instructed while he sipped the coffee.

"Won't anyone suffice?" Marcus asked.

"Well, the answer is both yes and no. When I'm hungry, yes, anyone will do. As you already know. You have fetched me hundreds of meals without any details or directions. But when I hunt, I'm not just looking for food, but also for souls. My master demands them for his army."

"So hunting is part of your origin? Where did you learn how to hunt? Heaven or Hell?"

"I learned how to fight in Heaven, and then hunt in Hell. Hunting allowed me to find my own food along with honoring my master. Once victims are eaten, their soul usually goes to Hell. My master can use it for whatever he wants. He tends to place them in his army."

"So, it's kind of like apple-picking. You pick the best apple, eat it, and then send him the core."

"Very good, Marcus. I need to clarify something before I continue my lesson. What I'm going to show you is the way my Fallen brethren survive on earth. My advertising industry antiquates this whole process. I collect souls on a massive scale in a more civilized, more progressive means. Nonetheless, it's a tradition, and I happen to enjoy it."

"So, this is not something you have to do to survive?"

"I need to feed off of others, but hunting is more of a way to honor my master. I see the confusion in your eyes. Because of God's free will, nothing is clear-cut. I am speaking to you in generalities. I will teach you the exceptions later," Andel warned. "I, well all angels, have certain powers. I can only take someone's soul for my master if, how should I put this, if my victim is in the right frame of mind. How do I explain this? Do you see that blonde woman crossing the street? She's somewhat young and wearing a long red coat."

"Yes, she's walking towards this cafe. Is she your victim for the night?"

"No, she's not worth my time. At this moment of her life, I am able to hear her thoughts," Andel said.

"What's she thinking?"

"She's thinking she's late. She was supposed to meet her lover at the motel up the street, but her husband surprised her at work and took her out for lunch. Right now, she wishes her husband were dead," Andel shared.

"So why is she not worth your time?"

"As of this moment, we already own her soul. Why steal something that is already yours. Fruitless. Now, see that man who just walked in here? He's at the end of the line," Andel motioned with his eyes towards the counter.

"The old man? What does his mind say?"

"I don't know. I can't hear his thoughts. He is the kind of prey I am looking for," Andel said as he sipped his coffee.

"So now what, Master? Do you want to follow him?"

"Not yet. It's still light out and I like the dark. We've got another hour until night fall," Andel cautioned.

"Please, Master, let me paraphrase my lesson. You pick out your prey based on whether you can read their minds? Thoughts that you hear are from souls that your master already owns, but thoughts that you can't hear are from souls you want to amass for your master?"

"Excellent. A+, Marcus. If you choose to change, this all has to be calculated into the hunt."

"Master, I've got some questions. For instance, let's say you chose that old man with the frappe, and he strongly believes in your nemesis, God. Could he call out to his own master for salvation? I guess I am asking is there a way for your plan to fail while you are sucking him dry?"

"Marcus, your scenario falls into the exception category. I will try to answer you during our next lesson. Again, today we will concentrate on the standard way the hunt is performed."

"Fair enough. Besides one's faith in God, are there other reasons you could not read someone's mind?"

"Marcus, be patient. More knowledge will come. To answer your question, I can't hear my own children's thoughts, but they can hear mine when I am near. It's now dark enough out for us. Oh, hunting we will go." Andel softly hummed as they left the coffee shop.

"So where do we go first? Church? Wouldn't that be the most obvious start," Marcus asked.

"Again, the answer is both yes and no. Your thinking-cap is really charged today. Why weren't you this analytical when you abducted my neighbor? Water under the bridge, my trusted servant. I prefer crime-ridden neighborhoods or other places that permeate indifference to death. I want to hunt in places that keep my profile low," Andel professed.

"Well, Master, you lead, and I will follow-all the way to the ends of the earth if you so wish."

Marcus drove the car and Andel searched the streets for hours throughout Philadelphia's most unsafe neighborhoods. The frigid weather kept most of the streets vacant.

"There's some teenage boys at the corner," Marcus said as he pointed to the right. Although the boys were dressed for the weather, their hats and colors advertised their gang affiliations. A Cadillac Escalade pulled up, and they crawled into the car. The Cadillac's driver parallel parked in the closest spot by their corner.

"I can hear them all, clear as a bell. Murder, drugs, and money. My master will be seeing them all soon enough. We need to keep moving. Turn left. There, can you see her? She's up a couple of blocks, taking the garbage can to the curb. She's the one. Stay back and watch," Andel said. He stepped out of the car and disappeared.

In less than a second, Marcus saw Andel drop from the sky and push the girl into the bushes in front of her porch. *What the fuck!* He was both terrified and aroused.

Marcus could barely see the attack but heard the girl's faint screams through the howling wind. She looked no older than fourteen. Andel didn't appear to struggle. He was amazingly fast and graceful. Once Andel latched onto her throat, Marcus saw her body go limp. It was a surreal experience watching Andel killed the girl in front of her house. The boys in the Escalade were in the view of the violence, but too busy to get involved with their dying neighbor.

Marcus, can you hear me?

Andel's voice was coming from inside his head.

"*Yes, Master. I see you draining the girl. Can I help?*" Marcus said aloud while he sat alone in Andel's car.

Drive east, I will meet you.

Marcus drove back to their original spot and passed the teens sitting in the Escalade. His presence made them paranoid. Two of the teens jumped out of the car, each with a gun, and ran towards Marcus' car.

"Who the fuck are you? You a pig? Who you work for? Get out of my zone before I kill ya," said the taller of the two boys as he waved a Beretta in Marcus's face.

Marcus accelerated the car away from the teens. He heard shots fired in his direction coming from both the boys on foot and the trailing Escalade. As he turned every corner, he managed to lose them. *They must have given up,* he thought. Now completely lost, he began to panic. A deafening thud on the car's roof made him scream. *Someone's shooting at me.*

Andel's upside down face and torso were plastered across the windshield. Marcus shrieked, then squealed the brakes and drove up the curb. Andel jumped into the car and they sped off.

"How...What..." Marcus muttered, unsure of what he just witnessed.

"The boys were a nuisance. Like I said, my master will be seeing them soon enough, probably about now," Andel calmly stated.

"You killed them? That's why they quit following me?"

"I got two of them. The ones in the Cadillac got away."

"But...the roof....was that a gun?" Marcus blathered, clearly in a daze.

"I see the amazement in your eyes. I am an angel; I can fly. That was me on the roof, not a gun shot. My movement is slightly slower than the speed of light," Andel said.

"What about the girl? Is she officially dead? Did you get her soul?"

"Yes, to both of your questions, and I shot her in the neck to make it look like gang violence. I will reveal more to you the next time," Andel said.

Chapter Fifteen

Eve woke up several times throughout the night, unable to sleep. The first day job jitters took control of her psyche. Insecurities about her job performance were making her stomach knot up into a ball.

By 4 a.m., she began primping for the first day of her new job. Most of her clothes were either too casual or too sexy for the advertising agency. As a former party girl, designer business suits were not an essential part of her wardrobe. Her recently worn black suit would have to do. For variety, she wore a different blouse than the one she had on for the interview, doubting Andel would keep tabs on her attire.

Hours later, Eve arrived much earlier than expected. However, the *Evil Empire* was wide awake. Almost every parking space in the regular lot was occupied. She took the last available space before resorting to the overflow lot.

The receptionist greeted her at the door then situated her in the largest cubicle on the floor. Claire's office was only a few feet away. Eve was given an email account and advised to check it several times a day. She was then informed about the staff meeting scheduled to begin in less than an hour.

Eve signed into her new email and already had seven messages. The first five were from colleagues welcoming her into the agency. The last two emails were from Claire and Andel. She opened Andel's first.

JJ and Sam from girlsareinsane.com request a professional site and a pop-up ad. Depending on your pitch, they might upgrade to a TV commercial in the near future. Pitch me today. They want their ad by Friday.
Andel

Eve clicked on the next email.

Hi Eve-Won't be in until this afternoon. Beast needs to go to the vet. Cover for me. You need to come up with something for girlsareinsane.com.
Claire

Oh great, sink or swim time, worried Eve. *I've got forty-five minutes until the staff meeting.* Eve attacked the keyboard in a frenzy and researched her first client and their respective competitors. She found an amateurish website of young drunken women in compromising positions which suggested the website was a form of erotica material. *My first client is in the porno industry.*

She furiously took notes about their business and current website. Her new client sold a series of downloadable videos, subscription website, cheap t-shirts, and lingerie. The free part of the website had links that led to brief video-clips. She noted her clients needed a completely new website along with animated pop-up ads embedded on related porno merchandise sites for additional promotion. Men who were on social media sites and clicked on sports and automobiles articles and ads would be the targets for her client. A possible late night TV commercial pitch would include two sexy models wearing the lingerie sold on the website. The two models would suggestively promote the user to pay for a teleconference with them for erotic conversation. These weren't the most creative ideas, but it was the best she could come up with for the time frame. *Good thing I came in early*, she thought.

Eve packed up her laptop and followed the herd of employees into the auditorium. Andel sat on a stool in the center of the stage waiting for everyone to enter.

"Eve, how's your first day going?" Andel politely asked as he saw her walk in.

"So far, so good," she answered.

"Nice suit....again," Andel sneered as he looked her over. "I'm paying you enough to expand your wardrobe."

Eve sulked in shame to the back row of the auditorium.

"Hi there. Is this seat taken?" asked Tony with a smile, looking like a Greek god. Eve remembered him from the day of her interview.

"No, Tony." She attempted to smile despite being shamed by the boss. He was dressed to the nines in a tailored Italian suit.

"You remember me. This must be your first day. Welcome, Eve. I couldn't help but overhear Andel snub your suit. Words of advice: spend some money on clothes! Don't worry, you will eventually have access to free designer labels. We have many high fashion clients. Andel is big on appearances. He treats this business like show business and wants us all to look the best we can," Tony said. "Little secret - he shunned my 'cheap suit' on the day of my interview and made me vow to buy decent clothes before my first day."

Eve could have kissed Tony right then and there. He just put some air back into her deflated ego and spared her from the potential tears that were watering only a moment before. "Thanks. I'm so embarrassed. And in awe. I've never been to a staff meeting in an auditorium. This place is identical to a professional theater. He's got a stage, seating, lighting, and even red velvet curtains."

"Andel is legendary for his dramatic flair. His clients eat this shit up. We have a staff meeting every other week or so. Andel also brings clients in here and then shows them our pitch. For the staff meetings, he likes to showcase recently finished ads. Everyone looks forward to these meetings. We get the opportunity to admire each other's work. It's also nice to be recognized by your peers. He is a pure marketing genius. Consumers are known to sell their souls for our clients' products. Simply the best in the business. He can be a real dick, but there is no one I'd rather work for."

The spotlight flicked on and surrounded Andel, now standing in the middle of the stage with a rhinestone microphone. He looked more like a movie star in his fitted dark green Valentino suit that accentuated his lean and muscular body. Every employee in the auditorium was mesmerized as he began to speak.

The lighting and sound were operated in an audio room behind the theater. The controller began the meeting by blaring Beethoven's Fifth Symphony through the speakers. The fanfare belonged to a Broadway production rather than a staff meeting. His staff's fidelity was obvious.

"Good morning and welcome to another staff meeting. First off, we have a new employee, Miss Eve Easterhouse. She's Claire's new assistant and the director of our newly created tech department. Please find the time to welcome her during your day. Next, I've retained three new clients and already matched them up to the best agents for their needs. I'll give all of you more details later. Right now, I would like to present some of our fabulous television, pay-per-clicks, and radio ads that were completed over the last couple of weeks. First up, Tony's and Gene's Glasnovkov vodka campaign."

The curtains opened and a big screen dropped down. The lights were dimmed and then the television commercial was projected onto the screen. Two very attractive and scantily clad women were flirting with each other while drinking the vodka at a chic city nightclub. The commercial was brimming with sexual innuendo. The end of commercial slogan simply stated, 'Glasnovkov, the only ice-breaker you need.' The commercial was well-received by the agency as everyone applauded.

Andel then promoted three other commercials for diet pills, a luxury sedan, and headache medicine. All elicited the same reaction as the vodka. The applause was loud and genuine.

Andel moved on to the print ads with still pictures displayed on the screen displaying cosmetic cream, basketball shoes, and tampons. He showed a pay-per-click ad in conjunction with Gogel, and then ended the presentation with a sound-only radio script advertising debt consolidation and insurance.

Eve was blown away. All the ads had a very attractive, sexy, and clever way of making her remember the product and wanting to buy it. After seeing such talent in progress, she felt even more out of her league.

"Thank you all for knocking the ball out of the park. Our clients loved these. Now, let me announce our new clients. First, we have the Alhmann's toothpaste account. They want a print ad and requested Roger and Sue. Okay you two, time to pitch us." Roger and Sue were already halfway up to the stage and ready to perform their idea.

Eve's heart rate doubled as anxiety consumed her. *I've got to go up there and tell the most creative people on the planet my ideas? I'm going to kill Claire.*

After Roger and Sue explained their pitch, Jim and Ned performed their radio script for a male arousal product. They were funny and smart, making the product very desirable. Finally, Eve and Claire were called. Eve meekly walked onto the stage alone. She was inaudible at first, but Andel coaxed her into asserting herself and sharing her ideas with everyone. She explained her plans for the porn site and its products, along with details of how the ad would look on the computer monitor. Once finished, Eve mustered up the courage to describe a potential television commercial that sold erotic teleconference conversation.

"Not bad for your first day! You're going to fit right in!" Andel grinned at Eve and then led another round of applause.

After the stress of the meeting, Eve ran to the bathroom and vomited. At that very moment she would have given anything for enough cocaine to cope with the rest of the day.

Chapter Sixteen

After a grueling first week at work, Eve made the time to take a road trip up to Wisconsin and have a look at the property her mother left her and her sister. She, Julia, and Bell were excited to see the mysterious home their mother kept secret.

Lake Geneva was a beautiful little tourist trap that featured a large lake only miles away from the Wisconsin and Illinois state-line. The town was a famous retreat for Chicago's most notorious and elite. Lake Geneva's celebrity residents had ranged from business tycoons such as the Wrigley and Schwinn families, to Playboy legend Hugh Hefner, mobsters, and even movie stars, like Spencer Tracy.

Once Eve, Julia and Bell drove into town, they scouted the area and easily found their new house. As they pulled into the driveway, all three of them were enchanted by the large historic craftsman decked with tapered white pillars and a wrap-around porch. The home had one of the best locations on the lake, and the view was stunning. The property also came with its own pier and boathouse.

"Wow! Mommy, Auntie, Grandma had a boat. Let's go see!" she exclaimed while running down the steep backyard towards the pier. Julia and Eve followed her to the water that was partially frozen. In the boathouse were two boats, a speed boat and fishing boat, suspended from the water and tightly covered for the winter months.

"Did you know Mom was into boats?" Julia asked.

"No, and frankly I'm a little pissed about it. She bought this place in '99? It would have been nice to enjoy this home with her when she was alive. As kids, we would have loved this place. I don't understand all the secrecy," Eve shrugged.

"We should go inside. It's cold and I'm beyond curious," Julia said.

They hiked up the steep backyard to the side entrance. Julia fiddled with the three keys on the ring, not sure which one unlocked the door. Eve could not help but notice the massive double deck attached to the back of the house. Each level was filled with multiple chairs, tables, and grills.

"Julia, did you see the decks? This place is an entertainer's paradise. I don't recall Mom as ever being a social butterfly. She didn't even know the names of our neighbors. This can't be our house," Eve reasoned.

Just then, Julia opened the deadbolt. "There, got it. The key works, so this must be the place. You're right, though. It's getting weirder and weirder."

The three of them slowly entered through the kitchen. Julia's maternal instincts willed her to scoop Bell into her arms and hold her tight.

"Wow, this kitchen is gorgeous. It looks and smells new. Everything is so clean, like it's never been used," Eve said as she opened every drawer and cabinet. "Everything seems to be in order."

The next room they entered was the dining room. A china hutch showcased several framed pages of the Bible and porcelain figurines of angels. On the wall hung several kinds of crosses around a large photograph of Eve, Julia, and an infant Bell.

"I remember when this was taken. All Mom wanted was a photograph of the three of us," Julia said. She then opened the china cabinet and took out one of the Bible pages. "I wonder why these are framed. Could they be worth something? They look very old and brittle. Look, some are in English, Latin, and then I think this one is in

Hebrew. I knew Mom was religious, but I didn't know about her collections."

"Religious? Is that what you call it? Our photo is in the center of at least thirty crosses on the wall," Eve remarked.

"Where's my painting? The one Grandma wanted me to have?" Bell asked completely at ease. She wiggled her way out of Julia's arms and began to explore.

"We've got plenty more house to go through. I'm sure we'll find it," Julia answered. As they walked into the foyer by the staircase, they saw melted down candles everywhere. They sat on the steps, shelves, floor, and end tables. More angel statues were displayed, but they were much larger and cast in bronze.

The next room they entered was the parlor which was converted into a library. The built-in bookcases held dozens of scholarly Christian-themed works of non-fiction. On the far wall hung a beautiful painting of angels dressed for battle descending onto the earth. One of the angel's faces resembled Lydia's.

"That's Grandma. Look, she's an angel," Bell pointed.

"Hey, could Mom have known the artist? Carlos Bacciani was his name," Julia said aloud.

The picture was framed in tarnished antique silver. Eve tried to lift it off the wall, but it was sealed tight. She felt along the frame's perimeter and found tiny hinges on the side. She pulled the other side of the painting, expecting it to open like a door, but it wouldn't budge. She felt along the other side and found a keyhole.

"Julia, toss me your keys." Eve tried all three of them, but they were too big. "We need a much smaller key. Maybe we'll find it in the house."

The remainder of the first floor held no surprises except for the full-sized harp that sat in the corner of the family room.

"Mom said she sold her harp years ago, after Will died. She just couldn't bear to play," Julia stated.

"I remember. I guess she couldn't bear to sell it either. Well, which way ladies? The basement or upstairs?" Eve asked.

Bell pointed to the basement. After descending the stairs, they found themselves in a game room and bar. The area was nicely finished with an open floor plan.

"Julia, what is going on? The secret house, the religious trinkets.... You spent a lot of time with Mom, especially after you had Bell. She baby-sat all the time," Eve accused. She suspected her sister knew more than she was letting on. Julia chose not to answer.

"Grandma was my best friend. I want her painting in my room," interjected Bell.

The only room, besides the bathroom, in the basement was a walk-in pantry. Except for some old dishes and linens, it was empty.

"Auntie Eve, Grandma wrote something. Look!" Bell pointed to scratches on the walls. After careful scrutiny, Eve and Julia agreed with Bell. The scratches were really symbols carved into the plaster. They looked similar to those etched onto Lydia's rock collection.

"Bell, what do you know about these symbols?" Eve asked.

"Well, I'm not sure. Grandma started to teach me, but I can't remember right now. It's how angels write," Bell answered.

Julia found a pad of paper and pen then carefully copied down each symbol in the order they were carved. "I have a friend who is a professor at Loyola. She'll know who to give this to."

"I wonder what kinds of relics Mom has for us to find upstairs," Eve said.

The house contained four bedrooms all roughly the same size. After breezing through each one, they figured the room with the attached master bath had to be their mother's. Like the kitchen, the bath and shower looked unused and new.

"This was probably another bedroom at one point which Mom had converted," Julia commented.

Eve noted that the materials and layout looked like the new bathrooms Julia remodeled back in Wheaton.

"This was her room. I recognize some of her clothes in the closet," Julia assured. "Let's ransack the place and look for the painting key."

After an hour of rummaging through their mother's room, Bell found a jewelry box behind the dresser. "Let me open it." The day was turning out to be a treasure hunt, and she was having a blast. Inside the box were several beautiful crucifixes. She pulled the satin padding out of the box's lid and yelled, "I found it! Let's go get my painting!"

They all ran downstairs and opened the painting. "Bell, you really did it!" Julia said. Once the picture opened, pink insulation was exposed. Julia frantically pulled it out from the wall and reached inside. "I feel a metal box. Some kind of case. It's sitting on top of a bunch of nails, to keep it in place. Wait!" She jumped with her whole arm stuffed up inside the wall. Julia managed to knock it loose, and then caught it as it fell. She gently pulled the box out of the picture opening.

They unlatched the case and took out its contents. All of them were both elated and aghast.

"Mom, wherever you are, we all wish that we knew you better. Who were you really? What were you involved in? Why did you hide all of this from us?" Eve mumbled as she looked up, assuming her mother made it to heaven.

Chapter Seventeen

Claire Jacobsen was grateful to her boss for filling Catalina Rojas' position. After one week on the job, Eve Easterhouse was already saving her hours of work. She could not help but wonder what happened to Catalina. She had called and stopped by her place dozens of times. Her whereabouts were still a mystery. Claire, along with most of *The Evil Empire's* staff, suspected foul play. Catalina wouldn't have walked off the job without any goodbyes.

Claire's suspicions were validated once more after overhearing an older woman's meltdown in the reception area. She noticed the woman's uncanny resemblance to Catalina. The woman was getting loud and beginning to cause a scene. Claire tried to diffuse the commotion.

"Hello, excuse me, I couldn't help but overhear Catalina's name. I'm Claire Jacobsen. We worked on several ads together before she left the agency. Are you a relative? You both look alike." Claire held out her hand for a formal handshake.

"I'm her mother, Lourdes Rojas. Claire, I've heard so much about you. Catalina thought of you as her mentor. She was enamored by your creativity and business savvy. And so ecstatic about working here. I just can't believe that she would up and quit," Lourdes said as she softly sobbed.

Claire couldn't help but notice how Catalina's mother was wording everything in the past tense, as if her daughter were dead.

"Ms. Rojas, let's sit down." Claire motioned to a couple of oversized leather chairs in front of the receptionist's desk. "I want to help in anyway. You're from Atlanta, right? Haven't you heard from her?"

"Not in weeks. The day before she supposedly quit was the last time, I spoke to her. We were as close as two peas in a pod. She called and emailed me all the time. I have no idea where she is. Just here to try and retrace her footsteps and get the police involved. Claire, you were her only friend here. Have you heard from her since she quit?" Lourdes desperately asked.

"No, and I've tried, and am still trying. You're right. She wouldn't quit without notice. And she would have told me before she actually did it," Claire said.

Lourdes nodded as tears rolled down her cheeks, causing her mascara to smudge. "This was her dream job. That boss of yours, you know he's a liar! He knows everything, and I bet he's the one responsible! He's evil! I'm growing more impatient as he dodges my questions. I have a right to look him in the eye. He's going to ..." Hysteria began to set in. She paused and regained her self-control. "What were you two working on before she disappeared?"

"Nothing unusual. We were in the middle of a huge campaign for a new pain reliever. She was instrumental in acquiring the account. Our clients were devastated once they learned she would not be back to finish it," Claire answered.

"Did she have a boyfriend? Any other friends at the agency?" Lourdes further inquired.

"I doubt she had the time for any social life. Although she and I worked ungodly hours together, we weren't really that close. She was very guarded and strictly business, as am I," Claire stated, deliberately omitting some details that would provide Lourdes more ammunition in her conjecture.

"I've been to her home and all her belongings are there. Food in fridge, clothes in the closet. If I must sit here forever, Andel will answer my questions. My next stop is the police."

"Lourdes, I don't blame you. People usually don't fall off the face of the earth. I'll pop in his office and let him know about your frustration." Lourdes was clearly unhinged, and Andel needed to contain her before she went ballistic.

"Claire, thank you for speaking with Ms. Rojas. She and I can speak in my office," Andel said, as he came out of nowhere into the reception area. He escorted her through the main floor of cubicles. Claire thought she saw a spark of recognition. Lourdes' face was lined with shock. Claire inferred they already knew each other.

Claire also assumed Catalina was dead, and suspected Andel was involved. Days before Catalina allegedly quit the agency, he wanted a report on all her communications. Claire assumed he no longer trusted Catalina. Her disappearance could not be a coincidence. Although she pitied Catalina's mother, her adoration for Andel trumped everything and everyone.

Almost three years ago, before Claire got sober, her life was spiraling out of control. Drugs, booze, and sex were no longer filling her self-loathing void. She wanted something or someone to take her to an even higher place. Andel's good looks, charm, and legendary good time ways became the aphrodisiac she was looking for.

She knew their affair was one of her biggest mistakes from the onset. At first, his sadistic ways gave her the sheer ecstasy and pleasure she craved. But as months went by, his insatiable appetite for the avant garde became exhausting. His sexual requests went way past perverted to almost deadly. Her refusal to be asphyxiated in the bedroom prompted him to throw her away as if she were nothing.

Claire's working relationship with Andel only complicated her feelings. At first, she desperately tried to reignite the passion they had earlier shared, but he moved on. Her lust turned into scorn. After vandalizing his car, she tried to kill him in the agency's entrance with one of the knives she took from his office display.

Claire jabbed the blade in Andel's chest, but he was miraculously unscathed. Six other employees witnessed her attack. His mocking smirk only encouraged her fury. Claire dropped the knife, and then lunged at him with her hands clamped around his neck. Her adrenaline gave her super strength. It took three other employees to pull her off him. She ran to her car and sped off.

Once at home, Claire assumed she was on the verge of arrest, and would probably be sentenced to spend decades in prison. Attempted murder incurred lengthy penalties. Rather than face the music, she swallowed a handful of sleeping pills then slashed her wrists over the kitchen sink. Blood spurt all over her kitchen, and she began to black out.

"Claire, open up." The voice sounded far away as did the pounding on the door.

I will go to sleep and never wake up.

Dazed and disorientated, she was barely aware of the dishtowels wrapped around her wrists. Someone carried her into a car. Several hours later, she awoke in a hospital, angry to be alive. She learned Tony from the agency had saved her from death. He worried about her after her violent breakdown at work.

Claire's peaceful hospital stay lasted for six months. Every night she dreamt of Andel. Her dreams were so vivid, that at times, she believed them to be real. In her mind, their romance continued, but on a much more profound level. He evolved into a god who accepted her as a disciple. During her dreams, she would bow down to his feet and kiss his hands. He was now deserving of her prayers.

Towards the end of her hospital stay, Andel came to visit her. Just like a dream redux, he promised not to press charges.

"Claire, I'm sorry. This is partly my fault. I should have realized how fragile you were. I want this incident to remain private. Please forgive me and come back to work. I've taken care of the hospital bills, so you won't have to worry," Andel said. Claire vowed to be forever in his debt. Her sobriety was the first step to maintaining her self-control.

Once back at work, Claire went from a jilted lover to one of Andel's most devout followers. Her allegiance had some imperfections. Jealously would occasionally rear its ugly head, especially when Andel showered Catalina with favoritism. Catalina disappearance was a relief.

Chapter Eighteen

Andel knew that Lourdes would eventually show up looking for her daughter. Her barrage of phone calls was not returned. There was no doubt that she would reject the story of Catalina walking off the job without notice. Like a good chess player, Andel planned several moves ahead for Lourdes' attack.

Andel watched Lourdes escalate in the reception area. Thankful that Claire was calming her down, he took over the potentially explosive situation. The resemblance between her and Catalina was uncanny. Although Lourdes had aged gracefully and kept herself in shape, she still looked like a woman in her late forties.

"Ms. Rojas, please walk with me, and I'll share with you all I know," Andel said as he escorted her to his office. He did not want any of his employees to know that Lourdes and he shared a history together. Once alone in his office, he asked, "How long has it been? You haven't changed a bit. Still beautiful as ever. Catalina could be your twin. Wish you were here under happier circumstances. Please sit down."

Ironically, Lourdes sat in the exact spot where Catalina was murdered. Andel took a seat behind his massive desk.

"Andel, you haven't aged a day. How is that possible?" Lourdes asked.

"In this business, we get all kinds of free products and I use them. What can I say, I'm more vain than a woman. So how have you been?"

"Upset. My daughter is probably dead. Listen, I'm not here to rehash the past. I came for some answers,"

Lourdes said, determined not to be sucked into his charm. She looked around the office, taking in all the details.

"Okay then. I don't blame you. It's been over two weeks since she quit, and no one has heard a thing. I'm getting the distinct feeling that you hold me responsible. Let me tell you everything I know. Catalina landed us a new client, a really big fish, a week or two before she left. She and Claire were launching a series of ads for them. Neconyl. It's a new pain reliever. Anyway, I don't know how she coaxed the company's CEOs to sign with us, and for a multi-million-dollar account, I didn't ask. Neconyl's people were so impressed with her, I assumed she quit to take on a more lucrative position with them. It's a new company who could use a marketing guru such as your daughter."

"Andel, she loved working here. She loved you. This place was the most exciting thing that ever happened to her. She never once mentioned another job offer. For the sake of your argument, let's say she did take on a new job. That still doesn't explain why I haven't heard from her. In fact, no one has heard from her. She was your daughter. I never told anyone, including Catalina, but I knew. Her blood type didn't match with mine or Hector's. I know you are somehow involved in this. Fair warning, I'm going to the police and pointing my finger in your direction."

"I thought she was mine when you originally called. She was my favorite employee. I treated her almost like family. I know you're worried, but I don't appreciate your accusation. I had nothing to do with her disappearance. And if you're pointing fingers, don't dismiss Neconyl's role in this."

"Don't play me. She didn't disappear or quit or leave! She's dead! And I'm going to find out who killed her!" Lourdes exclaimed.

Andel stared at her for a long moment then asked, "I want to show you something. Walk with me. Did you ever hear of a tachistoscope?"

Shaking with anger, yet curious about her daughter's last whereabouts, Lourdes played along and followed Andel out of his office to the other side of the building. They walked into the massive auditorium.

"Here. This is it." He showed her the instrument. It looked like an antiquated view finder. He then explained how the projector-like machine worked. With a shutter, much like a camera's, it flashed images for only milli-seconds during a commercial broadcast. "This machine was the first used for subliminal advertising. Bear with me, I have a point. Let me demonstrate its usefulness."

Andel lowered the screen and ran an old commercial from the 1970's for a game. While the commercial ran, the tachistoscope clicked, but Lourdes didn't see anything on the screen besides the commercial.

"Let me slow this down by several speeds," Andel said.

During the thirty-second commercial, Lourdes could now see several messages flashing throughout. The messages read 'buy me', 'go get this', and 'your kid wants this.'

"Andel, this is all fascinating, but what does this have to do with my daughter?" Lourdes questioned.

"Catalina was using a much more sophisticated instrument. It gave off some really powerful messages. You see, Catalina believed that commercials were not the only way companies could advertise on television and the Internet. Although this is unethical, her computerized version of the tachistoscope was digitized and compatible with actual TV programming. Messages could be flashed throughout an entire TV show, movie, sporting event, or any kind of media. It could work in real time broadcasts or streamed in material. The flashes you just watched are now much faster and more frequent. Let me show you what Catalina had designed for Neconyl."

Andel ran a hit TV sit-com with a new Neconyl commercial.

"Neconyl paid several million dollars to have their flashes run throughout this program. Because of the speed, viewers wouldn't be interrupted from their show, but on a subconscious level, their psyche would be bombarded with prompts to encourage them to purchase the item. Please, let me show you a new way of advertising," Andel said.

Lourdes sat down, not sure if any of this was relevant. As she watched the TV program without any regular commercials, she was confused. At the end of the TV show, she asked where the commercial was.

Andel slowed down the video. The first flash said, "Neconyl will ease your pain."

"Oh, now I get it. Yes, its flashed during the TV program," Lourdes exclaimed in a trance-like state. Her entire demeanor was replaced with a pleasant and amicable one. "It's been wonderful to visit. I'm sure Catalina will surface. She probably met someone and ran off on a romantic getaway. Good to see you and keep in touch."

Andel gloated with respite. The hypnosis was working. He had replaced Neconyl's messages with ones that fit his own agenda for the moment. While Lourdes watched the sit-com, her subconscious read:

Andel is innocent
Catalina is on a romantic vacation
Worship me
Catalina will surface
Don't go to the police
I will save you
Neconyl is guilty
Catalina is alive
Go home and leave this alone

Andel's instrument was one of his greatest inventions. His new and improved subliminal advertising machine worked wonders for mind control. His only regret was showing it to Catalina.

Chapter Nineteen

Bell, Julia, and Eve stared in disbelief at the contents of a large metal box found behind a painting of their newly inherited lake house. The gray toolbox was deceiving. Once opened, the old banged-up box surprisingly was lined with velvet. Several stacks of cash, a sealed scroll, and a broken piece of an odd shiny metal excited the three of them.

"There's got to be close to two million dollars in cash!" exclaimed Julia.

"This house, the cash, where did Mom get that kind of money?" asked Eve.

"Don't know, but we don't have to worry about taxes and property upkeep anymore. Look at this scroll. It looks like it should be in a museum," Julia said.

The scroll's seal matched the box's lining. The color was foreign to Eve, Julia, and Bell, but they agreed that indigo was the closest it came to any of the colors on the spectrum. The scroll was much thicker and softer than paper.

"This must be some kind of animal skin," remarked Eve.

The last item in the box was a piece of curved metal. The edges along its outer rim were ridged in an elaborate pattern. It looked like a cracked piece of a charger that once was part of an elegant set of china. Eve tried to pick it up but was initially electrocuted. The electric charge did not stop her from trying to hold it. She picked it up a few more times. Once neutralized, she held it to the light in the room.

"This looks like a piece of scrap metal. Obviously, it had major importance or Mom wouldn't have gone to such measures in hiding it. It's not gold, silver, or even platinum. But it's shiny, like tin. It's almost weightless. I thought it would be much heavier." Eve said.

"It's Grandma's. I've seen her wear it in my dreams. There's another piece that matches it and makes a circle. She puts in the back of her head, and it glows. She must have hidden the other piece," Bell said.

"Glows? Like an angel's halo?" Julia asked. She walked over to the painting. "Like in this painting? Is this what Grandma looks like in your dreams?"

"Yes, but that angel in the picture also looks like you. You and Grandma were practically twins."

"I do look like her. Do you know where the other piece is?" Julia asked.

"No, but maybe Lonnie does. I'll ask him when we get home," Bell said, referring to her ventriloquist doll.

"So, Mom was an angel?" Eve asked. "Based on her home décor, she must have thought so. I now understand all the secrets. She knew she was losing her mind. What do psychologists call it? Illusions of grandeur?"

"Auntie Eve, Grandma was not crazy. She is always an angel in my dreams. The artist of this picture must have had the same dream."

"But angels don't exist. And even if they did, Mom was a good person, but definitely not an angel. She had faults just like the rest of us," Julia said.

"Bell's right about the halo. There's got to be a matching piece also hidden. Maybe we'll find it and try bonding the pieces back together," Eve reasoned. "All of these religious baubles, the décor, the artwork and framed Bible pages can be purchased at churches, home shopping channels, flea markets, and the Internet. Maybe this collection is worth something. This scroll, for example, I'd bust the seal and see what's inside, but that might devalue it's worth. You know, kind of like opening a pack of baseball cards. Whatever it is, I doubt it's written in English. Too old. We'll need to get the scroll and Bible pages translated. Maybe your professor friend can lead us in the right direction. And the artist, Carlos Bacciani, we must check into his family. Could Mom have hired him to paint this for her? Why is she in the painting? If this angel is her, then who are the other three? And who is the man they are pointing their swords at?"

"It's definitely a strange portrait, but Sean says it's worth a fortune. This guy must be considered as a modern-day Picasso. We'll take it home and hang it up in Bell's room. It's been a long day. Do you want to sleep here? We can light a fire and order a pizza, then go home tomorrow?" Julia suggested.

"A sleepover! Maybe Grandma's ghost will come to visit us!" Bell exclaimed.

"Bell, there is no such things as ghosts," Julia said.

"I saw a Ouija board in the bookcase. We can all play after dinner!" Bell squealed.

"Sounds like a party! Count me in, little girl. Maybe Mom's spirit will come and tells us what all this junk is worth," teased Eve.

"Auntie Eve is going to play! This is going to be so fun."

"Thanks for egging her on! She's six years old. What's wrong with you? We were in high school when we first played. Bell, how do you even know what a Ouija board is?" Julia asked.

"I used to play with Grandma. There's a board back at home too. Please Mom, it's so fun," begged Bell.

"Hmmm, what's wrong with me? That's really rich, Julia. You're the one who left her with our crazy mother all the time. Listen to her. She and her grandma played Ouija and read angel's writing. Totally normal things to do with your grandchild. I say we play and see what your daughter knows about all of this stuff," Eve said.

Their insistence chipped away at Julia's resolve. After dinner, Bell joyfully brought the board to the table.

She then grabbed an armful of candles to set the mood. Once Eve lit them, they were ready.

The planchette moved across the board like lightning before it was even taken out of the box. The game piece then pointed to Bell.

"What the f....? This is a really bad idea," screamed Julia.

"Calm down. Maybe we'll get some answers. I'm trying to have an open mind to all of this. Bell might be able to help. She knew Mom better than we did. Bell, I think it must be your turn," Eve said.

Julia apprehensively went along, watching her daughter's royal blue eyes light up in the eerie candlelight.

"This is how we play." Bell demonstrated by taking her fingertips and placing them on each side of the planchette. She moved the piece in a circular motion over the board. "When it's your turn, the planchette will point to you. Okay, we are not alone. There is a spirit among us. Is that you, Grandma?" Bell's hands were yanked to the "yes" word on the Ouija board. "Hi Grandma. We miss you. You've got a real nice place here. Thanks for the painting. It's really beautiful. Is that you in it?"

Bell's hands jolted to the "yes" word on the board.

"Are you an angel? Like in the painting?" Bell asked.

Her hands suddenly raced to the "no" word and then spelled N, E, P, H, I, L, I, M. All three of them looked puzzled.

"Never heard of that word. I guess we better look it up," Eve said and then quickly looked up the definition on her phone. She read all of the versions of the word and then paraphrased, "It's an offspring of male angels and females. Like a half breed of some sorts."

"Grandma, are you still there?" Bell questioned as her hands stopped moving. The planchette re-energized and moved to the "yes" word. "Can you see us right now?"

Bell's fingers moved over the letters E, V, I, L. "Eeee v il, evil," Bell read as she sounded out the word. The planchette began wildly spinning then flung out of her hands. She screamed and then began to cry.

"That's enough! I knew this was a bad idea. Sweetie, it's okay. We are not staying here tonight. Let's pack up Grandma's things and go home," Julia said.

Chapter Twenty

Marcus Reinsing was everything that his master wasn't. His puny body, social ineptitude, and eccentricities kept him isolated from the other employees. He also dressed to not impress. His sandy brown hair was always greasy, and his casual clothes were raggedy and worn out. No one ever initiated a conversation with him, and he was just as aloof. Most assumed he was a friend or family member of Andel's. Nepotism was the only explanation for his employment. His job description was vague, and he kept irregular hours without anyone knowing what he was working on. At staff meetings and client presentations, he ran the lighting, sound, and video, but other duties were unclear. Judging by his appearance, some thought he might be part of the maintenance crew. But they never spoke to Marcus either. Andel gave him a nice office, which evoked jealousy among some of the hardest working agents still stuck inside of cubicles.

Marcus' outcast persona needed a makeover. Later that evening, his master invited him into his lair. Marcus wallowed in the extra attention as their relationship ascended to the next level.

"Marcus, I have so much to teach you and so little time to do it. Remember when we went hunting? It's time for you to find your own food. Do you still want to change?" Marcus bubbled with enthusiasm. "Then today is your day. We are going to do this in stages. First, I need you to bow down and take a sacred oath to revere me, worship me, adore me, obey me, serve me, and die for me. Are you willing?" Andel asked with his fangs elongating out of his mouth.

"Oh yes, Master. All of that and more. I love you," Marcus swore while on his knees looking up to Andel. His excitement led to arousal. He didn't want Andel to see his erection.

Andel leaned down, latched onto his neck, and sucked. The feeling was like a hundred orgasms rolled into one. Marcus could not help but ejaculate. Once Andel released his neck, he fainted.

Hours later, still in Andel's basement, Marcus woke up famished, but invincible. His reflection was subtly different. His gaunt face became more defined and chiseled, and his thinning brown hair was fuller. Never able to perform a simple push-up, he got down on the floor and did a quick and easy set of a hundred. His decades of servitude finally paid off.

"Master? Are you here?" Marcus called as he climbed the stairs and followed the sweet smell of blood into Andel's kitchen. The scent emanated from the refrigerator. He helped himself to a bottle of blood. Before he took the first sip, he heard Andel scream.

"What are you doing? Never, and I mean never, take what is mine without my permission. If this ever happens again, I will eat you from the inside out. You need to feed yourself. I am your master, not your mommy! Make sure you eat far away from my neighborhood!"

Marcus begged for forgiveness, and then left in his new pick-up truck that Andel recently purchased and headed west. After driving for over an hour, he stopped at an all-night gas station to find out where he was.

"You're in DeKalb, son. You know, Northern Illinois campus. You're about two hours west of Chicago. Are you lost? Do you need a map?" the cashier asked.

"No, no. I've got navigation. Just need to use it. Never been out this way before." Marcus got in his car and parked two blocks away on a deserted street, almost sick with gut-wrenching hunger.

It was past midnight and several degrees below zero. Marcus didn't even feel the wind-chill. He got out of his car and began to run. A few miles into the town, there was the main intersection full of restaurants and bars. The night was still young for a college town. He entered an Irish pub looking for prey.

"Red wine, please," Marcus ordered as he sat at the bar.

"You're soaked. Did you get splashed?" the bartender asked. She was a cute blonde that smelled like stale beer and cigarettes. Marcus thought she looked extra juicy with the few pounds of extra weight she was carrying.

"No, uh, I'm a runner. Was just working out, training for a marathon," Marcus said, trying to brag. At least he was wearing a sweatshirt and track pants, looking the part. He was proud of himself for attempting a conversation. Maybe the glass of wine didn't quite fit his story, but he paid for his drink and kept the change. The bartender's demeanor instantly turned sour. He then realized he forgot to tip her. *Too late now*, he thought. As he looked around the tavern, he noticed that half the tables were filled. *Not bad for a blustery Monday. The weekend has got to be jammed*, Marcus noted.

A middle-aged woman sat alone in a booth, looking inebriated. Marcus tried to read her thoughts to see if she had a soul worth stealing but drew a blank. His hunger superseded the hunting rules Andel had taught him. He bee-lined over to her seat, hoping she would be drunk enough to leave with him.

"Hi, I'm....Jerry. Can I buy a pretty lady a drink?" Marcus asked, surprised he sounded so smooth. With exception to prostitutes, he didn't communicate with women.

The woman accepted then gestured for him to sit down. She was drunker than he figured. Her slurred speech rambled about her husband who was filing for divorce. Marcus' impatience and hunger grew.

"So, do you want to get out of here and continue this party somewhere else? Perhaps my motel room?" he propositioned, even though he didn't have a motel room. She seemed receptive to his offer. Barely able to stand, Marcus helped her put on her coat. After a couple of steps, she fell. He tried to help her up, but she became angry.

"You son-of-a-bitch! You're all alike! You just want to get laid!" she screamed, causing a scene. Like a deer frozen in headlights, Marcus stood still while all eyes in the bar were staring him down. The woman swung a powerful left hook at his jaw. Humiliated and seen by several witnesses, he decided to hunt somewhere else.

As Marcus walked up and down the main intersection, all the bars were now closing with groups of people loitering the streets. Fear kept him from feeding. He did not want to attract any unnecessary attention. Then he saw the woman who just slugged him stagger down the block. He followed her to her apartment and waited. She fumbled with the keys and then opened the door. Before she could scream, he pushed her inside then sunk his teeth into her neck. She passed out in his arms.

Marcus sucked for several minutes. The blood was filled with vodka, but still satisfied his hunger. Once he was full, he took her hat and scarf and covered his face then carried her to his car. On the way home, he dumped her in the Fox River.

The first week of March showed no signs of winter relief. As the saying went, "March had come in like a lion", and everyone hoped it left like a lamb. The Midwest was buried in snow. As the employees walked into the *Evil Empire's* entrance, floors became very slippery and dirty. Marcus filled in for the receptionist who was running late.

"Marcus, I almost fell down in the entrance way. Do you mind hitting the floors with a mop? Maybe shovel the walkway?" Tony asked. "Don't want anyone to get hurt."

Marcus could feel his eye-teeth grow as his anger rose. One of these days he planned on making Tony pay for his arrogance. Because of his loyalty to Andel, he practiced self-control.

"We have a service to do that, but they are running behind due to the weather. Certainly, I don't want Andel to get sued. I've got it," Marcus replied with a forced smile. He hated all Andel's top agents, especially Tony.

The speaker at the reception desk blared. "Marcus, can you step into my office for a moment?"

Andel sounded upset. Marcus submissively left the reception area unattended and walked over to his master's office.

"Sit down, please. I can smell your fury through the walls of this office. I know. You don't like how people treat you. One of your biggest problems is your image. If you're going to replace me, you've got to come out of your shell. Advertising plants such a powerful seed. It's allowed me to recruit more souls than all my fallen brethren combined. I've hooked consumers for decades by simply using the seven deadly sins of greed, gluttony, sloth, pride, wrath, lust, and envy in my advertisements. I saw this industry's potential and take full credit for what it has evolved into. If you are going to replace me, you've got to replace your mannerisms. This pathetic lackey routine has to change."

"Yes, Master. But you know that I'm not good with people. Please teach me how to be well-liked and popular. I want to make you proud," Marcus said with his head bowed down to the floor.

"To begin with, I'm going to change your stature. People respect titles more than people. Congratulations. You are the new Vice President of the *Evil Empire*. Don't worry. You won't have to do a thing. You'll be too busy learning my ways. I will get you an assistant to launch some kind of newly created division. Ned will help you redecorate your office. You need to be polite, but authoritative in explaining the décor you want. I would suggest something traditional or contemporary, but I'll let you pick out the new furnishings. The title will muster up some free points in the respect department, but we still need a reason for everyone to kiss up to you. I know, you will oversee the Clio Award submissions. If this doesn't make you the most popular man here, I don't what else will. We only submit a couple within each category, and you'll be the one deciding," Andel said.

Marcus was going to enjoy every second of everyone's groveling and flattery. After years of being snubbed, he was finally getting his moment in the sun. Tony's submissions would go directly in the garbage. In fact, the only person at the agency who hadn't slighted him was the new employee, Eve. She would be rewarded for her civility.

"Master, how can I ever thank you? You treat me too well."

Chapter Twenty-One

Sean Slattery was one of the most trustworthy lawyers in all of Chicagoland. At $800 an hour, he prided himself on the straightforwardness his clients relied upon. Because Sean was a wealthy man in his own right, his career gave him the luxury of being honest.

Sean felt a sharp dose of guilt after lying to Lydia Easterhouse's heirs. It wasn't the kind of lie his sleazy colleagues repetitively made throughout the day; it was far worse. Omission was turning him into the kind of person he despised. His fondness of Julia and her daughter, Bell, made it more difficult to start fresh.

Sean Slattery had a long list of traits that single women found most desirable. At forty-two years old, he had the perfect Internet dating profile, but he had no interest in meeting someone off a computer.

Sean's ex-wife foolishly left him for a man of substantially lower caliber. His friends and family set him up on numerous blind dates, but he hadn't felt any chemistry. On the flip side, the women he dated were instantly smitten and always disappointed when he didn't call. All of that changed when Lydia Easterhouse walked into his office several months before her death.

Lydia had the height of the supermodel with the body to match. Her shoulder-length blonde hair enhanced her cheekbones and enormous cornflower blue eyes. Sean was unsure of her age but estimated her somewhere in her mid-thirties.

Sean had never put much effort into charming a woman. His looks and money did all the work for him. Lydia didn't seem to notice. She was all business as she hired him to draw up her will. After he took down all the details regarding her assets, she insisted on waiting until he was finished. Not only was Sean swamped with other work, he planned on taking his time with Lydia's will in hopes of getting the courage to ask her out. Her offer to triple his rate made it clear she was not playing games.

"Are you dying?" Sean asked which he knew was none of his business, but she didn't seem to mind his nosiness.

"No, but soon I will be dead."

"Does someone want to kill you?"

"What will be is what will be. We all fall victim to fate."

"I can finish this by tomorrow. Will you have lunch or dinner with me? I can point out all of the legalese you wanted," Sean asked.

"Why not. You have my address. Pick me up tomorrow at 5:00 p.m. I like to eat early," Lydia said, and then smiled for the first time during their meeting. Her paper white teeth sparkled.

After Sean took care of the business of her will, they enjoyed a delicious Italian dinner and light conversation. He couldn't help but comment after pouring each of them a third glass of wine, "I can't believe you have a granddaughter." He was curious about her age, but she wasn't offering any kind of explanation. Not that it mattered. He didn't care if she was 100 years old. Lydia had cast her spell. His obsession was born. Their dinner led to a series of dinners and an affair he would never forget.

Now that Lydia was gone, Sean had kept their affair to himself. He also neglected to tell her children the time he spent at her Lake Geneva home. He also left out how he had seen the painting referred to in the will. He remembered the day she ended their romance. His devastation was exponentially worse than when his wife left him. Then he heard about her fatal car crash, and he knew why she ended their relationship. Lydia might have been dead, but his love for her wasn't. He wanted to know everything about her.

Sean attended Lydia's funeral and immediately recognized her daughter, Julia, from photos hung in Lydia's homes. He would have recognized her regardless. Julia could have been sisters with her mother. Her daughter, Bell, was also a carbon copy of both mother and grandmother. They were three generations of blonde, blue-eyed beauties. Sean remembered her other daughter, Eve, was also beautiful, but had entirely different coloring. She was not in attendance, as he later learned, because of incarceration. During the funeral, Sean memorized every relative and friend that came. He tried to disguise his prying questions with idle chitchat about Lydia.

The casket was closed and rumored to hold a few of Lydia's charred, dismembered appendages, the only remains found after the explosive car crash. Sean fantasized she was still alive.

The service was small and took place in a non-denominational church. Per Lydia's will, she was buried at a Christian cemetery in her hometown next to her son.

Afterward, Sean hired Abe Silverman, one of the best private detectives in Chicago, to dig up some background. He gave him a list of family names to help begin his search. A few weeks later, Abe dropped by Sean's office.

"Lydia Easterhouse was born in '70 to Harriet East in Los Angeles. Harriet was born in '49. No father listed on either of the birth certificates, but the last name East somehow became Easterhouse. Both Lydia's father and her children's father are unknown. These women don't seem to marry. Lydia had two brothers, Jonathon, 2 years older, and Terrence, 3 years younger, making them 54 and 49. As you know, Lydia had two daughters, Julia, 34, and Eve, 32. One granddaughter, Bell, 6 years old," Abe listed off from a report he had printed.

"Are you sure both Lydia and her mother never married? Kind of odd for the times – children out of wedlock," questioned Sean.

"Not that odd. What do you want me to say? They must have been real swingers?" Abe sarcastically said.

Sean tensed, but held his tongue. Abe assumed this was a routine job, and he thought it was best not to tell him about the relationship he shared with Lydia. Abe continued his report, mentioning her late son, Will.

"Will died at 16 years old. Suicide. Hung himself in the attic. He was buried same place as the mother. Eve, her youngest, was just released from prison. Served over two years for intent to sell. She's a cocaine addict who is now in recovery. What else, oh, as you know, Lydia was currently a member of Community Christian, but she used to belong to a Yelizism temple on the north-side of Chicago. She had all three of her children baptized there."

"Hold up. What is Yelizism?" Sean asked, unfamiliar with the religion.

"As I just learned, it's really a unique religion. Kind of like a cult, a cult of angel worshipers," Abe said.

That explains her choice of interior design and art, thought Sean.

"Anyway, she changed religions. Just giving you the facts. But she did have a prominent place with the Yelizis. In the 1990's brochures I dug up, she was listed under their ministry," Abe said, as he handed him a few church fliers. "Here's an interesting detail. All her children were born poly-dactyl, you know, six-fingered. Don't know about the granddaughter. Lydia had their extra digits removed when they were babies. I don't know if she ever told them."

"What about the artist? Did you get anything on him?" Sean asked.

"Just getting to that. Carlos Bacciani. Born and lived in Florence, Italy. Lydia knew him. She took numerous trips to Europe to visit, and he also flew here to Chicago. Here's a photo of them in the paper at an art show. Can see why his shit is worth so much money," Abe chuckled. "Another complete psycho, like that Van Gogh fellow. Listen to this. He died over five years ago at the age of 46. His body was found in his apartment. Authorities knew it was a suicide, but because of family pressure, ruled it as an accidental death. I talked with one of the cops who found him. He fucking impaled himself on an old sword, some kind of artifact. His family insisted on getting the sword back. It was part of an expensive collection they had. It gets better. His bedroom was wall-papered with pages of Hebrew scripture. Carlos spoke Italian and English."

"What scripture did he hang?" Sean asked.

"Book of Enoch and Jubilees. They aren't in the Bible, but they considered holy. He was obsessed with.... what's the word?" Abe searched his mind.

"Angels?" Sean answered.

"No, nephilim. That's it. They are like angels, but different. So far, that's all I got. Want me to keep going? Gonna cost you another 20Gs plus expenses," Abe stated.

"Yeah. Get more on Lydia's family. Her mother, brothers, aunts, anything you can. Would like to know more about Carlos Bacciani. Was he her boyfriend?" Abe nodded as Sean cut him another check.

Chapter Twenty-Two

The Clio is to the advertising industry as the Oscar is to the Academy Awards. It exemplifies the standard to which advertising executives strive for. The award ceremony airs in the spring, with deadlines for submissions ending in late winter. The award holds the power to advance agencies and careers.

***

Every year Andel Talistokov planned his grandest staff meeting around the Clio nomination process. He hosted his own ceremony with staff presenting their submissions in a formal flair. Sparing no expense, he arranged for gourmet catering, live bands, and other forms of entertainment each year before the event's deadline.

The meeting lasted most of the day in the auditorium. Although Andel had always been the Master of Ceremonies for the agents' presentations, this year he was passing the torch to Marcus, as promised. He hired someone else to run the sound and lighting, while giving Marcus a complete makeover.

Andel looked especially debonair in a designer tux. He hired a professional photographer to take photos for his company's newsletter. For fun, he had a best and worst dressed column that used humiliation to reinforce his formal attire request. Agents presenting their best ad were always perfectly coiffed and elegantly dressed.

Marcus sat in the front row of the auditorium, several pounds beefier and barely recognizable, wearing an expensive designer tux, along with a modern haircut and manicure. His cloudy blue eyes mutated to a vibrant shade of turquoise. Andel would be introducing him as the new Vice President.

"Thank you all for another year of brilliance. This is the *Evil Empire's* fourth annual Clio party, third one here in our Wheaton office. You all know about my longstanding tradition of making this a special event. In the past, I've taken the best advertisements and submitted them to the Clios. All nominees chosen by the judges' panel got a paid week of vacation in New York for their attendance. I also gave a very generous expense account that could be used for clothes, food, entertainment, you name it. This year things will be a little different. I'm entrusting this task to the *Evil Empire's* new Vice President, Marcus Reinsing. For those of you who don't know Marcus, he's been with me for twenty years. Please make time to congratulate him on his well-deserved and long overdue promotion. His office is still in the same location but will be undergoing some minor renovations. Anyone with interior design expertise, please introduce yourself later and offer Marcus some help. Today I'm stepping down from our pre-Clio celebration and having Marcus MC. Let's all give him a hand."

All applauded ingenuously, both surprised and shocked about Andel's announcement. Marcus was seen by most of the agents as a few ladder-rungs below the company custodian. Tony Manghella was among the most surprised.

Deliberately seated next to Eve, Tony leaned towards her ear and whispered, "I can't believe that schmuck is in charge of the Clios."

"Tony, don't you think he must know something about this business? He's been with Andel for twenty years."

"He's good at ordering file cabinets and running the sound system," Tony quipped.

"You wouldn't be jealous now, would you? Maybe you know of someone more deserving," Eve teased.

While Marcus sat in the front row awaiting his cue to take the microphone, he listened to the audience instead of his boss. Since he was bitten, his hearing surpassed all human levels. With focus, he could hear everything within the auditorium. He heard the shockwave reverberate after Andel's announcement. He heard Tony mock his new position to Eve. Her defense was touching. Tony and his allies would not be going to the Clios.

"And now let me give the mic over to our new V.P.," Andel cued.

Marcus strutted onto the stage with his back straight instead of hunched over and his head held high as if he were a king looking down upon his minions. He confidently joked in between each agent's presentations and the audience laughed. He filled in the lulls with witty facts about the company while the agents made their way to the stage. For the first time in his life, he was not the creep who everyone avoided. He was popular.

Eve wore a red designer suit and expensive black heels, looking every bit the part of an advertising exec, but she still was out of place. The term "dress really nice for tomorrow" in the e-vite meant wear a designer evening gown. On the other hand, Claire looked like an Academy Award nominee. Her long, caramel hair was pinned in a fancy up-do and her makeup looked professionally done. She wore a magenta strapless gown with a diamond choker. She proudly submitted a weight-loss ad that she and Catalina Rojas created months ago.

Eve would have appreciated more details about the day, but the ceremony was not about her. She was still too new to compete. As she watched, the creativity blew her away. Each ad was better than the next. Her favorite was the exciting TV commercial Tony created for a video game.

He ended his presentation by giving everyone a code for the game.

At the end of the company's ceremony, each agent received their own *Evil Empire* statue and expensive swag-bag. Everyone moved into the banquet room and partook in the elaborate festivities that Andel had provided. Eve grabbed a plate of food and sat down at an empty table. She pulled out her laptop from her tote bag and logged onto the video game, using Tony's code. She was somewhat of a gamer and also intrigued by his ad.

Paradise Found was a video game modeled after John Milton's epic poem, *"Paradise Lost."* The game's main characters, like Milton's, were God, Jesus, Raphael, Michael, Adam, Eve, and Satan. The video used famous quotes from Milton such as "Better to reign in hell, than serve in heaven" when the player descended into the fiery lake. Some religious zealots and literature buffs protested the game because of its offensive nature. Their rebuke only added to the game's success. While playing the game, Eve could see their perspective, but also believed some educational value was involved. The objectives of the game worked like an interactive cliff-note of the story.

While she enjoyed herself, Marcus approached her wanting to see the popular video game everyone was so enthralled with.

"I see you didn't wear the jewels and the evening gown," Marcus commented.

"No, I just dressed nice, like the memo said to. I feel stupid with everyone so formal."

"You shouldn't. You're so pretty; it doesn't matter what you wear," Marcus said. "Do you like the game?"

Embarrassed, but flattered by the compliment, Eve smiled. "Thanks. And yes, I do like the game, but it's different than what I'm used to. Tony's ad is much better than the product."

"Would it be alright if I took a turn?" Eve nodded. Marcus pulled up a rolling chair while she added another player to the game.

"The object is to get back to Eden," Eve explained. She showed him the control and began to play. The two challenged each other for the rest of the luncheon.

"You're right. The game gets boring after the second level and you're also right, the ad is good," Marcus said.

The next day, Tony found an excuse to hover over Eve's cubicle. He wanted her input on his video game commercial and the actual game itself. She honestly told him her likes and dislikes. Running out of conversation, he desperately racked his brain for a new topic. "I have a computer problem. How do you convert one type of file in another type to use in another application?"

Eve opened an unimportant file to demonstrate. "First you pull down this window and then..."

"I'm sorry. I'm lying. I already know how to do that. Just wanted an excuse to talk to you. Would you have dinner with me tomorrow evening?" Tony asked.

Eve accepted. She wanted him to ask her out since her interview.

On the other side of the immense office floor stood Marcus, hearing every word Eve and Tony uttered. He hated Tony even more, if that was possible. With Andel leaving town to attend to other agencies, Marcus had a window of opportunity for some justice. Without the ever watchful eye of Andel, Tony would be out of his way soon enough.

Chapter Twenty-Three

"Mom, please hang my picture up," Bell reminded.

Julia purchased a gilded frame for the canvas. While she tautly nailed the canvas inside the frame, she couldn't help but admire the detail given to her mother's face. The artist seemed to have captured her soul. The other three angels in the painting were set in the distance of the scene, but also had swords in their hands. The man they were battling looked to be on the defensive. His face was covered with his arm as the Lydia-look-alike angel militantly attacked. *This must have symbolized something very important to Mom.*

Julia finished the mini-project and then hung the painting above Bell's headboard. She took a mental note to get the painting appraised and insured later during the week.

Both Julia and Eve were eager to find out about their mother's relics left behind at the Lake Geneva home. As promised, Julia looked up an old friend from high school, Doctor Sandra Jackson, who currently held a post at Loyola University. She hoped that her friend, Sandra, or one of her colleagues could identify the script and point Julia in the right direction in finding out its translation. If luck were on her side, they would be able to answer all of her questions.

Julia quickly found Sandra online listed under the College of Arts and Sciences. She called her at work, and Sandra was available to talk. They quickly caught up with each other's lives until Sandra got down to business.

"Julia, I'm so glad you called. Is this a purely social call or is there anything I can help you with?" Sandra asked, sensing that Julia was withholding something from her.

"Well, yes. I'm embarrassed to call after all these years of failing to keep in touch. And now when I could use your help, here I am. I'm a lousy friend. Please forgive me," Julia begged.

"It's okay. I haven't called either, so I'm also a lousy friend as well. Please, I'd love the chance to help. What can I do?"

Julia remained as vague and elusive as possible, briefly describing some of the carvings found in the basement wall. She told Sandra that she copied down the markings and wanted to know what they meant. She also described the old scroll, without commenting about the *who's, where's, and when's.* She purposely omitted other things.

"Julia, this all sounds very mysterious. Please bring what you have and come around lunchtime, tomorrow. We're all here in our cubicles. If I can't help you, I'm confident one of my colleagues can. See you then."

Later that evening, Julia informed Eve about the meeting with the Loyola staff.

"These heirlooms will bring us fame and fortune. They are our 'holy grail'! I feel like Indiana Jones!" Eve exclaimed.

"Don't get too blissful. They might not be able to help," Julia cautioned.

Overhearing the conversation, Bell became upset. "But Mom, who is gonna pick me up from school?"

"Holly's mom is. You're going to stay there until I get back, probably around dinner time," Julia assured.

"Mommy, those Loyola people are strangers! You just can't be showing them Grandma's things! It's not right! It's not what she would have wanted! Lonnie doesn't trust your friend!" Bell's petulance escalated. In desperation, she threw her aunt into the argument. "Auntie Eve, don't let her do this! Especially Grandma's scroll! It's too dangerous!"

Although Eve was uneasy about her niece's behavior, she was not going to let a six-year-old manipulate Julia's and her plans. "Sweetie, your mother and I are curious about Grandma's stuff. She is taking these things to a very smart bunch of people who may be able to help us. No one is going to wreck it or steal it."

"I already know what it is! Grandma was an angel, or a nephilim! Why don't you believe me?" Bell screamed as she raced up to her room.

The next day, Julia packed up her own drawing of her mother's carved wall, the scroll, and the piece of metal. Her excitement put her in a giddy mood. Once parked and in front of Loyola's main entrance, her friend Sandra met her in the foyer and escorted her back to the Arts and Science College. Sandra took Julia to their lounge and introduced her to six other professors who were equally interested in seeing her finds. All of them specialized in fields that had to do with the ancient world.

Julia began with unveiling her own copy of the symbols she drew from her mother's basement.

"I appreciate all of your attention. Can anyone tell me what this is, and if possible, what it means? Each symbol was copied down in the order it was etched into the wall," Julia said.

One professor immediately took the paper and made a copy. This made Julia uncomfortable. He asked, "Where did you find this?"

"Again, none of that matters," Julia stuttered. Her daughter's omen chimed throughout her brain. The man intuitively put up her defenses.

"Doctor Nrogbi's English is somewhat limited. He's not trying to be pushy or rude," Sandra explained.

"This is Angelic script, also known as Adamite language, alphabet of the Ark, or even Enochian. It's the first written language of this world. Angels used it to communicate with God. The first humans also used it before the Fall," Doctor Nrogbi lectured.

"Before what fall?" Julia asked, very confused. *How could Bell have known all of this?*

"Before Adam and Eve sinned. Before they were kicked out of Eden. It pre-dates Hebrew, Sanskrit, Aramaic, and other ancient languages. It's very sophisticated and difficult to translate. These symbols look like a key, invocation, or lyric. Let me get something off my bookshelf."

While he frantically flipped through several of his books, other professors rattled off bits and pieces of their own views concerning the script. Julia learned that Enoch didn't name the language, but his name was used in its classification. Enoch was famous for his communications inside of Heaven.

The professors spoke of John Dee, a famous mathematician, cartographer, and seer of Queen Elizabeth I. He had a revelation about angelic script and later recorded it. Sir Edward Kelley, his colleague, also witnessed the revelation and recorded additional symbols called Keys or Calls. Their legitimacy has been debated for centuries.

"Ah, I found it. What you have here is a Key. Angel script is read left to right. These symbols together are sort of like a prayer. A rough translation in English means, 'Forever fallen is forever damned, until one can unlock from within.' I wish I knew where you found this. The context would help cypher the meaning," Doctor Nrogbi stated.

"Anyone have an inkling to what the passage could mean?" Julia asked.

"I can only guess that fallen is either man, as in Adam, or possibly angels, as in the Fallen that waged war with Satan against God. He and all his angels were cast out of Heaven and damned to Hell. However, there could be a loophole – 'unlock from within.' Don't know, just a guess, answered Doctor Barry Lowenstein, an ancient comparative literature professor.

"Julia, you said you had a few more items to show us. Can we see? The anticipation is eating away!" Sandra said. Everyone else was thinking the same thing.

"Okay, I have a scroll that might be of some interest," Julia answered as she gingerly took it out of her large tote and laid it down on a long table. All the professors' jaws dropped in astonishment. They all hovered over the scroll, whispering theories of what it might be. Doctor Nrogbi quickly grabbed his cell phone and began taking photos. The rest of the professors followed suit.

"Tanned animal hide, probably lamb or ram, of the highest quality for ancient times. This must be dated as far back as 500 B.C., maybe even a 1000 B.C. We need to carbon-date this. It's in perfect condition. What was this stored in?" Doctor Lowenstein questioned.

"It came in a box. I didn't bring it with me," Julia replied, feeling suffocated and wanting to leave.

"We could use a combination of steam and chemicals to remove the seal so that it doesn't break. That way we could read the scroll. Can you leave this with Sandra for the next couple of days?" asked Doctor Litner, an art history professor and expert in document preservation.

Can you bring in the box? Can you take us to where this was found? Can you leave this for display? Can we take this to the Smithsonian? Can you, Can you, Can you.... Julia's head was about to explode. She changed her mind about letting them examine the ornate metal she still had in her purse.

"I'll call Sandra and we can do this another time. Thank you all for your help," Julia abruptly announced. She packed up her things and rushed out of the university.

Not paying attention, she almost got hit by a car. Once in her Lincoln Navigator, she calmed down. Rush hour traffic on the Eisenhower Expressway gave her time to process.

As Julia snailed down the highway, she began to rethink her plan of seeing the professors. All of them were too enthusiastic and pushy. She couldn't pinpoint her doubts, but they threatened her, especially Professor Nrogbi. Julia racked through her brain about all the new things she had learned. *Angel script, fallen angels, weird paintings, couldn't be. But Bell's claims were supported independently by a bunch of scholars. This is crazy. Eve is right. Mom must have lost her mind. But then there was the Ouija board, nephilim....*

The long drive allowed Julia to delve deep into her thoughts. A seagull flew on the hood of her car. The bird seemed perfectly content to sit there while Julia snailed along through the traffic.

By the time Julia reached her exit, another two seagulls joined the first one. As Julia accelerated, she was surprised the birds just stayed on the car hood. While stopped at a red light, more birds joined her hood. By the time she was almost home, over a dozen seagulls sat on her car hood. Julia didn't see the other ones on her roof.

Fear of the unknown took hold. Julia began swerving, beeping, and turning on her wipers in attempt to get the birds off her car. They all turned their heads in unison and began pecking at her windshield. The ones on her roof pecked on the sunroof and rear window. In hysterics, Julia floored the gas pedal, desperate to get them off. Screaming, the last thing she saw was blackness.

Chapter Twenty-Four

The search party in Andel's neighborhood grew rapidly. Phillip Krakowski had been missing for over a month. Some of the most hard-working and creative people had dedicated endless hours to finding him. Mass emails with a rough sketch of Marcus and photo of the make and model of his car were sent all over Illinois. Phil's Chicago Bears scarf was found only yards away from where a resident had seen Marcus. Circulation about Phillip and his potential perpetrator had reached over half of the Illinois population. Some of the *Evil Empire* employees had already shared and retweeted the 'missing man' social media posts. The story gained traction in Illinois and neighboring states. It was only a matter of time before someone took a good hard look.

Marcus worried about getting recognized. Luckily, the sketch of him wasn't definitive. He was relieved that Andel would be out of town attending to his other agencies. He now had the opportunity to make executive decisions that his new job title demanded without being under his master's thumb. Andel left him with a brief itinerary of deadlines and meetings.

Once Andel left, Marcus was bombarded with agents who wanted consideration for the Clio submissions. He had less than a week to send in a maximum of twenty entries. Those who had disrespected him were easily eliminated, but that barely put a dent into the piles of work he had to review. He felt overwhelmed and needed help. This was his chance to spend some time with Eve.

Marcus saw Eve in Claire's office and interrupted. "Hi Ladies. I know you are both busy, but I need Eve to help me sort through these entries. Eve, I thought you, being new and all, you know, immune to office politics with exception to Claire, of course, could see the advertisements for their merits. Your input would be greatly appreciated."

Claire was thrilled for obvious reasons and almost pushed Eve out the door. "Go help him. And don't forget about my terrific weight-loss campaign for film and radio."

"Couldn't forget it if I tried," said Marcus. He enjoyed her shameless plug.

Marcus and Eve took their laptops and the entries to the auditorium to review. Eve's long glossy black-brown hair smelled like flowers. Her lithe figure and soft olive skin were another pleasant distraction. His mind wandered.

"For the best in film, I thought Tony's was the most unique. He used some really sophisticated special effects and the commercial made me want to play the video game. And I legitimately thought Claire's weight-loss radio ad is the best for that category. Which ones do you like?" Eve asked, after they reviewed all the television and radio commercials.

Marcus was not going to submit any of Tony's work. "I liked Claire's and Catalina's weight-loss series in both TV and radio. They are very funny, clever, and different than the same old 'fat celebrity gets skinny' advertisement. The ad's submissions in both categories would also honor Catalina Rojas, who you replaced," Marcus decided. Claire was one of the few employees who had always been civil towards him, making the choice easy.

"That's really sweet. What ever happened to her?" Eve asked. She saw Catalina's hysterical mother a week ago by the reception desk.

"Claire didn't tell you?"

"No. All I've heard was that she quit, but no one, including her very upset mother, has heard from her. Do you think she's dead?" Eve questioned, trying not to sound gossipy.

"It sure looks that way. Maybe she was murdered. She was an amazing agent and Andel's favorite. No one really knew her that well except maybe Tony. They seemed quite friendly before she disappeared," Marcus lied, not sure how she would take the innuendo.

Although Marcus liked to trash Tony, he would have preferred to tell Eve every secret he ever had. She had such a nonjudgmental way about her, but murder was something most people did not understand. Her companionship made the job task and afternoon enjoyable. By the end of the day, they selected over half of the submissions and were ahead of schedule.

"We'll leave everything here and finish up on Monday. I hope you have a great weekend," said Marcus as they left the auditorium. As he walked towards his office, he watched Tony approach Eve's cubicle.

"Hey, are we still on for tonight?" Tony asked. "I know this great French restaurant that just opened up. Pick you up at 7:00p.m.?"

Marcus was seething with jealousy. He caught a reflection of himself from a hallway mirror. His blue eyes almost glowed. He needed to collect himself before anyone noticed. It appeared as if Eve was currently dating his office enemy, Tony. Once again, he felt kicked below the proverbial belt. Besides his eyes, the jealous anger elongated his eye-teeth. He knew he had to isolate himself before he lost control. As he headed back to the auditorium, he heard the receptionist interrupt the two new lovebirds.

"Eve, there's been an accident. Central Dupage Hospital has been trying to call you on your cell for the last twenty minutes." Eve checked her phone. She had the volume muted and immediately turned up the sound. The receptionist continued. "Listen, the hospital got through to me at the reception desk. Your sister, she's in the hospital. There's been a car wreck."

"Oh no. Tony, raincheck on tonight. I've got to go. My niece. I got to make some calls," Eve mumbled to herself as she grabbed her things and bolted out of the agency. She was on verge of full-blown panic.

Marcus smiled. Tony would be eating alone. An opportunity had just presented itself.

It was an unusually warm, March night. Restaurants, clubs, and bars were crowded with people excited to be out from being cooped up throughout the long winter. Marcus drove past Tony's townhouse and saw his Lexus in the driveway. Curious if he would change his plans, Marcus staked out his home. Tony lived alongside the train tracks in downtown Wheaton. Several businesses, including a coffee shop, were located across the street. Marcus bought a cappuccino, took a window seat from inside the café and waited.

An hour later, Tony was outside on his tiny porch, locking up his front door and then heading towards his red two-seater Lexus. Marcus hurried back to his truck and pulled up a few cars behind Tony. Tony was oblivious that he was being followed. He finally pulled into a nightclub several towns away in Schaumburg. Marcus passed the club, and then turned around a few minutes later. The place was enormous, trendy, and crowded. Almost every parking spot was taken. Marcus found Tony's Lexus and watched it for an hour. Once it became apparent Tony was not leaving, Marcus headed back to his townhouse.

Tony predictably had a hide-a-key located in his tiny backyard. Marcus found it in less than ten minutes hidden behind his AC unit. He let himself inside. Without turning on the lights, his eyes naturally adjusted to the night; he could see perfectly. Tony's home was spotless. The only thing Marcus could smell was cleaning products. His place was sparsely finished with neutral colors and couch covers, giving it a shabby-chic look. Televisions hung on the walls of every room. Taped up boxes were stored in his extra bedrooms. Tony had yet to unpack, in spite of moving from Los Angeles since the agency opened. Marcus was hungry and had nothing to do but wait for Tony to come home. He found Tony's laptop on the kitchen table. He turned it on and browsed through his emails and files. The computer had no password log-on and remembered Tony's passwords, making it extra easy for Marcus to snoop. *Oh shit! He's got an email with my sketch on the missing Winfield man. And he's saving it. I bet he suspects I killed Phillip Krakowski.* As he deleted the email, he heard Tony's garage door raise.

Marcus slammed the computer shut and dodged behind the long, darkening drapes in the living room. The element of surprise and his new super-human strength would make the kill easy.

"You're so funny," slurred a female voice. Someone flicked on the lights.

Tony had company. *Damn that bitch for wrecking my timing.* Marcus could smell fruit, rum, and daiquiri mix.

"Would you care for another drink?" Tony asked.

"I want to party with you all night long. Make me your house specialty. Nice place you got," she said, and then plopped down on the sectional couch only feet away from Marcus. He could see her profile through the long drape. Tony's guest was an attractive strawberry blonde.

Marcus could hear Tony using the blender in the kitchen. He wasn't sure if he wanted to kill Tony's guest along with Tony, or just leave the place hungry. He could always postpone his plans for revenge. His confidence dwindled. Missing people within the same general location were starting to accumulate.

Tony sat very close to the woman. Marcus wished they would go to the bedroom so that he could leave.

They both guzzled their drinks, and Tony made his move. They were kissing and fondling each other. Tony gently pushed her down on the couch and massaged her breasts. He then kissed her neck, and she passionately moaned. As Marcus watched, something was not right. The woman got too quiet. Blood trickled on the woman's blouse and she began to go into a seizure.

In shock, Marcus almost screamed and gave himself away. *No! Not him, too! He's feeding!*

Chapter Twenty-Five

Abe Silverman dropped a ton of bricks on top of Sean Slattery. The bizarre information pertaining to his dead girlfriend, Lydia Easterhouse, only indulged his obsession. Sean poured himself a large scotch and stayed up all night re-reading Abe's report.

Abe was very expensive, but extremely thorough. Each piece of information he found was backed up with addresses, websites, copies, or any relevant details concerning the job. Sean banged away on his laptop looking up Lydia's family, her friend Carlos Bacciani, her church, and any other lead Abe had to offer. Lydia's old church was the easiest for him to investigate. The Yelizi-inspired church had a service the following morning, and Sean planned on attending.

The church was located on the north-side of Chicago. The building was old, but nicely maintained. The red bricks and stained-glass windows looked benign enough for Sean to enter. Because of limited parking, Sean had to circle the block several times before finding a space. This setback caused him to be several minutes late for the service.

He noticed all the beautiful hand-painted tile over the walls and floors. The interior of the building had an Arab mosque design. Elaborate mosaics of peacocks and angels bordered the four-story cathedral ceiling.

The service had already begun, and Sean did not want to walk in and draw attention to himself. Instead, he watched through the nave door's small, rectangular window. Since the lobby was empty, he walked around and helped himself to some extra programs and brochures neatly stacked on a breakfront.

One of the fliers explained the religion's Iraqi origins while making a plea for donations to their sister Kurdish congregations. Yelizism was an obscure Middle Eastern practice that slowly and quietly spread throughout Europe and the United States. The religion adapted to western culture by adding their own rituals. The Chicago branch, like the Middle East practitioners, remained faithful to Malak Tawas, the peacock angel. Many angels were worshiped, but Malak was the religion's main avatar.

Sean had researched the religion the night before and learned that Malak Tawas was also known as Satan in other parts of the world. Critics of the religion deemed it as a cult of devil worshipers. As a staunch Catholic, this was not the kind of religion that he could tolerate. He tried to keep an open mind while reminding himself that Lydia had left the church decades ago.

Through the window, Sean could see everyone praying. He assumed they were speaking in tongues because of the odd pronunciation and sounds. Expecting to see the pews filled mainly with Middle Eastern people, he was astonished to see such diversity among the congregation.

Sean noticed Lydia's two brothers with their wives standing by the altar, and assumed they held a prominent position within the church, much like a deacon or elder. They wore long white robes with teal satin trim. Large gold medallions with odd symbols and pearls hung around their necks. Several members of the congregation wore smaller versions as jewelry.

The congregation sang a cacophonous melody that made Sean wince. During the hymn, Lydia's brothers set four bird cages on the altar then let them fly out once the song ended. Tame doves and seagulls greeted the church members. Some of the birds landed on their shoulders, seats, and even their hands. Everyone whispered their prayers and then formed a line, taking turns in bowing down to a bird sculpture they called Anfar. The service officially ended after an ultra-quick baptism and local announcements.

Sean had so many questions, but worried about being intrusive. Lydia's brothers doubtfully remembered him. He felt like a stalker of the dead with his obsession getting more disturbing by the minute.

Lydia's brothers and their wives were listed on the program as part of the diocese's ministry. After everyone cleared out, Sean approached the priest with a sizable check, hoping the money might buy some of his time.

As the priest gradually put the birds back into their cages, Sean walked into the assembly and introduced himself.

"Hi there. I'm Sean Slattery. Quite a service. Do you always end it with the birds? Very interesting," he said as he offered his hand to shake.

"Yes, we do. It's part of our worship ritual. May I help you?" asked the priest. He was a small, old man with dark, brooding eyes, gray hair, and a thick Italian accent. He shook Sean's hand, yet remained skeptical to the stranger.

"I would like to make a donation to your church. I'm sure you will put it to good use. If you could just enlighten me about this fascinating religion?"

The priest readily took Sean's $500 check and became more receptive. "Gratitude, Mr. Slattery. I'm Father Sardenelli. You are in a church that practices Yelizism, the oldest religion on earth. We worship God's angels. These birds symbolize their wings. That bird or peacock is Malak Tawas, head of the angels," explained the priest as he pointed to the stained-glass window. "This particular church has been here for close to a century. This is not...We don't engage in missions...How do I say this without offending you?"

"Please, Father, I respect your religion's ways and will not be offended. Go ahead," Sean said.

"I appreciate the donation, but if you're looking to join our congregation, we only invite new members via referral of existing members or ancestry. I apologize, but we are not open to the public. Usually, our doors are locked, and visitors are not allowed in. So that there are no hard feelings." The priest apologized, handing Sean back his check.

"Father, you misunderstand. Please keep the donation. I've come here out of curiosity, nothing more. A good friend of mine used to attend these services. Me coming here is my way of getting to know her. She died a few months ago and, I'm embarrassed to say, I can't stop thinking about her. I didn't know her as well as I thought, but I was in love with her. I saw her family at your service. They don't know me," Sean poignantly shared.

"Your sadness shows; you wear your grief on your sleeve. What was her name?" the priest inquired.

"Lydia. Lydia Easterhouse. This must seem really pathetic, just showing up to your service. I'm sorry," Sean said.

"I never met Lydia, but I do know of her. Both her brothers and her mother still worship here. I know that the family had some sort of falling out and Lydia stopped attending years before I was transferred. They rarely speak her name. But others claim that she was known as an extraordinary being. I now understand why you have come here," Father said.

"Isn't her family the founders of this church? I saw their names listed under your ministry," Sean pried. He saw the regret in the priest's eyes for telling him about her family.

"They have done much for our faith. Would you like me to pass them your phone number and you can directly ask them about their connection to this church? Maybe they can ease some of your grief."

"We don't know each other. It would be too awkward. I never knew they had a falling out. Lydia never talked about them," Sean said.

"Mr. Slattery, maybe I've said too much. If you don't mind, I have a great deal of work to do," the priest dismissively said while motioning Sean towards the exit.

"Of course, Father. Thank you for your time. You've been most helpful. Please allow me one last question. One of Lydia's favorite artists, Carlos Bacciani, loved to paint and sculpt angels. Was he well known within your religious circles?" Sean asked.

"We have one of his early works in our lobby. It was here before I was. You can take a look at it, but then you must go." Father Sardenelli showed him the peacock and the Anfar painting. Seconds later, the priest opened the front door for Sean and directed him to leave.

Sean's head was spinning. The church service and the priest only raised more questions for him to fixate upon. He ran through their conversation several times on his ride back home. Many things didn't sit well. The church made him uncomfortable.

Lydia, wherever you are, I wish you trusted me. I loved you so much. Anything you may have done wouldn't have mattered. For the first time since her death Sean cried.

Father Sardenelli watched Sean walk down the block to his Mercedes and drive off. He rushed into his back office and dialed the phone.

"It's Dominick. We might have a problem. Why don't you come to my office as soon as you can?"

Chapter Twenty-Six

Eve raced to the hospital after the agency's receptionist told her about her sister's accident. She screeched her tires in front of the emergency entrance and tossed the valet her keys. Her sister was being monitored in the ICU.

"Her airbag didn't go off. She slammed into a traffic post. Her head hit the windshield and her left arm is broken from the impact. There's some internal bleeding, a cracked rib, but she'll be alright. Right now, we want her to stay overnight for observation. Her head injury might be worse than we think. Hopefully, it's just a bad concussion. Soon we're going to move her to her own room," the doctor said upon meeting Eve in the waiting room. Eve looked at the woman's freckles and red hair woven back in a French braid. She looked more like a cheerleader in high school.

An old, overweight black nurse stood next to the doctor and held Julia's coat and purse. After the doctor was finished speaking, the nurse said, "Here, this was salvaged by the paramedics. Her car was towed to a nearby Lincoln dealership." The nurse handed Eve her sister's personal items and a business card as the doctor rushed off. "Don't worry. That woman might look young, but she was top of her class at University of Chicago. Have some faith. Everything will be okay. She'll need some things from home to make her stay more comfortable. She might be here tomorrow night as well. She said she has a daughter. Are you available to pick her up?"

"Yes, but I'm not sure where she even is," Eve worried.

"The phone inside of her bag has been ringing a lot. Check it. I'll bet you it's her daughter," the nurse said, and then walked back into the ICU.

The nurse was right. Eve easily found Bell and then picked her up from her friend's house. Together they went home and packed Julia's toiletries and pajamas. They picked out an enormous bouquet of roses from the floral shop to bring up to Julia's room.

Julia was groggy and emotional, but soon drifted back to sleep. Eve and Bell watched the Disney channel on Eve's laptop until Bell fell sound asleep on the small couch. Eve's eyes were drooping. She got up and collected their things. It was time to go home. Julia's eyes suddenly opened.

"She asleep?" Julia asked while looking at Bell.

"Yeah, I was just getting ready to take her home," Eve said.

"Can you take care of her until I'm released?"

"Of course. You don't need to even ask. Just let me know her regular routine so that I can clear it at work," Eve said.

"Where's my purse?" Julia asked. She looked frightened as she looked around at the machines that were monitoring her.

"Don't freak out. They think you're going to be fine. You might get off with some broken bones and a concussion if we all are lucky…"

Unfazed or interested in her health issues, Juliet snarled, "Listen, Eve, where's my purse?"

"Sorry. Your purse, the nurse gave it to me. And your coat, too. I dropped them off at home. Don't worry about your car. It's at the Lincoln dealership here in town. Do you want me to just have them fix it or do you want me to get some estimates?"

"I don't give a shit about my car. It's my purse that I am concerned about. It's got Mom's things inside. I went to Loyola this afternoon to see Sandra and her colleagues," Julia snapped.

"I'll look inside and make sure everything is still there once we're home. What's going on? You seem very upset," Eve asked.

"Upset? I'm far beyond upset. You're going to think I'm crazy, just like Mom, but I'm going to tell you this anyway," Julia whispered. She looked at her hospital room's door and empty bed next to her. Eve felt the hairs on her neck stand up from her sister's paranoia.

"I'm listening. I almost forgot about your meeting. So, things didn't go well?"

"Didn't go well? Are you fucking serious? Look at me. Look where I am right now. This is not because I lost control of the car. It was a bad idea looking up Sandra Jackson. She and her professor friends wanted me to leave the scroll with them," Julia whispered.

"I'm not following you. Are you surprised they would ask that? I would think that they would need to do some tests, you know, like check the scroll's authenticity. And then find out about the chemical makeup of the piece of metal, possibly?"

"They never saw the metal. Something told be to run before I took it out of my bag," Julia interrupted. "And Bell is right about everything. Those carvings in Mom's basement are angel script. Mom was conditioning Bell for something. You are so wrong about our mother. She was not insane. She knew about something, something big. Something to do with religion."

"You need to calm down. You're getting loud and hysterical. Do you need a tranquilizer, perhaps? The accident has frightened you," Eve said.

"Calm down? Don't patronize me. Do you know how I cracked up the car? A pack or gaggle or school or whatever you call a bunch of fucking seagulls landed on my car while I was driving. They wouldn't fly away. Then they all started pecking at my windows – at the same time, in synch! I couldn't see. I accelerated the car, swerved around, and honked my horn trying to get them off, but they weren't moving. Then I crashed. I'm lucky to be alive right now. Mom died in a car accident! Coincidence?"

Eve listened to her sister and wondered if she was delusional. "But Mom's car exploded after crashing it into a truck. This is different. You're okay," Eve reasoned. "Do you think you were setup? Do you think Mom was set up?"

"Check to make sure Bell is asleep, okay?" Julia asked, looking at Bell.

"Yes, she's in a very deep sleep right now. Probably dreaming about Grandma, the angel," Eve said as she rolled her eyes.

Julia continued with her insinuation. "Yes, I think I was 'set up', and yes, someone tried to kill me, and yes, I think someone succeeded in killing Mom. Think about it. Our grandmother, uncles, aunts, cousins, everybody in our family-We only see them at funerals, not even weddings. When we were little, we saw them all the time. Then there is our brother, Will. He's dead. Our father? Please, we don't even know who he is. We barely remember a man in the house, and who is to say he was our father. The only pictures Mom had of him were of him alone; there was no one else in the photos. Could be anybody for all we know. Another question – Who is to say that we even have the same father? Will and I looked alike, but you and I don't."

"I always thought I had another father. That's why I am the black sheep of the family," Eve replied.

"Black sheep? The whole family is one big fucking black sheep. It's all a lie. Everything she ever told us. Let's face it, Mom was living a secret life, and she was protecting us from it. Now all we have left are remnants about who she really was," Julia said.

"I've wondered, too. But a nephilim or an angel? C'mon. That's a tough pill to swallow," Eve countered.

"Listen, I'm ashamed to admit this, but when I was doing all that remodeling, I found more of those big rocks she liked to use for her garden inside of the wall. They had the same weird symbols as the wall in the basement of her lake house. Today I learned it's called Enochian or Adamite writing. It's the language between God, His angels, and the first humans ever created. Do you know what else I found? Will's suicide note: the one he supposedly never wrote. There was more cash, a great deal more. When I get out of here, we're holding another séance. Mom's Ouija board was some kind of portal for communicating," Julia said. Her blue eyes danced with madness.

Eve took all of this in with skepticism. Julia was either a stark raving lunatic or telling her the most incredulous true story she had ever heard.

"We are getting some information from our grandma. It's about time for her to share the family's secrets," Julia rambled.

"I'm exhausted. See you tomorrow, okay?" Eve couldn't listen to any more of her rantings. She carried Bell to her car, went home, and then tucked her into bed. It was after 2:00 a.m. and the phone rang.

"Hello," Eve answered.

"My purse. Check it please," Julia asked with urgency.

"Everything you took is still inside of it. Get some rest. I'll bring it to the hospital tomorrow if you want," Eve offered.

"No, put it inside the floor of my closet for now and thanks. I love you," Julia said.

Eve easily found Julia's secret hiding spot underneath the carpet of the closet floor. She had way too much money stashed inside. She also found Will's letter, instantly recognizing the choppy handwriting.

Mom, Julia, and Eve,

Do not blame yourselves. I love all of you but need to leave this world before it swallows my soul. I can no longer bear the voices inside my head, or the demons that visit me in my dreams. The line between good and evil is all but erased and I am unsure about which side I am supposed to take. I want God to decide my destiny, not genetics. My ancestors' free will has poisoned me. I am not a human, but a being that does not deserve worship. I refuse to alter any one's soul for any purpose. May your fate be one of ignorance.

See you on the other side,

Will

Did Will think he was an angel or nephilim? A demon? Voices in his head? I wonder if they are the same voices that I used to hear. The same ones that I quieted with cocaine. The same ones that I still hear from within.

Eve read the letter again and sobbed. The vision of his limp body swaying as he hung from the attic's rafters would be tattooed on her memory bank forever.

Chapter Twenty-Seven

Marcus' heart almost exploded as he watched Tony feed from a woman in his living room. Tony failed to see him hidden behind the long drapes, but Marcus could see an outline of them through the fabric.

Once Tony was finished with the woman, he rolled her dead body in the couch cover, revealing plastic covered couch cushions underneath. Because of Tony's anticipated clean-up, Marcus concluded this was not his first time. Once Tony was done wiping down the couch, he slung the body over his shoulders and went inside his attached garage. Marcus beelined towards the back door and dashed several yards away until he was out of sight. A few minutes later, Tony's garage door rose, and he drove off, presumably to dispose of the body.

I can't fucking believe this! This guy has everything: good-looking, charismatic, successful, and even superhuman! I thought I was the only one. How dare Andel change him! Or did he? Is it possible that Andel doesn't know anything about this? Marcus felt incredibly betrayed and needed Andel to address his concerns.

The following Monday, Marcus heard that Eve would be taking care of her six-year-old niece until her sister was ready to be released from the hospital. He saw an opportunity to get closer.

"Why don't you bring Bell here when she gets out of school? I've got several children's ads to go through for the Clio awards. Her input would greatly help the process, and she might even enjoy it. I've got some toy samples to give her," Marcus offered.

"What a wonderful idea! Thanks for suggesting it. The change of scenery might do her some good. The last six months have been difficult. Parents divorced. Her grandmother died. And now, her mother is in the hospital. The poor kid needs a diversion," Eve replied.

Throughout the morning Marcus and Eve chatted in the auditorium while selecting Clio submissions. Both instantly felt at ease with each other and took their conversation beyond small talk.

"My parents died a long time ago. Terrible accident. And the rest of my family is completely dysfunctional. I've been estranged from them for years. Andel is both a friend and father to me. He's the only family I have," Marcus explained.

"I also have family I'm not close with. There must have been a falling out with my mother and my grandmother and uncles. I barely remember them. Right now, all I got are my niece and my sister, but I'm very grateful," Eve said.

"You could always call them or write. Excuse me for being blunt, but you're a beautiful, smart, and kind woman. One day you'll have your own family. Tony, for one, seems to have feelings for you," Marcus said, fishing for the status quo of their relationship.

"Well, it's all very pre-mature. We haven't even gone out on a date. Right now, I'm just focused on my job," Eve said as she blushed. This information was music to Marcus' ears.

Lunchtime was approaching, and Marcus was about to offer some take-out for a working meal. Tony walked into the auditorium and squelched his plans.

"Just here to see if Eve would like to take a short break and eat with me in my office. I got a stuffed pizza, the best in Chicago."

You prick! It's not even noon and you ace me out of her lunchtime company. If I didn't hate you so much, I would try to learn something from you, thought Marcus.

"Are you hungry? Marcus, would you mind if she took a quick break?"

Sure, Marcus thought. *If I say 'yes, I do mind', then I look like a real asshole.* "Go right ahead. I'll be here."

Marcus also needed a break. He went into his newly renovated office, surprised to learn it was complete. His name and vice president title were painted on the door. The office was a contemporary masterpiece filled with elegant hues of grays and smoky blues. Mahogany furniture and built-in bookcases gave the room a touch of character. On the wall hung a colorful painting of a peacock with his feathers fully fanned out. A card was tucked in the corner. A gift for your new office. My master is now yours. Andel

Marcus wasn't sure of the significance of the painting and the card but would ask Andel once he returned. He flipped the remote aimed at his hanging flat-screen TV and searched for the local news. The broadcaster reported the day's top stories, and then updated the Chicago area about the still-missing Phil Krakowski. A rough sketch of Marcus was shown on the news program. There was a likeness, but no one had yet to mention it to him. A new haircut and some facial hair would completely distance himself from the sketch.

Over an hour had passed, and Marcus was ready to get back to work. He was astounded to see Eve already back from her lunch, going through the print ads.

"Hi. Just comparing these magazine ads. They are stunning. I don't use any of these cosmetics; they are much too expensive. But the models all look so flawless. I'm tempted to treat myself to some new make-up," Eve said as she showed him the glossy ads.

"Then these ads are doing their job. But the models really aren't that gorgeous, and the make-up isn't that good. It's the photographer that Andel uses. He's a genius at taking the attractive and making it irresistible. He also uses photo manipulation," Marcus said.

"So, these gorgeous women don't look like this?" Eve asked.

"They are that skinny, even skinnier than in the photo, but no, they are not that pretty. I'll take you to one of his photo shoots next time we use him. Hold on, I'll be right back," Marcus said. He returned with a couple of boxes of cosmetics. "Take what you want. There's at least ten different lipstick colors, mascara, foundation, you name it. Try it out and let me know if this stuff is really worth $80 a tube."

"Thank you, but this is too much. Just a few things and it adds up to $300 worth of make-up," Eve said.

"Take it all. Give some to Claire. It's been back there for a while," Marcus proposed, pleased with himself for thinking of it. Since his change, communicating with women was much easier.

"I'm going to give my sister and Claire a couple of these lipsticks. Again, thanks. And before I forget, this lipstick ad is my favorite. I love the woman's wild hair and jungle background. Her lips are such a deep bronze. Gorgeous girl and gorgeous ad."

"Then we'll stick with that one. I wouldn't know how to pick some of these entries without you," Marcus remarked.

"It's almost 3:00 p.m., and I've got to pick up my niece. I'll be back soon. Her school is just a few miles from here."

Once Eve pulled away from the parking lot, Claire Jacobsen came into the auditorium wanting to speak with Marcus.

"Hi. Just wanted to say thanks. Eve told me you chose Catalina's and my weight-loss campaign for a few different categories. Much appreciated," Claire said.

"You both did an outstanding job. Our client was very satisfied, and best of all, sales significantly rose as a result."

"Again, thanks. I also wanted to talk with you about Eve," Claire said with caution.

"She's wonderful. Thank you for referring her to the agency. Sorry to have taken her from you. We are almost finished, and you'll get her back soon," Marcus replied, oblivious to her tone.

"No, it's not that. I know she's the new girl, and really pretty, eager to please. It's just that she's not part of our inner circle. You know, she doesn't live and breathe for Andel. She's never going to be one of his disciples," Claire said.

Marcus wasn't sure how to respond and instantly became defensive. "It wasn't that long ago when you tried to kill him. And now you consider yourself his disciple? I'm the only disciple he has. And as far as Eve is concerned, what would be so wrong if she chose to worship him?"

"Listen, I'm not trying to offend you. Eve and I go to AA together. We're friends. She's got a lot of problems and doesn't need to get involved with some of the hedonism that goes on around here. That's all," she affirmed.

"I respect that, but you should be reserving your lecture for Tony. He's been asking her out for a week."

"I apologize. I just thought...I got the wrong man. He's going to be getting a repeat performance of my big mouth. I just don't want her to end up like Catalina."

Eve shortly returned with Bell who was greeted with swarms of attention. Eve escorted her back to the auditorium and introduced her to Marcus. He gave her candy and toys to win her affection.

"Okay Bell, we need your expertise. Let's start with the catalogs. I have three toy catalogs but can only enter one in this award show called the Clios. It's going to be on TV in a couple of months, and I need you to tell me which one makes you want to beg your mom or your aunt for the toys it sells," Marcus instructed.

Bell studied each catalog trying to assess every item. "These catalogs are so fun. Look, Auntie Eve, this doll book has hidden letters right here on the first page."

"Bell, they aren't puzzle books. It's a catalog, you know, a magazine that lets you conveniently buy things without going to the store," Eve explained.

"Auntie Eve, I know what a catalog is! Look closer! See? There's a "W" in the fold of her dress, and then an "O." Her dog has a "RSH" on his tag, and then the wagon has an "I" and "P." W O R S H I P, worship, right? That's what that spells."

"Give me that." Eve impatiently grabbed the catalog out of her hands and studied the first page. The letters were crystal clear and intentionally placed in the ad.

Oh no, Eve thought. Julia's comment *'Bell is right about everything'* thundered in her mind. She wondered if all the ads were somehow riddled with messages.

"Bell, can I see? Oh yes, she is so right! You are such the smart one!" Marcus exclaimed. He already knew Andel was using subliminal messages in most of his ads, but didn't realize they were so blatant.

"Marcus, look. On this page you can see angel script. Right there. That's how angels write. My grandma knew how to write like this." In the same catalog Bell pointed to the symbol disguised in the doll's hat.

Marcus had seen the angel script before, but never knew what it was. Andel kept religion out of their relationship. "Bell, what exactly is angel script?"

"It's symbols angels used to write with. My grandma knew all about it. She was an angel, or a nephilim."

"Wow, such a vocabulary. I've never heard of that word. Does it also mean angel?" Marcus asked.

"It's someone who is half angel and half human, like my grandma," Bell explained.

Eve hoped he took her comments figuratively and wanted to leave before the conversation turned even more abnormal. "Marcus, it's dinnertime. Can we finish this up tomorrow? I was going to pick up dinner and visit my sister in the hospital."

"Terrific. One question before you leave. What's your favorite catalog?" Marcus questioned.

"I like this one the best. There's lots of toys and it's the only one without hidden letters or angel script."

The other catalog also had subliminal messages, contemplated Eve.

"Then this is the one I will send to the Clios. Thank you, Bell. You are a delight. I hope you come here more often. And don't forget your toys," Marcus said.

Chapter Twenty-Eight

Abe Silverman had investigated over five hundred cases throughout his twelve years as a private investigator and thirty years as a policeman. At sixty-three years old, he had thought he had seen it all. Having seen all seven deadly sins at their ugliest, he was still unprepared for his latest case involving Lydia Easterhouse.

Sean Slattery, Abe's long-time associate, neglected to tell him about the mine field he was about to step in. He was already suspicious. For the first time in their decade-long relationship, Sean was unconcerned with fees and expenses. Abe was given a carte blanche in following any trail that stemmed from Lydia and took full advantage. Always wanting to see Italy, he chose to dig up more information about the death of Carlos Bacciani, Lydia's favorite artist and former boyfriend.

Abe set up a meeting in Florence with Detective Magliano. For five thousand U.S. dollars, the detective promised him copies of the file with an English translation. He also agreed to add more information and theories about the Bacciani family.

Abe checked into a nicer hotel than he was used to. His suite had all the amenities of an apartment along with a breathtaking view of the Arno River. He planned on staying a full week to soak in some sight-seeing in between work-related tasks. Florence was filled with art, architecture, and culture. Always dreaming of an Italian vacation, he was not going to waste an opportunity of mixing business with pleasure.

Abe met Detective Magliano in his hotel lobby. The short, heavy-set policeman preferred to conduct their business in the privacy of Abe's room.

"So off-the-record, what are we dealing with?" Abe asked after the exchange.

"Per our arrangement, I'll tell you everything I know. I'm not surprised to see a private investigator poking around this case," observed the detective in perfect English. Abe offered him a Coke from the room's mini bar. The Italian guzzled half the can. "First, a little background you may or may not know. Carlos came from old money. Long line of blue bloods, clergymen, government officials, leaders in industry, just about anybody who is somebody. They are all part of the Yelizi religion. As I understand it, they tend to worship the fallen angels over the ones that still live in Heaven. Birds are used in their ceremonies." Abe's ears perked up. This was the second time this obscure religion was brought up during the week.

"Peacocks?" Abe inquired, already familiar.

"Yes, peacocks are their mascot. Carlos was born into this. He was a brilliant artist. His paintings and sculptures were commissioned by his family's church and other Yelizi churches that exist throughout Europe and the U.S. Something happened. He wanted to distance himself from the church, his family, and all his clients. He began to paint and sculpt in an entirely different style. From whimsical and abstract, he changed to classical, like Raphael. He publicly renounced his old works and tried to buy them all back. He managed to get his hands on half a dozen or so and then publicly burned them," informed the detective.

"Do you have pictures of the pieces he burned?" asked Abe.

"In the file are a few photos of them. I also included his newer works that hang in public museums around Europe. Here's a newspaper article I saved. See the woman in the picture? That's Lydia Easterhouse. I think she was his girlfriend. She's an American. Is that why you are here?"

said Detective Magliano, as he handed Abe the pictures of the paintings. "Attractive couple."

Abe felt uncomfortable sharing information with the policeman. "I'd rather not say at this point. But I do want to know why he renounced his old works."

"Yes of course. And I'm sorry for over-stepping. I don't know why he burned his paintings, but I think everything seems to be related to this angel cult. Once he left his church, he wanted all traces of himself, including his soul, gone," Detective Magliano said.

"So, his family worships fallen angels? Yelizism is devil worship, correct?"

"You've done your homework, Mr. Silverman. Yes, very similar. I don't know if you're religious, but they mainly worship Satan, the most infamous angel of them all. He was an archangel before he tried to become God. As Christianity states, Satan was cast down with a third of all the angels who sided with him. That's where the peacocks come in. They represent Malak Tawas otherwise known as Satan. The Bacciani family and their elite friends opened the first church of this kind right here in Florence. It's not open to the public, so you'll have to sneak in to have a look around if you are curious. They have Friday and Saturday services both day and night, but I'm of course not suggesting you do anything illegal."

"Of course not. That would be against the law," smirked Abe. He now had himself something to do this upcoming Friday night. "You originally told me the artist had papered his apartment in holy scripture."

Detective Magliano flipped through the file and handed more photos to Abe. They were of Carlos' luxury apartment the day he impaled himself.

"These walls were covered with Enoch, Jubilees, and Isaiah. Seems the only common denominator they all have is verses about angels such as cherubim, seraphim, nephilim, arch angels, angels with names, or anything related. This picture is the wall that his bed's headboard was bumped up against. These carvings are called Enochian keys. Don't know much about them except they might be the language of angels."

"Where did this religion come from? I've never heard of it before," Abe asked.

"It originated in the Middle East. Some Kurds still practice it today. Centuries ago, one of Carlos' ancestors traveled there, and became stranded in Iraq. A clan of Kurds accepted him into their inner circle after he saved their clergy's daughter. He learned everything about their culture, including their ancient practice of Yelizism, and brought it back with him to Florence. The family's power, money, and status ascended, as did their religion. Gossip, now legend, stated that the Baccianis successfully summoned an angel and held fertility rituals in hopes of breeding him with a human female."

"So, Carlos checked out?"

"Yes. Or maybe someone found him to be a threat and wanted him to permanently shut up."

"Detective, you are really giving my client his money's worth."

"I know. And I do realize I could have gotten you to give me more money, but it's not about that. My partner and I aren't allowed to continue investigating the Baccianis. I'm curious, but my hands are tied. His family shut us down in record time. We had to cite the whole thing as an accident and close the file. Who 'accidentally' falls on a sword? It was an old sword that Carlos stole from his parents' artifact collection. It must symbolize something. Or else he would have overdosed or blown his brains out or something like that."

"Detective, I'm not here because of Carlos Bacciani. As you alluded to earlier, I'm here because of Lydia Easterhouse. She had some of Carlos' artwork, which is what led me here. I believe she and Carlos were romantically involved at some point. He painted her face in one of his paintings."

"Any chance you could give me a quick synopsis of her?" asked the detective.

"She's also dead. Car wreck. The car exploded, leaving her body charred and mangled. Another 'accident.' Same religion." Abe knew he said more than he should, but so did Detective Magliano. His curiosity seemed like a sincere professional interest. "Detective, what about Carlos' family? They aren't talking?"

"Hell no. Their team of lawyers does all the talking for them. Abe, if you need anything that I could possibly help you with, please call. Free of charge. I'm too obsessed to just let all of this go."

After the detective left, Abe took his tiny rent-a-car out for a drive around the city. He became sidetracked with the Pitti Palace and its Boboli Gardens. He then passed the Ponte Vecchio and paused. It was the oldest and only bridge in Florence that wasn't destroyed during World War II. *What a beautiful city. Marie, if only you were here with me*, Abe thought as he admired the view and missed his wife. *Back to work for now and then tomorrow I will enjoy the masterpieces of Botticelli, Da Vinci, Michelangelo, and Raphael at the Galleria degli Uffizi.*

Abe drove past Carlos' city apartment, his parents' castle-like estate, and finally the church. There were only a couple of cars in the parking lot. He took down the make, model, and plates with plans of calling his new friend, Detective Magliano, for further information.

Chapter Twenty-Nine

Father Dominick Sardenelli was angry with his volunteers. One of their tasks was to lock the doors promptly after the service began. They were then expected to guard the front door and lobby for any late comers. The routine enabled them to sit down about halfway through the service. Their complacency had cost them an unwanted visitor. Dominick was grateful that the service for the day was a conventional one. Some of their other rituals could easily be misunderstood.

Dominick believed the stranger, Sean Slattery, entered his church because he was in love Lydia Easterhouse. His curiosity must have led him to her old parish. However, Sean's unexpected presence along with an odd phone call from a Loyola professor prompted the priest to summon Jonathan Easterhouse back to the church for a private conversation.

Father Sardenelli remembered the beginning of his career as a priest in a small town outside of Florence. Since boyhood, the Catholic church left him psychological scars that would never heal. Despite his resentment, he submitted to the wishes of his mother and became a Catholic priest. After years of second-guessing his faith, he traded his Catholicism for the Yelizism. The religion allowed him to witness and interact with celestial beings. As much as he enjoyed seeing the paranormal, a gnawing voice inside his head questioned the morality of it all. This same voice tried to use logic to prove how his new religion could never have existed without God, yet the priest chose to ignore all the signs. Seeing the charms and magic of the angels gave him the spirituality that he had always craved.

Father Sardenelli had a talent in communicating with others. He fluently knew a half of a dozen languages and was familiar with a half of a dozen more. He also had the ability to connect with the underworld. The Catholic church recognized his unique talent and provided him with extensive training in exorcisms. An experience left him bitter. The very spirit that he had tried to exorcise led him to the Yelizi church in Florence. Almost twenty years later, Father Sardenelli remained both faithful and an integral part of their religious expansion.

The Easterhouse family held the most prominence in the church. They had revealed to Dominick and the congregation the kinds of miracles that secured everyone's beliefs. The family was separately worshiped and revered as idols.

By early afternoon, Jonathan Easterhouse and his brother, Terrence, came back to the church to speak with Father Sardenelli.

"So, Lydia left a love-sick puppy dog behind? Not too threatening. We have his name, address, and even his money from the check he left. This won't be too hard to keep tabs on him. He is probably telling the truth. Our sister could cast her spells," Jonathan said.

"Yes, but Lydia hated us. Who knows what she said to him? We need to see Julia and Eve. They could end up being a problem. I wonder what they know. Maybe Sean is working with them," Terrence said.

"Both of those girls have to be carriers of the Adonite gene. We engineered it for the highest probability. Julia's daughter might be like us. The other one doesn't have any children, but if she did? Hmmm," Jonathan contemplated.

"I doubt Lydia told them anything. She wanted out and never looked back. Remember what happened to Will when he found out," Terrence added.

While the brothers talked over him, Father Sardenelli questioned their ethics. Genes were part of breeding. Crossing angels with humans was forbidden within the church. The priest chose to remain silent about his suspicions.

"You both should know that Sean Slattery isn't the only irregularity we've had this week. Yesterday afternoon I received a phone call from a Doctor Nrogbi and Doctor Jackson of Loyola University. They were seeking our expertise on angel script translation. They claimed a woman came to their college asking questions about carved script she found, along with an ancient scroll with a purple seal. I denied knowing about the script, and I told them it was a lost part of the religion. However, in the light of Sean's unexpected visit, we have attracted some unwanted attention. All of this can't be a coincidence," Father Sardenelli said.

"We'll get to the bottom of this," Terrence promised.

***

Sean found out about Julia's accident and immediately became concerned. After a brief conversation with Eve, his prying questions had made her uncomfortable, and she abruptly hung up. *She knows something.* He called back in urgency.

"Don't hang up again. I don't blame you for finding me suspicious; I am. I've been holding out on you and Julia. Your mother made me swear to tell you as little as possible. I was only supposed to handle her will. Now it's too dangerous to honor her wishes," Sean pleaded.

Something in his voice kept Eve from dismissing him as a stalker. "She should be out of the hospital by the end of the week," she said.

"That might be too late. I don't want to upset you or her, but the three of us need to talk," Sean interrupted, not sure if he was alarming her.

"What are you suggesting? Do you think we are in danger?"

"Yes, that's exactly what I think. Your mother was probably murdered, and even if she wasn't, lightning doesn't strike twice. Someone tried to kill Julia as well. Tonight, at the hospital, can we meet? Without Bell?" Sean inquired.

Eve agreed, still unsure about trusting Sean. After work she headed to the hospital surprised to see Sean already there with dozens of flowers. Julia had tubes and bandages all over her body. Her delicate face had some bruising. Sean looked comfortable sitting in chair by her side, as if he had been there for some time. Eve took a seat on the small couch against the wall.

"Eve, I'm so glad you came. I haven't been upfront with either of you," Sean confessed. He sentimentally spoke of Lydia and their affair. Abe Silverman's findings were also divulged. Finally, he mentioned the odd church he had recently visited. "I think I saw your uncles and grandmother. Did both of you know that you were baptized there? They ended the service with birds. It was really strange."

"What kinds of birds?" nervously asked Julia.

"Seagulls and doves," Sean replied.

Both sisters obliquely gave each other a fearful glance.

"What do you know about the birds?" Sean demanded.

Julia didn't know if Sean was worth trusting, but he was the only one who held the same suspicions. She decided to take a chance. "A flock of seagulls. That's why I'm here. Sounds crazy, but I went to Loyola for some answers about some peculiar stuff that was in my mom's

Lake Geneva house. On the way home, after I practically ran out of the building, dozens of seagulls covered my car, and in unison, pecked at my windows. I freaked out and slammed right into a traffic light."

"This was not an accident. Someone wants something from you enough to kill you. Your mother knew she was going to die. She hoped her silence would keep you both safe. It's too late for that. Julia, I never meant to lead you or your family on, just wanted to get closer to all of you. I loved your mother so much. All I want is to find out what really happened to her," Sean cried.

Sean's sincerity melted away all reservations. He promised to update them on all information his private detective could find.

By the time Eve picked Bell up from the babysitter's and got her ready for bed, it was after midnight. She relaxed in bed while looking over a work file on a new campaign. The phone rang, and she nearly jumped out of her skin.

"Hello."

"Hi, is this Eve? Julia? It's your Uncle Jonathan. Do you remember me?"

Chapter Thirty

Andel Talistokov left his newest agency in Wheaton, Illinois to check on the ones he most neglected. He routed his business trip to begin in Memphis and end in Europe, with six other stops in between. Hoping for some additional pleasure, he remained vague on the time frame of his return.

Andel's leadership excited and inspired his agents. He was both a genius and legend in the advertising world. His diabolical use of subliminal messaging, backmasking, and audio messages spoken or sang backwards had been ingratiating his clients and his own master for several decades.

Like the *Evil Empire*, Andel had kept a movie theme for the names of each of his agencies. Like the movies, his top-ranking executives literally rolled out the red carpet upon his arrival.

The agencies were set up almost identical to each other. Andel liked the uniformity of his business chain. In the auditorium his agents gallantly presented him with their best ads that were submitted to the Clio awards. Like a proud father, he admired each advertisement. They enabled him to see, hear, touch, smell, or even taste his master's damning agenda.

While Andel watched his agents, he thought about his earthly contributions. Without having to threaten, coerce, or ever bribe, he honored Satan's wishes. He alone had revolutionized the conglomeration of souls, yet he was unjustly condemned. With every passing day, he became more bitter. He often fantasized about reigning over his own kingdom. Now he was pushed into rebellion. Other fallen angels for other reasons also wanted to secede.

Together they stood a chance in breaking free from Satan's rule.

Very few of Andel's employees knew about his true nature, but those who knew him would cater to his preferences when he came to town. Their loyalty was appreciated, but their efforts had grown stale. He was craving more than they could offer. Even orgies with gorgeous men and women had become monotonous. At the whims of his growing appetite, the good times were now ending in murder. To appease his thirst for blood, his lackeys brought him an endless supply of prostitutes to devour.

Under Satan's Manifesto, fallen angels were denied all forms of worship. They could be admired, respected, and even celebrated, but adoration and prayer were solely reserved for Satan himself. So that his celestial army would never forget, he had this law tattooed on all their skulls.

Andel had not been playing by the rules for decades. He hated sharing deification with Satan, the peacock. Marcus was the first to give him a taste of complete adoration. He kept Marcus' soul for himself, and then hid it in a safe place. He remembered Marcus' prayers felt like a surge of energy that was pure and focused. It empowered him, giving him superior strength in and intelligence. While some of the Yelizis worshiped him, they also worshiped Satan and other angels. Their worship was diluted. Now subjected to borrowed time, he wanted his own followers.

What's the worst thing that could happen to me? he thought. *I'm going to Hell anyway.*

Andel's last and favorite stop was in Florence, Italy. While hearing the prayers of his beloved Yelizi church, his mind weighed with blasphemy. Andel, or Armaros, his angelic name, had appeared before his congregation several times for fertility and prosperity rituals. After taking care of his Italian agency's business, he agreed to make an appearance at his parish. His long-time patrons, the Bacciani family, had a sacrifice to offer him. With their help, he planned on taking Satan out of the worship service.

***

Abe Silverman was thoroughly enjoying Florence's sites and ambiance in between accumulating information on the Bacciani family and their link to Lydia Easterhouse. Through the file that Detective Magliano gave him, Abe learned more about the Bacciani family's background, tracing their ancestry back to the Renaissance era. They were descendants of kings, government officials, giants of industry, and the backbone of Italian banking. They lived better than most royalty by owning several castles and chateaus across Europe. Although a private family, many had accused them of using their influence to dictate foreign and domestic policy of Italy.

In between sight-seeing, Abe had been staking out the Bacciani's church for days. He found nothing unusual about the people seen going in and out of the building. All drove nice cars and were fashionably dressed in spring-time clothes.

The church had a decent security system. All who entered required a key card that had to be swiped to gain entry.

Friday, the formal day of the church's morning and evening services, had two older gentlemen holding the doors open for the church goers. Abe took a chance and blended in with the crowd, managing to walk in without raising suspicion. He sat in the back row next to a young family, looking as if he was with them.

The church was decorated with Persian décor and paled in comparison to the great cathedrals of Italy. What the church lacked in ornamentation, they made up for in modernity. Three enormous theater screens hung in the front of the church. The screens displayed song lyrics, announcements, videos, and slide shows of events related to the congregation. Masterpieces of art, architecture, music, and technology flashed in between songs.

The service had a ceremonial format of most churches with the only surprise being the release of dozens of birds into the congregation. Once the service ended, Abe casually walked downstairs to investigate.

The staircase ended in a massive room that was being used as an aviary. Cages of pigeons, doves, seagulls, sparrows, and finches lined the room's perimeter. In the corner was a long piece of metal fencing that closed in four peacocks. *There are the peacocks I've heard so much about – the symbol of Satan. They must have two kinds of services, the tame morning gathering and then one that bows down to Satan. The rest of the birds must represent the lesser angels that fought with him in Heaven,* he thought. The chirping and rustling diluted the silence, enabling him to move around without worry.

As Abe navigated his way through the enormous basement, he came across a second ceremonial room that was much smaller than the one upstairs. There was a small stage with an enormous altar set in the middle. An elaborate peacock mosaic decorated its tabletop. Bright banners hung on the back wall. The center banner featured a quilt of a peacock with an upright halo behind its head.

Abe still had five more hours to wait until the evening service. He wondered if the next one would be held in the basement. Not sure if he could easily get back into the building, he decided to stay in hiding.

The rest of the basement had separate classrooms, closets, and public bathrooms. At the end of the hallway was one more room that could have been easily missed. The door was located around a sharp corner and farthest away from the aviary. As Abe approached the door's tiny window, he kept looking over his shoulder in fear of being seen. He peered in the small round window and froze with shock.

The room was devoid of all furniture with exception to a built-in bench and a toilet. A teenaged girl lay on the floor. She was either dead or in a drug-induced sleep. Abe tried to get the steel door open, but it was bolted shut. He grabbed his cell phone and started taking photos through the window. He punched a few more buttons and emailed them to himself with every intention of passing them onto Detective Magliano, his Florentine contact. He heard faint voices and had to move fast.

Abe ducked into the basement's church and frantically looked for a hiding place. In the far corner, behind the stage, he found an adjoining storage closet. Without a second to spare, he lunged inside. The voices were now only feet away. Two men were speaking Italian. He could tell they were in a good mood by their laughter and merry tone in their voices. They turned on the lights and then left. He had the feeling they would be back and decided to remain hidden.

Parched with thirst, Abe noticed a minifridge on the floor. Inside were bottles of water and carafes of a red liquid he had assumed to be wine. After guzzling down some water, he inspected the red liquid more closely. It smelled rancid and felt sticky. He put a few drops onto his tongue and confirmed it was blood. He snapped a few pictures with his phone, and again emailed himself the shots. The rest of the storage room contained cleaning products, toilet paper, candles, flags, and several trinkets with angel script engravings.

An hour later Abe heard voices outside of the storage room. As he remained motionless and crouched underneath the flags, a man walked in and grabbed an armful of candles. He returned for a few more trips. Abe could hear the pews being moved. Once the men left the ceremony room, he slowly erected from the uncomfortable crouched position and moaned. Every joint in his body ached. *I'm getting too old for this shit.* He peeked out of the door's tiny stained-glass window. The hall was empty, so he ventured out of the storage closet.

The cathedral was lit everywhere with white candles and torches. A soft, beautiful glow made the stark room look divine. Around the altar were large white candles and several of the carafes filled with blood. In the center of the stage sat a massive five-foot golden candlestick with a giant teal candle. Velvet throws in bright hues of blues and greens were tossed over the altar and stage floor. *This is going to be one hell of a party,* Abe thought.

Several minutes later, Abe could hear a multitude of footsteps and a variety of voices coming from the huge reception area that housed all of birds. He carefully left the safety of his closet to spy on the new arrivals.

With one look at the dozens of people conversing, Abe was dumbstruck with fear. *Run! Run, you stupid old man! These people are evil!* said the inner voice inside of his head. *I could wait in an empty classroom until they all enter the church and then quietly leave. Within a half an hour, I could have the police break down the steel door and rescue the girl I just saw.* But he remained transfixed, allowing curiosity to override common sense. He wanted to witness the ritual.

There were approximately three dozen people wearing red velvet robes, and masked in white porcelain, all expressionless and identical. A variety of bird feathers decorated the plain masks, giving each person their own individual look. Each mask was tied to the back of their heads with a colorful taffeta ribbon, and every one's hair was concealed with a coordinating satin skull cap. The ensemble was androgynous. Gender could only be determined through their voice. Abe discreetly took more photos for Sean Slattery.

After an hour reception of drinks and appetizers, a gong vibrated which signified everyone to bow down before their priest. Anticipating the service would soon begin, Abe slipped back into the storage closet. The door's stained-glass window kept him invisible while giving him a partial view of the stage.

As Abe expected, everyone piled into the ceremony room. Chants in an unknown dialect and language calling out for Armaros began the service. In unison, everyone ended at once, and then stood up and took off their velvet robes, wearing nothing but their masks and skull caps.

A young, handsome man dropped onto the stage, both naked and unmasked. From Abe's perspective, he could see the man's profile from the tiny window. A couple of congregation members brought in other birds, allowing them to fly around throughout the service. The man on stage took a bow towards his captivated audience and said something undecipherable. He jumped off the stage and carried a teenage boy from the congregation back onto the stage. He bent the boy over the altar, and he meekly obeyed. The man took a dagger already set on the altar and raised his arms. A pigeon gently landed on his shoulder. As the man sodomized the boy, all bowed down and chanted. The man cut up the pigeon while he penetrated and dripped its blood all over the boy's back.

Only feet away, Abe shook in terror, but couldn't bring himself to leave his viewing position. While the ritual was performed, he tried taking pictures. They came out blurry from the stained-glass, but he was hopeful they could be sharpened for more clarity.

"Armaros, Armaros, Armaros," they chanted. In the far back corner of the stage a bongo drummer got louder and faster.

The proximity of the storage closet left a blind spot from the door's window. Abe could not see a man approaching the closet until it was too late. The door opened and knocked him in the face. He fell back into the cleaning supplies, causing a ruckus. The man in the storage room saw Abe and sinisterly smiled.

"Look what I found," he yelled.

Chapter Thirty-One

Marcus Reinsing was enjoying his debut at playing the agency's chief executive while Andel was away. As predicted, his status meteorically rose from a worthless peon to highly respected superstar. Even Tony, his nemesis, treated him with the utmost civility. As his obsession for Eve grew, he still feared her rejection. Once her sister was released from the hospital, he planned on asking her out.

Marcus and Eve had worked tirelessly on the Clio submissions and finally finished. Nominations would be announced within the next several weeks. Marcus hoped to attend the Clio gala as *The Evil Empire's* representative. The opportunity of being seen as an important man fed his flourishing ego.

Marcus' transformation had given him the strength, confidence, and stamina that he had always desired. Although he could still eat and drink anything he wanted, food was no longer necessary for his existence. Blood plasma was the only thing required to sustain his energy. Without it, he would hibernate indefinitely. Two weeks had passed since his last feast. He began to weaken, and he needed immediate nourishment. After finishing the Clio entries, he left for an afternoon hair appointment and an evening of hunting.

Because Marcus' sketch was spammed all over the state of Illinois, he went to an expensive salon for a vogue make-over. The stylist gave him a new haircut and trimmed the facial hair he had begun to grow. She accidentally cut him while she shaved. Surprisingly, only a drop of blood excreted from his face. He was almost bone dry.

Marcus came home to get ready for his evening. As his master taught him, hunting was best performed in crime ridden areas far away from home. Plans of hitting the casino would offer up some ready-made whores who would make his meal-planning easy.

Marcus rapidly continued to weaken. Almost tempted to go into Andel's lair and take a bottle of blood from his fridge, he was stopped cold in his tracks. Andel had the basement entrances sealed shut and highly secured. *What am I thinking? I've been warned and it's for the best. Master would be enraged if he noticed anything missing.*

While Marcus put on a Colts sweatshirt and jeans, he admired himself in the mirror. He was still lean, but with a six-pack of abs and cut arms. He looked young and buff. As he stepped onto the scale, he was pleased to see a fifty-pound weight gain, making him a healthy one hundred and seventy pounds. Some of the new clothes that he purchased were now too small. He couldn't be happier with the way he looked. He felt confident that a female piece of meat at the Indiana casino would feel the same way.

As Marcus was getting ready to leave, a police car pulled onto the driveway. Two men knocked on the front door. He was indecisive, but eventually chose to answer.

"Hi, I'm Officer Novak and this is Fred Singer. He's one of your neighbors. You've probably heard on the news by now that Phillip Krakowski, your neighbor, has gone missing for almost a month. Here's a picture of him. Do you know him?"

"Never met him," Marcus quietly said as he took the photo through the small opening of the partially opened door.

"Are you the owner of this house? Andel Talistokov?" questioned the cop.

"No, I'm a friend. I'm house-sitting for Andel. He's currently out of town. Do you want me to leave this picture for him to look at?" Marcus nervously offered.

"Colts fan, huh? Indiana boy?" asked the cop, referring to Marcus' sweatshirt.

"Yes. Is there anything else?"

"As a matter of fact, there is. Here's a sketch of a man seen in the area where Phil walked his dog. He kind of looks like you, doesn't he?" the cop commented as he handed Marcus the next picture.

"He looks like a lot of people, Officer," Marcus retorted.

"You got me there. Do you live here too?" asked the cop who seemed to be getting more invasive.

"Again, I'm house-sitting."

"Right. Your name is?" fished Officer Novak.

"Marcus." His self-control was deteriorating.

"Marcus, your friend has a beautiful place here. What does he do for a living?" asked the cop.

"He owns a business. I'm in a hurry, Officer. If there's anything else?" Marcus asked dismissively.

"No, thank you very much for your time Mister? What'd you say your last name was?"

"I didn't. Good day." Marcus shut the door in almost a full-blown paranoia.

Do they think I'm the one in the sketch? Am I a suspect? Are they following me? Maybe I shouldn't go to Indiana. But I'm so hungry; I need a Plan B.

Marcus had plenty of experience with animal mutilation, but never thought of drinking their blood. With a suspicious cop that might have him under surveillance, he thought animal blood would be a safe alternative.

Marcus drove to a large pet store he had been to before on the south-side of Chicago. Every few seconds, he scanned his rear-view mirror in fear of being followed. It appeared no one was tailing him.

The pet store was overcrowded with dogs. Most considered the business to be a third-rate puppy mill filled with inbred mutts with phony kennel papers. Marcus examined the merchandise. By the front door were three discounted dogs in a large pen. They were no longer puppies, but neither fully grown. *They will have to do*, he settled.

Doing some mathematical configurations, Marcus computed that he needed at least 130lbs worth of dogs to feed from. This number equalized his last feast of a one hundred thirty-pound woman. Theoretically, the three dogs in the clearance pen should have contained enough blood to satisfy him. There was a Rottweiler, boxer, and large poodle, or at least that was what their description and certificates read. The store claimed they were purebreds with papers citing their lineage from some unknown kennel club.

"These dogs are from a long line of champions. They are going to be gorgeous," said the store clerk, trying her best to sell the dogs.

Marcus was much more interested in their weight. Not that it mattered, but the Rottweiler looked part beagle by its long floppy ears, and the poodle had silky black hair. The only dog that could pass as a purebred was the boxer, and that was still questionable by his size.

"I'll take all three," he said, and then paid in cash.

"Do you want to buy some dog food? Bowls? Treats? They come with their leashes."

"I have all that stuff at home," he claimed.

Marcus could smell the cashier. *What is that putrid odor? Fear? She is afraid of me. I must try to act happy about my new 'pets.' I don't want her to remember me.*

"You know, I'll take some of these Kong balls, and a dozen of these pig ears, some of these puppy ropes, and maybe these squeaky toys. They should like all of this stuff, right?"

She nodded and her smell seemed to dissipate.

All three of the dogs got along well in the backseat of Marcus' truck. *They were probably penned up together for months*, he figured. He was so hungry that he could no longer wait to drive all the way home. Passing a forest preserve, he pulled off into the parking lot and took the Rottweiler-beagle for a walk while leaving the other two dogs in the car. Several yards away, he pulled the dog off the path and walked him deep in the wooded landscape. Behind an enormous pine, his fangs dropped down. Without even touching the dog, it could smell danger and tried to break free. Before he could clamp his jaw into the dog's neck, it mangled part of his arm.

"You bastard!" Marcus screamed. "You're just like that fucking Old English Sheepdog! You're not getting away from me!" Filled with anger, he pinned the dog down and sank his teeth into its neck, draining him dry. He then tossed the body under the pine tree and left. The dog bite was nasty, but it didn't hurt. By the time he was home, his arm was almost healed.

Compared to the sweet taste of human blood, Marcus found the dog blood bitter and pungent. He couldn't feed on animals for the rest of his existence, but learned their blood was much like dieting. Still hungry, he could at least function. A few hours later he sampled the other dogs and fully regained his strength.

***

"Why didn't you arrest him?" asked Fred Singer, who lived a few blocks away.

"What for? Being a Colts fan? I'll admit the guy was suspicious, but I don't have any probable cause, and like he pointed out, the picture does look like a lot of white guys. Jackie, our only potential witness, said she saw the man in the area. She didn't say Phil was with him. It was dark and cold out, hard to see. All we got is a sketch."

"Can't you bring him in for a line-up? Jackie might be able to identify him. She said he could have been with Phil, but she didn't see the man in the front seat; he was passed out, or even could have been dead. This is our guy. Don't drop the ball," Fred rebutted.

"We'll keep an eye on him," promised Officer Novak.

Fred was disgusted with his local law enforcement. *They hand out tickets all day long to increase the town revenues, but they're plain old chicken shit when it comes to busting someone for murder. If this guy was inconvenienced for a few hours and Jackie didn't recognize him, so what. Life goes on,* thought Fred. *But if the cops weren't going to do anything, then maybe some neighbors and I should take the law into our own hands.*

Chapter Thirty-Two

After a week of being hospitalized, Julia Easterhouse was elated to be back home. She still needed several sessions of physical therapy for full range of motion. Her broken left arm forced her to use her other one.

Julia's first night back was relaxing, but chaos loomed around the corner. She had several messages from Sean Slattery, Doctor Sandra Jackson, and her uncles and grandmother. Bell retreated to using her ventriloquist doll, Lonnie, as her primary means of communication. She and the doll had disturbing conversations. *Hospitalization wasn't so bad after all*, Julia thought as Eve caught her back up to speed. The problems inside of her head were louder than a monster truck rally.

Eve mentioned her long conversations with their oldest uncle and grandmother, both of whom she barely knew. With her mother's passing, they seemed eager to begin a familial relationship.

"I invited them all over this Sunday for a late lunch or an early dinner. I told them you were just getting out of the hospital so everything would be pretty simple. They're coming, but without their wives. Grandmother wants to 'clear the air', as she put it. I told them Mom never mentioned their dispute, but we assumed there must have been hard feelings. I doubt we can trust them," Eve informed.

Bell was eavesdropping in the next room with Lonnie in her arms. "Lydia hates them. She doesn't want them here," Bell said through Lonnie, the puppet.

"Bell, we are having a grown-up conversation. You need to play in your room, the backyard, or someplace where you cannot hear us," Julia scolded. She dreaded their upcoming family reunion, but she needed some answers that only her grandmother and uncles could provide. Sean had enlightened both sisters about their family's odd religion of angel worship and use of birds within the ceremonies. Julia didn't believe her car accident was a coincidence. "Sunday dinner then, but I'm not kissing their asses. You ask the questions."

The sisters synchronized the information and questions they would bring up during the visit. The stress was eating away at them.

Sunday quickly approached. Eve ordered a few trays of Italian food from a local bistro with plans of pawning them off as her own home cooking. She brought Bell along to help load up the car with their meal.

"Auntie Eve, Lonnie says Grandma's mother and brothers are very bad. They did something awful to her. And that's why she quit being part of their family," Bell sadly said in the car ride to the bistro.

"What did they do?"

"He wouldn't tell me. He said I was too young to understand. Lonnie said Grandma's mom should have protected her, but she was really mean. Auntie Eve, I'm scared of them and wish you and Mom wouldn't invite them over," Bell said with a maturity and sincerity that exceeded her six years of life.

"I don't know what they've done, and doubt they'll tell me, but you can tell Lonnie that he's right. Your mom and I don't trust them. However, Grandma left behind a real puzzle, and they might help put some of the pieces together for us. Just wish we knew her better. Bell, consider yourself very special. Grandma trusted you most with her secrets."

"Auntie Eve, she never told you or Mommy anything because she thought you both wouldn't believe her. All she ever wanted was to be safe. She worried we all might end up like her."

"What do you mean 'like her'?"

"Become an angel, or nephilim, like her. And a breeding machine," Bell said and then reached for her aunt's hand.

A breeding machine? Nephilim? Where is she getting these delusional fantasies? Eve took her hand and squeezed it tight. She loved her niece as if she were her own. The disturbing comments that came out of Bell's mouth scared her. She worried that her niece might be in dire need of psychiatric help. *Or she's not crazy.* The second option terrified Eve even more.

Eve kissed Bell's cheek and asked, "Can we play Ouija board again? You, me, your mom, maybe even Sean, our lawyer? He loved Grandma."

"I know he did. And Grandma loved him back. She would like to talk with him again," Bell answered. "Maybe after the bad people leave?"

Eve hugged her niece and promised to give the Ouija board another try. She and her little helper took the trays of food into the house and transferred them all into bakeware, leaving no signs of take-out containers.

Eve's and Julia's grandmother and uncles arrived early. Their timing did not make a difference. Everything was already set up for the afternoon. Their stomachs knotted at the sight of the of the strangers who called themselves family, yet still welcomed them with disingenuous enthusiasm as they hugged them upon entry and hung their overcoats.

Eve brought a tray of iced tea and bruschetta into the living room.

"I can't believe how much you and your daughter look like Lydia," remarked Grandma Harriet. "And Eve, you look like me forty years ago, but much prettier. What happened to your arm, Julia?"

"Car accident. I crashed into a traffic post; a flock of birds distracted me," Julia answered.

"What do you mean they distracted you?" asked Harriet, as she shot her sons a worried glance.

"Nothing. I'll be fine."

Eve contemplated something stronger than the iced tea, but she made it through the afternoon sober. As their small talk evaporated, all parties searched for something light to chat about. The deafening silence forced Eve to rush everyone into the dining room for lunch. She placed the disguised take-out onto the set table as everyone took a seat.

Terrence, Jonathan, and Harriet were exceptionally good-looking. Their uncles were fair, like Lydia, while their grandmother shared Eve's dark hair and eye coloring. Harriet had to be in her seventies, yet like her mother, had cheated the humbling effects of time. Both her middle-aged uncles were also remarkably youthful looking.

"Shall we say 'Grace'?" asked Julia, with a tiny edge of contempt.

"Let's just eat," politely answered Harriet.

The only sounds in the room were the clanking of silverware and dull thuds of glasses being set down onto the table. Eve had to fill the void. "Well, thank you all for coming over. Wish your wives could have made it. This is nice. Awkward, but nice. As you all can imagine, we have a lot of questions. Our mother kept her feelings to herself. We hope this afternoon could mend some fences along with understanding her a little better. We remember all of you from many years ago coming over for the holidays, and us then visiting you. We were once a close family, and then something happened. We'd like to know what that something was all about."

"Completely understandable, but our reasons never had anything to do with you," said Harriet, looking regretful at Julia and Eve. "Too many years have gone by. It's time to put the past behind us. We're a family, and in the end, that's all you ever have."

"The timing seems to coincide with Will's...accident. After he died, Mom threw herself into a local Christian church. She volunteered, donated, attended all kinds of studies, you name it. At first, we thought she felt responsible for Will's death. The whole church thing acted as a kind of absolution. But then she cut all ties to you," Julia said.

"Our problems began long before Will took his life, but religion did take its hold on Lydia. And it's not the religion she was brought up with. We are Yelizi, as was your mother, as were you. It's a big part of our lives, but your mother always questioned the faith. More so after becoming a parent with three kids. She introduced herself to other kinds of religion, wanting spirituality, but not sure where to find it. She had strayed from our church years before Will died, but afterward she refused to talk to us. She blamed me for her unhappiness. The last service she ever attended was right after his death. I'll never forget it. She came alone and caused quite a scene. Many looked at her with pity, a mother who just lost a child. I'm not going to lie to you, her outburst is still talked about today. We were humiliated and angry," Harriet said.

"What did she do?" Eve asked, feeling a twinge of admiration. Lydia was courageous to stand up to a whole church.

"She publicly renounced us, the church, and everything we cherish. She hailed false accusations about our ministry. I don't know if your mother ever told you this, but we have a longstanding tradition and history within the church. My parents were its founders," Harriet explained.

"Why do you use the birds?" blurted out Eve, sounding confrontational and defensive of her mother.

"You know we use birds in our ceremonies? Your mother told you that?" asked Terrence. Eve shook her head in denial. "Well, as you might know, our beliefs originated in Iraq, by the Kurdish people. Yelizism is the oldest religion in the world. We use common birds such as sea gulls, pigeons, sparrows, whatever is available as a symbol and offering to the angels that we worship."

Harriet expanded about their faith by using the Disney version of their benign religion, subtly vilifying their mother as some rebel without a cause. Julia and Eve exchanged scornful glances meant for their extended family. Every word their grandmother said left a poisonous aftertaste.

Bell, the only voice of reason, did what was needed to be done. "Great-Grandma and Uncles, my grandma hated you all. Whatever you want from us, you'll never get. I want you to leave my grandmother's house. You're not welcome."

Their Uncle Terrence stood up from the dining room table, prepared to leave. He was surprised how the little girl did not get reprimanded for such disrespect. "This was a mistake."

"Terrence, sit down and shut up. I'm still the matriarch of this family and we'll leave after I have said my peace. Did your mother ever tell you about her role in our congregation? She was celebrated, almost worshiped, just like her children were, you were. When she left us, it caused doubt among the congregation. We were devastated. Many parishioners quit the church because of your mother's influence. We almost went under. She made us all out to be monsters and refused to let us see you. We were angry, but we still kept tabs on your lives. Eve, we know about your addiction and incarceration. You got out of jail a month or two ago? Are you working yet? And Julia, we know you are recently divorced. Are you seeing anyone? Working?" A long pause with refusal to answer followed Harriet's questions. "I understand, you don't want to share your private lives. We knew your mother had a boyfriend. His name is Sean Slattery. He recently attended our last service to see what it was all about. All this sneaking around, well,

I am tired of it. I just want to know you. You are my grandchildren and my great-grandchild," Harriet pleaded. Tears streamed down her beautiful face as she spoke with the utmost sincerity.

"There's a few things we know about you as well. Your church isn't what you portray. We know about the peacocks and the devil worship that goes on," Julia said with venom.

Jonathan wondered what else they knew that they chose to keep to themselves. "It's not that simple. We worship angels, God's celestial beings. Satan started off as an angel, so yes, he's part of it."

"So why was our mother so revered in your church? Why us? Why would our brother want to kill himself?" demanded Eve.

"Lydia's father, your grandfather-He was an angel, and your mom took after him, not me," Harriet announced.

"Our grandfather was an angel? Look, some pretty weird things have been going on, and I don't know what to believe or who to believe. I do think you all are insane. To echo my daughter, get out of our home! This is not going to work out!" Julia yelled.

"You aren't safe. You have no idea what you are up against. None of you even know what you are or what you can do. Will knew and chose not to participate, but all of you just live out your lives not knowing. Your mother's death left behind some unfinished business. Julia, you said there were birds that distracted you while driving, and that's why you crashed your car. Someone sent those birds to kill you. Your mother must have left you something very valuable. I can help. Trust me, and I can show you its importance. If you don't, things are going to get much worse for all of you," warned Harriet.

Julia opened the front door with her good arm and shook with anger. "Leave now!"

Per Eve's twelve step program, she had to refrain from cocaine and all drugs including alcohol. After her extended family left, she no longer cared about sobriety. Booze was the only thing that could dull her shaky nerves and quiet the screaming voices inside of her head. She hurried to the wet bar and poured herself a large glass of Amaretto.

"Eve, pour me one too," Julia ordered.

The sisters sat at the uncleared dining room table and guzzled their drinks without speaking. Minutes later, Eve brought the bottle of booze to the table and refilled their glasses.

"That went well," Eve smirked.

Bell tottered down the staircase with Lonnie in one arm and a Ouija board in the other. "Grandma left me this and I want to play. Let's call Sean and see if she'll talk to us again."

Chapter Thirty-Three

Tony Manghella's real name was not Tony Manghella. Throughout the decades he had changed it numerous times. At one hundred and thirteen years old, his youthful appearance frequently forced him to change jobs, relationships, cities, and names in order to avoid suspicion. Tony still loved looking at his handsome face and muscular body in the mirror. Youth and strength were the greatest benefit to being transformed. He would look twenty-eight years old forever.

Tony, originally Francis Luciano, was shot in an alley on New York City's lower east side by one of Johnny Torrio's men. He was abandoned, left to bleed to death. In his agony, he silently prayed, not wanting to die. A guardian angel of sorts personally answered him. He introduced himself as Mammon, the angel of greed, as he lapped up Francis' spilled blood. A deal too good to pass up was struck between the former angel and Francis. He was bound by the laws of Hell to carry out an array of conditions in exchange for eternity on earth. Mammon bit into his neck and left him for dead in the same alleyway.

The next morning Francis woke up. Thinking he had been dreaming, he soon found himself getting quicker, stronger, and smarter. He felt invincible. Instead of seeking retribution on his Mafioso family, he left New York City and traveled the world. Of all the places he had visited, the United States was his favorite playground. Murder no longer required a gun, just a sharp set of canines. A couple of decades later, he came back and settled old scores. The reaction on his mobster family's faces was like manna from Heaven.

Mammon guided Francis, presently calling himself Tony, through multiple careers that enabled him to carry out their lord's agenda. Tony had been a night-club owner, minister, motivational speaker, gun dealer, and policeman, but like Andel, found advertising the most productive means of collecting souls for his master. Almost five years ago, he interviewed with Andel at his Los Angeles agency, the *Gotham City*. Instinctively, he knew he was among his own kind.

Andel also sensed Tony was not a human. He could hear the familiar echoes inside of Tony's head, and his lack of mammal scent had also provided Andel with another clue. Tony's mere presence was a threat, which caused Andel's fangs to drop as a defense mechanism. He wondered which of his brethren was responsible for Tony's creation.

Tony sensed Andel's uneasiness. He broke the tension by stating, "I didn't come here as an enemy, but as a potential asset to your agency. We have much in common – the same goals, same lord. Your work is the envy of the fallen, and Mammon, my guardian, is who sent me here to be part of it."

Friends close and enemies closer. Words to live by, except I have no friends, thought Andel. To keep peace with Mammon, one of Satan's lieutenants, Andel hired Tony as an executive and then transferred him to his new Wheaton branch. Tony turned into one of Andel's top producing agents. His innovations and strong-arm tactics helped both the advertising business and Satan's agenda. Tony felt a sense of job security.

Lately, Tony had felt both jealous and suspicious of Marcus, Andel's new Vice President. His improved physical appearance, fading human scent, and current high standing within the agency made Tony feel vulnerable. Marcus was clearly being groomed for bigger and better things, while Tony remained stagnant. When he saw a sketch of a man who resembled Marcus both on TV and the Internet, he felt empowered. There was no doubt it was Marcus. Mistakes were common at the beginning of a change, but Tony expressed no empathy. He chose to hold onto this information like the ace of spades, prepared to trump Marcus when necessary.

To Tony, there were two kinds of women: those you have a relationship with and those you ate. Eve Easterhouse fell into the former category. Upon their first introduction, he became obsessively infatuated. Her long brown hair shone like glass, and her brown eyes hypnotically radiated flecks of gold. She had an unusual scent that acted as an aphrodisiac. Disappointed their dinner plans were put on hold, he patiently waited for the right time to ask her out.

Tony could see he wasn't the only stallion in her barn. Marcus was also vying for her attention. He had always thought of himself as superior to most men, especially Marcus. However, Eve seemed to hang on his every word. He hoped her actions were because of Marcus' new position, but she was difficult to read. Marcus' monopoly of her workday became an inconvenience, and Tony wanted him out of the way. He wondered if Marcus knew about his transformation. If not, soon Marcus would be able to smell him.

Sunday night, after cleaning himself from a kill, Tony drove by Eve's house. The lights inside were on so he pulled over and called her from his cell phone.

"Hi. It's Tony. How's your sister doing? Did she get out of the hospital as planned?" he asked, trying to sound concerned.

"She's been out since Friday. Thanks for asking," Eve said.

Her languid voice excited Tony as a man, not a demon. "Is it possible to get together tonight and maybe go for some ice cream or something?"

"Tony, my family was just over, and we got some business to sift through. I will take a rain check on the ice cream and the dinner you promised me last week. It's really nice of you to call," Eve answered.

Tony wasn't going to give up that easily. There was nothing more attractive than a woman lukewarm to his advances. "Can I come over? Bring a pizza and DVD? Maybe meet your family?"

"I would love that. Maybe next weekend. Right now, I've got to go."

"Next weekend then. I'll hold you to it. Goodnight," Tony said. He parked the car the next block over and invisibly staked out Eve's property. The porch and foyer lights were on, as if she expected company. Tony climbed a mature oak tree with the agility of an orangutan. He perched himself upon a tree branch and enjoyed her closeness. Several minutes later, a good-looking man in a Mercedes pulled up to the front door and was immediately let into the house. Jealousy consumed him. As a result, his fangs elongated. He tried to calm himself down by coming up with other explanations for the man's visit, but still was compelled to find out what it entailed.

Tony jumped from the tree and scaled the house. Once he reached the roof, he searched for an opening. The home had three chimneys. All the flues were closed, but he knew how to pry them open. His rubber-like flexibility enabled him to collapse his body and descend within the chimney. *I'm a real fucking Santa Claus*, he thought as he became cramped inside. He quickly pried open the flue, knowing he had to be on the second floor. As he edged himself onto the hearth, he was happy to find himself in an empty bedroom.

Tony spent many decades on Earth, never marrying, though he'd been in relationships. They always ended badly for his girlfriends. Jealousy, arguments, and unrealistic expectations caused him to lose control. If they didn't leave him, they usually ended up as his next meal. Eve seemed different. He thought she could be the one to end his loneliness.

Tony crept through the upstairs hallway until reaching the stair railings of the two-story foyer. Only a small lamp illuminated the immense area. Faint voices came from downstairs. Tony concentrated, able to pick up four distinct voices. He heard Eve, a little girl, a man, and another female's voice who he presumed to be her sister. They were not having a conversation, but engaged in a game.

No, couldn't be. Eve couldn't possibly be a part of that world. Tony could hear their chanting. *Did she worship the same master?* Tony moved in to listen. In his amazement they were talking to a spirit.

Chapter Thirty-Four

Abe Silverman was barely conscious after getting knocked down from the door of the storage closet that he was looking through. He had been caught spying at the night service of the Yelizi church. Fear almost paralyzed him. He instantly remembered his phone and the several pictures he had taken. Quietly, he turned it off with one hand behind his back and slid it under a tablecloth on the floor. The phone was his only hope in his survival.

"Who the hell are you?" asked a young man with a cocked smile.

"I'm a parishioner at your church. My name is Umberto," Abe lied.

Armaros and several others rushed to the tiny doorway of the closet for a look at the intruder.

"*Credere in demone?*" asked Andel.

"No Italiano, Senore. I'm an American here visiting my cousin. He took me here this morning. I'm also Yelizi, no worries," Abe answered.

"Do you believe in demons?" Andel repeated in English.

"Absolutely. I just came back here because I left my passport from this morning's service, and I'm a very foolish old man. I hid in the closet because you all came in here and took off your robes. I felt uncomfortable and embarrassed. My cousin is waiting for me, so I'll be going. Don't want to interrupt your service," Abe explained. He was convincing as Umberto, the shy American, but sensed the naked man without a mask doubted his story.

"I love America, Umberto, our new American friend. Your cousin can wait. We want you to have an extra fantastic time at our evening service. You will be our guest of honor and allowed to partake in the same indulgences as me, the great Armaros, one of Satan's fallen angels. What is your cousin's name?"

"Michael Angelo," answered Abe. Being put on the spot, he couldn't think of a more original name, and sensed he was being toyed with.

"Umberto, you will be elevated tonight, elevated like I will be," said Andel.

Abe looked into Armaros' eyes and saw flames. Before he could scream, his body was levitated up to the high basement ceiling.

"Everyone, please return to your places. Our new friend Umberto will honor us with his participation." Armaros ordered while staring up at Abe.

Abe looked down from the ceiling at the congregation as he hovered in the air. *These people aren't human. Their eyes glow yellow and look at me with lust. Armaros is going to kill me.* Once Abe was lowered to the ground, he was ordered to undress.

"We all wear nothing. With exception of myself, the guest of honor, and now you, our surprise visitor, everyone wears a mask and skull cap. Tonight, we perform an ancient fertility ritual. I will tell you the part you are to play throughout the service."

A man in the back of the church brought in the four peacocks separately caged. Andel motioned for him to put them back in the aviary.

"Tonight, we will forgo the peacock and all of you will pray directly to me. Pray that I may spread my seed to the four corners of the earth," Andel announced.

The man with the peacocks became angry and rushed the stage. "Armaros, great fallen angel of Satan, per our lord's doctrine and our Black Book, you must relinquish your command. You are modifying our lord's word. You, one of the ancient and infamous of King

Caligastia, are not above his laws. The peacocks need to receive worship for this ceremony to proceed."

"Are you divine? Have you been to both Heaven and Hell? Do you possess celestial power?" roared Andel. "I think not! Umberto, what shall we do with this dissenter, this disobedient simpleton, or anyone who disobeys the rituals of this church, my rituals? Umberto, you don't know?"

Abe stood a few feet away from Andel and urinated on the stage. He could no longer pretend to belong.

"Those of you who adore me, how shall I handle this blasphemy?" Andel vibrated.

The people who filled the room were at a loss. The evening's scheduled rituals had jumped off the track, leaving the congregation in a state of confusion. A lone voice shouted 'fire.' The rest of the parish erupted. Their chants sounded like a symphony to Andel's ears.

"Since I love all of you, fire it is."

Two men jumped the dissenter before he could get away. A metal pole and matching base were quickly assembled by a couple of congregation members as the crowd went wild. Tarps were laid around the poll. Two women began to pass out crystal goblets. Andel took carafes Abe had seen from the mini-fridge and partially filled each cup. Abe prayed God would spare him of all this madness, and if not, then lead someone who was not part of this evil directly to his phone.

"This blood represents life, life that you will pledge to me. Let us vow and drink." All obeyed, pledging their souls, heart, mind, and body to Armaros, their new savior.

"Umberto, drink, drink. You do what I do, remember?" Andel said. His eyes shimmered flames of gold and orange, and his fangs stretched below his lip. His naked body pulsed with his thick veins after each breath he took. Abe wondered if he was already dead and in hell.

"Umberto, our surprise guest and new friend, you will do the honors of burning our traitor. First, you must douse him with gasoline," Andel instructed.

Abe dutifully took a gas can from a naked woman Andel had cued, and then poured it all over the traitor who was bound to the metal pole. Without emotion, Abe kept reminding himself he was dousing a man who preferred Satan to Armaros. Evil was evil, and mercy wasn't an option.

Once Abe emptied the gas tank, he was handed a pack of long matchsticks.

"Umberto, you know what needs to be done. Light him up!" Andel ordered. A couple of congregation members stood close by with extinguishers as a precaution.

Abe hesitated. He had killed before as a policeman. Shooting someone in self-defense was very different than burning a tied-up man to death. He took the long match and slowly brushed it along the side of the box. The sulfur made his eyes water. For a moment, he stared at the flame and then gingerly threw it by the traitor's feet. He instantly ignited. The sound of his horrific screams and the smell of his burning flesh were hypnotic. Abe watched in both horror and fascination. *God forgive me.*

Drums began to beat. Everyone formed two circles around the burning man. Each circle went in a different direction as the church members performed a tribal-like dance. The burning man stopped screaming and the drums got louder with more intricate rhythm patterns.

"Armaros, Armaros, Armaros," they chanted as they danced. Their cries stayed in sync with the drums. As the fire burned down, Armaros stood with the charred dead man in the center of the circle. Abe was pushed into the circle to dance. He watched wings manifest from Armaros' shoulder blades. They were a thick, black cartilage with few feathers, and reminded Abe of a giant bat. Armaros then flapped in convulsions and flew with the loose birds throughout the church. Abe listened to his bird-like shrills and sobbed.

Two women supported the same teenager Abe saw earlier in a holding cell out onto the stage. She was dressed in a white toga and wore several pieces of gold jewelry etched with odd symbols. She was clearly drugged, but somewhat lucid. Her eyes glazed with repugnance. *She is not one of them,* concluded Abe. When the fire was completely extinguished, Armaros commanded everyone to line up before the stage and bow before him.

"Umberto and I are going to perform the fertility part of our ceremony. This virgin is a gift and not a sacrifice. Her temperature is right! Pray that I impregnate her!" Andel shouted. He led the prayer, and the worshippers echoed his words right back.

A naked woman dancer dominated the stage with a sexual and skilled solo while the drummers played. Her hips swayed with grace and flexibility. She had the entire room mesmerized. At the end of her routine, she took the teenaged girl's toga off her body, leaving her even more terrified and vulnerable. Armaros mounted her and penetrated. While he thrusted, the drums played with the accompaniment of a flute. The girl's face was frozen with a screaming expression. Tears rolled out of her eyes like rain. Several minutes later, Armaros was finished. Abe was commanded to be the girl's second lover of the night. Her repulsion mutated to catatonic indifference. Abe shook his head and looked down at his flaccid penis thinking his impotence was enough to refuse.

"Miranda, help the old man get ready for our ritual," Armaros said. The dancer knelt to the floor and placed Abe's penis inside of her mouth to prepare his arousal. He instantly received an erection.

"Our American friend is now ready," Armaros hissed, showing his animal eyeteeth.

Feeling helpless and trapped, Abe obeyed. His copulation began with humility, but a carnal passion overcame him. He forgot about the girl's dread and let himself go. Without ever looking at her expressionless face, he orgasmed with the most profound ecstasy he ever experienced. *God, I want to die.*

This time Armaros had heard his thoughts. "Umberto, you shall get your wish." He leaned into Abe's jugular and pierced his neck, sucking him almost dry. "Everyone, please feast."

The congregation rushed the stage with the determination of a swarm of mosquitos towards an open sore wound. Abe's limp body was scavenged by Armaros' new followers. They violently writhed through each other in a feeding frenzy. Within minutes, all that was left of Abe Silverman was his bones.

Chapter Thirty-Five

Harriet East and her two sons, Jonathan and Terrence, left her granddaughters' home in anger. They were rejected and humiliated. Like their mother, Eve and Julia wanted all family ties to remain severed. Vital information they sought had to remain unknown.

"Lydia has raised some incredibly crude daughters. And how about Bell? For a six-year-old, she is very outspoken. What a peculiar child," said Terrence, as he headed towards the north-side of Chicago.

"Could she possibly have the Adonite gene? Julia's ex-husband couldn't have been a carrier," Jonathan said.

"It's not genetically impossible, but extremely rare with only one parent bearing the gene," Harriet said. "Is there any way we can find out if Bell was born with a deformity?"

"Julia certainly won't tell us, and Lydia refused to let us into the hospital when she was born. Her husband seems to be out of the picture," Terrence said.

"It breaks my heart. Bad enough my own daughter betrayed me, but she also poisoned her children against us. Through death, she is still lashing out at me," Harriet cried. She turned off the car stereo so that they could have a serious conversation on the ride home.

"Did you know about the phone call Father Sardenelli received? It came from a college professor requesting an angel script translation. It was the same day, and probably the same time as Julia's car accident. I doubt these two events are coincidental. I wonder what Julia showed them," said Jonathan.

"Lydia always claimed to have the scroll," cited Terrence.

"But she had to be bluffing," Harriet said.

"We don't know that. Her daughters know more than they let on," Jonathan warned. "Do you think Lydia left them her halo?"

"If she did, they wouldn't know what it was or what to do with it," Terrence said. Both his mother and brother agreed, but still did not want the halo to get into the wrong hands.

"In spite of it all, it was really nice to see them, to interact with them, to eat with them. Everyone always remarked how Julia looked just like her mother, but I think she has your eyes," Harriet said as she looked at Jonathan, Julia's real father.

"You think? She's beautiful. This was the first time I got to see my granddaughter, and she's a real brat," Jonathan said and smiled. "Wish we were closer."

"Soon. It takes time. They'll come around once they know everything. We're a family. Blood is thicker than water," said Harriet.

"Some say it tastes better, too," said Jonathan and laughed.

"They better come around before we are extinct," Terrence said. "You both need to get your heads out of the clouds. We are never going to be one big happy family. We killed their mother, and I'm pretty sure they know it."

"Someday they will learn about the mess Lydia left us with. If we hesitated, if we spared her, she would have been martyred. The church couldn't have handled the schism," Harriet defended.

"If Julia has the scroll, then Father Sardenelli is our only chance of peacefully getting it back," said Jonathan.

***

Lydia's words hung over Father Sardenelli's once protected ministry like a black cloud. His private church had reached the interests of professors in the academic realm.

Professor Nrogbi called him a second time. The pastor deleted the message again and hoped the man would give up. But the professor only became even more pushy. He camped out on the front stoop of Dominick's modest Chicago home with every intention of talking to Dominick about the artifacts that Lydia Easterhouse had shown him. The priest opened the front door wearing his bathrobe.

"I hate to bother you, Father, but your knowledge is needed. All I want is a moment of your time," explained Doctor Nrogbi in desperation.

"Ah, you still think I can translate the angel script. I'm afraid the symbols from the Enochian keys are obsolete to my congregation. Again, I can't help you," Dominick said with brevity.

"Father, I'm parked in front of your home. If I have to sleep in my car, I will. Please, I beg of you, just a minute. Your ministry is the only one in Illinois, and one of the few in the Midwest. If you could just look at my pictures, your memory might stir," pleaded the African professor.

Dominick opened his front door and let the man inside. He led him into his home office and motioned for the professor to sit down in the leather chair in front of his desk.

"Please call me Dinda. And thank you for seeing me." The professor fiddled around in this briefcase and pulled out some pictures. "Here, these are copies of symbols that were carved into a wall. Any thoughts?"

Irritated with the insistent stranger, Dominick tied his robe to cover his pajamas. The evening was still early, but he just wanted to relax. The African was a nuisance that needed to go away. After glancing at the copies, his attitude softened. The enigmatic passage intrigued him, but he chose to keep it to himself. *Lydia, wherever you are, I know you have something to do with this,* he thought. "I'm sorry, Dinda. I just don't know what they mean. Goodnight," the priest lied.

Dinda smiled. The priest had just tipped his hand. "Father, do not take offense to this, but I looked into your background. I know you used to be a Catholic priest in Italy. My sources tell me you are an extremely private man who has spent your life looking for truth. We are alike in that way. I've heard you lost your original faith during an exorcism you performed. According to my source, the demon left his host and invaded your body. You were lured into the Yelizi ways."

"Dr. Nrogbi, you must be a good teacher because you've clearly done your homework. Your surprise ambush has left me at an unfair advantage. I have not had the opportunity to go behind your back and dig up malicious rumors. That tidbit of fiction was what my former clergymen said to explain my resignation. It's easier to ruin one's reputation than to admit that your religion does not practice what they preach. Any questions about the church were always answered with obscure words of faith."

"*Forever fallen is forever damned until one can unlock from within,*" translated Dinda from the copy of wall carvings he held in his hand.

"Doctor Nrogbi, you owe me an explanation. Why are you really here? You obviously don't need me to translate the Enochian script," said Dominick, boiling with rage. He felt like a pawn in a game in which he didn't know how to play.

"Guess I have your attention. Here are some photos of an ancient artifact that were brought to me and my colleagues last Friday. This is the real reason why I'm here, so let's quit pretending, shall we. I need some answers," remarked Dinda. His enormous, dark brown eyes blazed with flames of gold. Tiny white points protruded from his upper lip. Dominick now knew what he was dealing with.

"You have my full cooperation. Let's see, this is overtly an old scroll. I can't attest to its authenticity, but if that's animal skin...."

"It is," Dinda interrupted.

"Then it could be as old as 1000 B.C. In this close-up, the scroll's seal is such an unusual color. It's like indigo, but different. Maybe purple? I've never seen this color in an ancient artifact," Dominick answered, both terrified and enamored.

"Very good, Father. The photo does not give it justice. It's much more vibrant to the eye. You and no one, including the art department at my university, has ever seen this hue. It's not on any color palette."

"Where did you get this?" asked Dominick.

"Father, if you can satisfy my curiosity, I will try to do the same. Do not fear me. You are in good company. In South Africa, my home, Yelizism was practiced by my family and our entire tribe. An angel they summoned turned me into a monster. I cursed the religion several decades ago but yield to its power. This scroll is very important to the angels who like to visit the Yelizis. I want to know why," Dinda said.

"Doctor, you've backed me into a corner. I honestly do not know its value, but the symbol on the seal means Elohim or angels, as I'm sure you already know. The seal, did you touch it?"

"Yes, why?"

"Did it feel like wax?" Dominick asked. He was forming a theory.

"No, it was sticky and smelled sweet, like sugar."

"Then it's got to be blood. And the color – it's blood before it's oxidized, except it's not human blood, but celestial blood."

"Angels? From Heaven or Hell?" asked the professor.

"I don't know. The only way to find out is to read the scroll. If it's from our peacock friend, then...." Dominick trailed off.

"But what if it's from God?" asked Dinda.

The two men looked at each other with trepidation.

"Julia Easterhouse has the scroll," announced Dinda, and then left Dominick's home.

Chapter Thirty-Six

After their uncles and grandmother left, Eve and Julia proceeded to get very drunk. Bell brought down her ventriloquist dummy, Lonnie, and her grandmother's old Ouija board, and patiently waited for them to finish their conversation. She put dozens of candles all over the dining room. As Julia opened another bottle of Amaretto, she did not even notice her six-year-old daughter lighting all of the candles.

"Bell, aren't you too young to play with lighters?" Eve slurred.

"I'm not playing. I'm setting the table. Can you call Sean? He wants to play too," Bell said.

"I'll call him, and you make the coffee. I don't want to pass out for our séance," stammered Julia.

Sean answered the phone on the first ring and eagerly accepted the invitation. Because he lived on the opposite side of town, he arrived at their house within minutes.

"Thanks for coming over on such short notice. You made it here in no time. It was Bell's idea to include you. Did you ever play this game?" Julia asked as she led Sean into the candlelit dining room. Bell had the room decorated like a fortune telling booth.

"No, never. Was always too scared. I was brought up by a strict Catholic family who thought using Ouija boards, palm reading, and mediums were sinful, and even blasphemous. To them, it was classed as inviting evil into your life."

"Yeah, that's because it is. Your parents are right," said Eve. "Are you in, or are you too chicken shit to play?"

"I'm here. Count me in. I'm assuming we are summoning Lydia tonight. Yes?" he asked as he sat down.

With one good arm and several trips to the dining room table, Julia managed to serve a fresh pot of coffee, cups, and several bottles of booze. Sean took a coffee cup and filled it to the rim with Scotch. "I need to catch up to both of you ladies," he said has he looked into their hazy eyes. Feeling slightly dizzy, Julia switched over to coffee.

"Our mom might feel like talking. The candles are burning. Bell, will you start the séance? I think Grandma would want it this way," Julia said.

"Hi, Sean. Thanks for coming. Grandma will be happy you are here," Bell said.

Sean's eyes filled with tears at the child's compassion. *How would she know if Lydia would have wanted me here?* he wondered. *She must have trusted Bell enough to tell her about me.*

"Okay, we will begin. Now, everyone needs to touch this. It's called a planchette. It might start going super-fast and knock your fingers off of it. Don't worry. It will go by the person it wants to talk through. So put your fingers on the sides," Bell explained.

The game piece remained motionless. Everyone had four fingertips on it and stared, waiting for something to happen.

"Sometimes it takes a while, and sometimes it doesn't move at all. Let me begin. Spirit world, I am Bell Hoffman, daughter of Julia Easterhouse, and granddaughter of Lydia Easterhouse. We seek my grandmother, my mom's and aunt's mother, and Sean's true love. Spirits, do you hear me?" Bell called out with the confidence and ease of someone who was very familiar with the game.

The planchette moved to the "yes" word on the board. Bell continued. "Grandma, is that you?"

The planchette began to wildly spin. Their fingertips could not control it. It spun off the board, ricocheted off the wall, and landed on Eve's lap.

"Auntie Eve, the spirit wants to talk to you. Pick up the planchette and put it on the board," Bell guided.

Eve did what Bell instructed and almost asked a question. The piece took on a life force of its own. It spelled U, F, O, U, N, D, M, E.

"Ufoundme. What does that mean? Anybody have a dictionary?" Eve asked.

"Eve, could it spell *you found me?*" rationalized Sean.

Eve thought long and hard about who the spirit could be. She remembered finding her brother's dead body hanging from the attic's rafters. "Will, is that you?"

The planchette moved to the "yes" spot.

"I found you dead, but I always regretted not finding you alive before you killed yourself. I miss you, brother. We all miss you so much. I read your letter. Mom had it hidden, but Julia recently found it. Was there any other way? Did you have to end it?"

The planchette moved to the "no" place and then spelled 4, U, T, H, E, R, E, I, S.

"Four uthereis?" Eve read aloud, not understanding.

"Auntie Eve, I think he meant *for you there is.*"

"Yes, of course. Oh Will, what about Julia and Bell?"

The planchette slid to the "yes" corner of the board and then spelled F, I, N, D, H, A, L, O, and K, I, L, L, A, R, M ...." The piece flew out of Eve's fingers and pinged against the walls. Everyone dove under the table to avoid getting hit. The plastic game piece smashed into several pieces, leaving nothing but the round, clear plastic in the piece's center. It landed on top of Lonnie, Bell's doll.

The doll's wooden mouth began to move. "We are not alone, evil can hear, we are not alone, evil is here. We are not alone." Lonnie repeated himself several times, and then with a throaty deep male voice, he blurted, "Danger!"

"Bell, stop it right now! This is no time for...." Julia scolded, and then stopped. Both of Bell's hands were on the table. The doll was operating by itself. Julia screamed.

Eve was too drunk to be frightened. Every nerve in her body was in a state of relaxation. Seeing the chaos still had not fully convinced her of the paranormal happenings that just occurred.

"We are in danger. Will, if you're still listening, the only one here who is not family is Sean. He's the evil one we are being warned about, isn't he?" Eve yelled.

The board flipped off the table and onto the floor. The board's spine was partially folded and stood on the floor like a tent. It then flapped its way out of the dining room and into the foyer. Everyone followed the moving board out of the room as it finally collapsed on the first step of the staircase. They all stood silent and listened. An upstairs window squeaked as it was being opened, and then a loud thud hit the front yard. Sean raced outside to catch the intruder. As fast and agile as he was, the intruder was much faster. The women and girl watched him run after a man into the darkness from the safety of their porch. They could hear pounding footsteps and the rustling bushes in the distance. Seconds later, they heard the faint sound of an ignition and the screech of tires as the car sped off into the night.

Not exactly sober, but much more alert, Eve apologized. "Sean, I'm so sorry for accusing you of such horrible things. If it weren't for you, who knows what could have happened to us. Someone just broke into our house. Forgive me, please."

"There is nothing to forgive. You were protecting your family." Sean hugged Eve. "Listen, I would have thought the same thing under the extraordinary circumstances. Hey, was I dreaming, or did the Ouija board edge itself to the front stair of your staircase?" Sean rolled his blue eyes and smiled nervously. "By the way, I never want to play Ouija with any of you again! I should have listened to my parents. Besides, you hogged your turn and wouldn't let anyone else play."

Everyone roared with laughter. It was all they could do before completely cracking up.

"Let's report this to the police," Sean said.

"Sean, can you spend the night here? I'm really scared," Bell cried.

Chapter Thirty-Seven

Detective Leonardo Magliano, Abe Silverman's Florentine contact, had not heard from Abe in over a week. Abe was under no obligation of updating him on his investigation of the Bacciani family and Yelizi church. However, he assumed that they had developed a friendly alliance after personal information was exchanged.

Leonardo was tempted to call Abe until he overheard some uniformed policemen discussing a rental car that was recently towed. He eavesdropped upon their conversation.

"That rental we picked up – it's leased to an American, Abraham Silverman. We found a notebook inside with some strange notations. It appears as if he was jotting down license plate numbers and the times in which he saw them. Like a stakeout," said the young policeman to his even younger colleague.

"CIA? Black-ops?" asked the other cop.

"Don't know. Abraham is registered at the Villa La Vedetta Firenze. No one answers the room when I call. How long can we hang on to the rental before we give it back to the company?"

Detective Magliano interrupted the two policemen. "Excuse me, guys, but I couldn't help but overhear. I know Abraham Silverman. I believe you have stumbled onto a missing persons case. Let Dino and me look further into this matter. We will keep you in the loop on what happens. Good work on finding the notebook with the car plates in Mister Silverman's car. I would appreciate it if you both ran the numbers and found out who the cars belonged to."

"Yes, detective, no problem," said one of the uniformed cops with the utmost enthusiasm.

"You did a great job with this. It will be noted in my report."

Leonardo tracked down his partner, Detective Dino Barone, and headed towards Abe's hotel.

"Is this the guy who paid us five thousand U.S?" Dino asked.

"Yes, that's why I poached the case. I can smell foul play. The Baccianis are somehow involved in this," Leonardo said.

"Even if you're right, they'll buy their way out of this just like before," Dino said.

"Maybe, but it will be harder this time. There's a foreigner involved."

They arrived at the elegant and old Villa La Vedetta Firenze. The building reeked of old-world charm and decadence. Foreigners without a budget adored the place. Dino and Leonardo approached the front desk and showed the hotel clerk their credentials.

"Mr. Silverman prepaid for a two week stay. Let me check the computer. There shows no activity on his key card over the last few days. His room's voicemail is full; he hasn't been checking his messages. Callers have been leaving messages with us at the front desk," said the hotel clerk. He handed Leonardo a handful of messages from Barb, Rachel, and Sean.

"Senore, can you check with housekeeping? Maybe he doesn't want to answer his messages," reasoned Dino, trying to rule out all other explanations besides Abe being missing.

"Absolutely. Detective, I will have them open the room. Oh my, what if...." the clerk said and then quit talking, afraid his guest was dead.

They rushed up to Abe's suite. It was empty and undisturbed. Housekeeping confirmed what everyone was already thinking. His clothes neatly hung in the closet and his toiletries remained unpacked on the vanity counter. It was obvious to all that Abe had not been there in days.

On the way to the car, Leonardo already was on his cell phone calling Barb, one of the messages left for Abe. She answered the phone on the first ring.

"Abe is that you? The foreign number came up on the caller i.d.," asked Barb, Abe's secretary.

"No, no Senora. I am Detective Leonardo Magliano. Call me Leo. And you are Barb?"

"Yes, Barb Grossman. I'm Abe's secretary and friend. Detective Magliano, you are his contact out in Florence. What happened?"

"Well, Abe has not been to his hotel room in days. We just picked up his abandoned rental car parked on the outskirts of town. We talked to the desk clerk, and he gave us Abe's messages, which is why I am calling," Leo said.

"Oh my God! He's dead!" Barb was close to hysterics.

"Senora Grossman, please calm down. We don't know that. There could be a dozen explanations to his whereabouts. For instance, he told me over a week ago that he planned on seeing Italy. He said he intentionally booked a longer stay to see the sights. Hopefully, that is all this is. But I need you to focus right now. When did you last speak with him?" Leonardo asked.

"Last Friday morning. He was sitting in front of a church telling me he was going to try and attend the service. He frequently called and checked in with me when on a case. He said he had met with you," Barb ranted hysterically. "I called his cell, but it didn't even ring, just dumped me into his voicemail, like he shut it off. Then his voicemail box at the hotel filled up with both my and Rachel's messages. We then started leaving them at the front desk. His flight back to Chicago is scheduled for this Saturday. Detectives, something is very wrong."

"Who are Rachel and Sean?"

"Rachel Silverman is his daughter, and Sean is his client. Sean Slattery. He's a lawyer in Wheaton, Illinois. Abe's done various work for him throughout the years. He is the one who sent Abe to Florence. I do not know why, just that he wanted information pertaining to the Baccianis and their church."

"Did Abe email you, or anyone?" asked Leonardo.

"Not me, but I'll ask around."

"Barb, I'm going to need you and his daughter to fill out a missing person's report in order for us to continue looking for him," Leo said.

"Rachel and I will be on the next flight."

"That's not necessary. Sit tight. I will fax it to both of you and you can sign and fax it back. We might get lucky. He could turn up for his flight or come back from an excursion. I'll keep you posted on a daily basis, okay?" Leo said, wrapping up the phone call.

"It's okay for now, Detective," Barb answered. Leonardo called both Rachel and Sean. Neither answered. He left messages directing them to Barb if he could not be reached.

"Leo, everything points to that church. I'm sure they'll remember us," said Dino, referring to Carlos Bacciani's 'accident.'

"Damn right, they will remember us. Let's do this."

Once the missing person's report was officially signed, Leonardo and Dino visited the Yelizi church. Both took the plate numbers of the four cars parked in the parking lot. Not surprisingly, they matched the ones written inside of Abe's notebook. Dino knocked on the front door incessantly for several minutes.

"We're not going away, you fricken wackos," Dino softly said to Leo as he kept on knocking. "They're probably in the middle of a virgin sacrifice right now and don't want to be disturbed."

After an eternity of waiting, the door was finally opened by Franco Bacciani, the patriarch of the powerful family.

"Hello. Well, well. Detectives Barone and Magliano. How could I ever forget you fine gentlemen? What brings you to our place of worship?" said Franco, as he stepped outside instead of asking the detectives in.

"Hello, Mr. Bacciani. I am flattered that you remember us. Since we all know each other, we will skip the formalities. We are here to ask you a few questions. First, were you at last Friday's church service?" Leo asked.

"Yes, I am the senior elder and always here. What's this all about?" Franco asked.

"A missing person's report was filed today. We have reason to believe Abraham Silverman attended your morning service. We cannot track him any further. Here's a recent picture of him," Leo said. While Franco examined the picture, Leo could not help but notice Franco's youthful appearance. He had to be well into his eighties, but he looked decades younger.

"Never heard of the man. He wasn't here last Friday or ever. You both know we don't welcome new members," Franco curtly replied as he handed back the photograph.

"He told his secretary that he was coming here, and his rental car was found abandoned just a block away. Are you sure? Want to look again?" Dino asked.

"No, I'm quite sure. If he did come here, our ushers would have turned him away," Franco said.

"He might have slipped in. Is it okay if we have a look around?" Leo asked.

"Do you have a warrant?" Dino shook his head. "Then no."

"Mr. Bacciani, we understand you have your rights, and you also do not like the way we handled your son's case, but we'll get our warrant. For your information, Abe Silverman was an American. If it takes getting the consulate involved, then so be it. If you remember anything, here is my card," Dino threatened obliquely.

"Of course. Good day," Franco said and then went back inside the church and locked the doors.

Within an hour of leaving the Yelizi church, Abe's excited secretary called Leonardo with information.

"Detective, Abe didn't email me. However, he emailed himself! I'm so mad for not checking sooner. As his secretary, I have his password and usually open his mail. I'm forwarding the pictures he had sent. Some of them are bizarre. Hope this helps."

Chapter Thirty-Eight

Eve arrived late for work looking ill. She wore no makeup and had dark circles under her eyes, making her look haggard. A night of drinking, communicating with the dead, and having her house broken into had taken its toll.

"You look terrible. Are you alright?" asked Claire Jacobsen.

"You don't want to know. I need caffeine to get me through the day," Eve said. "Want a cup?" Claire nodded and Eve helped herself at the coffee machine. She brought both cups into Claire's office and sat down.

"Are you hungover?"

"Is it that obvious?"

"We should hit a meeting after work. You can't let yourself fall apart again," Claire warned.

Not wanting to discuss her sublime evening, Eve jumped right into work. "What are we doing today?"

"Marcus, your biggest fan, has given us a very cushy assignment. Thank you, Eve, for advancing our careers."

"Imagine that. I haven't even slept with the guy. He's actually really nice. Tell me what my irresistible charm landed us."

"Product placement for RE, or Regular Electric. They want us to incorporate their products in several TV programs, all on the same network," Claire said. "If all goes well, then they might want their products placed on a few Netflix shows."

"Back up, Claire. What's product placement?" Eve asked. "Don't forget that I am a computer geek who is a wanna-be ad exec."

"I keep forgetting you are new to this. But that's because you are such a quick study! Okay, our client, RE, will have their products placed in strategic and noticeable spots during several TV shows instead of a typical 30 second spot. They can be sitting on the table, mentioned by a character, used as a prop. An example would be the Manolo Blahnik shoes in *Sex in the City*. Or the *James Bond* movies with his Range Rover or BMW. Both those car companies paid a ton of money for him to drive their cars in the film. On *American Idol*, the judges always had Coke glasses in front of them. Probably the most famous product placement ad is the Reese's Pieces used in *E.T.*"

"Now I get it. Kind of like the influencers on social media. So, our job is to weave RE's products within the scripts of selected TV shows. Like a character commenting about what a great lightbulb they are changing or using an RE stove while they are cooking. RE would pay the network and then us a commission for the ad, right? Which network?" Eve asked.

"The one with the peacock logo. This is a very effective way to advertise. Consumers are sick of ads placed in their face all day long. This format is much more subtle, yet really works on a subconscious level when a particular show or character is popular."

"Do you use subliminal messages as well?"

"I didn't think of that. Please expand. This is an interesting point you just brought up," Claire said.

"I got the idea from Marcus when we were sorting through all of the submissions for the Clio awards. He gave Bell three toy catalogs and wanted to know which one she liked the best. She noticed letters placed by the toys. They spelled messages inside two of the catalogs. At first, I didn't believe her, but then she pointed to the letters. Marcus admitted this agency does this all the time. Why not for the advertisement placement?" Eve reasoned.

Claire was alarmed that the catalogs were so obvious yet liked adding the idea to their campaign. "We should run this by Marcus. If he thinks it's a good idea, we'll build it into our pitch."

"To take the idea one step further, did you or anyone ever design a placement ad that was disguised as a TV show?"

"No, and never even thought of that. This sounds fascinating," Claire said.

"Well, some of the shows that Bell watches are really just ads for other branches of the same corporation. An example would be the Disney channel. Their TV show plugs the musical downloads, which plugs the toys that go with the show, which plugs the book and magazine pertaining to the show, which plugs the movie which spins off the show, etc.," Eve explained.

"Yeah, it's brilliant. Cross-marketing. They just promote other divisions of their corporation."

"Yes, but besides placing the products all over the setting of the TV show, there would be subliminal messages throughout the program. They could be flashed with one of those new tachistoscopes. On an audio level the messages could be hummed in the background or even back masked with the sound barely audible. The whole show would be the commercial," Eve described.

"Genius! Evil genius, but genius! You should fall off the wagon more often. Marcus is going to love this idea. He'll probably bring it to Andel," Claire said.

Chapter Thirty-Nine

Marcus Reinsing was famished. After the police knocked on his door and asked questions about Phillip Krakowski, his paranoia prevented him from hunting. Marcus shot Andel's neighbor with a tranquilizer gun, and then feasted on his remains. Almost two months later, loose ends that were originally ignored had now gained momentum within the community. Afraid of being followed, he settled for animal blood instead of hunting in Indiana as he had planned. The dogs he purchased tasted hollow and did not satisfy him like human blood. Only days later, he needed to eat. His veins bulged with starvation.

Monday morning Marcus came into the office very late. Andel had just gotten back from his business trip and intently listened to his agents tell him about the chosen Clio submissions and new clientele. He saw Marcus and immediately called him into his office.

"You look sick. When is the last time you ate?" Andel asked. "I can see several of your veins because your skin is so translucent. Soon you'll go into hibernation. That's what happens when you become malnourished."

"Master, I'm so glad you're back. I ate last Friday, but not human blood. I bought three dogs and fed off of them," Marcus explained.

"Where did you get that idea? That's not what I taught you. That's like eating celery sticks when you are starving. If you don't want to hunt every week, then you need to hold someone captive. Blood regenerates in humans. You can feed, but you have to have enough control to keep the victim alive. Then every few days or so you can needle yourself. It's not recommended, but if you think you are being followed, then it's an option. You can't

193 • Peacocks, Pedestals, and Prayers

work like this. Here, take some of mine before you pass out. Tonight, you can hunt."

Andel offered his forearm to Marcus. He sucked the sweet blood that pulsated through Andel's veins. It tasted so good. Marcus became so absorbed, that he failed to hear Andel's command.

"I said stop!" Andel roared, his eyes flamed bursts of yellow and his fangs dropped below his lower lip. Marcus obeyed.

"I'm so sorry, Master. I got carried away and forgot. Oh, forgive me," Marcus wept.

"Your instincts took over. I understand. Blood is an addiction; you start to drink, and you don't want to stop until it's all gone. Do you feel better?" Marcus nodded. He was no longer weak.

"Your skin has retained its color. Now I'm going to scold you. What possessed you to substitute the dog blood for human blood?"

Marcus knew Andel would be angry, but told him everything about Phillip Krakowski, and the police sketch of him that was circulating in everyone's emails. He lastly included the visit he received from the police at Andel's home, and worried he was being followed. Andel contained his disappointment.

"Marcus, I need to relocate you very soon. All of these mistakes, well, it's just too much to fix," Andel coolly announced.

"But Master, I like it here. Please don't make me leave. For the first time in my life people talk to me as if I matter. I beg you to give me a chance and make things right," Marcus cried.

"People treat you well because of me, and don't you forget it," Andel snarled. "If I were not up against a wall right now, I would destroy you. As my protégé you have become a liability. However, timing is everything. And I'm running out of time. You'll get your chance to make things right, but if you don't, forget about relocating to another agency. You'll be going to my hometown, the depths of Hell. I can tell you firsthand that earth is much more fun. There aren't any pretty girls like Eve down there."

Marcus was embarrassed that Andel noticed his interest. Determined to end the neighborhood witch hunt, he began formulating his options.

***

Jackie Winthrop saw Marcus and another man slumped over in the passenger seat of his car on the fatal night of Phillip Krakowski's disappearance. She closely articulated Marcus' facial features to the police sketch artist. In addition to Jackie's help, other neighbors had got involved, forming their own version of a crime stoppers group with goals of finding Phil, dead or alive, and his captor. Marcus was not worried about their first objective. He and Andel feasted on Phil's flesh and blood and then properly disposed of his bones. What he found most threatening was the group's organization and pressure they had put upon the police. He first needed to get rid of Jackie, who could identify him on that blustery winter's night.

Jackie was easy to find. Not only was she listed in the White Pages, but also on Central Dupage Hospital's directory as a nurse. *Got to love Google*, Marcus thought. *It's a stalker's dream.*

Monday night, immediately after Andel threatened relocation, and then an eternity in Hell, Marcus was highly motivated to end all his problems. He easily found Jackie's car in the hospital parking lot, parked several blocks away, and waited. It was a cold night in March, but Marcus did not feel the climate. He crouched behind Jackie's wheel of her minivan and waited. Hours later, she exited the hospital. *There's that nosy bitch who is intent on ruining my life.*

Marcus could hear Jackie's idle chit-chat with colleagues, and then she walked towards her car. Once she started the ignition, he jumped inside with a gun that wasn't even loaded and commanded her to drive away. He ducked down until she exited the hospital.

"What do you want? My purse?" Jackie asked with tears in her eyes.

"It's me, the man you described to the sketch artist. Thanks to you, the police suspect me in Phillip Krakowski's disappearance."

Jackie slowly looked over and recognized him. "I never said you were responsible, only that I saw you there, struggling, with a man that didn't seem to be conscious."

"Whose idea was it to email the entire state of Illinois my sketch?" Marcus asked as he sat up in the passenger seat.

"It was all of ours. We had a neighborhood meeting about it," Jackie answered.

"I want names. Who is Fred Singer? He and a cop came to my house!" Marcus demanded.

"He and John King are the ones in charge of finding Phil. They arrange all of the neighborhood meetings and keep in contact with the press. Are you going to kill me? You don't have to. Fred wants confirmation it was you that I saw that night. He and I planned to stakeout your house this week with a camera. He was going to take photos with a zoom lens, and then post them side by side with the police sketch. All of it would be recirculated through email, social media, and the news. I could end your troubles permanently if you let me go. I could tell Fred that it wasn't you. We could pretend that all of this never happened. I have a husband and kids, please. You have nothing to worry about. I don't even know Phillip Krakowski, and right now, I don't care what you did to him. Just let me go and I'll clean up this mess."

Jackie's offer was very tempting. If she kept her word, Marcus could kiss all his troubles good-bye. But if she didn't, he had the ultra-warm climate of Hell to look forward to. He knew he was playing with fire and literally didn't want to get burned.

Marcus' original plan had two benefits: Jackie would be used for food, and she would no longer be around as a potential witness for the police. He flashed back to the conversation he held earlier with Andel, *blood regenerates in humans.* She could be used as his first host.

Marcus took Jackie to Andel's home and had her park in the garage. It was close to ten o'clock. Most people in his neighborhood were in bed watching TV. He doubted anyone seen her or her car. At gunpoint, he took her upstairs into an empty bedroom and tied her up. Before doing anything, he placed a plastic tarp around her so that there wouldn't be a mess on the carpet. *She's a big woman. Plenty of blood to drink. Kind of pretty, too.*

"What's going on?" Jackie cried. She looked down on the floor every time Marcus would give her one of his hungry and salacious looks.

She thinks I want to fuck her. No idea that's she's my food. "Just a precaution," Marcus said as he sneered. His eyeteeth were already elongating from excitement. He was so hungry. The couple of pints Andel shared was not enough to sustain him. He wanted his master's advice on how to feed without killing his victim. He knew Andel was home, and he opted to call his cell.

"Hi, it's me. I'm upstairs right now in the bedroom. Are you available for another lesson?" Marcus asked.

"I'll be right there."

Andel looked at the large woman the way a man looks at a Kansas City steak before he grills. Jackie was enough to satisfy then both. He was quite impressed that Marcus took the initiative in fixing his problems.

197 • Peacocks, Pedestals, and Prayers

"Nice work, Marcus. There is a trick to this. You must know when enough is enough, or there goes your future supply. Here, watch me and count how many seconds I take."

Despite the gag Marcus put inside of her mouth, Jackie was still sobbing loudly. Andel drilled his fangs into her wrist and sucked.

"1001, 1002, 1003, 1004, 1005, ….," Marcus counted for almost a minute, until Andel was through feeding off of Jackie. He licked up the open bite mark and wiped the blood off his handsome face. Jackie had passed out.

"That's about as much blood as you can drink without changing her. Be very careful. When she wakes up, it's your turn. The hardest part is stopping. It's our nature to suck our food dry. But with practice, you don't have to hunt as often. With her size, I'm going to estimate that she'll last us throughout the month."

"Thank you, Master, for giving me a second chance and showing me more of your ways. I won't disappoint you."

Chapter Forty

Sean Slattery experienced the most extraordinary evening of his life. He and the Easterhouse family participated in a supernatural Ouija board game which was interrupted by an intruder. After Sean chased him off the property, they reported the break-in to the police. The fireplace flue and window in the master bedroom were both left open. Because nothing was stolen, the police neglected to perform an extensive investigation. Their visit amounted to nothing more than an empty promise of patrolling the area more often.

Sean fixed the flue and barricaded all the fireplaces. Because of Bell's request, he spent the night on the sofa. The excitement of the evening had deprived everyone of sleep.

Sean had returned home by late morning and had several voicemails to play back. Barb Grossman, Rachel Silverman, and Detective Leonardo Magliano left messages regarding Abe Silverman. He went missing in Florence, and a report was filed. He could hear a twinge of blame in Rachel's recorded voice message and felt responsible.

"Mr. Slattery, I am calling because of your private detective, Abe Silverman. We last tracked him down to the Yelizi church you were interested in," said Detective Magliano's recording. Sean replayed it several times. His thick Italian accent was hard to understand. Once he had the number, he frantically returned the detective's call.

"Hello, Detective Magliano? Sean Slattery. Abe's missing? I can't believe...."

"Yes, he's missing. Thanks for getting back to me so quickly. I've been dealing with Barb, and his daughter, Rachel. Because they were both hysterical, I didn't tell them that I strongly suspect he's dead. Abe did leave a trail of breadcrumbs as you Americans say. He took some photos inside of the church. The good news is that he emailed them to himself, and Barb just forwarded them to me. I think most of them were shot in the basement. The pictures are enough to get us a warrant. Without one, the church will not cooperate. The Bacciani family who runs the church has deep connections within our judicial system," reported the detective.

"This is all my fault. I'm taking the first plane out," Sean declared.

"Don't blame yourself. I was very happy about him following up on this case, and even encouraged him to investigate the church in spite of knowing how dangerous these people can be. Just sit tight. We are doing everything we can," Leonardo said.

"I can't. Actually, I might be able to help. I'm an American lawyer and know how to scare the right people with legalese, if you know what I mean. As a citizen, I could get the U.S. Embassy involved. We'll find out what happened to him one way or another."

"Your international expertise would be useful. The Baccianis might tie our hands like they have done before. I want you to know that I salvaged a very expensive item from Abe's hotel room."

Sean knew he was talking about the information he purchased through Abe about Carlos Bacciani. "I'll call you when I land."

Sean feared for the safety of the Easterhouse family but was still compelled to leave the country. To ease his guilt, he dropped by before his flight with a few accessories.

Julia and Bell were home while Eve dragged herself to work. The house was lit up with numerous candles that lined the perimeter of the house. Crosses were hung all over the walls. Bell and Julia stacked dozens of Bibles on the dining room table. Mother and daughter were cutting out certain pages from them.

"What's going on here? Another séance?" Sean uncomfortably said.

"We're arming ourselves with God," Julia said.

"Me and Mommy went shopping this morning and I told her what to buy," Bell said proudly.

"Julia, this is a fire hazard. You're not protecting yourself or your daughter from fire. Do you really need all these candles on the floor?" Sean asked.

"This is how my mother handled things every time she felt threatened. She used God to ward off evil. In the end evil got to her, but she had a good run. My mother visited Bell in a dream last night and told her to do this. Bell dreamt of her before, but I assumed it all was a childhood fantasy. Now I'm not so sure. I'll take my chances with causing a fire. Right now, Bell and I are just trying to live a bit longer," Julia said.

"What about her dad? Can she stay with him for a few days?"

"Her father is pretty much out of the picture. He was paying support, but just stopped. And hasn't called her or taken her for the weekend in months," Julia said.

"I'm so sorry. He's a fool," Sean said.

"He left me for another woman, and they are about to get married."

"Like I said, he's a fool. Don't feel bad. You're not the only one. My wife left me, too."

"She's also a fool," Julia said.

Sean blushed and changed the conversation back to where it had started. "Well, just in case your mother was wrong, or Bell's dream was wrong, I want to leave my gun. I've got to leave town."

"Out of town? Why? Where?" Bell shouted, listening in on their conversation.

Sean knelt to be closer to Bell and put his hand on her shoulder. "I'll be back, but right now, I've got to find my friend. You know that painting your grandmother left you?" Bell nodded. "I wanted some more information on the artist. He was very good friends with your grandmother. My friend went to Italy, where the artist was from, in hopes of finding out more about him and more about your grandmother. Long story short, there was a connection. Now he's in trouble and I've got to find out why."

Bell started crying. She felt an unusual attachment to Sean and wanted him to stay. "You're going to Florence? It's not safe there. Stay here with me and Mommy."

"I won't be long," Sean said. Before he left, he gave Julia a quick lesson on how to use the gun.

Before his plane took off, Sean thought of the Easterhouse women. He already missed Julia, Bell, and even Eve. They were becoming like family. He felt dirty for having romantic feelings about Julia. She looked so much like her mother, yet her personality was very different. He tried to push those feelings away but couldn't help imagining being with her. The very idea calmed his nerves and helped him sleep through his long flight to Florence.

With the time change, the day had elapsed into the early daybreak hours of the next. After landing in Florence, Italy, Sean rented tiny hatchback with a navigation system. He punched in the address of the police station and called Detective Magliano from his cell. The detective and his partner, Dino Barone, were already at the station waiting for him. Introductions were made and then they got down to the basics of the situation.

"Here's the file you bought. Dino and I were the lead detectives who handled Carlos' suicide, or murder. We really don't know. Carlos was an interesting guy. He renounced both his church and family a few years before he died. And after that, he seemed to have gone crazy. Abe believed the Yelizi church held the answers to all our questions. Now that you are here, you can utilize the American Embassy for extra leverage in the Baccianis' cooperation. We will head over there within an hour. An American statesman is going to meet us. Sean, who is your client? Who are you representing that is so interested in angel worship and Carlos Bacciani?" Leonardo bluntly asked.

"I certainly don't have to tell you that. It's confidential, but under the current circumstances, I will. It's me. I'm my own client. I was in love with Lydia Easterhouse. My interest with Carlos Bacciani began with a painting he gave to her. He used her face for one of the angels in the scene. Now her granddaughter has the picture. Like Carlos, Lydia also had a suspicious accident. Everything keeps leading to this angel cult," Sean said.

"Since we have a few minutes before our meeting, let me show you the pictures Abe emailed himself. I believe most of them were taken in the church's basement," Leo said.

Sean sat in front of the computer on Leonardo's desk and clicked onto each one, examining them very closely. He knew Abe had stumbled onto something insidious.

"These birds were at the service I crashed in Chicago. They opened the cages and let them fly out during the last ten minutes of the sermon. They represent the angels these people worship. And the peacock, well you know who that represents, Satan. But I didn't see one in the Chicago branch," Sean said.

"We have reason to believe that the peacocks are only used during special occasions," Dino said.

"Going by their elaborate attire or lack of attire, this was definitely a special occasion. Red robes and masks, like a masquerade party, kind of. This is an odd picture. Are these carafes of wine in a minifridge? Why did he take a picture of this? The background of the room looks like some kind of storage area," Sean said while he flipped through more pictures. He then came upon the girl Abe photographed inside of a room without furniture and fell silent.

"We don't know who she is. Don't know if she's dead or sleeping. This is the shot that got us our warrant. All the other ones are going to be dismissed if you can believe that. There are three other pictures that have a yellowish cast, as if Abe took them through a yellow glass window. Our computer lab is working on them as we speak. We better get going," said Dino.

They all arrived at the church by daybreak. A few cars lingered in the parking lot, but the building appeared empty. Once Sean and the two Italian detectives got out of the car, a seagull landed on Dino's shoulder. Sean remembered the astounding story about the birds Julia shared. At the time, he just placated her, thinking fear caused her mind to play tricks. Now he sensed an omen.

"Where's the American?" Sean asked, referring to their consulate connection that was supposed to meet with them.

"I don't know. He's not answering his phone. Dino, shew that bird off you. It's creeping me out," Leonardo said. "Okay, boys. I'm going to give them a few minutes to answer. If no one does, we are going to break down the front door. Let's do this."

They knocked for several minutes and then got ready for the next stage of the warrant. Just before the uniformed cops took out their axes from the car, Franco Bacciani, and his brother Pasquale, answered the door.

"We have a warrant to look around your premises. This is your copy. Come on boys," yelled Leonardo.

The brothers remained quiet, and Franco texted his lawyer. Expecting this to happen, he and other members within the church planned ahead. Leonardo's unit photographed every inch of the place, verifying Abe's pictures were taken in the basement. The room the girl was photographed in was now vacant. They found the storage closet behind the stage of the assembly room and assumed it was Abe's hiding place. Dino checked the contents of the mini-fridge and found it empty. The door of the closet had amber and yellow stained glass. Dino deducted Abe must have been photographing the happenings through the door's window. Abe's perspective would have privileged him to a side view close-up of the stage. *Abe, what were you trying to tell us?* he wondered aloud.

Dino went through every item inside the closet. When he thought he had finished, a shiny electronic device underneath a tote bag caught his eye. He reached for it and turned it on. Surprised the battery still had a tiny bit of a charge, he identified the phone as Abe's property. The pictures he sent himself were in the phone's memory.

The rest of the squad were scattered all over the basement. Many paid special attention to the aviary, whereas others searched the empty rooms for the girl Abe had photographed. Everyone stopped after hearing Dino scream. "I've got it! Arrest the men. They have to be interrogated at the station!" He proudly held the cellphone up for everyone to see. The other police applauded. Leonardo and Dino finished up by dusting for prints inside of the closet. Unfortunately, it looked as if the tiny room had been recently cleaned. Still, they might get lucky.

Franco and Pasquale mutely cursed themselves. Their only mistake had them cuffed and shoved into the back of one of the squad cars. Once the detectives were finished, they commended each other for such great work. On the way out of the church, a seagull again landed on Dino.

"All these birds are starting to scare me. Did you see that wild little zoo they had downstairs? I'm no animal lover. It must be my cologne," Dino said trying to explain the attraction the bird had for him.

Another seagull landed on Dino's other shoulder. Soon sparrows, ravens, and more seagulls hovered around his body. The first one that landed on him began to peck.

"What the hell! Ouch! Do something!" Dino screamed.

Leonardo took out his gun and started shooting it in the air. The birds wouldn't budge, and more of them began to peck. They fought for a place to peck at Dino's face. He shrieked in horror. Blood spurted all over. Leonardo tried shooting the ones that were not very close to Dino's head, but they all flapped so fast. Too many bullets were wasted. Leonardo accidentally shot Dino in the leg. He buckled down to the pavement, screeching in pain. Almost two dozen birds were still pecking at his head. Leonardo went through the rest of his bullets, only killing a few of them. While he reloaded, Dino's eyes were plucked out of his head. Blood spilled like two waterfalls out of his sockets. Still alive, the birds continued to peck. Sean took off his jacket and started whipping it at them. This mildly slowed them down, but they drilled an opening into Dino's neck with their beaks. Like a tapped oil rig, Dino gushed all over the pavement. He died in front of the Yelizi church, attacked by birds.

Chapter Forty-One

Tuesday morning, before the blare of most agents' alarm clocks, Claire and Eve met at the *Evil Empire* to fine tune their pitch. They first planned on running it by Marcus. If everything went well, Andel would listen to their idea before presenting it to their prospective client, Regular Electric. Not only was their pitch original, but it could revolutionize both TV and advertising. Once they had all their facts and figures, they approached Marcus in his office.

"Marcus, as you already know, R.E. has numerous products to offer the public. Instead of a typical thirty-second spot that consumers are blocking out by going to the bathroom, getting a snack, or whatever, the ad can be built inside of the TV show," Claire opened.

"Also, don't forget about the people who record their favorite shows and fast forward through the commercials. With our idea, they would be forced to see the ad," Eve supported.

"Our idea is to showcase all of their products with strategic placement, flashing images, even back-masking. We could use the theme song to play slogans in the background. Maybe the back-up singers could vocalize *'buy RE'* backwards. The characters would use, and even talk about the products throughout the show," Claire said.

"Wow, what an ambitious idea. It's bold. I like it. Hold on, let me get Andel in here." Marcus rang his extension and he readily agreed to listen. Within minutes, he entered Marcus' office and made himself comfortable on the sofa.

"Okay, let's hear what Marcus is so excited about," Andel said.

Claire pitched the idea again, but with more details and enthusiasm than the first time. Her exhilaration was heightening. Andel appeared to be genuinely fascinated. When she finished, he asked, "Whose idea was this?"

"Mine. Eve and I have been working non-stop. I think RE will really like it," Claire lied.

Andel knew Claire was poaching credit for Eve's vision. He paused, waiting for Eve to defend herself. *C'mon, girl. This is the part where you 'throw her under the bus', add some drama, and demand both a raise and new partner. That's what you are supposed to do in this backstabbing industry.* But Eve remained tacit. He was daunted by his inability to read her thoughts and actions. He didn't like the uncertainty she brought to his business.

On the contrary, Eve knew exactly what he was thinking. His thoughts murmured along with heavy static inside of her head. His laser-like eyes attempted to burn his way into her mind. She became uneasy around him. Up until this moment, work had been somewhat of a sanctuary compared to her home life. Andel took that security away and invoked her 'fight or flight' instinct. Once again, she questioned her own sanity.

"Can you two provide R.E. with an example?" Andel asked.

"Of course," Claire reassured.

"I'll get the CEO in here by next week. Will you be ready?" Both women nodded. Claire was elated with such an enormous account, but Eve felt nauseated.

"I want to see what you're pitching them first," Andel ordered.

As Eve and Claire packed up their files, Eve could again hear Andel's murmurs. *I could put my own messages in sitcoms, dramas, news programs, mini-series, sporting events- The endless possibilities. I could keep the souls for myself, and even share with my fallen brethren. My work would reach an all-new level. Maybe I could stay.*

Eve looked at him in horror. He didn't see her expression because he was too absorbed within his thoughts. Although she found him confusing, her intuition confirmed his raw diabolical nature. *This man is evil, evil like my grandmother, like my uncles. And I'm stuck in the middle of it. Something is not right.*

"Okay, we got lots of work to do. Any suggestions on how to give R.E. an example of what we're trying to accomplish?" Claire asked.

If she wanted extra brownie points with the boss, then good for her, thought Eve. Only mildly upset with her partner, her mind weighed heavily on all the cursed events she and her family were experiencing. Convinced she was losing her mind Eve welcomed the diversion of putting together an intricate campaign. Work would keep her mind off things throughout the day. The sleepless nights worried her most.

"Maybe we can write a script based on a hit TV show and perform a scene right here on the stage. It would be enough for R.E. to get the idea. We can use an array of their products as props, write a hokey version of a theme song with their product subversively mentioned, and even have some of the song's words piped in backwards. We could use those flashing images that you advertising people like so much throughout the scene. Marcus could even help us. He does know all about the effects of both the stage and screen in the auditorium. We can make it funny," Eve rambled.

"Brilliant. Here is my company credit card. Roughly order a dozen or so of R.E.'s products for props. Once we know what we are advertising, we'll write the script around their products. We've only got a week. Let's get started."

While Eve worked away the morning, Tony approached her desk.

"Are you still up for dinner this Friday? Remember? You promised to reschedule with me?" Tony reminded.

"You know, with the crappy week I've been having, I would love nothing more than to blow off some steam with you. Are you promising a night on the town?" Eve asked.

"I'll show you an evening you'll never forget," Tony said flirtatiously. "Having a tough week? What happened?" He was curious about the details of his secret visit.

"You wouldn't believe me if I told you. But to brief you about my problems, we had a break-in last Sunday, my sister broke her arm and is recuperating from a car accident, and my niece is having emotional problems. I'm really stressed. I hope you like to party, Tony. I could really use an escape."

Friday evening, after a grueling week, Eve was looking forward to having some fun. She dressed like the sexy party girl she used to be. Tony came early, but Eve made Julia promise not to let him inside. Her sister's and niece's new decorum was enough to scare him off. Julia and Bell had cleaned out every Hallmark store within a ten-mile radius for candles and crosses. To a stranger, the family looked like stark raving religious fanatics.

"Aren't you going to let me in?" Tony asked, unsure of why she was being rude.

"No, we're kind of remodeling and the place is a mess. I'm too embarrassed with it being our first date and all."

"First date, I like the sound of that, like maybe they'll be a second," Tony said. Eve thought he was beyond salacious. His teeth were so white, like a movie star's. He looked metro chic in his black t-shirt and jeans.

Tony was equally impressed with Eve. Her long legs were accentuated in a sequined mini-skirt and four-inch heels. They got into his red Lexus and sped off towards Chicago.

"You said you wanted to party, so I thought we'd go downtown, you know, get some dinner, then hit some clubs. Do you like to dance?"

Eve nodded.

The evening couldn't have been more enjoyable. Tony knew how to show a woman a great time. He took her to an expensive restaurant where they feasted on filets and Cristal champagne. They danced until closing at the trendiest bars the city had to offer. He brought along an endless supply of cocaine which Eve took full advantage of. Both drunk and high, she felt ten years younger, and free from all her current problems.

By 4:00 a.m., Tony took her back to his townhouse. They passionately kissed and peeled off each other's clothes. Skipping all foreplay, they headed straight to his bedroom. His size, technique, and stamina gave her pleasure that she had never before experienced. He was a very primal, yet sensitive lover. Three hours later, exhaustion from their lovemaking marathon had set in, and Eve wanted to go home.

"Stay with me. We could spend the day together. It's like spring outside. Do you like to play golf? Horseback ride? You name it; your wish is my command," Tony pleaded. He kissed her all over, not wanting her to leave him.

"I can't. I need some sleep. Claire and I have to work tonight and tomorrow. We've got a big presentation next week."

Tony was hurt but tried not to show it. Eve was a woman of many layers. He was smitten with her unpredictability. One day he planned on having her all to himself.

Chapter Forty-Two

The day after Sean Slattery jetted off to Florence, Bell slept with Julia, periodically waking up throughout the night with violent outbursts. Despite her recurring nightmares, she still wanted to go to school because of a St. Patrick's Day party her kindergarten teacher was having. Julia agreed that school might help her forget about all the strange happenings.

School was a day of fun activities and lots of food. Bell proudly helped bake cupcakes in the morning before class. While all the children were enjoying their sugary treats, she dropped her plate and glass of Kool-Aid onto the floor. Her mouth was wide open, yet not a sound came out of it. Her blue eyes projected the kind of terror only seen by a victim before her violent end. She was almost immobilized, with exception of an occasional tremor. Not knowing what to do, the teacher used her intercom and summoned the school nurse to the classroom. Her behavior set off panic among the rest of her classmates. A clamor of screams echoed throughout the school hallway. An ambulance escorted her directly to the emergency room.

Julia met the ambulance at the hospital. After several hours of tests, Bell was given a clean bill of health. Upon her discharge, the doctor handed Julia a packet.

"Ms. Easterhouse, you might want to take her to a child psychiatrist. I have plenty of fine doctors to refer. Your daughter's attack was brought on by her psyche; there's no other explanation. A doctor can help her unload her troubles," said the E.R. physician.

"Thank you. I'll look into that right away," Julia replied. On the way out of the hospital she threw the list in the garbage and headed home.

Julia made her daughter some soup and then sat down with her as she ate. "Do you want to talk about what happened at school today? Your teacher and the nurse said you were frozen, and then would shake from time to time."

"Mom, I don't want you to worry, but I saw Sean in Italy, and it was horrible," Bell cried. She needed her mother to comfort her. Over an hour later, she stopped crying and recapped her vision. She saw a man Sean was with get his eyes plucked out by birds in a parking lot.

After listening to Bell describe the horrific vision she encountered, Julia called Sean Slattery's cell phone.

"Sean, are you alright?" Julia cried.

"I'm fine, but one of the detectives, well, it was a tragedy, a freak accident. Oh God! Out of nowhere, birds, lots and lots of birds, different kinds, pecked Detective Barone to death. We tried everything. One of the detectives was shooting at them. I was whipping them with my jacket, but they wouldn't stop. It was as if they were possessed. Oh God! It could have happened to you. I mean, it did happen to you. You are so lucky, Julia! They would have killed you! I'm so sorry. I thought you were in a state of shock; I just didn't …."

"Sean, it's okay. Did the detective find anything important, maybe something about Abe? Did the birds go for his eyes?" Julia interrupted.

"Well, yes. He found Abe's cell at the church. Then right there in the parking lot…that's where it happened, the attack! How did you know?"

"Bell saw you in a vision. She saw the birds, church, everything. It happened at while she was at school. She appeared catatonic, so they rushed her to the emergency room. She's calmed down for now. What's going on? I don't know how much more of this we can all take," Julia said as she sobbed.

"Julia, I think Abe is dead, and the Bacciani family is behind it. In fact, I think they are behind everything.

There are rumors that have followed them around for centuries. I'll explain all of this later. Right now, I'm at the police station with Detective Magliano. He is motioning me to hang up. I'll call you when I get a chance. I love you," Sean said.

There was a pause in the conversation that made Julia elated yet uncomfortable.

"Sean, I don't know what to say."

"I'm sorry, forget it. I meant that you, Bell, and Eve are, well, I care for all of you. Good night."

"Good night, Sean. And we love you, too. I love you, too," Julia said. She could not tell if her feelings were altruistic or brought on by despair and vulnerability. None of it mattered. She was beginning to fall in love with him, just like her mother.

Detective Magliano approached Sean with a grave expression. The joy Sean felt after Julia echoed those three words he longed to hear was short-lived and temporarily forgotten.

"I'm so sorry about your partner. Someone is controlling those birds, and we're going to nail him," Sean said.

"Dino was going to retire this summer. He planned to live out his days with his wife on the Italian Riviera. His daughter lives there. She's expecting her first child, Dino's first grandchild. His wife is a mess. Someone's going to pay, even if I have to spend the rest of my life searching. This is far from over. Sean, do you remember the American diplomat who was supposed to meet us this morning? He jumped out the window at approximately 9:10 a.m. His body is splattered all over the Embassy parking lot. They are calling it a suicide," Leonardo said in a low, hushed voice as he scanned the station for signs of anyone who might be listening to their conversation.

"Jumped? Timing couldn't be more suspicious. Are you sure he wasn't pushed?" Sean asked. "Do you think the Baccianis are behind this?"

"Senore Slattery, please keep it down. You are way too loud and attracting unwanted attention. And yes, the Baccianis are involved somehow, some way. I can't even prove they were even on the premises. They could have hired someone, but I can't prove that either. I'm about to question Franco and Pasquale, separately of course. There's a two-way mirror and a small viewing area on the other side of the interrogation room. Care to watch? Their lawyer is here to make sure they don't incriminate themselves, but maybe they'll slip," Leonardo said.

Sean sat with a couple other police officers inside of the viewing room. They had a front row seat in witnessing sheer evil. Franco Bacciani, the older brother and priest of the parish, was questioned first.

Detective Magliano drilled him about their church service, the discovery of the uninvited Abe Silverman, and use of birds inside of their ritual.

"Are you persecuting my client for his religious views? I'm deeply sorry for you and your partner's family. This morning's incident was a tragedy and nothing more. To insinuate that my clients had anything to do with those malicious birds, well, you know better. They were cuffed and sitting in a squad car while Detective Barone was attacked," adamantly defended Bacciani's lawyer. "Now, if there's nothing else, we are done here."

Detective Magliano still had one more card to play. "Mr. Bacciani, who is this young woman lying on the basement floor of your church? Abe Silverman took this picture before you killed him," Leonardo said with dramatic flair. He slammed the picture that he printed from Abe's camera down on the table for Franco and his lawyer to see.

Without flinching, Franco looked him straight in the eye and answered. "She's my granddaughter, Carmen Bacciani."

"Even if she is your granddaughter, locking up minors and holding them captive is against the law in Italy, no matter what your religion is," Leonardo stated.

"Listen, you mock our ways, but they are thousands of years old. Our faith is the oldest practice in the world. Carmen turned fourteen in that picture. We held a confirmation of sorts. That room is not a cell, but a waiting room to sit or lay before approaching the altar."

"Is Carmen the daughter of Carlos Bacciani?" Leonardo asked.

"Yes. He abandoned her, along with his wife, and all of us when he publicly renounced our ways, and then killed himself," Franco said.

"I'm going to have to talk to her in order to verify your story," Leo insisted.

"Of course. It's late. Tomorrow morning, I'll have her mother bring her here," Franco promised.

Leonardo continued to accuse and interrogate, hoping Franco would falter, but his lawyer protected him from the slick line of questioning. Pasquale, the younger brother, had an almost identical story. While both brothers were individually being questioned, they both stared at Sean through the two-way mirror. At first, he thought he must be imagining the eye contact, but the two other policemen in the room also noticed their gazes.

"Is it possible to see us in here?" Sean nervously asked. Both brothers made the hair in the back of his neck stand up.

"No, not at all. But they know they are being watched."

Without Abe's body or the girl, Leonardo did not have enough to make an arrest. Abe's cell phone and the lurid ritual photos were not substantial evidence. Again, the Baccianis walked away from the police unscathed.

As both brothers and their attorney were on their way out of the building, Franco caught Sean's eye and deliberately approached him. He softly whispered, "We're going to get the scroll back one way or another."

Chapter Forty-Three

Eve had one of the most amazing dates of her life. She and Tony Manghella, her colleague, partied the night away, and then ended up in bed. After relapsing from her twelve-step program, feelings of guilt and remorse were surprisingly absent. She had so easily forgotten about the multiple problems, including prison time, that drugs had given her. Deep down inside, she knew that Tony was toxic for her and her sobriety, but she couldn't resist his charm and attention. The day after their date, dozens of flower bouquets, each with a personally composed card, were delivered at her home.

Eve worked with Claire for the remainder of the weekend, finishing up the final touches of their presentation. Andel would be viewing it the following Thursday, and Regular Electric would then be pitched the day after. Because her home life was jinxed, work gave her the perfect excuse of not having to confront her problems.

The beginning of the week proved to be more hectic than the weekend. All the appliances and electronics Eve ordered were being delivered to work. She consciously ordered items that were light enough for Claire and her to carry. Neither of them had the space to store all the boxes. Marcus volunteered the usage of the basement then gave them the keys.

Once they both moved over a dozen small appliances into the basement, Eve and Claire stopped for a short break to catch their breath.

"We'll have to move all of this back upstairs in a few days to set up on stage," Claire said. "I can't believe everyone is using the auditorium this week."

"That's fine. For what he pays us, it's not a big deal," Eve said.

"The bonus on the account will make our salaries look like chump change. I really want this. We are the envy of every agent here. Speaking of other agents, what happened with Tony? You haven't mentioned him all weekend, and I thought you two were going on your big date," Claire teased.

"We did go out Friday. I just want to keep this hush-hush. You won't tell anyone, will you?" Eve pleaded.

"No, of course not. I completely agree with keeping your personal life out of your work life. Now spill! I want all the details."

"He's the whole package. Smart, funny, sexy, sweet, a good time. What do you know about him? Has he dated anyone else here?"

"I don't know. There were rumors that he and Catalina, my old partner, dated. They never seemed like a couple. For all I know, they weren't. I can tell you this. After Andel dumped me, I kind of went psycho. Drugs and my emotions took over all my common sense. I never told you this, but you'll eventually find out anyway. People gossip. Before I got sober, I tried to kill him right outside in the parking lot, in front of everybody. I went home, completely hysterical. Then I tried to kill myself by overdosing and slashing my wrists. It was Tony who cared enough to stop by and check up on me. I'm alive because of him. I know he used to be a player, but he seems more focused. You are so lucky. He's a great guy. I always wished he would have asked me out, but he didn't want to get involved with the crazy ex-girlfriend of the boss, and I can't say I blame him. I hope the two of you work out. So anyway, where did he take you?"

Eve downplayed the evening, only mentioning the phenomenal dinner she had with him in Chicago. Because

219 • Peacocks, Pedestals, and Prayers

Claire was her program sponsor, she didn't want her to know about the bars, drinks, and cocaine.

"Did you sleep with him?" Claire asked.

"Is it that obvious?" Eve blushed.

"Was it the first time you had sex since you've been out of prison?"

Eve nodded. "And it was out of this fucking world! Sign me up for a second helping! He was amazing!"

The two women laughed while finishing up taking their purchases out of the boxes.

"We're going to blow these R.E. bastards away! All we need is the network to go along. Hey, what's over there?" Claire pointed to a door on the far side of the enormous basement.

They approached the door, turning light after light on, to illuminate their way through the vacant darkness. It was locked. Eve tried several keys on the key ring until she found the one that worked. She opened the door and found a light switch on the inside of the wall.

"Look, it's another basement. A basement to the basement. I guess that would make it a sub-basement," said Eve. "Feeling nosy? Let's check it out."

Inside the door was a spiral staircase that descended another twenty feet below ground level. The stairs emptied out into an unfinished, large room with concrete walls and floor. Cheap metal racks lined one of the walls, stacked with various sundries like juice, medical supplies, and canned goods. Along the side of another wall was a refrigerator, utility sink, and an electric stove.

"Could this be a bomb shelter? Or maybe a prepper cellar?" asked Claire, unsure of the strange and secretive layout.

"Or possibly a panic room?"

"Yes, that's what it is. Here's a camera to the upstairs. It's turned off, but you're right," Claire agreed.

"You thirsty? Here's some cans of Diet Coke," Eve suggested.

Claire nodded. Eve found two plastic cups then went into the freezer for some ice. As she opened the top freezer door, she dropped the cups and screamed. They were too far underground for anyone to hear.

In a split second, Claire rushed to her side and saw what Eve was screaming about. Inside the freezer box, was the preserved, beautiful, and frozen head of Catalina Rojas.

Chapter Forty-Four

Professor Dinda Nrogbi left Father Sardenelli's house somewhat satisfied with the information he had divulged. Julia Easterhouse had brought her own copy of angel script carvings and an ancient scroll to his faculty's attention a few weeks prior. She abruptly left the university after being asked to leave her scroll for artifact testing. Her defiance had angered him enough to order the birds to hunt her down.

As Dinda suspected, the Yelizi priest verified the scroll's celestial origins. Father Sardenelli added that he thought the seal was set with angelic blood. *This could be it,* thought Dinda. *And to think I held it in my hands. So close.* The scroll had the possibility of being written before mankind.

For almost two centuries, Dinda roamed the earth as a monster who was involuntarily changed at thirty-five years old. One frightful night at his tribe's ceremony, they conjured up Armaros, one of Satan's favorite generals, during a ritual. Dinda's father insisted he be used as a sexual offering for the revered angel. He resisted, and in turn, was bit by Armaros. His father's pleas persuaded the bloodthirsty angel to stop sucking, which resulted in his eternal transformation into a demon. Dinda would have preferred death. Forever cursed, he hunted the innocent to ensure his own survival. The only reason he had not tried to destroy himself was his innate fear of the alternative - Hell.

Dinda had been searching for Armaros since his change. Once found, he planned on begging the angel for his humanity back. Julia Easterhouse's scroll had changed his future plea, giving him something to bargain with. A normal life in exchange for the scroll would get Armaros' attention. Maybe Dinda could even negotiate getting his soul back.

Unlike most changed humans, Dinda refused to worship angels. He blamed them for all the evil he had committed. Nonetheless, they still had the ability to take away his free will and leave him a prisoner to his instincts. Although he could never find Armaros, he could feel his presence and hear his words. The closer he was to his master, the clearer his voice became when a communication was sent.

Six months ago, Dinda moved to Chicago after hearing Armaros sing a hymn. Almost two centuries later, this was the closest he ever came to finding him. Julia Easterhouse couldn't have entered his life at a more opportune time.

Dinda left Julia several messages after meeting her at Loyola University, but she would not return his calls. He was puzzled at how she even fit into the saga. After some research, he found her mother and uncles were part of Father Sardenelli's weekly angel worship service. Instead of asking her family about her findings, she chose Loyola's academia. *Some kind of family schism? Did she steal it from them? Why was she being secretive?* Dinda wondered.

During Monday early afternoon, Dinda drove past Julia's Cape Cod mansion. His blood pulsated with excitement. Hopefully, Julia would let him inside. There was an SUV parked in the driveway. Light illuminating from the windows assured him that she was home. He hesitantly knocked on the double doors. Something about the house felt familiar.

Julia saw Doctor Nrogbi through her front door window and recognized him. She distrusted the man immensely, but she wasn't afraid.

He tapped on the glass window of the door and yelled with a strong South African accent. "Ms. Easterhouse, I have vital information for you. Please, you won't return my calls, so I'm forced to pay you a visit. Only five minutes of your time."

"Mommy, don't let him in," Bell whispered as she clutched her mother's leg.

"It's all right. Just stay in your room. I'll give him his five minutes and then he'll leave," Julia said.

Julia threw on a sweatshirt with her good arm and stepped out on the porch to talk, without letting Doctor Nrogbi inside.

"I remember you from Loyola. We met through my friend, Doctor Jackson. What is your visit all about?"

"I had the pleasure of speaking with Father Sardenelli. Do you know him?" She shook her head. "He's the only Yelizi priest in the Midwest. I believe your family attends his services on the north-side of Chicago. Their names are printed on the church's program."

"I am estranged from my extended family. The priest and the church are unknown to me," Julia answered.

"Of course. You did come to us at Loyola instead of your family. I didn't realize it at the time, but I wanted more information on the angel script, so I went to the local expert. I had no idea there was any connection with Father Sardenelli and you."

"There isn't. But I can't help feeling there's a connection now. Professor, you didn't give him my name, did you?" Julia asked.

"Uh, maybe. I'm very sorry. I had no idea. Can I come in? It's important."

Against all logic, Julia let him inside her house. Curiosity superseded everything, including her and her daughter's safety.

Julia noticed the fearful look in Doctor Nrogbi's eyes as he looked around the walls that were lined with Bible passages and crucifixes. Candles cluttered the furniture surfaces and steps. The professor had interrupted her from lighting them all.

"Disregard the house. We are in the process of redecorating," Julia defended.

"Redecorating? Or keeping something away?" Julia looked down, refusing to answer. "I'm sorry, it's none of my business, and your home décor has nothing to do with why I'm even here," Dinda said.

Bell appeared at the top of the stairs watching their every move. Terror filled her eyes. The almost seven foot tall African with black eyes and bulging muscles looked intimidating to the little girl.

"Well, hello there, who do we have upstairs?" he asked. "No school today?"

"That's my daughter, and she's home sick," Julia answered. "Bell, go back to your room."

For the moment, Bell obeyed her mother.

Julia noticed Dinda looking at her broken arm. A flicker of terror pulsed through her body, but she ignored it.

"I showed Father Sardenelli the photos I took of your scroll. He seems to think it's a celestial document," Dinda said.

"A what?"

"It was composed by angels, maybe even Satan himself. It might be written before mankind was created. Please, I beg of you, just one more look. I won't take any pictures. I just want a closer look at the seal. There was an embossed symbol inside of it that I need to see."

"Why?" asked Julia.

"The odd color might be a mixture of angel's blood. I'm begging you, just one little peek and I'm gone," Dinda asked, looking genuinely sincere.

Once again, without reason, Julia's compulsion for some answers to her mother's belongings prevailed. She ascended the stairs and went straight to her closet. While digging for the box she hid under her carpet, she heard Bell enter the room.

"Mommy, do you need help?"

"No, honey. I've got..." Julia screamed, dropping the metal box that contained the scroll. To her horror, Dinda held Bell in a choke hold. As she dangled from his long arms, she began to cry.

Julia studied his ever-changing face. His black eyes now had flecks of gold and shrank into slits instead of the huge round shape they had been before. His beautiful smile now showed pointy animal-like teeth. Bell was right again. She should have never let him inside.

"Please, don't hurt her. She's only six years old. You can have the whole box with the scroll, just let her go," she begged, sliding the box in his direction.

Dinda let go of Bell and pushed her into her mother. He opened the box and sinisterly smiled as he took the scroll out and admired it. He then noticed the halo. "What's this? Scrap metal?" he asked, referring to the broken semi-circle of metal. "Ouch!" Dinda tried to pick up the metal, but it seared his hands. He flung his burnt fingers in front of Julia's face.

"It's part of a halo. A holy and divine halo," Julia replied in fear.

Dinda examined the scroll's seal. "Definitely angel blood," he muttered. "This will be my salvation. My curse will soon be lifted. Thank you. In return, I will not kill either of you." He gently put the scroll back into the box.

"You're not taking my grandmother's things!" screamed Bell.

The broken halo spun out of the box like a circular saw, cutting Dinda's burnt hand as he tried to catch it in mid-air. It kept spinning until landing in Bell's hand.

Dinda hissed in rage at Bell. He lunged towards Julia and attempted to bite her forearm.

Bell shrilled, "No!" She took the broken halo and flicked it with her wrist, like a Frisbee, at Dinda. It spun so fast that it was almost invisible, slicing him in the neck. With boomerang ability, the halo spun right back to her.

Without hesitation, she flicked it at him again. This time it sliced into his skull.

While Dinda doubled over in pain, Julia took the box away from him and slid it back inside her closet. Bell kept pummeling the halo at him until his body was full of deep cuts.

Without emotion, she said, "Mommy, he isn't dead yet. You've got to burn him. Take the crucifix and place it on his face. Then take your lighter and light."

Julia grabbed a cross off the wall and then pushed it deep down into his face. His skin sizzled like a pan of burning bacon. Per her daughter's directions, she flicked her lighter at Dinda's freshly branded face. He instantly was consumed by a contained fire. The blaze threw a wave of furnace-like heat, but then the fire was gone, leaving no trace of his body or any other damage in the room.

"Mommy, you did it!" Bell squealed.

"Me? How about you! Like David and Goliath! You took him down with part of a halo! That was amazing," Julia scooped up her daughter with her good arm and held her tight while tears streamed down her face.

"Mommy?"

"Yes?"

"He's not the only one who wants the scroll. We are going to need the other piece of this halo," Bell forewarned.

Chapter Forty-Five

Fred Singer called Jackie Winthrop Tuesday morning. He wanted her to review some photographs he had taken earlier of Marcus Reinsing. He had a gut feeling that Marcus was involved in Phil Krakowski's disappearance. Officer Novak and Fred briefly met Marcus when canvassing the neighborhood together. Jackie Winthrop's police sketch could have passed for Marcus' facial features. Fred wanted him arrested and questioned, but the officer lacked probable cause in detaining him.

After tailing Marcus for a few days, Fred learned his name and work address. Not surprisingly, he found the owner of the house, Andel Talistokov, was also the owner of the ad agency that Marcus worked at. Fred assumed they were living as a gay couple, and Andel, his boyfriend, must have known something about Phil's disappearance.

"Hi. Is Jackie there? This is Fred Singer. I was wondering if I could come over this afternoon, before dinner? Jackie and I had tentative plans of reviewing some pictures that I have taken," Fred asked. He figured the man on the other end of the phone was Jackie's husband.

"Fred, this is Lance, Jackie's husband. She hasn't been home since Friday. I reported her missing yesterday. She was last seen driving away from the hospital after work. No one has seen her, and her car is unaccounted for. I'm sorry, but I forgot all about your meeting. I haven't slept. There's no good explanation for any of this. Our marriage was okay, but even if Jackie wanted to leave me, she would never have done it without the kids. I can't help but think that she is dead. And the police are actually acting as if I might be responsible. I can't help but blame you for all of this. You are the one that's been spear-heading this whole search party for Phil. The emails, social media campaigns, police pressure, and even the press…Yet still no one has found him. Meanwhile, my wife might be the only one who could help piece together what happened, and now she's missing," Lance said.

"I understand where you are coming from. You want someone to blame, then go ahead and blame me. Phil, now your wife – it's not a coincidence. She saw the bastard alright, and that's why she's missing. We've got a serial killer on the loose right now, and we need to find him before more people end up d...," Fred said, catching himself from further upsetting Lance.

"I don't think you understand. I don't want your help! I've got two kids to think about. Just let the police do their job. Jackie's strong. Maybe she's still alive," Lance cried.

Fred didn't argue with the grieving spouse, but he went to the police with his photos and accusations.

***

Marcus converted the master bedroom in Andel's mansion as a makeshift prison cell for his new food source. He boarded up the windows in the bedroom and master bath, while also removing all furniture with exception of a sole bare mattress that lay on the floor. He installed cameras at the highest peak of the vaulted ceilings of both the bedroom and the bathroom, far from her reach. This enabled him to watch her every move. He made sure she was well-hydrated and fed with crushed-up hefty dosages of tranquilizers to keep her subdued. His new prison cell was not infallible, but effective.

He and Andel took turns feeding off of Jackie. She had punctures all over her neck and extremities from both men's consumption. Marcus was thankful for the food, but he only ate enough to keep himself nourished, and not satisfied. He asked Andel if he could add another source to the mix.

"We could, but it would be risky to keep them in the same room. Who knows what they could do as a team? They might figure out how to escape," Andel answered.

"Master, this house is so enormous. How about if I prepare another bedroom for a new host?"

"No need. I have a room in my basement that isn't being used," Andel offered. He was referring to his worship room. "I'll tell you what, find another host and give me first pick, alright? We have to dispose them by April. Otherwise, it's too hazardous."

They entered the master bedroom. Marcus watched as Andel fed from Jackie's collarbone. She no longer cried, just stared at the wall devoid of all emotion. She was too weak from the drugs and blood loss to fight. She repetitively told herself she was having a nightmare and soon would wake up.

While Andel fed, he was interrupted by pains of agony. He stopped sucking Jackie's blood and doubled over to the floor. "Oh, make the noise stop! I'm burning! Please, spare me from this!" he shrilled. Andel began to scream in a language that didn't even sound human.

Jackie snapped out of her indifference, trying to assess what was wrong with him. As an emergency nurse, Andel's ailment was one she had never seen. After screaming and crying, Andel curled up onto the floor in a fetal position and sucked his thumb.

"Master, what is wrong? What can I do?" Marcus knelt beside him and stroked his hair with worry.

Several minutes later, they witnessed Andel partake in an emotional breakdown and seizure. He finally stood up and steadied himself.

"I'm fine. It's now over. One of my creations was just destroyed. You know I've fathered more children than I care to count, but I have only transformed and created a handful of humans, including you, Marcus."

"But I thought I would live forever. What do you mean destroyed?" Marcus asked.

"You will live forever. I will hunt down whoever did this and bring down my wrath. When one of my own creations is destroyed, it's like part of myself died along with it."

"But Master," Marcus said as he looked over towards Jackie.

"No need to worry about what she hears. Soon she'll be dead," Andel said.

Chapter Forty-Six

Father Sardenelli headed towards Harriet East's Glencoe estate unannounced. After a frightening visit by the Loyola professor, the priest deserved some answers. Lydia Easterhouse had left her family an ancient scroll that caught the interest of the academic realm. After seeing the photograph Doctor Nrogbi showed him, Father Sardenelli had his own ideas about the scroll's importance. He needed Harriet to clarify some of her family secrets first. Although he was very much an insider of the Yelizi church, the Easterhouse family remained aloof to everyone except their own kind.

Dominick pulled onto Harriet's long driveway very late at night, after Dinda Nrogbi threatened him inside of his house. The gigantic house was dark and looked empty, but Dominick was determined to get some answers. He researched Harriet's lineage before coming to her home. Now armed with a theory, he could no longer wait. After tracing back the East/Easterhouse family tree, the priest feared her grandchildren were in imminent danger.

Dominick rang the doorbell and expected a servant to answer. He was surprised to see Harriet open the door. She wore a bathrobe, but she appeared to still be awake. "Father, what brings you here at this hour?"

"Yesterday I had a visitor. We need to talk. Your family might be in trouble."

"Come in and sit down. Now tell me about your visit," Harriet asked. "Can I get you anything to eat or drink?"

"A glass of wine would be great. Actually, change that to a bottle of wine and a glass," Father Sardenelli requested. His body shook from adrenalin despite his lack of sleep.

"One of those days, huh. I understand. What has gotten you so shaken up?" Harriet led the priest into the immense dining hall where he sat down at table long enough to seat twenty people. She took a bottle of white wine from the buffet, opened it, and poured them both a glass. "I've got something stronger if you need it. What on earth has you here so late at night, Dominick?"

"First off, thanks for the wine and thanks for letting me in at this hour." Dominick gulped down the glass and refilled it. "Harriet, you need to level with me. Your family tree is very cryptic. I want to know why your granddaughter would have a celestial scroll written by angels."

Harriet's interest turned into alarm. "Is this scroll made from vellum with a bluish seal on it?"

Father Sardenelli nodded.

"Before you came to our parish and before you were a glorified altar boy for the Baccianis, I gave birth to three very special children. I want you to know that I always loved them, in spite of everything. Even Lydia, who betrayed me and this family," Harriet explained.

"I know you love them. It seems like Lydia passed the scroll onto her children. Why would she have one of the oldest documents ever written?"

"All three of my children have a unique father. Before our church got so big, we as a parish would frequently try to conjure an angel up through ancient rituals. As you know, we still do this, but back then it was different. The rituals are still the same. You've conducted them yourself, but we had different intentions back then."

"Like breeding humans with angels?"

"Please, let me explain. All the young women dreamed of having a baby with an angel. It was considered to be an honor, a gift from Malak Tawas. The baby was considered an extension of him. We would fornicate with the angels who answered our calling. I was the only one who ever got pregnant. The first time was with Jonathan, and then I kept on going. Next there was Lydia, and then Terrence. I had a fourth child, but she died as a toddler. After that, I quit calling out to the angels. As the first human woman to ever successfully breed, I was also an object of worship, almost like an icon in some circles. Later on, it was discovered that I had the Adonite gene which was why I got pregnant. It's a recessive gene that very few people in the world have, and even fewer are aware that they have it. Genetically speaking, it's useless..."

"Except when you breed with angels?" Dominick interrupted.

"Yes, Father. If you're familiar with a Punnett square, you can figure out what happens. However, unlike other genes, this gene controls the DNA. To simply put it, offspring take on traits determined by the Adonite gene and not the parents' characteristics. Like my children and then their children.

"Lydia's children were born with six fingers. Some believe angels were created with extra digits on their hands and toes. Armaros only has five fingers on each hand, but he could have gotten the extra ones removed to blend more in with society. Those who share the gene can sometimes hear each other without speaking. I've often wondered if that was the reason Will killed himself. He went crazy," Harriet explained.

"Is Armaros the father of your children?" the priest asked.

"Yes. I know he's close to us, somewhere in Chicago area. I can feel him, even hear him at times," Harriet recollected.

Father Sardenelli thought back to when he first met the angel while he was a Catholic priest performing an exorcism. He remained silent, unsure if Harriet knew about their previous relationship.

"So Lydia's children are different than Terrence and Jonathan's children? Or do all of your grandchildren have the Adonite gene? Technically, your children are Nephilim," added Dominick.

"Father, you are correct. My boys married outside of our kind. Their kids might be carriers, but they have lost much of their race when crossed with their human wives," Harriet answered.

"But Lydia didn't breed outside of her race, did she?" asked the priest.

"Bravo, Father. You've figured it out," Harriet sadly praised.

"Who did she breed with? Your sons? You wanted to see if inbreeding could get you closer to producing an angel in the family, didn't you?" accused the priest.

Harriet cried. "Yes, I did. That's why she hated me. She told our entire parish that I made her have sexual intercourse at fourteen years old, and she wanted me in prison for child abuse. She made me look like a monster, or some kind of demented pimp. Some of my humiliation was spared. She failed to broadcast that her brothers fathered her first two children. We had both Jonathan and Lydia fornicate at a private ritual right here at my house. At first Lydia didn't get pregnant. We had to try several times and almost gave up. Almost a year later, she got pregnant with Julia. We repeated the process with Terrence, and then Lydia got pregnant with Will. They both were born with an extra finger. We knew right away they were nephilim," Harriet admitted.

"But not Eve. Why? What made her so special?" softly slurred Dominick. The wine was making him drunk and sleepy.

"I think you already know," Harriet sobbed. "I'm going to burn for this, aren't I?"

"We all are. Don't tell me Eve's father is Armaros. That would make him both her grandfather and her father," said the priest.

"Yes, he was Lydia's father, and then we bred them both together, getting Eve. Lydia didn't know he was her father. She was in love with him. They were inseparable for months. But then he left her before Eve was born. She was destroyed. Once he left her, she began to question our church. Years later, she found out Armaros was also her father. That's when she officially cut all ties with me," Harriet said.

"Do you blame her? You were the one summoning him to conceive an angel. You weren't happy with having nephilim children. You wanted something closer to the celestial gene pool. So, you used your own daughter like a dog breeder uses a bitch! Their consummation would make Eve three quarters angel, and one quarter human. Does she even know the kind of power she has? Malak Tawas doesn't create, he changes. By creating, you are trying to play God. Nephilim are by nature half-breeds, but you wanted a celestial being," the priest charged.

"Don't be so naive. We have been trying to breed our own angels for centuries. Eve is the first that I know of to ever live past adolescence. Most end up like Will, and he was only half celestial," spoke Harriet.

"What about Bell, Julia's daughter? How does she fit into all of this?" asked Dominick.

"I don't know. When she was born, Julia wouldn't allow me to visit. Her father is probably human. However, there is a chance that she's a nephilim. We saw her for the first time over a week ago. Fearless for six years old," Harriet said with a smile.

"Do you have any feelings for them at all? I came here to warn you that they may all be in danger. A demon, Doctor Dinda Nrogbi, paid me a visit. He was one of the Loyola professors Julia had shown the scroll to. He flashed me his beautiful pointy smile once I stated I didn't know anything. After that, my memory started working. I told him I thought the scroll was divine but was unsure of which side it was written by. He is going to try and steal it from Julia and Eve. Probably break into their house and even kill them for it. He thinks it can save him. Do you even care?" said the priest.

"Of course, I care. But somehow, I'm not afraid for any of them. I think they can easily take on an angelic-made demon. Their instincts will know what to do when faced with that kind of evil. I also need the scroll. It's not safe with Julia. We have got to get it back into the right hands," demanded Harriet.

I can't believe this woman. All she cares about is the scroll. Father Sardenelli nodded and left Harriet's estate.

Chapter Forty-Seven

Carmen Bacciani did not sleep the night before she was expected to give her statement to the Florentine police. Her grandfather, Franco Bacciani, and his attorney coached her for hours on what she was allowed to say. Part of her wanted to please him. When her father, Carlos Bacciani, left her, Franco had taken over the role. She was grateful to him for everything he had given her and her mother. However, the ritual he had made her participate in gave her nightmares. She was locked up in a room awaiting to be raped. Part of her wanted to tell the police about how deviant her grandfather and his church were.

Carmen grew up with private tutors, boarding schools, and controlled friendships. Her family sheltered her in every aspect of her life. Subconsciously, she knew their ways were immoral. She always hated her father for leaving her, but now she understood why. Now she hated him for not taking her with him. Together they might have been strong enough to break away from his family. Daydreams of killing herself filled every moment of her day.

Carmen remembered her fourteenth birthday with the same accuracy as a tortured POW who survives. The event would be tattooed to her memory bank forever. Her grandfather told her that because she was so extraordinary, angels desired to have a baby with her. She was also told that her child would change the world. Born with a genetic defect of an extra finger, Carmen certainly never felt normal. Her family elected not to have it removed. Her fourteenth birthday was built up to be the most significant experience of her life. Not only did it fall short of her expectations, but it amounted to the kind of anguish that made her question everything her family stood for.

Carmen's birthday began in the basement of her family's church. She was taken to an empty room with a toilet drilled into the corner. Heavily drugged, she passed out on the concrete floor for most of the day. By night fall, she was groggy, but able to stay awake. She vividly remembered her grandfather coming into the room. At first, she didn't recognize him. He wore a red robe and a mask, but he assured her with his voice.

"Tonight, is all about you, your right of passage into womanhood! I want you to have this. Please put it on for the ceremony. Armaros has come a long way. He is the one we put on the pedestal. He has picked you to have his baby. Don't be afraid. He is very powerful. Your first time might hurt. We will all be by your side watching. Oh, what a glorious day!" exclaimed her grandfather.

Carmen hurriedly put on the white silk dress and modeled it for her grandfather. It had an unstructured fit, like that of a toga. "You look beautiful, but you are forgetting the belt," he said as he handed her a long gold chain with angel script engraved into each link.

"Wow, Papa! This is beautiful. I have never seen anything like it," Carmen gratefully claimed. It was the last time she would ever feel loved as a person. Looking back at the evening, she now felt like a lab experiment.

"It's time, Carmen. We're going to make you beautiful for Armaros," said Carmen's mother. She and her grandmother whisked her backstage to paint her face and braid her long caramel hair. Once they finished, Carmen peeked out the stage's side and became both repulsed and confused. The smell of ashes and charred flesh fumigated the large assembly hall. A strange man levitated above the stage with the screeching birds among the chaos.

Is that Armaros? That's not an angel. And who is that naked old man? thought Carmen.

The old stranger waited for the dancer's performance to end. Carmen was carried onto the stage by four men in a gilded chariot. The dancer approached and slipped off Carmen's silk dress. The masked church members chanted his name, Armaros. As the birds violently flapped above them, he penetrated her on the immense pedestal on stage. She bit the sides of her mouth so hard, they bled. Tears streamed down her face, but no one made him stop. He took her face and cupped it in his hands. His eyes glowed different colors and his fangs glistened in the candlelight.

"Hey Umberto, you go. It's your turn," Armaros bullied.

Carmen saw his face as she laid there. After he was finished, he looked her in the eye and said, "Forgive me. God, I want to die."

Carmen whispered back, "Me too." She was envious when the angel and his congregation devoured the old man alive. Her own family took part in the feeding. *At least the old man was spared from any more of their torment,* she sympathetically thought.

Carmen later learned that the old man who raped her was Abe Silverman. He was not a member of their church, and he had the police and an American looking for him. Her grandfather spent a tremendous amount of money to have her coached on what to say during her official police statement. Carmen was expected to deny ever meeting him, along with the entire ritual.

As promised, Franco Bacciani, Carmen, and his lawyer arrived at the police station the next morning. Detective Magliano gave them lattes, and then had them wait inside the interrogation room.

***

"Sean, glad you're here. I want to show you this before we begin," Leonardo said, handing him one of the photos Abe had snapped from his phone camera. The detective had the yellowed one digitally sharpened. Two men were having sex on an altar. One was wearing a mask.

"Wow, I can't believe you cleaned this picture up so well. Is that sodomy? Part of their ritual?" Sean inquired.

"If so, it certainly is not mainstream knowledge. This man might be who they worship. Look at this picture. See how they all have masks. But the man in this picture doesn't. Here, we've blown up his face, but it's still hard to see. If you look hard enough, you can see some defining facial features," Leonardo said as he outlined the man's face with his finger.

Sean examined the close-up. "Something is off. Do you have a magnifying glass?"

Leo hurriedly fetched one from his desk and handed it to Sean.

"If this were a better photo, I could be more certain, but it looks like this man's teeth are extended past the outside of his lips, like fangs. He looks more like a monster," Sean replied.

"You're right," Leonardo agreed. "Wait, look again at Abe's pictures. The wine in the minifridge isn't wine, but blood. Why else would he take it? Sean, go sit in the viewing room and watch me question these sick fucks. This has got to stop."

Leonardo grilled the fourteen-year-old girl. She looked even younger than her age, and she was clearly frightened. He was sure that she was hiding something.

Leo tried his best to be passive and nonthreatening towards the child, but he was losing his patience. He could tell she was holding back. Franco's legal coaching was paying off.

Finally, Leo raised his voice. "Carmen, quit playing games with me. You are in a police station right now. A man is missing, probably dead. If you know something, you've got to speak up. It's the right thing to do. He's got a family and friends who love him. You know much more than you're saying. Let's try this again. What was Abe doing when you saw him at the ceremony?"

"I told you; I never saw him!" Carmen cried. She stated that the church service was devoted to her and others reaching their confirmation. She repeated several more times that she never saw Abe, nor heard of him.

Leonardo slammed the pictures onto the table. "He was there! These are the pictures he took at your confirmation! Look at this one! It was taken from the storage room off the side of the stage. Do you know this man?" Carmen shook her head. "Is this how all the confirmations start off? A man sodomizes a boy on the church's pedestal? Was it the boy's confirmation too?"

Carmen was uncontrollably crying. Her lawyer interjected on her behalf. "She was backstage getting ready. She has no knowledge of this. And that is not a boy, but a grown man. They must have been fooling around before the service. I know it's disgusting, but gays have no respect for the sanctity of church in any denomination."

"Sanctity of this church?" laughed Leonardo. "Please Carmen, who is he? Is he one of the angels you all worship?" he screamed. Her resolve was beginning to break.

"She's fourteen! Is it necessary to yell? She told you everything she knows," barked the family lawyer.

"Carmen, what they are making you do is a sin! It's wrong to lie! You are in the company of some very sick people! I can help you if you just tell me what happened that night."

Carmen stopped crying. Her baby face was filled with oppression. As her eyes nervously shifted, Leonardo could feel her cracking. *Five more minutes ought to do.*

A knock was heard at the door. Leonardo's police chief interrupted. "Leo, I need to talk to you for a second."

"Can't it wait? I'm in the middle of an interrogation..."

"I know! One second," the chief commanded.

Leonardo stepped outside the room. Once they had some privacy, Leonardo was told to drop the case before they sued for harassment.

"Are you fucking with me? That pervert in there is abusing children! And we're supposed to let him go? I know he is involved with Abe Silverman. And who knows what he did to his granddaughter. How can you sleep at night?" Leo screeched.

"I'm not asking you but telling you to let the family go. One more word, and I'll suspend you without pay," the chief dictated.

Leo punched the wall and almost busted his hand. "Fine, you win. This isn't worth losing my pension over, and who knows what else, but you tell them. Tell them 'happy fucking birthday! Hope everyone's birthday was as fun as hers! Once again, the great Baccianis are immune to arrest," Leo ranted, as he stomped off in a huff.

Without hearing their conversation, Sean knew what had happened. He saw the chief let the Baccianis go. He rushed out of the viewing room and tried to catch up to Leonardo.

"Hey, I'm sorry," Sean said, as he jogged to keep up.

"Nothing you can do. This is what happened to Dino and me last time. Oh God, poor Dino! His death is for nothing! I'm sorry. We almost had the girl. Something sinister is going on, and we're helpless in stopping it."

"Meet me tonight for drinks. I'm going to the American Embassy for some answers," Sean said.

Sean drove by the Il Duomo Cathedral and admired its beauty. He wished he were in this romantic city under different circumstances. He envisioned himself taking Julia around Tuscany to enjoy the famous vineyards. Almost passing up the Consulate General of the United States, he had to quickly snap out of his fantasy. He handed the security his passport then parallel parked down the block.

The old, stately building sat on a riverbank. Sean climbed up the stairs and admired the creamy brick, red tiled roof, and American flag. He was confronted with security upon entry. "Hello, my name is Sean Slattery. I'm an American citizen and lawyer. I need to talk to someone right away. An American is missing. I'm here as a representative of the family."

The guard nodded and motioned him through a metal detector and conveyor belt. After he passed through clearance, Sean was escorted into a director's office waiting room and told to fill out some paperwork. *Busywork,* he thought. *They need time to figure out who I am and why I'm here.*

An hour later, Sean was allowed into the office. He sat down in front of Tim Bollier, Director of American Diplomacy. He was a short, young man with a receding hairline. Extending his hand, he said, "Thank you for seeing me without an appointment."

"Says here that you are representing the Silverman family. Abraham Silverman has disappeared, and he was last seen right here in Florence. Looks like the Florentine police are already involved and working on the case," Tim recapped as he referred to Sean's form that he just filled out.

"Who is reassigned to Abe's case?" Sean asked.

"Excuse me?" asked the diplomat.

"I understand the ambassador who was originally assigned to the case recently jumped out of a window and killed himself just days ago," Sean said, staring the man right in his tired, blue eyes.

"Well, how did you know? That's not public information. We're in the process of...."

"Let's cut through all the tape, shall we. I've been here for a couple of days. I was invited to tag along with the Florentine police. Detective Dino Barone was attacked and killed by a flock of birds in the parking lot of the Yelizi church. At the same time, your guy decides to end it all while the police are expecting him to join them for a warranted search. Today, Carmen Bacciani, Franco's granddaughter, was questioned. She clearly knew something, but the chief of the Florentine police let the family go home. As an American citizen I have the right to know why this family is above the law. All evidence reeks of their scent, yet it all gets swept under the rug. I thought politics were not part of your diplomacy when it came to getting our citizens out of trouble. I need an explanation as to what the holdup is."

"Mr. Slattery, you're understandably angry. We're doing all we can right now while this case is being reassigned. I guarantee you it is of imminent importance," said Tim with authority. While the diplomat lectured, he passed Sean a note he had just written on a piece of computer paper. *Meet me at the Mercato Centrale in an hour.*

Sean read the piece of paper as Tim continued to lecture. He nodded and played along. "If you're handling everything, I will get out of your way. Please call me when you have more information."

Sean headed straight to the market and leisurely strolled around. It was filled with all kinds of food stands, cooking shops, and cafes. The tourist trap was a very large strip that was overcrowded. He could not fathom how the ambassador would find him. Exactly an hour later, he got tapped on the back of the shoulder.

"Mr. Slattery, thank you for meeting me outside of the embassy. Sometimes the walls have ears, if you know what I mean. I came here to warn you. The Baccianis are an old and influential Florentine family who have made themselves an important ally to the United States several decades ago, beginning in World War II. They have offered their ships, planes, and homes during war time, and they even exchanged messages between the U.S. and Italy. They are the unofficial royals of Tuscany. They have been getting away with horrific crimes for centuries. We've got a file on them as thick as the dictionary. We all joke how they are like the supernatural Mafia.

"Hal Kaufmann was his name. Oh, God. He was a good man with a great family." The American diplomat wiped away a stray tear that had fallen down his cheek. "He was the diplomat who was supposed to meet with you and the police the other day. He read their file and was enthusiastic in getting the opportunity of nailing them. We, and many of their victims, have wanted to stop them for years. Their cult has brought strange accidents to all who seem to get in their way. At the last minute, something happened to Hal, something I can't explain. His secretary was taking notes for him. He just looked at her, or as she says, he looked through her. She thought he was about to have a stroke. In less than a minute, he got up from his chair, and without warning, opened his window from the top floor and jumped. The secretary described his demeanor as a type of demonic possession. Most dismissed her account, but those of us who have been around for a few decades knew she was telling the truth. Mr. Slattery, we are diplomats, not the Green Beret. No one wants to get involved."

"What? These people are sociopaths! Pure, unadulterated evil! Their mascot, the peacock, represents Satan! Somebody has got to stop them. You didn't see Detective Barone get his eyes plucked out of his head in their church parking lot. I did. He was the one who found Abe's phone, the only piece of hard evidence the cops had that proved Abe was there!" Sean exclaimed.

"On the record, we're working night and day to try and find Abe. Off the record, get yourself a priest and find out what you're dealing with. A man of faith is your only hope." The U.S. ambassador walked away as silently as he came.

Later in the evening, Sean met Detective Magliano at Santino II, a trendy bar located in the heart of Florence. Both men took a seat in the back of the lounge and ordered a couple of martinis. After catching up with each other's the dead-end stories of the day, they began to postulate their next move, both determined to bring down the Bacciani family. "Your own government told you to get a priest? Fuck America! All of your country's manpower and technology cannot bring these assholes down, huh? Very ironic. Rome is so close, and priests are plentiful. Does this priest have to believe in God?" asked Leonardo, in awe of the suggestion. As an atheist, he always felt that Christians, particularly Catholics, were the most hypocritical people on earth.

"He didn't say, but I kind of figured God would somehow play a role in all of this. I actually know of a priest back in Chicago. He's from here, Tuscany. He switched sides on the Holy See, and now preaches for the Yelizis. That's where Lydia's family attends church," Sean shared. "I obviously couldn't trust him."

"But if you could, he'd be the one," Leonardo stated. The two men said their goodbyes and promised to keep in touch while the detective drove Sean to the airport. While waiting for his plane, Sean kept rewinding his thoughts back to the last thing Leo had said to him, *he'd be the one.* Father Sardenelli just might be the key to the Yelizi downfall.

Chapter Forty-Eight

Eve stood in front of the freezer within the sub-basement of the *Evil Empire* and screamed. The only other soul that could hear her was Claire Jacobsen. Both were too isolated from being detected. Claire understood. Catalina Rojas' head was lain on its side in the otherwise empty ice box.

Claire had found the secretive room below the basement while they were storing RE products. Unlike Eve, she didn't scream. She had suspected that Andel was behind Catalina's disappearance from the beginning.

"I knew it. Eve, meet Catalina Rojas, my old partner." Looking at the frozen head, Claire directly said, "Cat, don't know what you did, but you certainly did not deserve this."

"Andel did this? I don't understand. Why would he kill her and then risk saving her head? Is this a souvenir for him?" Eve asked after getting over her initial shock. She began searching the rest of the sub-basement, wondering what other body parts might turn up. She saw carafes inside of the refrigerator. "He's got a frozen head, sodas, snacks, and now wine in his panic room? This is more like some kind of horror hideout. Claire, you need to come clean with me before I go to the police."

"Wait, I'll go with you. Andel needs to pay for this. We can go together, but first hear me out. No one knows we've found this room, so we got time. Please, let's wait until the end of the week. If RE signs with us, we both will get over a million dollars in commissions. And that's just the beginning. I've seen your house. I know you've inherited some money from your mother, but I'm in financial ruin. When I was using, I spent every dime and tens of thousands more, all on credit. This deal can put me out of debt. I can start over. This is our chance. Eve, I beg you, I really need this. Just a few more days. She's not going to be deader than she is right now. Then I'll promise to go to the police."

"Why would he do this?" Eve asked.

"I don't know. Some rumors circulated that they were having an affair, but I never caught that vibe. I know she went behind my back, and she was developing some kind of computerized tachistoscope. It had faster flashing images with more persuading messaging, but I couldn't tell you the details. Andel had me track all her communications, you know, like undercover, the week before she died. I don't know if you remember, but her mother came in here shortly after you were hired, completely hysterical. But he magically calmed her down."

While Claire rambled, Eve stared at Catalina's frozen head inside of the freezer, oddly feeling a strange impulse to touch it. She reached out and grasped her frozen jawbone. An electric shock jolted throughout her body. Her arm was used like an access cable into Catalina's memories. Bombarded with visual stimuli, Catalina's life flashed before Eve's eyes. Terrified, Eve was still compelled to grasp her frozen face. The flashes gave her a sense of Catalina while she was growing up. Catalina seemed like a content child. Then the visual flashes decelerated, making it much easier for Eve to perceive. She felt Catalina splintering off into an alternative persona, coinciding with the same time she moved and began working for Andel.

As the stimuli slowed down to the speed of a video, Eve had the ability to see through Catalina's eyes and get her perspective as she began a transformation. With each step, Eve could feel Catalina running down a gravelly path with the speed of a jaguar during the middle of the night. A man attacked her, but Catalina bit him, and then exhausted him of all his blood. More victims and more blood were shown. The catastrophic visions were much more graphic than the goriest horror movie. *Catalina was a vampire*, Eve concluded.

The next series of clips that reverberated through Eve's mind were unsuccessful suicide attempts; carbon monoxide inside of a garage, slashed wrist, and overdoses of narcotics were not potent enough to kill her. Once Catalina gave up on killing herself, she turned her violent tendencies towards Andel. For some reason, she blamed him for her compunctions. She stormed into his office with a gun and tried to shoot him. Eve watched the scene with terror. He revealed his fangs to Catalina, and then knocked the gun out of her hand. With inhuman speed and agility, he had effortlessly latched onto her neck. Eve then heard the last words Catalina ever said, "Father, I will see you in Hell." The screen inside of Eve's mind went blank.

While Eve was in a deep hypnotic state, Claire tried to shake her. She was deterred by an electric shock that emitted off Eve's body. In repugnance, she watched Eve blankly stare at the frozen head while touching it. Finally, Eve released her grasp and awoke from her spell. She was so dizzy that she needed to hug the wall to keep from collapsing.

"What the hell just happened to you? I got shocked trying to shake you out of your trance. Are you alright?" Claire asked.

"I think I know what happened. Catalina was Andel's daughter," Eve dreamily said.

"Impossible! He's our age. She was in her mid-twenties," Claire replied, very confused.

"I need a drink," Eve said, shaking like a leaf. She reached into the refrigerator and grabbed a carafe, then took a big gulp, and swallowed. Coughing, her face soured. "What the f...."

"It's not wine, is it? I suspected as much. I should have warned you," Claire apologized.

Eve opened several cans of Diet Coke and stood over the sink, swishing the pop inside of her mouth, and then spitting it out. The taste of blood made her want to vomit. "What kind of animal, no, that's too good of a word, what kind of devil is he? I don't feel so good. I've got to go home," Eve cried.

"Promise to hold off on the police for a few days? Please, I'm begging you."

"Promise, but my silence is only temporary," cautioned Eve.

"You should go home. You look pale green. I'll clean-up and lock up, now go. Don't let anyone see you. You look as if you just saw a ghost."

I just did, Catalina Rojas, thought Eve.

"Be here Thursday and Friday for our presentation? I need you; you're my wing-man."

"I'll be here. Once we sign for bonuses, I'm going straight to the police. We've got to find ourselves new jobs."

Eve ducked out of the agency in the afternoon without anyone noticing. *I'm working for a vampire,* she distressed. On the way home, she made a quick stop at the liquor store, and picked up a fifth of bourbon. She needed something to steady her nerves. Unsure of her next move, she hoped Julia would be home for some advice. To her disappointment, her sister was out. She assumed Julia was probably at physical therapy, yet she failed to check her cell phone or notice the note left on the kitchen island.

Eve wasted no time in pouring herself some bourbon into a large coffee mug. *Better than drinking it straight from the bottle from a paper bag.* As she quickly depleted her first drink, she got on her laptop and began Googling "Catalina Rojas." While she kept eliminating others with the same name, Eve finally found her Wheaton address, both parents' separate addresses, and other bits and pieces. There were no records of Catalina reported missing, let alone dead. Eve began to wind down from all the stress. She clicked on "Lourdes Rojas", remembering the hysterical woman making a scene in the office shortly after she was hired. Her Atlanta address and phone number popped right up.

Eve poured herself more bourbon and contemplated whether to call Catalina's mother. She noticed half of the bottle was gone. *This puts a whole new twist onto drunk dialing. Fuck it. I didn't promise Claire not to call Catalina's mother.* She fished her cell phone out of her purse and dialed.

"Hello, Mrs. Rojas?"

After giving Lourdes a brief biography on who she was, Eve bluntly asked if she had recently spoken with her daughter.

"No, but Andel told me she was hired on as a consultant for one of the companies that you ad execs do business with. I believe the name is Neconyl."

"Did you ever call them and confirm what he told you?" Eve pressed.

Lourdes seemed confused, as if she were in some kind of haze. Her lack of worry alarmed Eve. She couldn't understand how the once distraught mother now seemed so indifferent.

"May I call you Lourdes? Was Catalina related to Andel Talistokov? Like father-daughter related?" Eve tactlessly asked.

"Who are you? Who told you this?" Lourdes cried. The mere question seemed to snap her out of her complacency.

"Catalina told me this, and she's dead," Eve slurred, very drunk from the bourbon.

Lourdes began to uncontrollably sob. "Yes, Andel is her father," she divulged, and then hung up the phone.

Chapter Forty-Nine

"You think Grandma has another piece to this halo?" Julia asked Bell, after killing Doctor Nrogbi in her master bedroom. "Do you think it's at Grandma's lake-house? Maybe even here?"

"It's somewhere at Grandma's other house. Lonnie told me Grandma hid each piece in a different spot. This broken piece is not going to work against an angel. It just works for the devils they create," Bell said.

"How did you know how to defend us against Doctor Nrogbi?" Julia questioned.

"The professor knew how important the scroll is and wanted it. Grandma knew too. That's why she hid it. She used to tell me stories all the time, and one story was about a little girl who used an angel's halo to slay the dragon. The story ended with the girl lighting the dragon on fire. That's how I knew," Bell explained.

"Should we break the seal and read it?" Julia asked.

"No, Mommy. Not yet. You won't understand it anyway. It's not like it was written in English," Bell replied.

"If not now, then when?"

"I don't know. Grandma only taught me so much. But in one of her stories, she told me about a scroll that Lucifer needed. It was kind of like his rules for his angels. Lonnie says he wants to fight God, and thinks the more souls he steals, the better his chances of winning," Bell answered.

Could Lonnie be real? Should I be taking Bell seriously? Julia wondered.

"Bell, pack up some sodas for the trip. I'm calling Auntie Eve." *Dammit, she's not picking up her phone. She better check her voicemails.* "Eve, going up to mom's other house. Haven't talked to you lately. Very important. Call me ASAP."

Once Julia reached Lake Geneva, Bell made her stop and buy some more candles, Bibles, and crosses. "I know Grandma has a lot of these, but I feel safer with my own."

They hauled their bags of mementos into the house. Bell set Lonnie down in a rocking chair and propped a crucifix onto his torso which made Julia feel uneasy. She decided not to say anything.

Julia grabbed all the Bible passages her mother had framed throughout the house and read parts of them to Bell.

"Okay, Bell. Let's start with this one. It looks so old. This is from Jubilees 5, and it's about the angels who lived on the earth.

.....*and they took themselves wives of all whom they chose, and they bare unto them sons and they were giants. And lawlessness increased on the earth and all flesh corrupted its way, alike men and cattle and beasts and birds and everything that walks on the earth -all of them corrupted their ways and their orders, and they began to devour each other, and lawlessness increased on the earth and every imagination of the thoughts of all men (was) thus evil continually.*

The verse continues about how upset God was, and, with exception to Noah and his family, obliterated the earth.

And against the angels whom He had sent upon the earth, He was exceedingly wroth, and He gave commandment to root them out of all their dominion, and He bade us to bind them in the depths of the earth, and behold they are bound in the midst of them, and are (kept) separate. And against their sons went forth a command

*from before His face that they should be smitten with the
sword, and be removed from under heaven.*

Bell, I searched Jubilees and it states that the book
is part of Jewish sacred writings considered to be the 'little
Genesis."

"Mommy, what does smitten by a sword mean?"
Bell asked, trying hard to understand the cryptic passages.

"It means to be struck down with divine power,
kind of like Doctor Nrogbi was smitten by Grandma's
halo," Julia explained. She continued to read passages from
Isaiah, Enoch, Revelation, and Corinthians. Each passage
had something to do with Satan's fall and/or the angels that
he brought with him.

"Mommy, what's this?" Bell asked, pointing to the
swirly design on the picture frame mat that held the page of
scripture.

"It's just a design," Julia replied.

"No, Mommy. Look!" Bell demanded as she traced
the cursive letters 'b, o, a, t.' "Boat. Do you see it?"

"Yes, but....."

"It's like the toy catalogs at Auntie Eve's work.
Submoninal?"

"Do you mean subliminal?" Julia corrected.

"Yes, that's it!" Bell exclaimed.

"Honey, that's used in advertising, not Grandma's
picture frames. I bet you can spell out a lot of words with
all of the curly designs."

"Okay, where?" Bell challenged.

Julia looked long and hard then finally conceded.
"Okay, I can't find any. You win. Let's go check out the
boat."

It was the middle of March, but the weather
remained cold. Both Julia and Bell rushed outside without
dressing properly for the almost freezing temperature.

Despite their shivers, both were determined to look more closely at Lydia's boat.

"I don't know, honey. Maybe 'boat' was just a coincidence. It's almost dark out," Julia said as she climbed into the suspended boat inside of the boathouse. She continued checking the boat's dashboard, seat cushions, and other storage spaces of the small speed boat. She then hopped into the fishing row boat with her good arm.

"Mommy, I know Grandma put it here. She's hiding it so no one else can find it but us. What are these ropes for?"

"They are used for the boats so that they don't float away," Julia explained.

"But those ropes around the post aren't holding anything, they are just wrapped around it, hanging down in the water," Bell argued.

"Let me prove to you the rope is nothing but an extra tether," Julia said. "Help me pull this up. I've only got one good arm, okay?" Bell nodded and they both yanked the rope up from the water. "What in the world...." A big metal box emerged. "Once again, you are right! Help me carry this inside."

***

After Lourdes Rojas hung up, Eve noticed a few messages on her phone screen. She checked her voicemail and listened. Julia kept leaving messages and sounded worried. Her last one sounded desperate: *'Where are you? I left a note on the counter. You're not picking up your work-line, your cell. I'm worried. We've got a lot to talk about. Call in sick and come up to Mom's lake-house. Call me when you get this.'*

Eve found the note in the kitchen, unsure of how she could have missed it before. It was the only thing on the kitchen island.

Oh shit! I'm way too drunk to drive up to Lake Geneva right now. Coffee! I've got to call Julia back. What's that, the doorbell? What the hell is Tony doing here?

"Hi, Tony. Come in," Eve said.

"Claire said you were sick. I stopped at Costco and got you some of their gourmet chicken noodle soup," Tony offered, as he set it down on the dining room table. He eyed her laptop and half empty bottle of Jack Daniels.

"You're having a mental health day? Sorry, I was told you left early with the flu," he said. "You mind? I'd love a drink."

"No, not at all. I was just making some coffee. I had a really stressful day and got carried away with taking the edge off," Eve defended herself as she handed Tony another coffee mug.

"Before you sober up, have a drink with me and tell me what set you off." Tony couldn't help but notice the web page of the computer screen that displayed Lourdes Rojas' personal information.

Oh, what the hell, I might as well unload. He also works there and is kind of my boyfriend. "Okay, you pour. As you can see, I looked up Catalina's mother online."

"Why? Did Catalina call you?"

"Catalina's dead. I found her head in the basement. Andel had it stuffed in a freezer."

"What? I thought she went to work for one of our clients. That's crazy! Want me to take you to the police?" Tony offered, feigning surprise.

"Claire wants me to wait. She wants to land the RE account first. The commission is too big to pass up."

"What are you going to do? I kind of can't blame Claire."

Eve explained her discovery, leaving out all the mystical details. She then confessed to calling Lourdes Rojas and confirming Catalina was Andel's daughter. Tony listened with the kind of concern and interest she wasn't used to. Their conversation led to other work-related matters and then Tony flashed his gorgeous smile.

"You know, I can't stop thinking about you. Whatever you want to do about Catalina, I'll support you. I just don't want you to shut me out."

"You are very sweet," Eve replied.

"I had such a great time with you last weekend. I'm glad you're not really sick. Just relax. Let me help you forget about your problems for a while," Tony offered, as he slid his hand up her leg.

Eve's loins moistened. Tony's touch was exhilarating. She touched him back, pleased to find him already engorged. She was enjoying the intimacy and then began to escape. Their petting turned into full-blown passion. As Tony kissed her neck, he carried her upstairs to her bedroom. Both were naked before they got through the door. Almost two hours went by while they explored every nook of each other's bodies, giving each other the kind of visceral pleasure that draws the mind blank.

Ring, ring, ring, ring, ring. 'You have reached Eve Easterhouse. Leave a message.'

"Hi, Eve. Where the hell are you? I'm worried to death. If you don't call me very soon, I'm going to start calling hospitals. We are knee deep in trouble. Bell and I found another part of our inheritance at the lake-house. Call me! And get up here as soon as you can!" Julia exclaimed.

Chapter Fifty

"Hi, Julia. It's so good to hear your voice. My flight just landed, and I'm back in Chicago. What? Attacked? Are you alright? Bell? Eve? She was at work... A professor from Loyola, Doctor Nrogbi....the one you saw before your accident? It will be late, but I'll meet you as soon as I can. I might be bringing a visitor," Sean said to Julia as he snapped his cell phone shut. He was bubbling with rage.

That Yelizi priest is going to help one way or another, he vowed.

Determined to track down Father Sardenelli, Sean called Abe's secretary who found his unlisted Chicago address in less than a minute. He hoped the priest would be swayed into sharing some religious secrets. Unlike most of the angel worshipers, Dominick Sardenelli was not born into the faith, but opted to join. As a former Catholic priest, he might be struggling with the guilt affiliated with massive evil. Sean drove straight from the airport to the priest's old brick home on the city's northside.

Knock, knock, knock, Sean pounded. He could see the priest cower through the sidelights. "Sean Slattery. Remember me? I crashed your Friday morning service a few weeks ago. I was a close friend of Lydia Easterhouse. I need to speak with you now."

"Mr. Slattery, I can't help you," yelled the priest through the glass.

"I'm not leaving until I get some answers from you," screamed Sean. He took his coat off and spread it on the front stoop, then sat down and waited. The houses were inches apart. Sean was on the verge of making a scene in front of Dominick's neighbors if Dominick didn't let him inside.

Five minutes dragged on like five hours. The temperature dipped to freezing level in the early spring evening. Sean was freezing and exhausted from the trip, yet he was prepared to stake out the priest's house for as long as it took. He needed some answers.

"Alright, Mr. Slattery, you win. But not here. I'll talk with you somewhere in public. There's a diner a block north of here, on the corner of Pulaski. I'll meet you there. You start walking, and I'll follow. To be blunt, I don't trust you."

Sean could see the fear in the priest's deep brown eyes. Maybe he, too, was under attack. His paranoia made Sean believe he was not the man's first unexpected visitor. Sean looked over his shoulder while he walked to the diner. The priest was shadowing him thirty yards back. Sean noticed the way he kept his hands inside of his overcoat, as though he was carrying a gun. The priest was clearly spooked. Sean calmed himself down, and switched gears. There was a slim chance of Father Sardenelli coming clean as long as he treaded lightly, without scaring him off.

Sean found the only diner on the intersection and walked in. It was a dump. The leather seats in the booths were split and held together by duct tape and the paint was pealing. Despite its run-down appearance, the place contained a considerable amount of customers eating past the dinner hour. Sean picked a quiet booth in the corner. Father Sardenelli joined him minutes later. Both men were immediately hit up by the waitress. Without looking at the menu, they both ordered coffee and cheeseburgers. Neither of them was hungry, but they wanted the appearance of two ordinary men eating dinner.

Without the pleasantries or formalities of idle conversation, Dominick immediately asked after the waitress walked away, "What's so important that compelled you to track me down?"

"Father, I...."

"Please, call me Dominick. I'm not feeling very priestly."

"Okay, Dominick. You look scared, and you should be. I am, too. I'm also angry, just not sure of who to be angry at. An hour ago, I got back from Florence, Italy. Wish I was there under pleasant circumstances. Beautiful city. Your hometown, right?" Sean began.

"Yes. And if you know that, then you probably know I was trained there as a Yelizi priest by the Bacciani family," Dominick admitted.

"That information was in a file that I paid a great deal of money for. You see, I hired a private investigator, Abe Silverman, to travel to Florence and gather information about Carlos Bacciani. I just couldn't understand why he would go stark raving mad and impale himself. He had everything: talent, money, fame, and Lydia. But he wasn't mad, was he?"

"Mr. Slattery, Sean, you are playing with fire. Just walk away," the priest warned.

"I can't. I won't. Too many dead bodies. I'm too involved," Sean declared.

"The Baccianis make the Easterhouse family look like marshmallows. They are the most fascinating people I ever met, but..."

"Is evil the word you are looking for? Seen plenty of that in my short trip to Florence. But back to Abe. To summarize his assignment, he told both the Florentine detective and his secretary that he was going to snoop around the Yelizi church. That's the last time any of us ever heard from him. We have proof he was there. One of the detectives found his cell phone in a storage closet. Know what happened to him?"

"Let me guess. He's dead and Franco Bacciani got the police to drop case," said Dominick without eye contact.

"Perfect guess. As if you were there and saw the whole thing go down. Do you know what happened to the detective who found his phone in the church?" Sean continued.

"No, but please tell me," said the priest, looking shamefully at the floor.

"He was attacked by a flock of birds right there in the parking lot and died in front of my face. An American ambassador was supposed to join us while we searched the church," Sean said with anger.

"He didn't make it either, did he?"

"Father, you are one smart fellow. He decided he'd rather jump out the window of the American Embassy than keep his appointment with the Florentine police and me. Let me do some math. We've got Will Easterhouse, who hung himself at sixteen years old, then Carlos Bacciani who impaled himself, Lydia Easterhouse who mysteriously died in an auto accident, my friend and private detective, Abe Silverman, body not found, but dead, Detective Barone who was pecked to death, and an American ambassador. That's a total of six people that I know of. What are the odds that six people who were involved with the Yelizi religion would either commit suicide or die in a freak accident? Julia Easterhouse could have been number seven. She was recently in a car accident too. She lost control of the car once several birds began to peck at her windshield. She got lucky, almost like a guardian angel was helping her. These angels are real, aren't they? But they aren't all good. Plenty of bad ones. More people are going to die if we don't stop them. Father, you were once a man of God. C'mon, talk to me," Sean demanded.

"The birds always fascinated me. The angels and those they change can control them. I can't. I'm just a mere human."

"What do you mean 'those they change?' Angels can change people? Into what?" Sean asked, desperate for answers.

"When Satan was cast down from heaven, he took plenty of angels with him, otherwise known as Caligastia's One Hundred. Now Caligastia is another name for devil or Satan or Lucifer. This legion was banned from Heaven by God, but not banned from earth, and of course Hell, their own kingdom. Although most people consider them to be demons, they were originally created as celestial beings. Whatever you want to call them, they have certain powers. They can't create with their own kind; all of them are male. But they can mutate someone into a much less powerful version of themselves. When they change a human, they change him or her into a monster, almost like a vampire. They are embodiments of evil. Because of their fall, distinct differences were created to separate them from their seraphim brethren. They've turned to humans to ensure their existence," explained the priest.

"Dominick, did you know all of this when you renounced God?"

"I never renounced Him. But I knew about the change, and I have been offered a transformation on more than one occasion. Everlasting life is the benefit of it all. My Yelizi congregation questions my choices, but I prefer my human status. As for Yelizism, I wanted to be part of a it, a witness to it, and even make decisions in it. God just waits and watches, whereas Malak Tawas acts and we act with him," defended Dominick.

"So that's why you quit the Catholic church? You wanted to see your faith in the flesh, even dictate its policy? Pride is why you converted?"

"Pride? Pride has nothing to do with it. Sean, don't think you know me, because you don't. I believed in God with all my heart, but He never believed in me. I was raped as a teenage boy by my own priest in God's house. Where was He then? While I was in the seminary, I saw men sneak off with each other after taking vows of celibacy, not very Godly. When I held my first post, outside of Florence, I witnessed the senior priest molest a boy. I reported the incident. Do you know what happened to that priest? He's now a cardinal. Pride is not the reason why I chose Yelizism."

"Dominick, I apologize. I, too, was raised Catholic. I'm an Irish boy from the Chicago suburbs. But I had a very different experience. I never had to endure the kind of twisted bullshit that you have," Sean sympathized, partly understanding the choices Dominick had to make.

"It happened long ago. One thing I had going for me was the ability to communicate with the spirit world. I've always been sensitive, and my talents were noticed. I was trained to perform exorcisms, and I was rather good at it. After banishing half a dozen spirits from their human hosts, I found one that I couldn't resist. It wasn't an exorcism like the others, but rather an exorcism of the household. A little girl around five years old prayed to angels every night. Finally, one came to visit her. His name is Armaros, and he's still around. Loves it when people pray. One of the few of Satan's legion who lives here on earth and desires attention. Anyway, I got him out of the little girl's house, but he led me to the Yelizi church. They welcomed me with open arms for knowing the great Armaros. That's how it all started. On the Catholic side of things, I got reprimanded for not destroying the angel while I had the chance," Dominick confessed.

"Do you ever think of going back? I mean back to God, not the Catholic church?"

"Well, I certainly don't agree with all the things they do, but I'm already damned, so what's the use," answered Dominick.

"They don't own your soul. Maybe that's the real reason you refused to be changed. Listen, you have a chance to redeem yourself. Hear me out. See this girl? That's Carmen Bacciani, Carlos' daughter. She's fourteen years old now. I printed this off the Internet. It's her with her grandfather, Franco," Sean said, then put the photograph Abe snapped from his cell phone next to the priest. "Here's the same girl on her birthday."

"She looks like she's sleeping on the floor."

"You don't recognize the room? It's in the basement of the Florentine church."

The waitress plopped down two cups of coffee and a bunch of creamers. Sean quickly took the photos off the table, paranoid that she might have seen something.

"It's okay. I come here often and she's not a snoop, just doing her job. As for the Florentine church, it's been almost twenty years. The basement was an enormous unfinished space." Dominick filled his coffee with cream and drained half of the cup. "I should have suggested a bar. This coffee isn't cutting it."

Sean also guzzled down his cup. "I'd rather have all of my wits about me for now. The coffee is just what I need. Look." Sean handed the priest the photos again. "The church is finished now, complete with this prison cell, a reception room, and another worshiping area. Is it common for adolescents to celebrate their birthdays in your church?"

"Yes. Fourteen is considered the passage into adulthood. The boy or girl usually dresses in white, gets a golden chain belt with angelic script, and recites passages from certain scripture. It's kind of like a confirmation. The family then decides if they want their child to learn the language, sigils, and writings of Enochian keys."

"Does the ritual include an angel trying to impregnate the girl?"

"Never. We have had angels come and visit, but it is against nature's laws to try to breed them to anyone, let alone teenagers. You are talking about rape," denied Dominick. Sean knew he was lying.

"Let me rephrase. Dominick, maybe you don't hold rituals like that, and maybe they are not formally condoned within your church, but are they known to happen?" Sean asked again.

Sean got the answer he was looking for just by observing the stunned look on Dominick's face. He wasn't sure how much the priest knew, but from experience, could tell he had hit a nerve.

The waitress came back with two platters of cheeseburgers and fries and then laid the check on the table. Both men didn't even look at their food and stared at each other. Sean took out his wallet and put a couple of twenty-dollar bills on the table.

Sean was the first to break the silence. "Dominick, here's another picture Abe took. He hid in a storage closet for this shot. It's a man sodomizing another man, possibly a boy. Can't tell because he is wearing a mask."

Sean saw the recognition in Dominick's eyes. "Is that Armaros?" He listened intently as Dominick explained how masks were worn during fertility rituals. He accentuated how children were not supposed to attend.

"Fertility for whom? Armaros? Look at Carmen's hands. She has six fingers on each of them. That's some kind of proof of celestial descent. Eve, Julia and Will Easterhouse had theirs removed when they were babies. Talk to me. One of these angels or changed humans, not sure which, just tried to kill Julia and Bell Easterhouse over a scroll Lydia left them. God was important to you once before. Please, I'm begging you to come with me. You can translate it, help combat these demons, even perform an exorcism if need be."

"Was it Doctor Nrogbi?" asked the priest.

"Yes. How did you know the name?" Sean asked.

"He came to see me about the scroll, and he told me Julia was at his university inquiring about it. I'm so sorry. I'm partly responsible for their attack. When he came to my house, I was scared. He threatened me by showing me his fangs. He wants the scroll because it's celestial. It could be some kind of manifesto, or even a treaty. Maybe it's an outline of the territory Satan has permission to enter after he lost the war in Heaven. The document could even provide the bylaws of Hell. I have lots of theories but can't tell you until it's opened."

"They also have a piece of metal which is believed to be part of a halo. You told me you wanted to take part in your faith, to witness it, to make decisions in it. Now's your chance. Come with me and help us."

"But Sean, He's never going to forgive me. How can you even trust me? I've spent over twenty years worshiping Satan."

"Father, and I am going to call you Father from now on, I don't have a choice. You are all I got."

Sean watched Dominick cry. He appeared to be praying. Sean needed to say a prayer as well. *Oh God, please make sure I picked the right guy to help us.*

"Alright, I'll go with you. But first, I need to pack up some of my things," Dominick said.

Chapter Fifty-One

Eve Easterhouse was experiencing the most intense climax as she rolled around with Tony in her bedroom suite. Their liaison worked as a magical recipe for making all problems disappear. She and Tony were exploring every fissure of each other's bodies until he tensed up and jumped off the bed.

"Someone's here," he announced.

Eve thought it might be Julia and Bell back from Lake Geneva. "The door's closed. Maybe you could lock it."

"I don't think it's your sister. Stay right here," Tony said as he threw on his pants.

Eve also got dressed, resenting the interruption of the wonderful time she was having. The protective role Tony was taking on made her nervous. She could hear distant voices from the first floor. He was right. There were uninvited guests in her house. An acute sense of fear quickly sobered her up.

As Eve listened, she plotted on how to grab her purse which held her phone, car keys, and other miscellaneous items that could be used as a weapon.

"Who the hell are you two guys?" Tony shouted.

"Who the hell are you?" echoed a male voice that sounded vaguely familiar.

"I'm Eve's boyfriend."

"We're her uncles. You need to leave. We have some family business to discuss with her," Jonathan said.

Eve crept down the staircase and grabbed her purse. She could smell the testosterone throughout the house. Seen by Terrence, Eve was forced into making her presence known. "Tony, these are my uncles, but I don't want you to leave. Terrence and Jonathan, you need to leave. I don't know how you got in here, but you aren't welcome."

"You left the door open," Jonathan said. Eve found that hard to believe, but she was pretty drunk, and safety wasn't a top priority. She stood in the foyer and pointed to the door.

"Get out!"

"Okay, Eve, if that's the way you want to play it. We'll leave after we get what we came for," Jonathan said.

Eve looked unsure of what they were talking about.

"I think you know what I mean," Jonathan reminded. "The scroll your mother left you." His face began to contort. Eve no longer recognized him.

"I don't know anything about a scroll," Eve bluffed, while her hand quietly felt the inside lining of her purse. She felt something hard and round, then covertly slipped it inside of her pocket. A thick tension filled the room, instinctively making her want to run. She suddenly smelt sulfur. Her instincts were on high alert.

In less than a blink of an eye, Jonathan managed to get from the far side of the dining room across the vast foyer. Terrified, Eve cowered against the wall. She could see his teeth protrude from his mouth. With every ounce of bravado she could muster, she placed her arm against him to defend herself from his advance. "What are you? A vampire?"

Jonathan took her purse and whipped it across the foyer. "If only you were that lucky. Unfortunately for you, I'm much more than that. I'm altered, transformed. An angel changed me to his likeness. An angel you have more in common with than you think. Now, I'm going to ask you one last time, Eve, dear sweet niece of mine, where's the fucking scroll?" Jonathan thundered with his blue eyes glowing.

Out of the corner of her eye, Eve could see Terrence and Tony struggling with each other. She put her hand in

269 • Peacocks, Pedestals, and Prayers

her pocket to feel the object she had just taken from her purse. She figured out that it was the rock Bell had given her after she took the job at the *Evil Empire,* the same rock that belonged to her mother. Out of the corner of her eye, she saw Tony handle Terrence and regretted he was dragged into this mess. But then she did a double take. Tony was holding his own against her other uncle. *Him too? I'm in a room with three monsters?*

Before Eve could blink, Jonathan had her in a choke hold. "I'll bite her, Tony, unless you leave my brother alone," Jonathan roared as he looked over at two monsters engaged in a brawl.

Terrified, Eve grabbed the rock she had in her pocket and bashed Jonathan in the head. She could smell the burning flesh and more sulfur. His hands fell from her neck, and she gasped for air.

"Ow! My forehead! What did you just do, you bitch! It burns!" Jonathan screamed as he seethed in pain. Eve broke free and watched in horror as Jonathan went down to his knees shrieking. She saw Tony vacantly looking at her, as if she was a stranger.

Eve watched as Terrence tried to strike. Tony reflexively blocked him from harming her. Both men had their fangs out and their eyes blazing. They were determined to fight to the death.

Eve intervened. "Tony, let me hit him with this." He nodded his newly changed hideous face, knowing what had to be done.

Tony led Terrence towards Eve's right hand, and then she swung the rock at his head. Terrence burned then sank down to the floor. Both of her uncles were only a few feet from each other.

As Eve watched Jonathan and Terrence writhe in pain, she looked at the engraved angel script wondering what the symbol meant. *Was this why Mom collected these rocks? For protection? Was Tony just like them? Sooner or later, he will try to kill me. I should finish him off, or at least cut him loose.*

As her uncles cried, Tony could read her mind. "I wouldn't hurt you. Please give me a chance. I thought you were this fun and sexy party girl, not some kind of demon slayer. I should have known. It was me who broke in and spied on all of you when you were playing with the Ouija board. You are chosen for something. Don't reject God like I did. It's too late for me and your uncles, but not too late for you. Let me tell you how to kill them."

"How? Do I keep hitting them with this rock?" she reasoned.

"No, that will just slow them down and keep them in pain. You need something that represents God," Tony said. Eve couldn't help but notice him look scared as he checked out the religious décor of the house.

"A cross?" Eve asked. He nodded.

Eve unhooked a large Celtic cross that hung in the foyer. "Now what?"

"Get a lighter or matches. Now take the cross and push it down on his face, and then flick the lighter close to his skin."

Eve pushed the cross into Terrence's forehead. He was too weak to fight her off. Howling like a wolf caught in an animal trap, he screamed, "No! You'll pay for this! I'll see you in ...." Terrence combusted into a fireball then disintegrated, leaving nothing but a few ashes and an odd smell behind.

"That smell, is it brimstone?" Eve asked, familiar with the term used throughout the Bible.

"Brimstone, sulfur, ashes, all of it. To kill our kind, you have to fight fire with fire. Do you trust me now? Try the other one."

"Eve, please! Julia is my daughter! Bell's my granddaughter! You don't want to do this! Have mercy upon me. I can show you the power of the scroll," Jonathan begged.

Eve was too transfixed with her lighter to pay attention to what he was saying. With the dexterity and ease of a veteran vampire slayer, she took another cross that was hung on the wall. This one was made of an acacia tree from Bethlehem. She smashed it into his forehead, and it sizzled like a raw hamburger patty on a hot griddle. He tried to hit her in defense, but he was paralyzed by the crucifix. The cross burnt an outline of itself onto his face. With the flick of a Bic, Jonathan was consumed in fire.

"Tony, why did you have to be one of them?" Eve asked. She really liked him. She sensed that he was a bad influence, but now he was much more; he was evil.

"I was changed by the angel, Mammon, decades ago. He's my master. I do some chores for him from time to time. He's a lot like Andel. You must know he's also an angel. At first, Andel was unaware of my own powers, but then he figured me out by my lack of smell. To keep the peace among the angels who live on earth, he put me on his payroll. These angels, most people call them demons, are very powerful. The crucifix isn't enough to burn through them. I'm not sure how to take one down. No one is. They're invincible. They've been around before the beginning of time."

"Tony, I got to meet my family. We're all in trouble," Eve said with urgency.

"Take me with you. I can protect you from the birds. They will be after you. Whoever sent your uncles will also send birds. C'mon, I'll just follow you anyway. I'm too afraid of you to try anything. Eve, I regret the choices I've made. You might get the privilege of seeing one of God's miracles. I want to be there. It's my only chance to tell Him I'm sorry. Please, I'll even let you kill me afterward."

Eve didn't know what to think. For all she knew, he, too, could be after the scroll. However, he did save her, and then taught her how to annihilate her uncles. She called her sister.

"Julia, it's..... Sorry. Please, quit screaming at me. I love you too. I'm leaving now. Be there as fast as I can drive. I've got to bring someone, Tony. He *could* be dangerous. If I don't bring him, he *will* be dangerous."

Chapter Fifty-Two

Each day that passed made Marcus more infatuated with Eve. Not only was she beautiful, but also intelligent; he was impressed with her aptitude for the advertising business. He knew she was dating Tony, but he had big plans for being the rebound guy. While he waited for their affair to end, he fantasized about saving her from Tony, and then killing him to end her fears. Marcus cast himself into the role of her knight and shining armor whose bravery was impossible to resist.

Without thinking, which was what Marcus did when around Eve, he gave her and Claire the keys to the basement early Tuesday morning. Later, he noticed Eve's absence. "Claire, where'd she go?"

"She's got the flu. I told her to go home before she gets us all sick," Claire answered.

Still not thinking, he asked Claire to pass along his condolences.

The next day, Eve was still absent. Marcus again asked how she was doing.

"She's really sick. Hopefully, she'll be better for tomorrow and Friday – we've got our big presentation for Andel, and then, if all goes well, RE," Claire replied.

Marcus, still not thinking, took Claire's word at face value. He had her order a 'get well' bouquet to be delivered to Eve's home. He then upped the flower sale to four dozen red roses while wishing her a quick recovery on the card.

That evening, Marcus went home hungry. Before nourishing himself with his new host, he played back the video that monitored her every action throughout the day. He noticed the once large woman of at least 200lbs. had considerably shrank in only five days of being held captive.

The tape proved that she was not eating the meals that he left her, and she spent almost all day and night sleeping. Had it not been for her large size, she would probably die by the end of the week. However, Andel claimed she had at least two more weeks of blood left to drink before dying. She was basically a corpse they were picking clean.

Thrilled it was his turn to eat, he fed off his prisoner, Jackie Winthrop. As he sucked on his compliant and almost lifeless victim, the day's events passed through his head. He knew that his victim's minivan had to be immediately disposed of. Andel would be angry if he saw it still inside the garage. He also wanted to find a second host for Andel. Sharing Jackie's blood worked, but he always felt hungry afterward, and he wanted to gorge. As he sucked, he lost count.

The blood invigorated Marcus. While he fed, he thought about his beloved Eve. She was not at work for a few days. He couldn't remember seeing Tony either. Anger began to swell. Before ire had a chance to take over his actions, a tiny voice inside his head hummed a hint of logic. *Basement – Catalina's head – Eve knows.* He bit into his zombie-like victim so hard, that she snapped out of her trance and screamed. *Fuck! I should have counted. I couldn't have been feeding for that long, could I? Need to get the head out of the basement.*

***

Attorney Fred Singer talked his neighbor, John King, into investigating the disappearance of Phil Krakowski and the recently missing person, Jackie Winthrop. Convinced that Marcus Reinsing was liable for kidnapping and probably killing them, they went to Andel Talistokov's house where Marcus lived to have a look around. They waited until dark, bringing both a crowbar and camera, and found a shaded window on the side of the brick garage for their entrance. The consequences of getting caught were not enough to deter them from finding both Phil and Jackie. Fred easily pried the window open, and then ripped the screen.

"John, I can't believe this opened up so fast. Just like the movies," Fred excitedly remarked as he stepped on John's hands for a boost inside. He wiggled his rolls of blubber through the tight opening and slowly lowered himself, headfirst onto the epoxy floor.

The 4-car garage was spotless and perfectly organized with metal cabinetry. Fred reached his hand back outside of the high set window and grabbed the camera John was holding. The only two cars inside were a new pickup truck, which he assumed to be Marcus', and an older minivan that fit the description of Jackie's car.

"We've got 'um!" Fred yelled as he snapped off a dozen pictures of the van, including the VIN and plates. He tossed the camera through the window back to John.

The window was high. Fred had to find something to stand on to get back outside. He quickly found a lawn chair and opened it up below the window as he heard John yell.

"Fred, what does Andel drive?"

"I think he drives a Cadillac."

"Get out now. He's turning onto this street. I'm running through his backyard and going to the police. Got to go!" John yelled.

"Shit!" Fred said under his breath. He had his torso out of the window and scrambled his legs for leverage against the wall as the garage door rose. Once he felt a hand on his leg, he knew he had been caught. The hand pulled him back inside, and then the garage door closed. Fred's only hope was the police getting to the house in time.

***

Andel was stunned that someone would be stupid enough to break into his house, let alone a grown man who had the look of an upstanding citizen.

"Well, well. What'd you take from me?" Andel calmly said with a smile.

"Nothing. I never made it to the inside of your house. You came home too soon. Call the police and have me arrested. I broke into your home, and I should go to jail. Please forgive me. I'm an idiot. Just desperate and this fancy house looked like it had a lot of good things to steal," Fred said.

"You don't look like a burglar," Andel said. His face was slowly changing from human to grotesque. He could see the man tremble with the kind of fear that one feels just before they know that they are going to die. He loved that look; it made him feel very powerful. The burglar soiled his pants while he shook. With supernatural speed, he approached the man and picked him up as if he were light as a feather, and at 275lbs., he wasn't. The man tried to defend himself, hitting Andel in the face. Effortlessly, Andel grabbed his arm and snapped it like a dried-up twig, and then dislocated his shoulder as he threw him down on the epoxy floor.

"Your name? Tell the truth," Andel snarled, displaying his jagged canines.

"Fred. Fred Singer," he cried.

"Marcus! We have a visitor!" Andel diabolically bellowed. He dragged his guest inside of the house from the attached entry door of the garage.

Marcus descended the staircase in response to his master's command.

"Look who I found snooping around in my garage. Do you know him? This is Fred Singer," Andel said.

"He was with the policeman. They were passing out a sketch of me along with photos of Phil Krakowski," Marcus answered.

Andel's intuition was correct; the man was definitely not a burglar. He wished he could read the man's thoughts. Fred had seen too much, and he had to die.

"I'm eating this one," Andel declared. He gnashed up Fred's neck while he sucked. Once almost all the blood was gone, Fred's body violently vibrated and then flopped down on the wooden floor of the laundry room. Surprisingly, his attack didn't leave much of a mess. Only a few droplets had spilled. Andel's hunger was satisfied, but he was still upset.

Marcus had once again forgotten to take care of a loose end: the woman's minivan. Andel's doubts about his protégé weighed heavily on his mind. With the utmost clarity, he knew Marcus was not smart enough to take over his empire. Unfortunately, loyalty was not enough. He still had time to find someone else as his replacement.

"Master, I think I screwed up," Marcus mumbled.

"Damn right you screwed up. I told you to get rid of that van a couple of days ago."

"It's not that," Marcus confessed, looking down at the ground, avoiding eye contact.

Andel exploded after learning that Eve and Claire had been in the basement with a set of his keys.

Chapter Fifty-Three

Once again, Julia was amazed by her daughter. Upon Bell's insistence, they pulled up an old metal box that was sitting on the bottom of Lake Geneva, tied to Lydia's boat dock. The gray metal box looked like a high-tech toolbox with handles on the top and the sides. After hauling the box inside of the house, Julia broke several kitchen utensils in attempt to pry it open. Finally, she found a screwdriver found in one of the kitchen drawers. She and Bell could hear a popping sound similar to a jar being twisted open for the first time as the toolbox lid lost its seal.

"Lonnie was right! It's the other part of the halo!" Bell exclaimed.

"Let's make sure," Julia said as she grabbed the other piece from her bag. "Perfect fit. Wonder how it broke."

"When the angel fell from Heaven. There's something else, Mommy. Look, it's like a knife."

Julia took it out of the box and examined the thick short blade. She held the sword vertically to the floor. It immediately expanded to the length of a full-size sword. "I don't understand. How did it do that? There are no brackets or seam to make this extend. What kind of metal is this? And there are five finger holes instead of four on the hilt. Oh wow, look at the beautiful metal design." Julia admired the intricate artisanship.

"It's out of this world! No wonder Grandma hid it. The metal of the sword looks like the metal of the halo, Mommy. Is Auntie Eve coming? I wish I could show her all of this."

"She should be here in an hour or two. She's bringing someone, and he might not be very nice."

"You mean like the professor? He wasn't that scary. Is Auntie Eve bringing him here so we can kill him?" Bell questioned. There was the gleam in her royal blue eye that suggested she had a thirst for killing the unholy. Julia found this disturbing, and even felt a twinge of fear. Her daughter was not normal, but she couldn't deal with another problem at the moment.

"I don't know why she's bringing a guest, but we'll find out once they are here. Sean is also on the way with another so-called friend. Almost like a party," Julia said. Her sarcasm went unnoticed with her daughter. "Bell, it's late, and everyone should be here by now."

"Mommy, Sean just pulled up. I see him through the window, and you're right, he did bring a, uh, not sure what they are called," Bell announced as she opened the front door. "Hi, Sean. How was your trip?" Bell politely asked as she motioned them in.

"Wish you and your mother were with me. This is Father Dominick Sardenelli. Don't be alarmed. He's wearing a robe and a collar like a priest. He used to be part of the Catholic clergy. As a matter of fact, he's originally from Florence. That's the same town I visited in Italy. He converted over to the Yelizi faith, and now he oversees the parish that your grandmother and uncles attend," Sean said as he introduced Dominick.

"And you brought him here? Father, no disrespect, but by affiliation to that part of my family, you are not welcome in my house. Sean, how could you do this?" Julia asked.

"Please, hear him out. Yes, he's made some past mistakes, but he wants to make things right. Besides, I don't know anyone else who can help us, and neither do you. Father Sardenelli speaks Hebrew, Greek, Latin, and of course Italian and English, and reads Angel Script. He was trained by both the Catholic church and the Baccianis. He knows both sides," Sean pointed out.

"You can read angel script! Grandma was trying to teach me that before she died. Can you teach me?" Bell interrupted.

"I would love to if your mother would let me. Listen Ms. Easterhouse, you have every right to throw me out of your house. Just say the word, and I'll go. But I want to warn you that your grandmother and uncles are willing to kill for the scroll. Sean also was threatened in Florence by Franco Bacciani. Some of the Yelizi members have broken the most sacred laws of their faith by fornicating with angels. These acts were also committed during the days of Noah. God was so angry that He destroyed the earth, only sparing Noah and his family," Father Sardenelli said. "No one wants that to happen again. And if these people don't stop......"

"I thought God flooded the world because people were wicked," interrupted Julia, unsure of his intentions.

"Yes, He did, but it is also written that the Watchers or fallen angels were mating with human women. Their offspring were called nephilim. Some thought they were physical giants, like Goliath, but others took the language figuratively, interpreting their powers as giant, as in supernatural. They were also polydactyl," explained the priest.

Julia sensed Father Sardenelli wasn't just giving them a Bible study lesson. *How could he have known about Bell? I had her extra lefthanded digit removed before she turned one year old.*

"Father, say what you want to say already. I'm too tired to read between the lines," Julia demanded.

The priest looked at Sean apprehensively and said, "Beginning with your grandmother, each generation all the way down to Bell is special."

Julia's impatience grew as the priest searched for the right word to say. "Define special." She saw the panic-stricken look in his eyes, and so did Sean.

"Look, what he's trying to say is that there are many family secrets that have been withheld from you and your sister. He knows about some of them. Give him a chance and let him stay. Is Eve coming?" Sean asked. The priest was still standing in the foyer with his coat on looking uncomfortable.

"Eve should be here soon," Julia replied.

"Good, can we wait until she's here? They'll be a lot of questions. Julia, if you trust me, then you gotta trust him. He came prepared, in case we have company," Sean said.

Julia remained guarded, but she took the priest's coat and invited him to sit down in the living room. He wore his vestments, along with several gold chains and medals hung around his neck and waist.

"Well, you certainly look holy. What's in the briefcase?" Julia asked.

"I'm not sure what could happen once the scroll is opened, so I came with my old weapons, or weapons from God," answered the priest.

"Father, are your weapons strong enough to protect us from the bad angels?" Bell asked.

"I hope so. They have worked in the past when I've used them to remove demons," he answered.

"Can I see them?" Bell enthusiastically questioned.

The priest opened his black case on the coffee table and revealed his old exorcism tools that were given to him by an archbishop during his extensive training. He carefully pulled out each item from the case and explained what they were.

"This is a Latin Bible, 16th century. Very old. It's a souvenir I took with me after I left the church. Then there is this book. It's called the *Rituale Romanum*. Kind of like a handbook for getting rid of evil. This is a wooden cross, and it has been blessed by dozens of clergymen throughout the centuries. Here's a bottle of holy water and a bottle of holy oil. This is a scapular. It's kind of like a necklace. This one has St. Benedict on one of the squares and his prayer on the other," the priest said. Despite the upcoming danger, he and Bell enjoyed going through all the belongings. "It's been almost twenty years since I even looked at these. Thanks for giving me a chance. This feels right, and I haven't felt right in years."

"Who's St. Benedict?" Bell asked, looking at the scapular.

"He was a priest who started several monasteries in Italy. His prayer, along with one for St. Michael the Archangel, is used in exorcisms. This is his medal," answered Father Sardenelli as he took off the medal necklace from his neck and gave it to Bell to study.

"These letters that are running up and down on the cross, CSSML, stand for Crux Sacra Sit Mihi Lux, or '*may the holy Cross be my light.*' And these letters that run across the cross, NDSMD, stand for Non Draco Sit Mihi Dux or '*Let not the dragon be my guide,*'" recited the priest.

"What's an exorcism?" Bell continued.

"It's when a priest or a person who can communicate with the spiritual world helps families get rid of demons that are in their house, in their body, or even in one of their objects. We cast the demons or even the devil away."

Bell's acceptance and interest in the priest softened Julia, but she still remained skeptical. "You brought an exorcist here? What for? Do you think we're possessed?"

Sean was about to answer, but Father Sardenelli cut him off. "I realize how crazy this seems, but I don't know what's inside that scroll. Once it is opened it might invoke some uninvited guests with certain powers that are beyond our control. I do know, as do you, that too many people are after it. Doctor Nrogbi for one; he almost killed you twice. Once with birds, and then once from a visit earlier today. Yet you and your six-year-old daughter out-maneuvered a monster. How is that possible?"

283 • Peacocks, Pedestals, and Prayers

"I don't know. You tell me," Julia said.

"I know, Mommy. I sliced him up with part of the halo, and then you took one of our crosses and burned him. You killed him when you lit him on fire! You made him disappear! We were like super-heroes!"

"Can I see this halo piece?" asked the priest.

Julia uneasily watched as Bell went to fetch the piece out of her bag.

"Here, Father. It was my grandmother's. Don't know where she got it, but she hid it real good," Bell said. Julia was thankful she didn't tell him about the other piece they just found along with the sword.

The priest studied the piece for several minutes while Bell watched him at the coffee table. "The hammered edging looks like musical notes," he commented.

"It does!" Bell exclaimed. "There's a harp in the family room. Do you play?"

"No, I never learned. May I hold it?" the priest asked.

"Go ahead," said Bell as she passed him the piece.

"Ouch! It zapped me. Must be static electricity. Ouch! It got me again!" the priest yelled.

Julia picked it up from the floor, uncertain of what the priest was yelling about. "Bell, does it hurt you when you touch it?" Bell took it without flinching. "Me neither," said Julia.

"Sean, what about you?" asked Father Sardenelli.

"Ahhhhh! That hurt! Like I was electrocuted. Owww! Geez, this thing is filled with a type of current. I can't touch it either," Sean said.

"It burned the professor," Bell added.

Julia caught the knowing looks both men gave each other. She began to have a panic attack brought on by paranoia. "What's going on? What aren't you telling me?" The words barely got out of her mouth as she began to hyperventilate.

"Calm down. This is definitely a piece of a halo. Father Sardenelli and I can't touch it because we don't share a bloodline with the celestial, or divine, or ...." Sean described.

"What are you talking about?" shouted Julia as she barely could catch her breath.

"Don't you see? Grandma was a nephilim. That's why she gave me that picture. Her blood runs through you, and it runs through me. That's why we can touch it. We're part angel, just like she was," Bell said as she hugged her distressed mother.

"But the halo is broken. Does that mean we are part of the fallen? Are we related to demons?" Julia cried.

A loud knock at the door temporarily discontinued their conversation.

Chapter Fifty-Four

Eve sobered up in record time after her uncles tried to kill her. Without Tony's help, she would have been dead. He insisted on joining her for her trip to Lake Geneva, warning her about the deadly birds that might follow. After revealing his demonic side, she was too scared to go with him and too scared to go without him.

As Tony predicted, all kinds of birds kept landing on her car's hood and rooftop. Before they could start pecking, he would shriek loud enough to scare them away as he drove. The inhuman sound made Eve shudder.

"Somebody wants you dead," he said.

"Could be you for all I know. This protector role you've created could be just an act," Eve bitterly remarked.

"I just saved your ass. There was no way you could have taken both of them on. And then I'm fool enough to show you not only how to kill them, but myself as well. I should be more scared of you than you are of me. You're the demon slayer with the lethal rock. You're probably going to kill me once I'm in your and your sister's lair," Tony argued.

"But you told me I could kill you. Or was that just a bluff? You know, maybe we shouldn't talk to each other the rest of the drive," she said. Silence followed after mutually finding a radio station to listen to. Eve's mood lightened after several minutes. "Tell me, how old are you?"

"One hundred and thirteen, but I'm young at heart," he quipped.

"You're dead at heart."

"For what it's worth, I was thinking of changing you, of course with your consent. Guess that's no longer an option. I had this crazy idea that we could live happily ever after. You are probably more disappointed in me, than I am with you."

"You got that right. By the way, fifty percent of marriages don't make it past ten years. Why would you ever think we could last for eternity? How did you end up like this anyway? Did you choose this life or was it forced on you?"

"Well, when I was human, I was a two-bit gangster from New York. Lost my accent over the decades. I was shot down like the piece of shit that I was and am, you know, live by the sword then die by the sword. As I was dying, Mammon, my guardian angel of sorts, came to me. He gave me a choice - either die and enter Hell right then and there or prolong the inevitable and live on earth as a changed man. Seemed like a no-brainer at the time. I promised him my soul and then he bit me."

"You worship this Mammon?" Eve asked.

"No, I worship Satan. It's part of my transformation. Mammon held a service for me at one of those Yelizi churches your uncles probably attend."

"What happened?"

"I took an oath not to talk about it, but I'll tell you anyway since it's a long drive and all," Tony said with a smile. "A ceremony was held. There was a goat made up to look like the Devil - makeup, horns, the whole nine yards. I had to kiss it in its private parts and then renounce God. I wrote my name in this book they call the *Book of Death,* and then I was marked or tattooed in my anus. Very painful. Afterward, the insides of my body felt sucked out by a giant vacuum. I felt so empty; that was when they took my soul. Seemed like a good idea at the time, but now I wish that I chose death. In my fantasies, I turned to God during my last breath and asked for His mercy, and He granted it to me. Too little, too late."

"Can you get your soul back?"

"No. You can't renege on the devil. Hey, take the steering wheel for a second!" Tony rolled down the window and screeched, warding off more flocks of birds.

"Listen, I really do appreciate you protecting me. And you're right. Somebody really wants me dead. But maybe you still have a choice."

"Demons don't get redemption. I've been here on earth for way too long. Everyone is starting to blend together. I keep meeting the same two people over and over: the good ones, and the bad ones. Every once in a while, I'll meet an undecided one. But you are different. I see both the good and bad within you. You're one complex and unpredictable lady."

Eve smiled. He had a way of cutting through all the bullshit and summarizing over one hundred years of life in a few sentences. She was flattered that he saw good within her because all she saw was the bad.

"What about Andel? How does he fit into this whole evil underground world?"

Tony scared off more birds with his inhuman screech. They flapped off the car but continued to fly over the car. "To answer your question, Andel is my boss, but not my master. I was placed with him as a token of peace between him and Mammon. But I'm really there to keep an eye on him, kind of like a spy. He's one of the most brilliant generals that Satan has. For decades, his advertising chains have weakened if not converted millions of souls. No one else has his kinds of numbers. He's like the MVP of the Fallen. However, his allegiance has been questionable for some time now."

"You mean you're not all united?"

"United? Hell no! Think about it. These aren't the most loyal beings. The ones chosen to roam the earth have turned into are megalomaniacs. They betrayed God, what's to stop them from doing it again? I'm sure many have dreamt of taking Satan down and beginning their own kingdom. Like they say, 'if you're going to lay down with dogs, then you're gonna get fleas.' That's basically what's happening. Andel has recruited quite the following for himself. Soon he has to go back inside the pit. I think he's preparing to make his move. Of all the talented people that work for him, he's training Marcus to take over the agencies. That incompetent bastard will destroy his empire. What a shame," Tony said.

"Do you think he's appeared to my uncles?" Eve asked.

"Yes, the Yelizis are his favorites. They are easy to manipulate. He's already got an edge because they worship Satan, or as they call him, Malak Tawas."

"My mom used to be a member, but she quit and raised us Christian. She died a few months ago in a mysterious car wreck."

"I don't know your mom, but I know how the Yelizis are when one of their own wants out. I'd be willing to bet these damn birds caused it. They probably were controlled by your sweet uncles."

"I think you're right. Tony, sometimes, when I'm close to Andel, I can hear his thoughts. Or at least I think I'm hearing his thoughts. Why is that?"

"Are you related to him?"

"No, I never met him until I began working at the agency," Eve answered. She thought of Catalina and wondered. *Could I be? Is that why I could get inside of Catalina's head?*

As the Lake Geneva signs popped up on the highway, Tony asked how Eve was going to introduce him.

"I'll tell them all that you are Tony Manghella, the vampire-like demon who used to be a two-bit gangsta," Eve said.

"It's gangster, not gangsta. There's a difference, smart-ass."

"Sorry, gangster." She laughed. Behind the mask of jovial banter lied the looming fear of entering the unknown. With each mile they covered, her stomach filled with dread. *He is coming for the scroll, and he will kill me and my family if we try to get in his way.*

***

"Finally! I'm so glad you're here," said Julia as she hugged her sister before she even got through the doorway. "I was worried."

"Glad to see you, too. And Bell, give me a hug. Hi Sean, and ….?

"Hello, I am Father Dominick Sardenelli. Sean brought me here." The priest extended his hand to both Tony and Eve.

"Everyone, this is Tony. We work together," Eve announced. Bell still clutched her arms around her aunt.

"Auntie Eve, I don't like your friend. Something about him," Bell whispered. Everyone in the living room still heard her.

"You are one perceptive kid. But bear with him for a bit. I'll explain," Eve whispered back. "Father, nice to meet you, but do you mind stepping out for a moment. There's some private things I need to go over with my family."

"Eve, it's alright. He's here to help. Please go on," Sean said.

Julia gave her the look to proceed.

"Very well, then. I've got a lot to tell over the last eight hours," Eve said. She brought everyone up to speed on her exhausting and horrifying day then thanked Bell. "Remember that rock you gave me? When I started working for the advertising agency? It saved my life. I burned both of our uncles with it, and then Tony taught me how to finish them off. They're gone. I lit them up, and poof!"

Julia and Bell gave a full and almost identical account of their day with Doctor Nrogbi.

"We must have just missed each other. Hey, Tony is here to help. He scared away hundreds of birds on the way up here that were violently attacking my car. I know that him being here is a huge risk. He's of the spiritual world, like our uncles and this Doctor Nrogbi, but he also has critical information to share. He's more scared of us than we are of him. Please, just let him stay for a while. He wants to help, and he's not afraid to die," defended Eve.

"I've got more of grandma's rocks. To feel safe, I'm going to pass them out in case your friend wants to try something funny," Bell said with both bravery and maturity. Eve couldn't help but notice the additional religious décor that Bell and Julia had added to the lake-house. Candles burned everywhere along with dozens of more crosses hung onto every wall.

"Tony, do you read angel script?" Father Sardenelli asked.

"Not much, just a few keys. I do know Latin. Never thought I'd use it, but I have since my change. Had to take it as a boy. Brought up Italian-Catholic. Wished I'd taken it all more seriously," Tony responded as he stared at the Latin Bible sitting on the coffee table.

"Shall we try to open the scroll? Let's do this in the dining room," Julia said as she led the group into the large room.

Everyone took a seat while the mood drastically changed from nervous to stoic. Father Sardenelli gingerly touched the seal and tried to rip it open, but to no avail. Next, he cautiously took his pocketknife and attempted to saw through the adhesive that held the seal to the rolled vellum. Again, the seal held firm. Getting frustrated, he gave up being careful, and pulled the seal and the end of the scroll in opposite directions for extra leverage. Eve worried that he was going to rip it, but before she could say anything, it became clear that the seal would not budge.

"Father, my mom just read me this Bible verse that ended with 'smitten with a sword.' I have an idea." Bell went into the toolbox propped next to her doll, Lonnie, and took out the sword. She put her four fingers in the finger holes of the hilt and the blade dropped down to full size. "Here it goes." She stabbed the seal with the sword.

All eyes in the room watched with awe as the indigo seal transformed into a red liquid.

Chapter Fifty-Five

Andel admitted to himself that he had made the wrong decision in choosing Marcus as his protégé. He had seen firsthand how Marcus' ineptitude spread like cancer, putting decades of hard work in jeopardy. Now he was left vulnerable. Marcus absentmindedly allowed Eve and Claire access to his sub-basement where Catalina Rojas' severed head was kept.

Andel fondly recalled the first time he met Marcus. He'd seen full-blown insanity many times throughout the centuries, but as he watched Marcus roll on the floor of his private padded cell, he caught a glimmer of something that he could use. Had Marcus been better prepared and armed with more foresight, he would have gotten away with his transgressions. Most of the people Andel knew would have ran after murdering their parents, but Marcus chose to dress them and serve them dinner every night while their bodies decomposed. Forgetting to cancel the cleaning service, the team of maids left the house in revulsion.

Andel rewarded Marcus for his pure heart and years of loyalty. However, time kept on ticking, and another replacement was needed to salvage his empire.

After finding out about the basement keys, Andel visited Claire at her nearby home. It had been a few years since he'd been there, but he remembered it well. She was one of the few women he had known that could keep up with his sexual predilections. He thoroughly enjoyed her adventurous spirit until she became too clingy.

Andel saw the fear in Claire's eyes when she answered the door. Despite the late hour, she was still dressed in clothes worn at the office. He easily read her thoughts of guilt, wondering how long it would take her to tell him what happened in the basement.

"Hello, Andel. I'm surprised to see you at this hour. Is something wrong?" Claire asked.

She wants to play.

"Just here to see how things are going. Aren't you going to invite me in and offer me a drink?" he seductively said with a smile.

"Yes, of course. Red wine if I recall," she said, grabbing a non-alcoholic bottle from her wine rack. "This is all I have. Still on the wagon. It's really expensive grape juice." Claire filled one wine glass and set it on the end table next to where he was sitting.

"So, how's the presentation going? Will you be ready to give me a sneak preview this Thursday? Hopefully pitch it to RE by Friday?" Andel inquired, toying with her for the moment.

"We are very prepared. You and RE will be wowed! Eve and I created a skit based on that new comedy, *Faust's Contract*. It's about a man who gives his soul to the devil in return for fame and fortune. Great show, and it's a big hit. We bought several of their items to show how placement would be used in the ad. By the way, I charged a couple of thousand on the company card," Claire confessed.

As she chatted away about their campaign, Andel contemplated the various ways he wanted to torture her. His patience was gone, and answers were needed. "See anything strange down in that basement?"

"No. Why? It's vacant. Marcus told us we could use it to store all the RE stuff," Claire lied. Andel could see her face was lined with tribulation. It was time. He stood up and pulled down all the blinds.

Claire dove for the front door, but Andel was too fast. He lunged, and then whipped her across the glossy hardwood floor. The wall stopped her speed. He smiled at the sound of her bones cracking.

Beast, her Anatolian Shepherd, appeared from the stairs and growled ferociously. Andel kicked Claire in the face to see what the dog would do. Beast knocked him to the ground and clamped onto his leg. He diabolically laughed at the dog in the same manner he laughed at Claire when she tried to kill him a few years back. He knew she and her dog were both powerless against him, but he enjoyed a good fight. She finally gave up, but her dog continued his vengeance.

Beast was frothing at the mouth and viciously ripping through his pants. He took his hands and clenched the dog's mouth open and then swirled the dog in a circle, like a father playing airplane with his kid. As he gained momentum, he released. The velocity sent the dog sailing into the freestanding bookcase, causing books, pictures, and other breakables to tumble on top of the animal. Beast laid on the floor and whimpered in pain. He slowly got up and whimpered up the stairs.

Andel jerked Claire by her long caramel hair, and then dragged her back into the living room. As she cried, he commanded her, "Tell me what you saw in the basement."

"Nothing," she moaned.

Andel's anger rose. He felt himself transforming into his fallen state. Grasping Claire's wrist, he lit it on fire with his breath, then watched her writhe in pain. He repeated, "What'd you see in the basement?"

"Just fucking kill me already!" she shrieked. Andel gleefully watched her wrist's skin incinerate off the bone.

"You want to die? Then tell me what you saw in the basement!"

"Okay, but first put the fire out. I can't think."
Andel pushed her wrist into the kitchen sink and ran the water. Black smoke plumed, and then the fire detector went

295 • Peacocks, Pedestals, and Prayers

off. He petulantly took a kitchen stool and whacked the alarm off the ceiling to stop the loud beeping sound.

"Well, I'm listening!" he screamed.

"Catalina's head! We found your secret room. Eve looked inside the freezer. I told her it was Catalina. We also found the blood in your refrigerator," Claire squealed.

"Did she go to the police?'

"No, at least I don't think so. I made her promise to wait until we got the RE account," Claire uttered.

"What else?"

"There's nothing else. She went home sick. The end."

"I know there's more. Think!" Andel raged, exhaling more fire as a warning.

"She touched Cat's head. It was odd, like a connection between them was made. She became mesmerized. After she was done, she told me that Catalina was your daughter."

How could she have known that? Unless.....

Andel's line of thinking was interrupted at the distant chanting of his name. Someone was praying to him. The woman's voice was familiar and sounded desperate. He knew he had to answer.

"You're a coward. I wish you killed yourself years ago. Now I'll do you the favor."

Andel thrusted his incisors straight into her neck, piercing through the skin then sucked the life right out of her.

***

Harriet East invited the Bacciani brothers to the Chicago church in hopes of retrieving the scroll. The three of them set the church up before they summoned Armaros, their patron angel.

Harriet briefly gave the brothers a synopsis of the events that led to the current predicament they were all in.

Their existence was in dire straits until the scroll was back in the right hands. While they prepared the church with candles, lanterns, incense, and birds, the Bacciani brothers had much to report on their own end in Florence, Italy.

"We met Sean Slattery over in Florence. He sent a private detective to spy on us. What can you tell us about him?" asked Franco.

"I saw him at my daughter's funeral, and suspect they were lovers," Harriet answered.

"He had us backed into a corner. I think he left town yesterday. We had the police and U.S. diplomats suffocating us. There wasn't a choice; some obstacles had to be eliminated. Armaros took care of the private detective. He used the guy as part of our fertility ritual. Anyway, one of the Florentine detectives found his phone in our church with pictures in it," Pasquale shared.

"What kind of pictures?" Harriet asked.

"Well, one was of our granddaughter in our holding room. She just turned fourteen. We hope she's pregnant. Another picture was of Armaros himself. We need to warn him," Franco Bacciani surmised.

"Let me finish getting everything ready before we summon him. May your granddaughter be with child. Armaros is very potent. As you know, I had two boys and a girl with him. Would have had another girl, but she died. He also impregnated my daughter with Eve. She's in her early thirties now. What scares me most is her genetic makeup. Her blood has more celestial DNA than human DNA. I don't even think she knows her potential. Lydia tried to raise them all 'normal.' With her bloodline and that scroll, well, I don't know what's going to happen. We need to get it back."

Harriet had everything meticulously ready. She and her two visitors knelt before the pedestal and prayed directly to Armaros. She began the prayer with praise and appreciation. Words of savior, father, king, and lord were chanted in between her own made-up verses. The birds fluttered around in confusion. All were let loose with exception of the peacock. Armaros wanted sole worship, without any reminders of Malak Tawas.

For decades both the East and Bacciani families prayed to Satan in hopes of him visiting their humble parishes, but he never came. Instead, Armaros paid them tribute, and in return, captured their loyalty. Almost half an hour elapsed, and they almost gave up on his arrival. Tonight, was the first time they really needed him. With jubilation, Harriet heard a tap on the skylight directly above them.

"It's him! Our master!" Harriet exclaimed. She opened the skylight for his quiet entrance. He stood on the stage, fully transformed into his full-blown demonic stature. Harriet's loins moistened. He still made her quiver. With his muscular physique, soot-stained and bat-like wings, blistered torso, and blazing fiery eyes, he looked magnificent. His teeth glistened in the candlelight, reminding Harriet of a smaller mouth of a raptor.

Without taking her eyes off of Armaros, Harriet, and her two guests bowed before him and explained their request. She told him about the scroll, his children, and other family secrets. As they talked, she felt ashamed for keeping everything to herself.

"Lydia died a few months ago? And our sons? Are they alive?" Andel asked while Harriet anointed his feet with perfume. Pasquale and Franco bowed down while they spoke.

"My lord, why do you ask? I sent them to our granddaughters' home to try to get the scroll back," Harriet said.

"Something must have happened. I feel as if part of me died."

"Armaros, you and Lydia had a child together. Forgive me my king. I never told you. Her name is Eve.

She is both your granddaughter and daughter. I think my boys might have underestimated her," Harriet confessed.

"A daughter? Lydia was already a nephilim, and then I'm of course a divine being. Your sons were no match for her. Why didn't you tell me?"

"Lydia was heartbroken when you left her. She was so young. And then she learned that she was pregnant. She begged me not to tell you, and even promised we could use her child as an object of worship right here in the church. I honored her wishes, but she never honored mine. She ended up betraying me and our whole family," Harriet said.

"None of my children ever had this much concentration of my genes. This is not a coincidence. Harriet, I have an employee named Eve Easterhouse who has recently become a threat to my empire," Armaros said. Harriet stopped massaging his feet and brought him some blood in a golden goblet.

"That's her. I didn't know she worked for you. Lydia changed the last name on all of her children's birth certificates from East to Easterhouse. She was embarrassed that she was never married. Now, looking back, she had plans since our grandchildren were babies of disassociating herself from this family. She never did forgive me."

"Eve Easterhouse? Did you put her up to applying at my agency? I should kill you right now!" he rumbled.

"I haven't spoken to her in years. I swear I had no idea. Please Andel. Sometimes fate can be cruel," Harriet cried.

Harriet, Pasquale, and Franco shuddered with fear as Armaros fluttered around the vaulted ceiling of the church. He fury escalated. He caught bird after bird with his claw-like hands then pelted them down on Harriet.

"Why didn't you tell me? I'm running out of time, and she's trying to ruin me!" he bellowed.

Chapter Fifty-Six

Father Sardenelli stood in awe of Bell as she stabbed the scroll. The bluish embossed seal melted onto the table and changed to a bright red. It quickly dried into a sugary wax-like substance on the dining room tablecloth.

"Bell, unroll the artifact," the priest said.

The scroll laid on one of the dining room chairs. Bell grabbed one of the scroll's rods and slowly unrolled it while the priest held the other end in place. Julia butted up more dining room chairs, making a surface for the scroll to set.

The scroll was almost as wide as the chairs' seat cushions, and once unwound, reached approximately eight feet in length. The characters imprinted on the scroll were made with a dye that matched the unbroken seal.

"This is angel script and cuneiform. The translations are going to be a little more difficult because of the cuneiform, so bear with me," Father Sardenelli said as he pointed to the two distinct kinds of characters. All stared in silence, waiting to learn what the scroll read.

The priest regretted wasting his talents on the Yelizis. They exploited him for his education and communication with the underworld. He briefly recalled the isolation that always followed an exorcism. This was so much different. Looking at the document, he felt a sudden burst of confidence. He had his tools. Translation of the scroll was possible. Just skimming through the symbols, the priest sensed that Satan was the author. The old vellum smelt of rot, brimstone, and sulfur. He needed God's protection and guidance to proceed. *Would He ever forgive me? Is it too late? Can I help this family in any way?* he thought before beginning with the translation.

"We all need to pray. Before I changed my faith, I extinguished demons for the Catholic church. Before each exorcism, I always prayed to St. Benedict. Bell, would you wear my medallion? A cardinal gave it to me many years ago." The little girl smiled. "Thank you, Bell. I'm honored. It's now yours. May it keep the demons away from you at all times." The priest took off the medal and hung it around her neck. The gold glistened with her yellow hair, making her look even more cherubic than she already did. Before he began his prayer, he warned Tony that it might cause some discomfort. Tony stepped outside of the circle they had formed around the dining room chairs and table.

"Thanks, Father. I'm here to help in any way. I know that I'm unholy. Whatever happens, whether I destruct or go straight to Hell, I want to say goodbye to Eve. I wish we had more time together. I know I'm not even human, but I think I love you. I don't know if it's even possible for me to love anyone, but you are as close as I've ever gotten to putting someone else's life before my own. And if I never see you again, you were worth it. Father, thanks for letting me hold you up. Please continue," Tony confessed. Because his soul belonged to Satan, he had the most to lose during the exorcism. Despite his sincerity, Father Sardenelli still did not trust him.

"Thank you, Tony. No offense, but everyone hold the rocks Bell gave you. Tony's instinct might supersede his noble intentions. Okay, let us pray. O Cross of the Holy Father Benedict, may the cross be a light for me. May the Devil not be my guide. Go away. Satan! Never suggest vain things for me. What you suggest are evil things. Drink your own poison."

Everyone screamed as Tony's ankle combusted into a fireball. Eve took off her cardigan and smothered it. His handsome, olive-skinned face began to gray as his demonic features took over. "I'm alright, Father. Just go on. May

God protect all of you from my evil ways. Beware, I'm going to get even more hideous with each prayer."

"I'm holding onto to everything holy, sacred, divine, and blessed. The Fallen are angry we opened this. They might even be able to hear me translate. I believe this document is an agreement, treaty, or maybe a pact between Satan and one hundred of his elite Fallen. The title of this reads *'Vows to Caligastia.'* That's another name for the Devil or Satan. I'm going to guess this was written after the Great Flood, when God destroyed the world and every living thing on it except for Noah and his ark. Historians typically believe it happened 1,656 years after Creation, or 4600 years ago."

A draft swept over the room and blew out several candles.

Father Sardenelli continued. "This document is not meant for human or holy eyes. It's solely written for Satan and his legion. There are forces that warn us to quit translating the scroll. I will try to be as quick as possible, so that we can all cut the forces' momentum. The beginning of the document reads like a preamble of sorts. To paraphrase, Satan admits his defeat of the war that he and one-third of all the angels waged in Heaven. Because of their Fall, they are all aligned forever. And because that bond was formed, Satan will eternally be their king. He selected one hundred angels from his legion to help him manage his army. These top-ranking officials all have special privileges that separate them from the rest of the Fallen, but not Satan himself. In their kingdom, Hell, there are rules and consequences they are all expected to follow. A numbered list follows. I think these may be his commandments."

The house began to shake, and more candles blew out.

"Well, we are definitely upsetting someone. I'll read them off in the order they are written.

Human will is free; it can never be coerced.
Humans are not allowed to be changed into our image.
Fallen angels are not allowed to breed with human women.
All pregnancies that result from intercourse with human women will be aborted.
Our appearance, language and dialect will differ from our former brethren; we have become our own society.
Earthly visitation is only allowed through charter.
Waging war against our own kind is treason and always forbidden.
All human prayers are directed and forwarded to me, Caligastia.
I and my 100 highest ranked will uphold and enforce these laws to the best of our abilities. Judgment procedures are in place for the disobedient.
No one will exalt themselves over me.
Violation will be heard in Sheol. All offenders will be subject to punishment decided by a small panel of my Fallen.
Signed with blood,
Caligastia

These markings below his name are the signatures of his 100 officers. I recognize some of the names. There is Beelzebub, Azazel, Mammon, Mephistopheles, Armaros... I know that angel. He likes the Yelizis. Then there is Nod....."

The house became very cold. Everyone could see the priest's breath as he read off more of the Fallen's signatures. The priest paused and looked around. He could almost touch the sinister presence within the room. The only candle that had yet to burn out was the one lit next to his 16th century Bible. Julia tried the lights, but the electricity was out. *Just like the old days*, he thought as he grabbed his wooden crucifix.

The house became breezy despite the closed windows. Father Sardenelli had a difficult time reading the remainder of the angelic signatures from the scroll as it wildly flapped. Eve and Bell held it tightly down so he could finish reading it. They rolled it back up and put it back into the velvet-lined toolbox.

Lonnie, Bell's ventriloquist doll, began chanting odd noises without manipulation. They all edged across the foyer and into the living room. In disbelief, the priest dropped his cross.

"The doll is speaking in tongues! It's warning us that evil is near," cried Father Sardenelli.

"Arm yourself with God, and it will be alright. Sean, Julia, Eve, and Bell-I love you," said the doll in an all too familiar voice. It's mouth moved while it talked.

"Don't go, Grandma! We love you, too!" yelled Bell. But it was too late. Her doll had gone limp and fell out of the chair Bell had set it in.

Chapter Fifty-Seven

Once Harriet revealed to Armaros that Eve was his daughter, he flapped his wings in rage, flying in circles with the birds through the high vaulted ceiling of the Yelizi church. His plans of staying on earth were in peril.

Armaros needed the scroll that Lydia left behind. Satan had wanted it back for centuries. It could be used as a means of negotiation for him to peacefully break away.

Armaros remembered when it was first drafted and signed thousands of years ago after God flooded the world. He was roaming earth when God sent down the Great Flood. At the time, he almost drowned. Had it not been for Satan's refuge, he would never have escaped. Using the disaster as an excuse to codify his reign, Satan, now called King Caligastia, declared himself their eternal king and gave them a set of rules to live by. For reasons of self-preservation, Armaros and other Fallen angels were forced to sign the agreement that curtailed their wills while submitting to Satan's rule in both Hell and earth. Dozens of centuries later, an opportunity arose. Unable to resist the temptation, he stole it and hid it in various safe places. Lydia Easterhouse found his last hiding space.

The Devil sealed the scroll with droplets of his Fallen's blood. Although the laws were never repealed, in recent centuries, Satan turned a blind eye to the broken promises of his top producing officers. Their success in soul accumulation was of the utmost importance. Another war with God would soon come, and Satan needed all the soldiers he could muster.

Other Fallen angels were not as talented as Armaros. Once caught participating in their forbidden pre-Flood ways, they were left to face the arbitrary and cruel punishment of their king. Armaros knew that he, too, was now awaiting the Devil's wrath. With nothing left to lose, he had plans of fleeing Hell and beginning his own kingdom, filled with worshipers and other outcasts. Ironically, his daughter, Eve Easterhouse, had the scroll and the genetic ability to unleash Satan upon him.

Armaros stopped his tantrum and flew down to the church's floor. He walked up to the altar and sat on its surface, listening for voices. He heard prayers, conversations, and thoughts of thousands, maybe even millions. No matter how much he concentrated, he could not hear Eve. However, he faintly heard Father Sardenelli's recitation of the Lord's Prayer. "Where is Dominick?" he bellowed.

Harriet, Franco, and Pasquale sat in the front pew of the church and looked at each other with fear and confusion. For the first time in their lives, they had seen the great warrior Armaros worried. His insecurity was contagious.

"We don't know. He wasn't invited to be here with us. Maybe he's at home," suggested Franco.

"Harriet, our sons are dead." Armaros said. She shook her head in grief.

"Like I said, they went to Julia's and Eve's, attempting to get back the scroll, but I haven't heard from them since this morning," Harriet cried.

"Today I cringed with such a crippling pain. The intensity can only mean one thing; part of me was destroyed. I changed them into my image. Their destruction will be avenged."

"My lord, are we in danger?" asked Franco.

"I'm not going to lie. Yes, but the rewards outweigh the risk. We need to prepare for war. Our own kingdom awaits! I come with some good news to bear. Franco, today I had a vision that your granddaughter, Carmen, is pregnant with my baby. Protect her. This child might be my last. If my rebellion fails, I want to thank all of you for your worship, patronage, and adoration. You would have been my generals," Armaros said.

He saw the tears within their bloodshot eyes. They also faced severe repercussions for positioning themselves with him.

"You are the Great Armaros! And it's far from over! We will help you in any way needed. Don't give up now," Franco pleaded.

"I can hear Father Sardenelli's prayers, and they are not for Satan, much less me. He is with Eve and Julia Easterhouse. They've opened the scroll. I need to kill them before it's too late. Soon I will summon you, and we will fight the ultimate fight for independence. May we be victorious!

Chapter Fifty-Eight

"*Our Father, Who art in Heaven...*" Father Sardenelli repeated for the fifth time. Tony shrieked in pain with each phrase. Small flames would periodically combust from thin air and lick his flesh. His soulless stature made him a victim to God's word.

The priest continued praying, occasionally switching gears to the *Apostle's Creed*. He watched Eve smother each flame that blistered Tony while thinking her efforts could endanger their lives.

Bell's doll, Lonnie, was being used as a portal for the spirit world. Lydia used it to warn her family of what was to come. As the doll laid on the floor, a cold gust of wind came from nowhere. Another spirit saw Lonnie as its entry way.

As the doll rose from the floor, its arms dropped from its wooden body. Two arms emerged from armholes on each side of the doll. Then the doll's legs popped off, replaced by hoof-like feet and muscular scabbed legs. The rest of the doll cracked off in pieces, displaying a growing small-horned, scaled monster with fiery yellow and orange eyes. Charcoal wings spurted out of his shoulder blades. The demon was unrecognizable to all in the room except Father Sardenelli. He had seen Armaros before in his full resplendence. The priest went on the defense and flicked holy water at the grotesque creature.

"Dominick Sardenelli," Armaros hissed. His abdomen rippled as though snakes were underneath his skin. "Always knew you were a traitor! You will never enjoy the eternal privileges of your congregation. All of this is in vain. Hell still awaits you."

Armaros looked around the room and saw Tony struggling with his own transformation in the foyer. "Tony Manghella? This is quite a surprise. Mammon, your master, will not be happy with the company that you are keeping. His anger will burn you to ashes, and then you will be sprinkled into the Lake of Fire!"

"....*And Christ, our Savior, will....*" Father Sardenelli chanted, not letting the angel distract him from God.

Armaros looked around and took in the new faces. "You must be Julia. I'm your grandfather. And you, little girl, must be Bell, that makes me your great-grandfather. I knew Lydia very well. She was my daughter, which makes her a Nephilim. Your uncles are my sons, or shall I say they were my sons."

Armaros's eyes burned through Eve as she looked down at the floor.

"Your uncles were mere carriers of the Adonite gene. Later, I changed them to an image similar to Tony's. Julia, your Uncle Jonathan was also your father. Your grandmother forced them to breed like dogs in order to give birth to a nephilim. Harriet did the same thing with Lydia and her other brother, your Uncle Terrence. He was Will's father. But she wanted more, she wanted to create a new race of nephilim. Their genes would eventually be purified to a cultured or man-made angel of sorts," Armaros snarled.

"It's all true, but don't look into his eyes! He's trying to hypnotize you!" Father Sardenelli admonished. The priest could see Bell edging her way towards her mother's tote bag and metal case that sat in the foyer. She inconspicuously took out the halo pieces and sword, preparing to fight. He continued with his prayers, flicking holy oil and water at the demon. It didn't expel him, but it contained him from an attack.

"Eve, nice to see you. You might not recognize me in my natural state of being. My earthly name is Andel, and I'm your boss. You are very special to me. I recently learned that you are both my granddaughter and daughter. With your three quarters of celestial blood, you were the apple of your grandmother's eye. Most nephilim with your genetic makeup never reach maturity. Adolescence is as far as your kind usually get, yet here you are. How'd you kill the voices from within? Drugs? Alcohol? Electric shock? Wait, that's right. You are a drug addict. It drowns everything out, doesn't it? Your cravings for drugs are really cravings for blood. Soon you will not be able to help yourself. Blood excited your brother. He even acted upon it. Maybe that's why he checked out. Catalina, your half-sister, also got thirsty. I heard that you met her in the freezer of my basement. She hated herself, and she tried to take it out on me. Don't you all see? Bell, Julia, and especially you, Eve, are part of me. I'm in your blood, your cells, your DNA. Don't deny what you are. Join me and help rule my new kingdom. We can do great things together!"

With exception to Father Sardenelli, all were too terrified to speak. Prayers were recited while the priest continued to splash both holy water and holy oil on Armaros. Each drop sizzled, causing unsightly cysts all over his body. The creature was in pain and wanted the stalemate to end.

"Give me the scroll! It's of no use to you!" Armaros demanded.

Out of the corner of his eye, the priest saw Bell give her mother one of the pieces of the halo. Julia took it with her good arm and waited. Father Sardenelli nodded, and she flicked it at the fallen angel. It hit his abdomen, but it didn't cut or burn him like it did with Doctor Nrogbi.

"That's my halo! Where did you get this?" Armaros blazed.

Father Sardenelli charged him, piercing through his collar bone with his wooden cross. The demon's flesh cooked. He floated to the ceiling in rage, screeching like an injured bird.

"Anfar, god of the birds, rain down your justice among these outlaws!" Armaros exclaimed.

Julia grabbed the sword from Bell and climbed on furniture. She swung at Armaros as he floated under the ceiling. "Get out of my house and leave my family alone! We will destroy you!" she yelled, but her broken arm impaired her effort.

Armaros was nicked by a few of her swings. Reflectively, he kicked the sword out of her hand, and sent it sailing into the foyer.

Tony tried to pick up the sword, but it burned his hands. He kicked it under the couch as Armaros lunged for it.

Father Sardenelli shifted his eyes to show Bell where the sword had slid. As she dove for the hilt, he whipped his rosary at Armaros. The beads lashed through his leg like a machete, dropping him to the floor. Once distracted, Bell took the sword from under the couch and stabbed his hoof-like foot.

Enveloped in wrath, Armaros breathed a fire ball in the little girl's direction. Sean used his body as a shield to protect her. His entire torso was aflame. As he writhed in pain, Eve grabbed a couch cushion and beat out the fire that was consuming his body. She took the sword by the blade from her niece. It didn't cut her fingers.

"You're our last chance! He's going to kill us and take the scroll!" screamed Father Sardenelli.

Eve put all her fingers inside of the five-holed hilt, including her thumb. The grip was uncomfortable, but she felt encouraged by the translucent blue-white light that emitted from the blade. The glow made Armaros pause in fear.

"Auntie Eve, here's both pieces of the halo," Bell said as she set them in Eve's other hand. They had magnetically bonded together and glowed in the same amazing light. Armed with the supernatural, Eve struck Armaros. The sword's grip gave her an oblique angle that punctured him through his chest cavity. With her left hand, she took the halo and drove the circular metal straight down his forehead. It cut like a diamond blade. Blood streamed out of the Armaros' head, leaving him injured.

"Alright, I'll go for now! You can even keep my halo. It was mine before I fell. But I must have the scroll. It's our laws, our rules," Andel cried. His demonic features began to fade, leaving him with a human appearance. His eyes no longer blazed, but alternated shades of brown and green while glittering in the light cast from the sword.

Father Sardenelli warned, "Behold, he is a wolf in sheep's clothing! Strike him again and give him nothing! It is you who now has the upper hand. Rid this demon from the earth before things change!"

"Eve, as your father, just hear me out. If you give me the scroll, then I'll leave all of you alone forever. This is how your mother would have wanted it," he softly stated.

Eve's mind raced with questions. She was half tempted to rid herself of the scroll, him, and the horror that it caused. However, she doubted if she would ever be free.

"Auntie Eve, what's the matter? Kill him! Before he kills us!" Bell shouted.

Eve calmly watched her father who now looked helpless, and said, "Like you said, I won't deny who I am. Now go to Hell!" She lunged at him with the glowing sword and hacked off his arm. Feeling powerful, she kept coming at him, but he was unbelievably quick. He hurled to the floor and retrieved his extremity. He flew out of the window, breaking the glass, like a bat out of hell.

"He's not gone, is he?" Julia asked.

"It's not over," answered Father Sardenelli, fearing that he would come back with some more company.

While they waited, the priest answered questions about the sword. "I'm not positive, but the sword might have been made in Heaven and meant only for celestial beings to use for battle. The five finger holes confirm that angels can have six fingers. Both the sword and the halo are part of what make you seraphic beings invincible. Armaros' halo was broken because of the Fall. Once it was his own weapon, but now can be used to destroy him."

As the priest continued explaining the celestial weapons, loud thuds pelted the roof. It sounded like ten-pound hail stones were falling on top of them.

The shrill squall of dozens of birds rang of madness. Some flew inside the house through the opening that Armaros left when he flew out the window. They attacked everyone except Tony. Using his own aviary skills, he scared some of them away while boarding up the window with the top of the dining room table. That held them long enough for Tony to draw the few that flew inside the house towards him while stomping them to death. The squawking sounds thundered as the hundreds of birds pelted into the sides of the house.

"I'm going outside! I'll try to get them out of here!" Tony yelled through the screeches. They watched him through the window use himself as bait for the birds to attack. Immune to their violence, he easily smashed each one of them. Despite his defense, he was completely outnumbered. More were finding ways of getting inside. Then he remembered Bell's rock collection. *Touch the birds with the rocks!*

One by one they fell, like an animal die-off. Sometimes Tony managed to kill two birds with one stone. But his hands looked like hot charcoal. Bell passed Tony a rock held by a pair of salad tongs through the door. "Here, I know these burn your hands. Maybe you can use the rock by holding it with this."

Tony swung the rock with the clasped tongs, killing the birds at a faster rate than stomping, snapping, and striking each bird. Soon he killed hundreds of pigeons, sea gulls, ravens, and robins outside of the house while everyone else killed the rest of the birds that flew inside.

Once the threat of the birds ceased, Tony came back in the house, and they celebrated their victory. Father Sardenelli shook his hand and apologized for his mistrust. Although he knew Hell's fire was at his heels, he enjoyed his role as their hero. For the first time in his life, both as human and as changed, he felt a glimmer of worthiness.

Eve reluctantly took on the leadership position. "We need to send him back to Hell. I think I know a way."

Chapter Fifty-Nine

Wednesday evening after work, Marcus checked his computer to see how his prisoner, Jackie Winthrop, was doing. The last time he fed off her she nearly died. He doubted that she could survive for much longer. He couldn't see her from the cameras inside of the room, and assumed she was passed out in one of the blind spots. Just as he was going to feed, Andel came home.

"Master, what happened? Your head, your chest? There is blood is all over your clothes," Marcus asked. He had never seen a scratch on Andel, let alone an injury.

Andel's eyes barely looked human. "I'm just here to pack up a few of my things. Then I'm leaving for good. We might face an attack. Come with me and fight for our freedom before Lucifer sends us to Hell," Andel demanded as he limped into the basement.

"But Master, what about your agency? Your church? The life you've made right here?" Marcus yelled down the staircase.

"None of that matters. Time has run out!"

Marcus went upstairs to eat what was left of his prisoner. The room was empty, and the deadbolts were punched out of the door. *How could she do this? Did someone save her? Did Fred Singer have a partner with him when we caught him in the garage?*

Marcus examined the door. The damage took place from the inside of the room. The windows were still boarded up. From the main floor he heard faint voices.

Marcus stopped at the top of the staircase. Looking down at the foyer he saw Jackie Winthrop and two police officers blocking the front doorway.

"Ms. Winthrop?" said Officer Novak. "Your husband reported you missing. A concerned neighbor tipped us off with some photos of your minivan that's parked in this garage."

Jackie nodded in confirmation. The policeman grabbed hold of his gun, and whispered, "Blink if he's watching." Jackie blinked. "Blink if you're under duress." She blinked again. "When the other policeman moves out of the doorway, run. Okay?"

The other officer edged away. Both policemen hadn't seen Marcus, but they checked the immense rooms on both sides of them. Jackie looked up at Marcus with a sinister grin. She lunged with supernatural speed and sunk her new razor-sharp teeth into Officer Novak's neck. The other policeman unloaded a full clip into her back, but she didn't flinch. Gasping for a breather, she shrieked, "The other one is for you! Go and get him!"

Although confused, Marcus' hunger overrode all logic. He pounced down the stairs and attacked, latching onto the other policeman's neck. Both finished their meals then laughed themselves into a manic hysteria. Blood oozed from their mouths and dripped on their shirts.

Andel rushed up from the basement, catching the tail end of the blood bath they had waged. "What are you doing? You changed her? Are you fucking crazy? I regret ever changing you, in fact, I regret even knowing you! I'd kill you right now, but three more squad cars are pulling up to my house. I've got to leave. You'll pay for this, I swear! Hell has a special place for you imbeciles!" Like a thief in the night, Andel slipped out the back and made his way to his Yelizi refuge.

"Master, I'll follow your lead," Jackie submissively stated.

Master, she called me Master. We just shared a moment. Marcus felt a warm spot in the cavity of where his heart used to be. He finally had someone to call his own.

Jackie would make him the perfect servant for the rest of eternity. After slaughtering seven more police together, they began to telepathically communicate. When there were no more cops left to kill, they admired the dead bodies that littered the front yard of Andel's mansion. They sped off in one of the squad cars and drove east until they saw the sunrise. They spent their time in bliss, murdering prey for both food and sport.

***

Andel headed towards his Chicago-based Yelizi church cursing Marcus and his new creation. Once there, he hibernated into a custom-made bedroom which was built years ago for his privacy and overnight stays. Thursday morning, he fed on a boy that Franco fetched from a nearby impoverished neighborhood. Once he ate, he regained some of his strength, and began to heal. Franco, Pasquale, and Harriet were his most trusted elders. Now that his time was almost up, he divulged some of his secrets.

"Here, I want you to have this. It's a map and deed to an isolated island off the coast of southern Italy. I bought it ten years ago. Even then, the idea of defection sat in the back of my mind. I want you to use this island as land for a new kingdom. It will be a place where you can develop a new race without being prosecuted and where nephilim and humans can live side by side."

"Thank you, Andel. We will prepare the island for your victory. Once we are situated, a throne and a castle will begin construction. Don't worry, when Satan gets back his scroll, he'll cut you lose without a battle," Franco assured.

Dubious about a peaceful separation, Andel disclosed some of his military tactics he'd be using to confiscate the scroll. Relying on guerrilla warfare, he and his small band of other Fallen angels and their own creations were going to raid King Caligastia's palace. His plan had many holes, the biggest was underestimating the Easterhouse family.

"Armaros, Eve has proved to you that she and her family are a force to reckon with. Look at yourself! They almost killed you! You act as if getting the scroll back is comparable to taking candy from a baby!" Franco exclaimed.

"I'll admit they had more courage than I thought. But I foolishly handled the situation alone. This time I'm teamed up with the fiercest warriors on earth. Go to my island and prepare for me and my celestial friends. Whether it's violence or negotiation, we will prevail," Andel announced.

***

After the attack at their lake-house, the Easterhouse family and their new allies retreated to their Wheaton home. The Lake Geneva house looked like it had been through a war. The inside of the house was razed, while the outside of the house had holes, bird blood, and unsecured pieces of trim that flapped in the breeze.

When they all arrived back to Wheaton, Eve asked Father Sardenelli to help her communicate with Satan. He insisted on using an evil backdrop as a portal. She knew the perfect place. The attic had always felt unholy, even before she found Will's lifeless body hanging from the rafters. He agreed that the room seemed to have an undercurrent needed for spiritual contact.

Knowing this was a delicate situation, Father Sardenelli began their meeting with a holy disclaimer. "Almighty Father, protect us from Lucifer, the one You cast down so long ago. We are armed with Your word, halo, and sword. We want Your permission to negotiate with Satan. Please give us a sign if You approve and You'll protect us!" The candles flickered. Once again, the halo magnetically fused, then glowed alongside the sword.

"Thank you, Lord, I believe that was a sign. We now have the faith and courage to continue. Let me try to summon him. I've done this in the past with the Yelizis, but he never came. Just Fallen angels, especially Armaros, would answer. Maybe now there is more at stake," said the priest.

Dominick and Eve knelt down. "Oh Satan, we do not call out to you as humble servants, but as Christians armed with God's protection. We seek not war, but negotiation. Please hear our offer."

The room remained silent for several minutes. "He might not hear us. I don't know what else to do but wait."

"Father Sardenelli, let me try. Lucifer, I have a proposition that might be of some interest. I have a scroll in my hand that you and your Fallen drew up centuries ago. I understand you want it back." Several more minutes of silence elapsed. Discouraged, Eve took out a lighter from her pocket and yelled, "If you don't want to talk with us, I'll just burn it. It's caused me and my family nothing but grief."

The candles blew out, and the room went pitch black. A rattling from a free-standing mirror placed in the middle of the room caused both Dominick and Eve to look. They failed to see their reflections, but instead looked into the amber eyes of a red blistered face with the horns of a demon. House flies from nowhere swarmed the attic, making a deafening buzzing sound. They could feel heat coming from the mirror.

"Lucifer, is that you?" asked Eve in fear.

"No. I'm Beelzebub, his first lieutenant, and authorized to act in his place for all negotiations. Alright, you have his attention. This scroll, I need to check its authenticity before we can proceed."

"Father, do you mind stepping out of the attic? I'd like to be alone with him and conduct our business in private," declared Eve.

Somewhat dejected, the priest gave her his gold cross and left the attic.

Eve opened the scroll in front of the mirror. The demon seemed pleased. He eagerly agreed to her terms for the exchange of the document. Eve rolled up the document and pointed it towards the mirror. And like a vacuum, the mirror suctioned the scroll through, and then the beast's reflection and the thousands of flies were gone.

***

The remainder of Armaros' congregation prayed to him one last time before he joined forces with the other Fallen angels. Over ninety black sedans encircled the church, yet everyone inside remained oblivious. A man with black sunglasses and an ID introduced himself as Agent Gaston.

"Andel Talistokov, I'm here to arrest you for the multiple murders of Phillip Krakowski, Catalina Rojas, and Claire Jacobsen. You are also a person of interest for several murders in other states. Come with me. We need to bring you in."

Armaros looked at the agent and saw something familiar in his icy blue eyes. He submitted, but he planned on snapping off the handcuffs and killing both the agent and driver once they were in motion. *A minor setback thanks to fucking Marcus*, he told himself. Agent Gaston pushed him outside of the church where the other cars were first noticed. *Am I on America's Most Wanted?* Lourdes Rojas, Susan Krakowski, and John King stood from the sidewalk and watched.

Uncomfortable and exhausted, Andel attempted to telepathically tell his brethren that he would be running late. Not sure if they heard him, he fell asleep in the back of the car. Once awake, he panicked. Several hours, if not days had passed. His head felt as if someone had dumped a cement truck on it. The handcuffs would not break, and he began to burn. As he looked out the window, he saw nothing but desert. And then it dawned on him.

"Nooooooooooooooo!!!!!!" Armaros bellowed. His black sedan, along with the others that followed, descended into the sands of Hell.

***

Forever fallen is forever damned, until one can unlock from within. A glinting white staircase appeared in the middle of the desolate desert. Lydia Easterhouse was freed and ascended to her rightful home.

Epilogue

"Julia, I just got off the phone with Father Sardenelli. He started his own church back in Florence. It's a nondenominational Christian parish. He was hitting me up for a contribution. I told him I needed to check with you first," Sean said.

"I think we can send him a little something. Did he mention the Baccianis? My grandmother?" Julia asked.

"He said the Baccianis are long gone, and the Yelizi church is now vacant. My old friend, Detective Magliano, connected another murder to their sect. This one must have been an open and shut case. Why else would they split? Maybe justice was served after all. He mentioned that Carmen Bacciani, Franco's granddaughter, tried to kill herself. Poor kid. She doesn't stand a chance with them. She told the nurse in the emergency room that she was pregnant, and now she's missing," Sean answered.

"They probably took her with them to another place for a fresh start."

"I sure hope not. The world's got enough evil in it already without them praying for more. Right now, I'm going to pretend they are gone. Julia, I was thinking. Florence is so beautiful, and we could visit Father Sardenelli at his new church, give him his donation in person, and maybe he could marry us. I love you." Sean got down on his knees and opened a blue velvet box that displayed an enormous diamond ring.

"Oh Sean, yes to all of it! I love you, too! Bell will be thrilled! Wow! This ring is exquisite!" Julia cried. Not only did she admire the diamond, but also admired the band. Two angel wings were handcrafted in platinum with an inscription of '*credere angelus*' on the inner ring. "I believe in angels too!"

***

Eve and Tony showed off their chemistry while pitching an advertisement for Regular Electric. Their skit showed the corporation how they could exclusively inundate their product on a popular television show. They made the CEOs laugh while portraying Johann Faust, a successful movie star, who wants to get his soul back from Lucifer. RE and the TV show's network signed the most lucrative contract in advertising history, leaving them with a gargantuan commission.

Eve used hair samples from both her and Andel to prove they shared the same DNA. As his only surviving daughter, *The Evil Empire*, along with two dozen other agencies were now hers. She put a few of them aside for Bell to take over once she reached adulthood. Julia was hired on as vice president of the conglomeration, with her future brother-in-law acting as head of their legal division.

By late spring, Eve had Tony move into her Wheaton home with Beast, Claire's dog who miraculously survived. Together, they scrubbed down every inch of the house with holy water, which no longer burned Tony's skin. His cravings for blood were replaced with steak tartar and pork blood stew.

The Clio Awards were scheduled during the last week of May. Eve and Tony took the whole family, including Bell who had just had her 7th birthday. They spent the day as pampered movie stars. *The Evil Empire* swept the awards, taking home seven different Clios. Eve accepted two of them posthumously won by Claire Jacobsen and Catalina Rojas. Unknown to her, Marcus submitted the first ad she ever worked on. She, too, ended up a winner. *If only I could have saved you,* Eve thought. Claire would be missed.

"Not being a sore loser, but I should have won. My video game ad wasn't even submitted. It would have slaughtered all of the others for the interactive category," Tony whined.

"Probably. But you ticked off Marcus, remember? He threw your submissions in the garbage. Wonder what happened to him."

"Glad he's gone. He was always such a weasel. So, I've got him to thank for walking away empty handed," Tony commented.

"How about a consolation prize?"

"That might lighten my mood. I'm very interested." Tony ran his hand up her leg, and she laughed.

"Would a baby do? I'm pregnant!"

About Dina Rae

Dina Rae lives with her husband and three dogs outside of Dallas. She is a Christian, avid tennis player, movie buff, teacher, and self-proclaimed expert on several conspiracy theories. She has been interviewed numerous times on blogs, newspapers, and syndicated radio programs. She enjoys reading about religion, UFOs, New World Order, government conspiracies, political intrigue, and other cultures. Peacocks, Pedestals, & Prayers is her eighth novel.

List of Works:

Peacocks, Pedestals, and Prayers (Halo of the Damned - Revised)

Crowns and Cabals

The Best Seller

The Sequel

Big Agri, Big Pharma, Big Conspiracy (nonfiction)

Love, Lust, and Revenge

Halo of the Damned 2012

Halo of the Nephilim

The Last Degree

Be Paranoid, Be Prepared (short story)

Social Media

Twitter: https://twitter.com/PeacockPedestal

Goodreads: https://www.goodreads.com/author/show/5747
496.Dina_Rae

Amazon: https://www.amazon.com/Dina-
Rae/e/B0085348DY?ref=sr_ntt_srch_lnk_1&qid=1594939
790&sr=8-1

Pinterest: https://www.pinterest.com/dinaraebooks/_created/

Facebook: https://www.facebook.com/DinaRaeBooks

Website: http://conspiracycrackpot.com/

Blog: https://conspiracycrackpot.home.blog/

Trailers:

The Sequel:
https://www.youtube.com/watch?v=ZAMlurlxPZs&t=16s

The Best Seller:
https://www.youtube.com/watch?v=JQER8wJmaf8

The Last Degree:
http://www.youtube.com/watch?v=nkbg6Yy8UKU

Halo of the Damned:
http://www.youtube.com/watch?v=4p89LXZNxOs

Peacocks, Pedestals, and Prayers:
https://youtu.be/HE45Nzd77ro

Printed in Great Britain
by Amazon

25240127R00185